THE SPIES

THAT BIND

Book 11 of the NEVER SAY SPY series

Diane Henders

THE SPIES THAT BIND
ISBN 978-1-927460-34-4
Copyright © 2016 Diane Henders

PEBKAC Publishing Inc.
P.O. Box 67, Station Main
Qualicum Beach, BC   V9K 1S7
www.pebkacpublishing.com

This book is a work of fiction. Names, characters, places and incidents are either the product of the author's imagination or are used fictitiously, and any resemblance to actual persons, living or dead, business establishments, events or locales is entirely coincidental.

First printed in paperback March 2016 by PEBKAC Publishing Inc.
v.4

Since You Asked...

People frequently ask if my protagonist, Aydan Kelly, is really me.

Yeah, you got me. These novels are an autobiography of my secret life as a government agent, working with highly-classified computer technology... Oh, wait, what's that? You want the *truth*? Um, you do realize fiction writers get paid to lie, don't you?

...well, shit, that's not nearly as much fun. It's also a long story.

I swore I'd never write fiction. "Too personal," I said. "People read novels and automatically assume the author is talking about him/herself."

Well, apparently I lied about the fiction-writing part. One day a story sprang into my head and wouldn't leave. The only way to get it out was to write it down. So I did.

But when I wrote that first book, I never intended to show it to anyone, so I created a character that looked like me just to thumb my nose at the stereotype. I've always had a defective sense of humour, and this time it turned around and bit me in the ass.

Because after I'd written the third novel, I realized I actually wanted other people to read my books. And when I went back to change my main character to *not* look like me, my beta readers wouldn't let me. They rose up against me and said, "No! Aydan is a tall woman with long red hair and brown eyes. End of discussion!"

Jeez, no wonder readers get the idea that authors write about themselves. So no, I'm not Aydan Kelly. I just look like her.

Oh, and the town of Silverside and all secret technologies are products of my imagination. If I'm abducted by grim-faced men wearing dark glasses, or if I die in an unexplained fiery car crash, you'll know I accidentally came a little too close to the truth.

I hope you enjoy the book!

For Phill

Thank you for being my technical advisor and the most tolerant husband ever. Much love!

To my beta readers/editors, especially Carol H., Judy B., and Phill B., with gratitude: Many thanks for all your time and effort in catching my spelling and grammar errors, telling me when I screwed up the plot or the characters' motivations, and generally keeping me honest.

To Rick and Sandy H. at Hand Crafted Images: Your talent makes my covers extra-special, and your sense of humour makes photo sessions fun even for a camera-hater like me. Thank you!

To Steve A. and the staff at The Shooting Edge: Thank you for lending us your excellent facilities for our cover photo sessions. You guys rock!

To everyone else, respectfully:
Canadian English is an unholy hybrid of British and American English, so I apologize if spellings in this book look odd to you. But if you find typos, please send an email to errors@dianehenders.com. Mistakes drive me nuts, and I'm sorry if any slipped through. Please let me know what the error is, and on which page (or at which position in e-versions). I'll make sure it gets fixed as soon as possible. Thanks!

CHAPTER 1

The monitor on my wrist vibrated for the umpteenth time. Even though I was expecting it, my heart lurched reflexively and my casual glance at the wristband's tiny screen was twitchier than I would have liked.

The image relayed from my surveillance cameras didn't soothe my nerves. Glancing around, I laid a surreptitious hand on the lethal weapon sitting beside me on my back deck.

John Kane, the lethal weapon in question, returned a smile that crinkled the sexy laugh lines around his grey eyes. "Nice party, Aydan," he said. His body heat radiated through my hand.

I hid my momentary breathlessness and squeezed his muscular forearm, wishing I could slide my grip up to that bulging bicep and go for a full-on fondle.

"It's about to get less nice," I warned quietly, and jutted my chin in the direction of the latest arrival.

Kane stiffened. "What the hell is he doing here? You didn't invite him, did you? Or have you temporarily lost your mind?"

I sighed. "No; and no." I tilted my chair onto its back legs, leaning against the safety of my house while I eyed Tyler Brock's pierced features and supercilious sneer with distaste. "He's with Tammy." I nodded toward the small plump woman who clutched Brock's arm with one hand and her white cane with the other, her round face beaming eagerly from behind dark glasses. "Spider invited her, but no handlers were available today and Brock is the only other person with a high enough security clearance to accompany her. And you know Spider; he'll always give people a second chance, even a dickhead like Brock."

Kane growled softly, a sound that sent shivers racing to parts of my body that had no business shivering in his presence. "Well, if he causes any trouble, I hope you have a good place to hide the body."

I feigned serious thought. "Could be tricky. If it wasn't August we could bury him in the garden. A little shitbag like him would do wonders for my vegetables, but I wouldn't want to disturb them this late in the season. I guess you'll just have to let him live."

Kane shook his head in mock chagrin. "The things I do for you."

Reluctantly removing my hand from his arm, I took a slug of ice-cold beer from the bottle sweating on the small table beside me. "Yeah, I know. I'll have to find some way to reward you."

That came out sounding more suggestive than I'd intended, and I cleared my throat and added, "It seems like everybody's enjoying the party, though. Who'd have thought Spider's generation would get as much of a kick out of Twister as we did?"

Eyeing the knot of bodies on the grass surrounded by cheering and heckling spectators, Kane chuckled. "Alcohol makes everything more fun." He raised his own beer bottle in a toast before taking a swig.

"Except that Spider doesn't drink," I pointed out.

Kane's strong square features softened into an indulgent smile as he gazed across the lawn at Spider's beanpole figure, Coke in one hand and his other arm around his diminutive fiancée. As we watched, Linda pressed closer to Spider, flashing her sparkling smile up at him. He stooped to kiss her, oblivious to the catcalls that rose from the crowd of young people scattered across my back yard.

I was turning back to Kane when my attention snagged on a middle-aged man who had trailed Brock and Tammy into the yard. The man's dress shirt and slacks were incongruous among the casually attired party-goers, and my pulse ticked up. Was he an invited guest? Or something more sinister?

That worrisome thought was interrupted by Kane's chuckle. "I swear Webb looks closer to seventeen than twenty-seven," he said. "I keep feeling as though I should ask for his ID whenever there's alcohol around."

Pulling my mind back to our conversation, I laughed. "Yeah. He's such a sweet kid." My smile turned to a grimace, and I slugged some more beer. "Since when did twenty-seven become 'a kid' to me? God, I'm old."

Kane sobered. "Forty-seven is nowhere near old. You're in better shape than most twenty-year-olds." The breeze wafted a strand of long hair across my face, and he reached over to tuck it behind my ear with a smile. "See? There's still more red than grey in your hair. And you're far more vibrant and desirable than any of these younger women. They're like cardboard cutouts by comparison."

"Thanks." A hot shiver chased down my spine, and I was about to topple into the warm grey of his eyes when good sense reasserted itself. Gulping another largish swallow of beer, I tore my gaze away from him to watch the well-dressed man talking to Brock.

They exchanged a few words, but the man was apparently turned off by Brock's attitude. After a short exchange he turned away, then crossed the yard and greeted Spider's parents with warm handshakes.

I sucked back another swallow of beer. *Jeez, woman, take a pill. It's a wedding shower, not an undercover op.*

But something about that guy set off my alarm bells...

Across the yard, Linda's Granny Lola caught my eye with a cheery wave before turning to say something to the two gray-haired women with her. They smirked and studied us avidly, and I waved back with a smile and muttered to Kane out of the corner of my mouth.

"I love her to death, but I'll never understand why anybody believes Lola's sweet-little-old-lady act."

Kane grinned across the yard at the tiny wrinkled figure with neon-pink hair, silver-studded black leather bustier, mini-skirt, and biker boots. "She's one of a kind. And you can't deny she's got style."

"No kidding. She should look ridiculous, but that outfit totally suits her."

My wristband buzzed again and I jerked it up to scan the surveillance image before letting out a breath. "Just some of the guests going down to the creek."

Kane nodded, stretching out his legs and reaching for his beer bottle. As he drank, his gaze flicked over the party with the habitual keen evaluation of a top agent, and I let out a small sigh. *If he was on the alert, too, was that good or bad?*

I hid a grimace behind my beer bottle. *It likely just meant we were both paranoid freaks.* I glanced over again, but the well-dressed guy was still visiting and looking like he belonged.

Let it go. Nothing to worry about.

Kane said idly, "Hellhound hasn't shown up. Is he coming?"

I snorted. "Are you kidding? Spider asked me to convince him, but as soon as Arnie heard 'wedding shower' he said he was allergic to weddings and started to back away. I tried to explain it was only a big backyard party, but he was already babbling something about having to wash the cat and then he turned and ran."

Kane guffawed. "Wash the *cat?* What kind of lame excuse is that?"

"I'm pretty sure it was just blind panic talking at that point. It was pretty funny to see Mr. Big Tough Biker running scared." I snickered into my beer.

Kane shook his head, still grinning. "He's one of the bravest men I know, but everybody has their limits." He drank some more beer before continuing, "It was good of you to host the party."

"I wanted to." I drew a deep breath, regarding my happy guests and letting the laughter and music wash over me. "I thought..." I swallowed. "I thought it was time to make some good memories on this farm."

His voice softened. "Yes. Long past time, I'd say." He hesitated. "How are you doing?" He nodded toward my wrist. "You still seem a little jumpy."

"I'm okay." I reached for my beer, decided against another swallow, and picked at the label instead. "It's just that I'm not used to quite so much activity on the monitor."

"But it's working well?" Kane inquired, eyeing my wristband with interest.

"Great!" I held out my wrist for inspection. "If there's movement anywhere on or around my yard it sends a picture to the screen, and I can switch to full-video if I want. It uses a satellite link so I never have to worry about getting out of range, and it doesn't affect my bug detector. And it's got a panic button linked to Sirius Dynamics."

"Good system." Kane nodded approval before returning his disturbingly observant gaze to my face, his voice gentling. "And does it make you feel safer?"

"Yeah." The word came out on a sigh, and I added, "I'm a lot better. I haven't had a flashback for quite a while, and I don't usually expect bullets flying through my walls anymore. How about you?"

"I'm doing better, too."

When I looked into his eyes I could see it was true. Instead of the haunted look of four months ago, now the ghosts only lurked at the edges of his clear grey gaze.

I smiled and squeezed his hand. "I'm glad."

"Me, too. It's been a difficult time."

We went back to watching the party in companionable silence. The afternoon heat was diminishing as the sun's rays lengthened to evening. Fading traces of barbeque scent mingled with crushed grass, warm hay from the surrounding fields, and the coconut aroma of suntan lotion. The air was soft on my face and arms, and even the holster concealed at my ankle seemed less sweaty and constricting.

Brock and Tammy had concluded their brief conversation with Spider and Linda and now they stood apart from the crowd. Tammy was still chattering at Brock and Brock was still sneering, incongruous in the happy crowd with his multiple piercings, skinny orange jeans, man-purse, and obvious personality defect.

And speaking of incongruous...

The well-dressed man shot a glance my way but didn't

approach, joining a different group to shake hands and chat instead.

I should go over and introduce myself. Say hello and find out he was somebody's favourite uncle, and then I could get over my irrational suspicion.

But what if my instincts were right?

My heart thudded a little faster. I didn't even want to think about the potential carnage if he pulled a gun...

My wrist monitor vibrated and I jerked so violently that Kane twitched, too. When I glanced at the display, dread tightened my throat.

"Oh, shit. This doesn't look good." My voice came out tight.

"What?" Kane demanded, his hand hovering near the holster concealed by the loose summer shirt he wore open over his T-shirt.

"Police car coming in my gate." I rose and hurried into the house with Kane on my heels.

Switching to full-video mode, I kept my gaze glued to the tiny screen while I fumbled a secured phone out of my kitchen drawer one-handed and pressed the speed dial button.

"Stemp." The brusque toneless greeting of the director of clandestine operations made me draw a breath of relief.

"There's a police car coming up to my house," I rapped out. "Are they legit?"

"Yes, I sent them. Please cooperate fully." His emotionless tone somehow managed to become even dryer. "Without revealing anything classified, of course."

"Right," I muttered.

"Have Kane call me immediately afterward. Was there anything else?" he asked as the doorbell chimed.

"No," I growled, and disconnected as I headed for the door. "Stemp sent them," I said over my shoulder to Kane. "He says to cooperate without revealing anything classified."

I swung open the inside door and regarded the two uniformed RCMP officers through the screen.

The female officer shuffled her feet, looking uncomfortable. "Hi, um... Aydan Kelly, isn't it?"

"Yeah. Hi, Constable Peters," I replied warily, resisting the urge to look away and shuffle my feet, too. Considering that she'd strip-searched me the only other time I'd met her, I wasn't quite sure of the proper etiquette.

"This is, uh, Constable Glen Birch from the Drumheller detachment," she went on, and the uniformed man beside her nodded a greeting. "We're looking for John Kane. His boss said we would likely find him here."

Fear constricted my throat. Oh, God. Had something terrible happened to John's father? Or worse, to Hellhound, for whom John would be listed as next-of-kin?

Oh, God, no. Police only came in person if somebody died...

"C-Come in," I managed through cold stiff lips, and pushed the screen door open.

CHAPTER 2

"Hi, John," Constable Birch greeted Kane with a strained smile.

"Glen." Kane's face and voice were in cop mode, controlled and expressionless. He nodded to the female officer. "Sandra. What's this about?"

"Uh..." Clearly uncomfortable, the two officers exchanged a glance before Constable Peters drew a deep breath. "Why don't you sit down, John?"

"I'll stand." Kane straightened into a parade rest that might have looked relaxed if not for the spring-steel tension vibrating in his shoulders. "Spit it out."

"It's, uh... it's about your ex-wife." Peters squared her shoulders.

Pain flared in Kane's eyes, crimping his mouth into a hard line. "Alicia's dead?"

"Uh? Oh, um, no...' Peters drew a deep breath. "When was the last time you saw Alicia? And would you please describe your movements today?"

"I last saw Alicia on Tuesday, June 22, 2004, at approximately four-fifteen in the afternoon at the house where we used to live in Calgary."

"Wow, that's really, um... specific... for something that

happened seven years ago," Birch mumbled, staring fixedly at his feet.

Kane gave him a bitter grimace. "That's when she served me with the divorce papers. And to answer your second question, this morning I woke up at five-thirty as usual and I was at the gym when they opened at six. I worked out for two hours, then went home. I was there until one-thirty this afternoon. I was alone, but if you check my telephone and computer records you'll see that I was online off and on between eight and eleven AM and at about eleven my dad phoned and we talked until about noon. I was cooking for our potluck dinner between noon and one-thirty but I spent about ten minutes online during that time. Then I drove here for the party, arriving about ten to two. Any of the guests can verify my presence here between then and now. Tell me what happened to Alicia!"

"Oh, good..." Peters pressed her lips together as if she hadn't meant to reveal her feelings, but both she and Birch looked relieved.

Birch withdrew a photo from his pocket and passed it over to Kane. "Do you know this man?"

Kane studied the photo briefly. "No." He turned it toward me, displaying an ordinary-looking fortyish man in a camo-printed jacket and matching ball cap. I shook my head.

Kane passed the photo back to Birch and was beginning to speak when Peters interrupted, "Does the name Arbuckle Murphy ring a bell?" She and Birch eyed Kane intently.

"No. Tell me what's going on."

"Are you sure?" Birch asked.

Kane frowned. "Of course I'm sure. I wouldn't forget a name like that."

"How about Buck Murphy?" Peters persisted.

"No. Who is he, and how does this relate to Alicia?"

Peters nodded as though he'd confirmed something she already knew. "Thank you, that's all we needed. The questions were really just a formality." She began to turn away.

"Sandra." The name snapped from Kane's lips with such authority that she froze in her tracks. "Glen." Birch stiffened to attention, too, as if unable to defy Kane's command. "Tell me what's happening," Kane rapped out. "Now!"

Peters and Birch exchanged a single defeated glance, and Birch hissed a long breath through his teeth. "I knew you wouldn't let us get away with this," he mumbled. "Look, John, just sit down for a minute, okay?"

"Tell. Me. *Now*." Kane's growl raised every hair on the back of my neck, and Birch took an involuntary step back.

"Okay... Okay." Birch exchanged another look with Peters and apparently decided to go with the 'ripping-off-the-Bandaid' approach. "Your ex-wife didn't realize she was pregnant when she served you with the divorce papers, and she never told you she'd given birth to your son. Today at about three-thirty PM he was abducted from a birthday party. She didn't want anyone to contact you but the Calgary police convinced her the biological father should be questioned just in case you had somehow discovered the truth and conspired to abduct your child."

The colour drained from Kane's face so fast I thought he might faint. I sprang to his side, gripping his elbow and trying to guide him to a chair, but I might as well have tried to move a mountain. His bloodless lips opened.

"That's not possible," he rasped. "She couldn't have children. The fertility specialist said there was no hope. She must have adopted a child. This is a mistake. A... misunderstanding."

Constable Peters stepped forward to lay a hand on his shoulder. "Without a paternity test we can't know for sure, but I really don't think she's lying, John. I'm sorry, I know this is a shock, but..." She drew a photo out of her pocket and handed it to him. "I doubt if it's a mistake. He looks just like you."

Together, Kane and I stared at the photo. Kane's grey eyes laughed back at us from a chubby childish face under dark hair that matched Kane's own.

"He's six," Constable Peters said softly. "His name is Daniel Wyatt Kane."

The name hit Kane like a gut-punch, half-folding him with a whoosh of air from his whitened lips.

"Sit!" I pushed him into a chair and clamped the back of his neck to press his head down. "Head between your knees. Breathe."

"I'm fine," he muttered, fending me off with an absent-minded sweep of his massive arm that sent me staggering back despite my hundred-and-sixty pounds and five-foot-ten height.

Kane shook his head like a boxer recovering from an uppercut. Then his shoulders squared and he sat up straight. "Give me the facts of the case." His cop face and cop voice were emotionless but the photo quivered in his white-knuckled grip. "And hurry. The clock's ticking."

As if sensing my confusion, he turned to me to explain, "The longer a child is missing, the greater the likelihood that they won't be found alive. The first forty-eight hours are the critical window." Returning his hard scrutiny to the two officers, he demanded, "Any ransom demands? Physical evidence? Witnesses?"

"John..." Birch reached over to clasp his shoulder. "I'm sorry, but you're not on the case. You're too close to it. Leave it to us."

Kane rocketed out of the chair, fists clenched. "You'll damn well tell m..." An instant later he caught himself and drew a deep breath, white lines of strain bracketing his mouth. "Sorry, Glen, Sandra; you're right. Thank you for telling me this much. Just..."

He drew another deep breath and offered the photo back to them, holding it as if it might break. "...keep me posted."

"We will. I promise everybody's doing their absolute best to find him." Birch nodded at the photo. "Keep it. We made copies."

"Thank you," Kane said raggedly.

Birch gave him a tight-lipped smile and Peters gripped his shoulder sympathetically before they let themselves out, leaving us standing in shattering silence.

"How..." Kane shook his head as if still reeling from the blow. He spoke again as if to himself. "How could she...?"

Helpless in the face of his pain, I took his hand and stroked it in silence.

His grip tightened, nearly crushing my fingers. "I have to talk to her," he muttered.

His hand tightened again and I let out a yelp. "Ease up, Superman!"

The moment the words left my mouth I willed them back with all my might, but the damage was done. His face twisted with pain, and I knew he was remembering the little boy who had gazed up with hero-worship shining in his eyes and called him Soopooman only a few months ago. Younger than his own son.

The son he'd lost without ever knowing of his existence.

Desperate to distract him, I pulled free of his grip and hurried over to extract another secured phone from the kitchen drawer.

"Call Stemp." I pushed the phone into his hand. "He said he wanted to talk to you right away."

"Stemp." Kane blinked at me like a sleepwalker mired in a waking nightmare. "What does he want?"

"I don't know, just phone him, okay? Here." I pressed the speed dial button and lifted his hand to his ear, phone and all.

He frowned at the crackle on the other end that was undoubtedly Stemp's curt greeting. Then he lowered the phone and I thought for a moment he was going to drop it and walk away, but he pressed the speaker button instead.

"It's Kane," he said flatly, and waited.

"You've spoken to the RCMP?" Stemp inquired.

"Yes."

"My sympathies. This must be very difficult for you."

A hint of surprise touched Kane's shell-shocked expression, but he didn't know about Stemp's secret daughter overseas. I alone understood how heartfelt Stemp's words truly were.

"Thank you," Kane mumbled.

"That said..." Stemp's voice regained its usual dispassionate crispness. "You are to have no professional involvement in this case whatsoever. That's a direct order. You're too close to it, and in any case it's outside the Department's mandate. Any interference with the official investigation will be grounds for disciplinary action, dishonourable discharge, and/or imprisonment. Is that clear?"

"Yes. That won't be a problem," Kane said with no inflection whatsoever. "Because I quit. Effective now. I'll drop off my written resignation when I have time."

"John!" I hissed. "Think about this! You can't just-"

"I just did."

As Kane moved to press the disconnect button, Stemp spoke again. "Your resignation is accepted. Surrender your weapon and report to Sirius Dynamics for debriefing immediately."

The robotic voice fell again from Kane's lips. "I'm giving my weapon to Aydan right now. She can turn it in. I'll come in later for my debriefing."

"Come in immedi-"

Before Stemp could finish the sentence Kane clicked off the phone. He was reaching for his holster when a commotion at the back door halted him.

"...F-fine," a too-loud voice insisted. "I'm f-" A hiccup interrupted the word before he finished, "Fine! Jus'... Jus' leemee 'lone..."

"Aydan!" Linda's call sounded strained. "Where are you?"

"Here!"

I hurried toward the voices, rounding the corner in time to see Spider stagger and carom off the wall next to the back door. His eyes were unfocused in his unnaturally flushed face and angry red blotches blazed on the pale skin of his throat. Linda braced her tiny frame against him in a futile attempt to stabilize him. On his other side, a slim baby-faced young man clung to Spider's arm, his forehead crinkled with worry.

"Aydan, I'm sorry, we'll have to go now. Thank you so much for hosting our wedding shower." Linda gave me a tight smile that was equal parts worry and anger. "Someone spiked Spider's drink, and he's allergic to alcohol."

"I'm sure it was that Tyler guy who came with his blind mother." The slim young man shot a venomous glance over his shoulder through the still-open door. "He's a total jerk, and I saw him with a hip flask."

"She's not his mother," Linda began, but I interrupted, studying Spider worriedly.

"Should I call an ambulance?"

"I think... umph." Linda nearly buckled as Spider staggered again, bracing himself on her shoulder with a heavy hand. "I think he'll be okay," she continued after righting them both. "I've already given him an antihistamine and if he was going to have an anaphylactic reaction he likely would have already, but the drug is intensifying the effect of the alcohol..."

"I'm really, reeeelly..." Noisy hiccup. "...drunk," Spider informed us with a lopsided grin. "But don' worry, Schw... Shweetie..." He attempted an inaccurate kiss and succeeded in thumping his forehead hard enough against Linda's to make them both stagger. "I'll be... f... f..." His eyelids drooped and he blinked heavily once. "...fine..."

The word faded as his eyes dropped shut and his knees buckled. Kane sprang from behind me to seize Spider's shoulders and lower him gently to the floor.

"Ohmigod!" The baby-faced young man fell to his knees beside them, patting Spider's face with shaking hands. "Spider! Spider! Ohmigod, say something!"

"Give him air," Kane said, and gently but firmly pushed the young man back.

Linda was already kneeling beside Spider, fingers on his pulse. He mumbled something unintelligible, still smiling, but his eyes didn't reopen.

"Calm down, Tim," Linda said. "I don't think he's in any danger. But I'm going to take him to the hospital just in case."

"Call an ambulance," I urged. "Don't take a chance on driving. If he gets worse..."

I trailed off, unable to even speak the words.

"I'll get our friends to drive so I can ride with him in the back. Tim, go and get Grant and Red." She turned back to me while Tim continued to wring his hands helplessly over Spider. "If there's any problem, I can call the ambulance from the car, and it'll be faster if we meet them on the way to town anyway." She frowned. "Tim! Go!"

He stared at her with his lips trembling, clearly beyond the point of any useful action, and she took him by the arm. "Aydan, John, please stay with Spider while I make the arrangements."

I nodded and she vanished out the door, a tiny but authoritative figure dragging the ineffectual Tim. In moments she returned with two burly young men and Lola, her wrinkled face uncharacteristically serious.

The two young men loaded Spider's pliant body into the car with a matter-of-fact mien that bespoke frequent experience with semi-conscious drunks, and minutes later they were gone.

Lola patted my arm. "Don't look so worried, honey," she comforted. "He's just a bit drunk. He'll be okay. Remember, Linda's a good nurse."

"I know..."

I spared a moment of guilt over the fact that I was less worried about Spider than I was about Kane. His face was expressionless, but his hands were clenched in white-knuckled fists and the ghosts haunted his eyes again.

No, not ghosts.

Demons.

The savage flames of his own personal hell flickered in his eyes, replaying his torturous march four months ago carrying a horribly abused child.

I shuddered and turned back to Lola. "Can you do me a huge favour?"

"Of course, honey. Name it."

Kane was heading for the door, looking ready to tear someone apart with his bare hands. I had no idea where he might be going, but it seemed like an exceptionally bad idea to let him go alone.

"Um, John's got a family emergency and we need to go." I snatched up my waist pouch from beside the door and grabbed a spare key out of my kitchen drawer to hand to Lola. "Could you please host the party until everybody's ready to leave and then lock up? Just snap the gate padlock shut on your way out and spin the combination."

"No problem." Her bigger-than-life voice was filled with reassurance. "Don't worry about a thing. I'll handle it."

The door closed behind Kane, and Lola pulled me down to her level to murmur, "How bad is it?"

I gulped, fighting the tightness in my throat, but all I could manage was a dry whisper.

"It's bad. It's really bad."

CHAPTER 3

Dashing out my front door, I caught up to Kane just as he was opening the driver's door of his black Expedition.

"Wait," I panted. "Where are you going?"

"Calgary." He swung into the driver's seat.

"Whoa, hang on!" I wedged myself into the opening before he could swing the door shut. "Are you okay to drive?"

"I've only had two beers over the last couple of hours. I'm not impaired."

I hadn't been referring to his blood-alcohol levels, but he looked ready to peel out of there with me clinging to his door handle so I didn't press the point.

"Okay." I eyed him worriedly. "I'm coming along. If I go around to the passenger's side, will you promise to let me in? Or do I need to crawl over top of you from here?"

The grim lines eased a fraction from his face and he pressed the lock release. "Go around. I promise to let you in."

"Thanks." I circled around the front of the vehicle just in case, but I made it into the passenger's seat without incident and he even waited for me to do up my seatbelt before stepping on the gas.

When we reached the highway a few minutes later, he accelerated to just over the speed limit before activating the cruise control. He usually drove without it, but I guessed he didn't trust himself today. His knuckles glowed white on the steering wheel.

I reached over to brush my fingertips lightly over the back of his hand. "Try to relax a bit. If you do that for the next two hours you won't be able to feel your hands by the time we get there."

He grunted assent and loosened his grip, then added, "Would you please call Hellhound? Put him on speaker."

I extracted my cell phone from my waist pouch and dialled, and a few moments later Hellhound's cheerful rasp filled the cab. "Hey, Aydan, how ya doin'? How's the party?"

"Hi, Arnie." I glanced at Kane's rigid face and decided not to waste time on pleasantries. "I'm fine, but we have a situation. John and I are on our way to Calgary. I've got you on speaker so we can all talk."

"Shit, what's wrong?"

The muscles in Kane's jaw rippled as though he was working to control his voice. "Do you know where Alicia is living now?"

A short pause. "Nah," Hellhound said cautiously. "Why?"

"Can you find out?"

"Well, sure, it ain't rocket science. But why d'ya wanna know? Thought ya didn't wanna have anythin' to do with her."

"Get me her address and phone number. I'll pay your usual P.I. rates."

"The hell ya will," Hellhound growled. "Ya don't hafta fuckin' pay me. But, Cap..." He hesitated. "Sorry, I gotta know what's goin' on."

"I just found out she was pregnant when she divorced me." Kane's voice was tight with pain or anger, or probably both. "I have a six-year-old son. He was abducted today. I wouldn't have known at all, except that the RCMP just finished questioning me."

"What the everlovin' *fuck?*" Hellhound demanded, his gravelly voice rising to an incredulous shout.

"I have to talk to her," Kane ground out. "I have to see her. Find out... The fertility specialist said it was impossible. But..." His fists were clenched on the wheel again. "The police showed me a photo. He looks just like me. And she named him Daniel Wyatt..." His voice choked off and he swallowed audibly.

"Fuck," Hellhound repeated.

"She must be lying." Kane swallowed again. "Or the police got it wrong. It just can't be. The specialist said it couldn't happen."

My heart clutched. I knew he wasn't denying it because he didn't want a child. He just didn't dare to hope.

Hellhound hesitated. "I dunno about that, Cap. Remember when we were sittin' in the bar after her last appointment? Ya said to me, 'The specialist said it would be practically impossible for Alicia to get pregnant. He suggested we consider adoption. It's over, Arnie; that was our last hope'. But it was you that said 'no hope', not the doc. 'Practically impossible' ain't the same thing."

Kane's lips twisted in a parody of a smile. "You and your photographic memory. If you say that's what I said, I believe you. So maybe I really do have a son." His jaw muscles rippled. "If he hasn't already been killed by the scumbag who abducted him. Find Alicia. Call me as soon as you have anything. If we get to Calgary before we hear from you, we'll come to your place."

"I'm on it." Hellhound's rasp softened. "Hang in there, Cap. Think good thoughts."

He disconnected, and I stowed my phone again before reaching over to massage Kane's neck. His muscles felt like iron under my touch.

"Try to relax a bit," I urged. "Tensing up like this won't help anyone, least of all you."

Kane hissed out a breath between his teeth. "I know." He shook his head as if trying to rid himself of dark thoughts. "I know better. I've been in situations like this before. I should be able to..."

He trailed off, and I said softly, "Maybe not exactly like this."

He blew out another breath. "Not exactly."

I kept rubbing in silence and after a while his muscles softened, probably due more to his own efforts to relax than to my ineffectual one-handed massage.

"Do you want to talk about it?" I inquired after a half-hour of silent driving. "It sounded as though his name is significant to you. Is he named after your brother?"

Kane spared me a glance before returning his attention to the highway. "Yes."

I thought he was going to fall silent again, but he added, "We were just starting to talk about having a family when Daniel was killed. We agreed that if our first baby was a boy, we'd name him Daniel."

"And Wyatt is your middle name, isn't it?" I prompted.

"Yes."

Silence fell again.

After several miles Kane spoke as though our

conversation had never lapsed. "So either she was honouring my wishes... or she was deliberately taunting me."

"She couldn't have been trying to hurt you." I sent up a silent prayer that it would be true. "If she wanted to taunt you she would have told you about him."

"Maybe."

"Was she, um..." I wasn't quite sure how to phrase the question. "Was your split, um... amicable? I mean, I know it's never easy, but..."

"Did she hate me that much?" Kane stared bleakly out the windshield. "I didn't think so, but obviously I was wrong." He barked out a mirthless laugh. "I guess my first hint should have been the way she slapped me with the divorce papers."

"Well, yeah, divorce papers are usually a bad sign..."

"No, I meant her timing." He stared straight ahead, his jaw working for a moment before he spoke again. "Maybe you thought it was odd that I remember the exact date and time."

"Um, well... I guess that kind of thing is... um... memorable..." I fumbled, trying for tact.

"You could say so," he said bitterly. "Do you remember the armed standoff in 2004 where ten hostages were killed? It started on June twentieth."

I nodded, my heart sinking with recognition. "I remember, but I'd forgotten the exact date."

"I was with the Emergency Response unit at the time," he went on. "A gunman held fifteen people hostage in a bank. We tried to negotiate..."

"...but he wasn't interested in negotiating, was he?" I finished. "He just wanted the media attention."

"Yes. He played us like a cat with mice." Kane spat the

words with disgust. "He killed a hostage every four hours. Each time he made a demand before the killing, but it didn't matter whether we complied with his demands or not. Six innocent people and the police negotiator were dead before we realized he was going to kill all the hostages anyway. So we had to take a chance on collateral damage when we stormed the building."

I squeezed my eyes shut. "I remember. That was a horrible no-win situation. He murdered four more and wounded the rest before the team killed him."

"Yes." Kane stared into the past, his shoulders bunched, hands clenched on the wheel.

When he didn't go on, I murmured, "So it was a bad time to get hit with divorce papers."

His face twisted. "We had been arguing when my pager went off. When I started with the RCMP I was assigned to remote areas. Alicia hated small-town living, so after a few years I transferred to the Emergency Response Team based in Calgary. But I had only been with the ERT six months and she was already nagging me to quit. I was angry because she was the reason I'd transferred in the first place, but she said she spent all her time worrying that I'd be killed and accused me of never being there for her. But when the pager went off, I had to go."

He swallowed. "I was gone for forty-eight hours. No sleep. Running on pure adrenaline. Finally I got home. The blood of innocents on my clothes. On my conscience. Staggered up the front steps and she met me at the door. She'd packed my clothes into suitcases. She slapped the papers against my chest and said, 'You're never here anyway. Don't be here when I get back.' Then she turned and walked away. Got in her car and drove away. That was the last time

I saw her."

He let out a breath. "Four-fifteen on June twenty-second. Two hours after the last bullet was fired, my marriage died."

My throat closed. "I'm so sorry," I whispered.

Kane twitched his shoulders. "We had been having problems for quite a while. It was bad timing, that's all." We rode in silence for a few more moments before he spoke again. "Aydan... thank you." His hand slid over to clasp mine. "It means a lot to have you in my corner at a time like this."

I squeezed his hand. "What are friends for?"

My phone rang, and I snatched it out of my waist pouch and glanced at the call display before punching the Talk button and activating the speaker. "Hi, Arnie, that was quick. I've got you on speaker again."

"Thanks, darlin'," he began, but Kane interrupted.

"Did you find her?"

"Hell, yeah. Easy. She's still livin' at your old place. Same phone number, too."

Kane let out a breath. "Good. Thank you."

"No problem. How 'bout if I head over there an' see if she's home-"

"No," Kane interrupted. "I don't want her to know I'm coming."

"I could put on my Al Hamlin disguise," Hellhound suggested. "Cruise past, make sure she's there, maybe set up a little surveillance-"

"No," Kane repeated. "The police will be there and I don't want to take a chance. I'll call you when we're at the edge of town and you can meet us over there." He hesitated. "...if you have time...?"

"Fuck, Cap, ya don't hafta ask. Anythin' ya need, I'm there."

When the outskirts of Calgary came into view after another hour of silent driving, Kane spoke at last.

"Would you please call Hellhound again? Tell him we'll meet him a block west of the house in forty-five minutes."

"Sure." I pulled out my phone and dialled.

The conversation was short, and after making the arrangements I disconnected and tucked my phone away again. Casting a sidelong glance at Kane's rigid form in the driver's seat, I cleared my throat and tried for a neutral tone.

"So, um... what do you plan to do when you get there?"

"I don't know." His jaw muscles bulged and his next words ground out between his teeth. "I don't know what to do. I don't know what to say to her. I can't..." He broke off with a hissing exhalation. "What the hell's wrong with me, Aydan? I'm an experienced agent. I should be able to handle this."

Sympathy constricted my throat. "It's nothing to do with your competence as an agent. You're a dad who's just found out his child is missing. There's no way to turn that off."

"A dad," he repeated bitterly. "I'm not a dad. I'm just a sperm donor."

"John..."

"It doesn't matter," he interrupted. "I have to let that go and stay focused." He shot me a single tortured glance before returning his gaze to the road. "My son's... Daniel's life might depend on it."

"No, you don't have to." When he shook his head and clenched his jaw, I reached over to grip his forearm and spoke more forcefully. "John, listen to me. This is not your case. The RCMP warned you off. Stemp warned you off. They're right; you're too close to it. And you weren't even back to active duty yet so you shouldn't be involved regardless. Talk to Alicia if you need to, but stay out of the investigation."

"Don't tell me that," he said flatly. "If it was your child..."

I sighed. "Yeah, I know, I'd be in there like a dirty shirt. But you're a professional. You know better."

"So do you." Kane's lips twisted in a humourless smile. "And it wouldn't stop you for an instant."

"But..."

I racked my brain for some useful rebuttal and came up empty. I couldn't preach from any moral high ground. He knew me too well.

We drove the remainder of the trip in silence while the fading sunset drained the western sky to black.

CHAPTER 4

When Kane pulled to a stop in a quiet residential area, Hellhound straightened from his slouch against his Harley Fatboy, leaving his leather jacket and helmet lying on its seat. He strode over to meet us as we got out of the Expedition, the harsh streetlights transforming his battle-scarred features into a forbidding mask of beard and shadowed eye sockets atop a mountain of tattooed muscle.

"What's the plan, Cap?" he rasped.

Kane hissed out a short breath between his teeth, flexing his hands as though trying to regain his circulation. "Let's go and find out."

Hellhound gave me a worried glance as we trailed behind Kane's long strides, and I returned a helpless shrug.

At the front door, Kane pressed the doorbell without hesitation and we waited.

After several moments that seemed longer than they probably were, the door opened and a man surveyed us expressionlessly. Despite his civilian clothes, his short-cropped hair and level gaze said 'cop' just as clearly as the badge clipped to his belt.

"Yes?" he prompted.

Kane squared off into parade rest. "We're here to see

Alicia."

The cop surveyed him with a frown, obviously picking up the 'cop' vibe from Kane in turn. "In what capacity?"

Kane drew a deep breath. "I'm John Kane. Daniel's biological father."

Sympathy transformed the other man's face. "I'm Carson Mayweather with the Calgary City Police. I'm handling your son's case. Please come in."

He stood back from the doorway and we filed in.

As we rounded the corner, a soft-looking brunette sprang up from the sofa and hurled herself at Kane with a choked cry. I glimpsed brown eyes in white strained features before she flung her arms around Kane and buried her face in his chest.

His arms closed around her automatically, but his eyes blazed grey fire in an expressionless face.

"Oh, John, thank God you're here," she babbled, her voice muffled by his shirt. "You have to help me, you have to get him back!"

Kane's gaze sought Officer Mayweather over her head. "Are there any new developments?" Kane asked. "Any ransom demands?"

Mayweather shook his head regretfully. "Nothing new."

"Alicia." Kane gently disengaged from her grip and stepped back. "Tell me what happened."

"He was at a birthday party. His... his best friend Sammy, just a few blocks away..." She dashed tears from her eyes with trembling hands, gazing up at Kane imploringly. "They said Buck... my ex-boyfriend... p-picked him up..." Her voice broke.

Officer Mayweather touched her elbow. "Why don't you sit down?"

She sniffled and turned away to pull a tissue out of the well-used box beside the sofa before perching on the edge of the cushions. Earlier today she might have been pretty, but terror had etched deep lines around her eyes and mouth, and her eyes were red-rimmed above blotchy cheeks.

A toy soldier lay half-concealed under the couch, and I sensed Kane's pain as he glanced at it and then looked away, his lips tightening.

As if coming back to the present, Alicia glanced at Arnie and me for the first time.

"Hey, Lish," Arnie rasped gently. "How ya holdin' up?"

"Don't call me that!" Red spots flared into her cheeks. "I hate it, I've *always* hated it!"

Hellhound blinked as though she'd slapped him. "Shit, Li... sorry, uh... Alicia, I wouldn't'a called ya that if I knew. Why didn't ya ever say anythin'?"

"It doesn't matter." She shredded the tissue without looking at it, her bloodshot gaze trained on the wall behind us. "It doesn't matter; nothing matters except Daniel. I'm..." She shook herself and focused on us again. "Please sit down."

We settled ourselves, Hellhound in the chair and Kane and I on the loveseat, and Alicia gave me a chilly once-over before turning to Kane. "I suppose this is your girlfriend."

"John and I work together," I said hurriedly. "Sorry I didn't introduce myself. I'm Aydan Kelly."

"Oh." Her expression softened into relief. "So you're a cop, too."

"Um, no..." I began, but Mayweather interrupted, giving Kane a keen glance.

"Peters and Birch said you'd probably show up here. You know each other pretty well?"

"Not really, we just work together sometimes," Kane said without inflection. "They're good officers."

"So you didn't know you had a son at all." Mayweather eyed him with the intensity I recognized from all the cops and agents I knew. Watching for lies.

"No. Not until they questioned me a couple of hours ago." Kane turned a burning look on Alicia.

"Don't you put this on me," she said defensively. "I told them not to contact you. I told them you didn't have anything to do with it."

"But I do," Kane said in a voice so soft it sent a shiver of primal fear down my spine. "He's my son, too. And you kept him from me."

The red spots were burning in Alicia's cheeks again. "No, *you* did that. You were never here while we were married, and then you left and never came back. It's your own fault that you never knew Daniel existed."

"You told me to leave and never come back!" Kane snapped. "What did you expect me to do?"

Alicia lunged to her feet. "I expected you to fight for me... for *us!* You're such a big hero, always ready to fight for everybody else, even total strangers in some horrid war on the other side of the world, but you wouldn't fight for *us!*"

Kane was on his feet, too. "You packed my bags! You had the divorce papers ready! I don't know what delusional world you live in, but life isn't like those romance novels you love so much! In real life a guy who refuses to leave and tries to force a reconciliation gets slapped with a restraining order and labelled a stalker!"

"*You didn't even try!*" Alicia was screaming up into Kane's face, and Mayweather intervened with a hand on her elbow.

"Let's cool it, folks," he said in the same 'everybody-stay-calm' cop voice that Kane so frequently used. "Alicia, John, let's just sit down. This isn't helping Daniel."

Alicia let him guide her back to the sofa while Kane sank onto the edge of the loveseat again, but he leaned forward, his gaze boring holes in Alicia.

"What did you tell him?" he asked in that deadly-quiet tone. "Did you tell him your boyfriend was his father?"

"No." She stared through him, cold and remote. "I told him that his father was John Wyatt Kane, a man I once loved very much. A brave soldier who died fighting in a war, in a place far away over the ocean."

"You told him I was *dead?*" Kane's fists knotted. "*You lied to him?*"

"It wasn't a lie." Alicia dropped her gaze to watch her hands throttling each other in her lap. "John Wyatt Kane died in that war," she whispered. "The man I loved never came back."

Kane went grey-white as though he'd been stabbed in the gut. My hand flew to his without a conscious decision on my part, earning a dirty look from Alicia.

"I'm sorry," Kane said hoarsely. "I tried. You have to know how hard I tried..." He swallowed. "But you should have told me you were pregnant. I would have-"

"Would have *what?*" Alicia demanded, her fists clenching. "Tried harder? I wasn't good enough when I was barren, but if I could give you a son maybe I was worth a little more effort? Is that it?" Her voice was rising again, her knuckles whitening. "Was I just a... a... *brood mare* to you?"

"No, of course not, I-"

"Folks," Officer Mayweather interrupted. "We're not accomplishing anything here. John, was there something specific you wanted?"

Kane squared his shoulders. "Yes. I'd like to know exactly what happened, please. And what's been done so far."

"Alicia, will you please tell it again?" Mayweather inquired. "I realize it's upsetting, but each time you tell it there's a chance that you might remember something more."

She nodded, her arms wrapped tightly around her body while she stared at the floor. "Daniel went to Sammy's party. He was so excited. It was all he'd talked about for weeks. Sammy is his best friend and they share a passion for toy soldiers." She shuddered. "They pretend they're soldiers fighting in a war. I should never have told him John was in the military."

"Please go on, Alicia," Mayweather encouraged.

"Yes. Well." She drew a deep breath, still hugging herself. "Anyway, the party was at two o'clock, and Marta..." She glanced briefly at Kane before returning her gaze to the carpet. "Marta is Sammy's mother. Marta said she'd walk Daniel home after the party ended at four o'clock. At four-thirty I started to wonder. At five o'clock I called her, and she said..." Her voice wavered. "She said... my ex had picked him up at three-thirty."

"Was she certain it was Murphy?" Kane snapped. "How well did she know him?"

"Yes. She knew him, and she didn't think anything was wrong. Arbuckle told her..." She trailed off at Hellhound's snicker and added, "Yes, his name is Arbuckle. Arbuckle Faulkner Murphy. His parents had great aspirations for their children. His brother's name is Penobscot Salinger Murphy. No wonder they go by Buck and Scot."

Hellhound stifled himself, scrubbing a hand over his

beard as Alicia went on, "Anyway, Buck told her I'd asked him to pick Daniel up from the birthday party so they could go camping. Marta was pleased that he was making the effort because Buck was often critical of Daniel. He called him a girly-boy." She glanced at Kane's thundercloud scowl and hastened to explain, "That's why we split up."

"Don't see what's girly about playin' with toy soldiers," Hellhound observed.

"No, Buck approved of that because it was manly. But Daniel liked..." Her voice caught on a sob, but she stiffened her spine and went on firmly, "...he *likes* to draw and paint. And he likes to help me bake cookies." She shot a defensive look at Kane. "I encourage him in whatever he enjoys. He's not..." She made angry air quotes. "...'girly' or 'manly'. He's just a happy child who loves soldiers and art and bugs and mud and puppies and kittens and baking and books... and... h-hockey..." Her words trailed off into a quaver.

"You're a good mother," Kane said gently. "I always knew you would be."

Tears welled up in her eyes. "And now he's gone..."

"We'll find him. Just focus," Kane encouraged, his cop voice strong and calm despite the tension vibrating in his shoulders. "So Murphy abducted Daniel as... what? Leverage? Revenge? What did you do when you discovered he'd taken Daniel?"

"I don't know why he'd take Daniel, he just wasn't that interested in children..." Alicia gulped. "Maybe... maybe this is all a big mistake and everything's fine and they're on their way home..." She threw an imploring look toward Mayweather, but I could tell she didn't believe her own words any more than he did. "Anyway," she went on shakily, "I... I wasn't too worried... at first. Angry, but not worried.

Buck had asked earlier to take Daniel camping this weekend, and although Daniel was excited about the idea, I had said no."

Kane's voice came out bleak as bone. "Why? Did you have reason to believe Murphy couldn't be trusted alone with Daniel?"

"No!" Alicia straightened, meeting Kane's eyes directly for the first time. "No, he would never molest a child. I..." She dropped her gaze again. "I actually hired a private investigator to check on him when we first started going out. He wasn't a pedophile."

She swallowed. "It was just that... I wasn't sure it was good for Daniel to continue seeing Buck when there was no chance we'd reconcile..." Alicia gulped back tears. "I c-called Buck's cell phone but it went to voicemail. I thought he was probably just ignoring me until they'd set up camp so I wouldn't have the heart to make him bring Daniel back. And..." She wiped her eyes with the crumpled tissue. "If... If he had called... I'm not sure I w-would have. Daniel was so... thrilled at the thought of camping, and he needs male influences..."

As if realizing she was twisting the knife, she gave Kane a guilty glance before continuing hurriedly, "But when he hadn't called by six, I started to worry in earnest. I called the police..." She threw an imploring look at Mayweather. "I'd been calling and calling Buck's cell phone b-but... I should have called the police right away, I should have..." She trailed off helplessly.

"If Murphy was contemptuous of Daniel and didn't like children, why the sudden interest in camping?" Kane asked. "Had Murphy been acting unusual lately? Any changes in routine? Changes in the way he interacted with Daniel? Did

Daniel say anything about him or act differently around him? Had anything changed recently in your relationship with him?" He broke off with an apologetic look at Mayweather. "Sorry, I'm sure you've already gone over this."

Mayweather nodded. "It's okay. It's worth going over again. We never know when we might uncover some new detail."

"Thank you," Kane said. "Alicia? Anything?"

She let her hand fall open limply in her lap. "No. Nothing had changed. I wasn't surprised by the camping trip because after we broke up it wasn't unusual for Buck to drop by on a whim and take Daniel out for a few hours." She wrinkled her nose. "He criticized the way I'm bringing Daniel up, and said he had to teach Daniel to be a man. But I think he just took Daniel to the park and tried to attract women by playing the doting dad. Poor Daniel lapped up the attention; he wanted a father so much..."

Kane made a small sound as if in pain, but if I hadn't known him so well I would have thought he was only clearing his throat. His impassive expression never wavered.

"Fuckin' sick!" Hellhound burst out. "What kinda sick fuckin' asshole uses a kid like that?"

Alicia hunched her shoulders, still staring at the floor. "Anyway, he 'borrowed' Daniel last weekend, so that's likely how he knew about the party at Sammy's house. But..." She jerked forward, reddened eyes burning in her white face. "Don't you see, it doesn't *matter* how he knew! It's too late for that! What if... oh, God, what if I was wrong about Buck? What if he sold Daniel to some horrible child prostitution ring?"

Hellhound shot a worried glance at Kane before returning his attention to Alicia. "Hush, now, darlin'," he murmured. "Stop imaginin' the worst. It's gonna be okay. We'll find him, an' he'll be fine."

"I'm not your darling!" Alicia snapped. "And what do you know anyway? You don't have children; you're nothing more than a big child yourself!"

Arnie's expression never changed, but I could see the hurt in his eyes.

"Take it easy," I said, my voice coming out with a bit more of an edge than I'd intended. "He's only trying to help."

Hellhound reached over to squeeze my hand. "It's okay, darlin', she's just gotta blow off some steam. I got broad shoulders, I can take it." He turned back to Alicia. "Go ahead. Get it outta your system. It'll do ya good."

Her face crumpled. "I h-hate you," she choked. "You always meant more to John than I did. Like... Like after that last appointment with the fertility specialist." She shot a bitter look at Kane. "You went to the bar with *him* instead of staying with me."

Kane jerked upright. "You said you wanted to be alone. You practically pushed me out the door. I was hurting, too-"

"*Then why didn't you show it?*" she shouted. "Why didn't you-"

"Hey, now," Hellhound intervened gently. "Ya were talkin' about how much ya hate me, remember?"

Alicia turned brimming eyes back to him, glaring through her tears. "*You!* You were always his excuse to withdraw whenever things got tough. You always came first. And *look* at you, you're ugly and vulgar and... and..."

"An' I called ya Lish for years," Hellhound finished comfortably. "I'm a real fuckin' asshole."

"*Oh...*" Tears streamed down her face. "I *hate* you!" She

lurched to her feet and flung herself at him.

Hellhound met her halfway, folding her into his arms and rocking her while she bunched her fists in his T-shirt and wept great wrenching sobs.

"It's okay, darlin', it's okay," he soothed. "Just let it out."

At last her weeping subsided into broken whimpers, then quieted. She relinquished her grip on Hellhound's T-shirt and hid her face in her hands.

Mayweather proffered the tissue box, and she mopped her face and blew her nose without looking at us. "I need to lie down for a while," she whispered and turned away, arms wrapped around her body as if to hold herself together through sheer physical effort.

"Want me to sit with ya for a bit?" Arnie asked softly.

She stopped. "No. My parents are flying in. They should be here in an hour or so." She turned and gave him a brief watery smile. "Remember, I still hate you."

His answering smile was full of compassion. "Yeah, I know."

She turned again to totter off down the hallway, leaning against the wall as if her legs could barely carry her weight.

CHAPTER 5

"What's been done so far?" Kane asked, and Mayweather leaned back in his chair, clearly relieved to be free of the conflict between Kane and Alicia.

"We put out an Amber Alert as soon as Alicia called us," he said. "So police, border guards, and the public are watching for Daniel and they have a description of Murphy and his vehicle. We've pulled all Murphy's credit, debit, and phone records. We know he bought gas with his debit card right before he picked Daniel up, and the gas station CCTV records show he was alone then. He was driving a black 2007 Chevy Silverado, registered in his name."

"What about-" Kane began, but Mayweather wasn't finished.

"We've also questioned all his friends, family, and work associates," he went on. "None of them noticed any change in his behaviour recently. We asked if they knew of any favourite camping spots Murphy might have had and they gave us a few suggestions, but we've searched those and found nothing. Murphy's phone records show that he talked to his brother this morning, but the brother says it was just a social call and Daniel wasn't mentioned. We searched Murphy's apartment and canvassed the neighbours. His cell phone was found in the apartment, and his neighbours said they hadn't seen him since early this morning and they'd never seen him with a child."

"So he's vanished," Kane said tightly. "With this much of a head start, they could be anywhere in several thousand square miles. Or if Daniel was delivered immediately to a contact in a human trafficking ring, he could even be out of the country by now."

I read the truth of Kane's statement in the thinning of Mayweather's lips, but he replied reassuringly, "We don't have any evidence of human trafficking. Try to put that out of your mind. This could still be perfectly innocent. Murphy may have dropped Daniel off at a friend's house and they don't even realize anything is wrong..."

Kane began to speak, but Mayweather held up a restraining hand and met Kane's gaze steadily. "John, you know as well as I do that torturing yourself over this won't help anybody. I promise, we're doing the best we can. It's getting late. Why don't you try to get some rest? Leave me your number and I'll call you if there are any developments."

Kane opened his mouth as if to argue, then closed it and nodded. Scribbling his number on a torn-out page from the small notebook he always carried, he handed the paper to Mayweather.

"May I call you if I have more questions?" Kane asked.

"Of course. Any time of the day or night." Mayweather tore the paper in half and wrote his own number on it before offering it to Kane.

"Thank you." Kane shook Mayweather's hand and we did the same before filing for the door.

When we reconvened under the streetlight next to Kane's Expedition, Hellhound said, "Come on back to my place. I got beer an' that bottle a' scotch ya left last time ya were there." I edged closer, shivering in the chilly evening air, and Hellhound wrapped his arm around me. "Come on, Cap," he urged. "Ya need to wind down a bit."

Kane shook his head. "I don't want to drink. I need to keep my head clear. I have to figure this out..."

He was about to speak again when Mayweather called his name from the doorway. When Mayweather beckoned, we all hurried back to the house.

"News?" Kane demanded.

"Yes." Mayweather didn't look happy, and my guts clenched. "Please sit down while I go and get Alicia," he added.

We all perched tensely in our original positions, and a moment later Mayweather emerged from the hallway with Alicia clinging to his arm, chalk-white.

"What is it?" Kane demanded, his face almost as pale as Alicia's.

Mayweather guided Alicia to the sofa and seated her before saying, "Arbuckle Murphy was killed in a single-vehicle rollover accident southwest of Rocky Mountain House, probably a couple of hours ago. He wasn't wearing his seatbelt. He was ejected and the truck rolled over him. The wreck wasn't discovered right away because his truck went over an embankment that made it invisible from the road. Fortunately some off-roaders saw headlights shining through the trees, or who knows when we might have found him."

"Daniel...?" Alicia's voice was a bare whisper.

"No sign of him," Mayweather said.

Kane's mouth flattened into a grim line. "You said it was a rollover. Any chance Daniel might... might have been ejected, too?"

"No."   Mayweather gave him a sympathetic look. "Responders searched all the way down the embankment as a matter of course, and once the truck was identified, the RCMP searched the entire area again just to be sure. They found a child's hat and a toy soldier in the truck so they brought in tracking dogs, but they found no scent anywhere around the scene." Mayweather let out a breath. "Daniel was never there."

"Show me exactly where it happened." Kane extracted his smartphone and rose. Mayweather stood, too, waiting while Kane brought up a map.

"Expand this area," Mayweather prompted, pointing at the screen. Kane did, and Mayweather leaned in to hover a fingertip over it. "About there. He was southbound on the forestry trunk road."

Kane turned the phone toward Hellhound and me, and I extracted my reading glasses for a better look.

"Do either of you know this area?" Kane asked.

I sighed. "Sorry, no."

Hellhound shook his head, too. "Nah. Took a bike trip through there once, but I was headin' up to Drayton Valley an' I stayed on pavement. Never went west a' Rocky Mountain House."

Kane returned his attention to Mayweather. "What else can you tell me?"

"The RCMP said it looked as though Murphy really was planning to go camping..." He frowned. "Or poaching. He was wearing camouflage clothing and he had a compound hunting bow and broadhead arrows, but the bowhunting season doesn't open for another couple of weeks."

Kane frowned, too. "Aydan, do you know of any archery

ranges up in that area?" When Mayweather gave him a quizzical look, he elaborated, "Aydan is an archer. She has medals from tournaments all over North America."

"Maybe..." I said slowly. "There are no big public ranges out there, and only a couple of small private ones. But the ranges don't usually allow broadheads. They slice up the butts too badly."

Hellhound snickered, and I prodded his ribs with an affectionate knuckle. "Wiseass. 'Butts' are the backboards where we pin our targets." I turned back to Kane and Mayweather. "You can buy special targets for broadhead practice so he might have been planning to set one up in the woods somewhere. Did he have anything that looked like a big foam cube in the vehicle? About eighteen inches square?"

Mayweather shook his head. "He had the bow, a hunting knife, and a cooler full of food and beer. There was an extra jacket in the truck, so he might have been planning to stay a while. The weather forecast is hot and dry for the next week so he wouldn't have needed that heavy jacket for the short term. The only odd thing was that he wasn't wearing any shoes, but..." Mayweather shrugged. "I've seen footwear end up long distances away in that kind of an accident."

Kane folded his arms over his massive chest and regarded the smaller man without expression. "You didn't mention a tent. Was there one in the vehicle?"

"No."

"So Murphy had already set up camp, and left Daniel there. Are they searching the campgrounds?" Kane demanded.

"Yes. But it's crown land out there, so lots of people pull off the road and camp anywhere they please. And we don't know whether Murphy was leaving his campsite or returning to it, so we have to search in both directions. We'll get a helicopter up at first light to try to spot any tents set up on the crown land, but in that kind of wooded terrain there's no guarantee they'd be able to see a tent from the air."

"So Daniel may be alone in a tent in the middle of the woods somewhere," Kane said grimly. "Or maybe the camping was just a ruse and Murphy already delivered Daniel to a buyer."

Mayweather sighed and scrubbed a hand over his face. "Officers are canvassing the restaurants and gas stations between here and Rocky Mountain House, but so far nobody remembers seeing Murphy or Daniel."

"So..." Alicia spoke for the first time, her voice a thin quaver. "Buck's d...dead... and... and Daniel could be anywhere..."

"If he's in that area, we'll find him," Mayweather said firmly. "We have the dogs, and we have a lot of volunteer searchers. At first light tomorrow we'll get even more personnel on it."

"And... if he's not there...?" Her voice broke.

I could tell Mayweather wanted to say something reassuring, but instead he tucked a hand under Alicia's elbow and raised her gently to her feet. "Lie down again," he said. "As soon as I know more, I'll let you know."

When Mayweather returned from guiding Alicia back to bed, Kane was already standing at the door, vibrating with the need for action. "I'm going to drive up to Rocky Mountain House tonight," he said.

Mayweather shook his head. "Stay here. We have our best people-"

"I have military Search and Rescue training," Kane

interrupted. "I'll pick up my gear and leave within the hour. Notify your team that I'll be joining them."

Mayweather opened his mouth as if to argue, then closed it again and nodded as if realizing it was futile. "They'll be starting at first light tomorrow," he said instead. "I'll call you with the information in the morning."

"Thank you," Kane said, and strode out.

Hellhound and I muttered awkward goodbyes and followed him.

Kane was waiting impatiently for us beside his Expedition, and as soon as we were within earshot he said, "Hellhound, can you take Aydan back to Silverside? I'm leaving as soon as I get my gear from the condo."

"Why don't ya get some sleep first..." Hellhound began before trailing off with a glance at Kane's jutting jaw. "Okay, Cap," he said instead. "We're comin', too. I just gotta stop off at my place an' pick up a change a' clothes an' my gear, an' then I'll be right behind ya. We're gonna need a base camp. Get two rooms an' call me with the name a' the hotel."

"Thank you," Kane said simply, but his eyes showed the depth of his gratitude.

"Um... sorry to be a pain," I interjected. "But I left with nothing but my waist pouch. I'll need to pick up a few things."

Kane eyed me quizzically. "Don't you have anything at Hellhound's place?"

"No." I sent an affectionate look Arnie's way. "That would be too much like commitment. If I left a toothbrush in his bathroom we'd both have to run for the hills."

Kane shook his head, but the corners of his mouth softened in what was almost a smile. "You two are completely messed up; you realize that, don't you?"

"Yep." Hellhound gave me a grin in return. "An' that's just the way we like it." He sobered. "Go on ahead, Cap. I'll take Aydan shoppin' an' follow ya later."

"Thanks. See you. Oh, wait..." Kane stepped into the shadow of the Expedition and unfastened his holster. "You'd better take this." He handed me his Sig, swung into the driver's seat of the Expedition, and drove away before I could protest.

"What the fuck?" Hellhound demanded.

I blew out a breath, the gun heavy in my hand. "He quit. Stemp told him to stay off this case and threatened disciplinary action if he didn't, and he just flat-out quit. Told Stemp he'd turn over his weapon to me, and hung up."

"Aw, shit." Hellhound stared at the holster in my hand. "Fuckin' goddam shit."

There didn't seem to be much more to say. We exchanged a helpless look, and after a moment of silence Hellhound gave a resigned shrug. "Well, leave it at my place for now, an' ya can turn it in to Stemp when ya get back." I handed it to him and he turned to tuck it into the Harley's saddlebag, exchanging the weapon for his spare helmet. "Here ya go, darlin'," he added.

I eyed the inadequate shell with trepidation. "Uh..."

"Come on, let's get goin'..." Hellhound began, shrugging on his leather jacket only to pause, his brow furrowing. "Aw, shit. Sorry. I know ya always use a full-face helmet, but this brain bucket's all I got. An' I ain't got any leathers for ya." He eyed my bare arms worriedly before shedding his jacket again and holding it out. "Put this on. D'ya wanna drive? I can ride on the P-pad if it'll make ya feel better."

I summoned a joke, trying to gather my courage. "I thought the 'P' in P-pad stood for 'pussy'. Didn't you tell me your dick would fall off if you had to ride on the back?"

He laughed. "Tonight I'm gonna say 'P' stands for 'passenger', an' my dick was only gonna fall off if I hadta ride the P-pad on that candy-ass little Honda Shadow ya had. The back a' my hog'll be okay."

Passing his jacket back and clinging to every ounce of trust I had in him, I managed a grin. "Your dick is far too important to me, so I won't take the chance. And there's room for two of me in that jacket. You wear it and drive. I'll be fine on the back."

"Are ya sure?" Hellhound sobered and studied me with concern. "'Cause seriously, darlin', I don't mind. I know how much ya hate doublin'.'"

"I'm sure." I buckled the helmet on, feeling horridly vulnerable. "It wouldn't be safe for me to drive. Your bike is a couple hundred pounds heavier than what I'm used to, and with you on the back I probably couldn't even keep it upright at a stoplight." I turned away to hide my fear. "Hurry up, let's go. At this time of the night the only place open is Shopper's Drug Mart, but at least I can get a toothbrush."

"Okay." He swung astride the bike.

As I mounted up behind him, the Harley woke with a roar that rattled the quiet street. I wrapped my arms around Hellhound, pressed my face into the snarling dog on the broad back of his leather jacket, and commended my spirit to whatever benevolent god might be willing to accept it.

CHAPTER 6

Enveloped in one of Hellhound's far-too-big hooded sweatshirts about an hour later, I settled into the passenger seat of his Subaru Forester with a sigh that came all the way from my toes.

He glanced over from the driver's side. "Okay, darlin'? Ya warm enough?"

"Yeah." I shivered and stifled a yawn that was part fatigue, part nerves. "I'm just bagged. Long day." I wouldn't admit exactly how frightened I'd been on the back of his bike, but he probably knew. His ribs were likely still aching from my deathgrip.

"Helluva long day," he agreed. "An' it ain't over yet." He put the SUV into gear and pulled out into the light traffic. "This's sure a helluva clusterfuck."

"Yeah." I shuddered. "I can't even imagine what John's going through." He grunted agreement, and I added, "So, um... is Alicia as much of a piece of work as she seemed tonight?"

"Nah, she's okay..." Hellhound trailed off uncertainly, then shrugged. "Well, hell, I dunno. Never knew how bitter she was." He sighed. "Poor Lish. An' poor John. They went through hell when they were together, an' now this. It fuckin' sucks."

"Yeah." I leaned back with a sigh. "When John and I were first getting to know each other, he mentioned he was pretty messed up when he came back from combat overseas. It's too bad he couldn't get the help he needed then."

Hellhound stared through the windshield. "He got as much help as he could, but shit like that changes ya forever. Lish didn't wanna believe that. She thought if he just tried hard enough he could get over it an' go back to the way he was. But that ain't the way it works."

I reached over to touch his hand, studying his expressionless profile. "You fought alongside him. It must have been just as bad for you."

"Nah. I was already fucked up beyond repair when I went over."

His matter-of-fact tone twisted my heart, and I brought his hand to my lips and brushed soft kisses over his scarred knuckles. "I wish I could wave a magic wand and make all that stuff go away for you, but... you know I love you exactly the way you are."

He swallowed, and when he spoke again his voice was hoarser than usual. "Thanks, Aydan, but that just goes to show how fucked up ya really are."

I grinned. "That's why you love me."

He smiled, the glow of the dashboard lights softening his battered features. "Nah. I'd love ya even if ya weren't fucked up."

We lapsed into a comfortable silence, driving through the darkness holding hands. After a few minutes I roused myself.

"I still don't see how she could have kept it from him."

Hellhound grunted. "I can't believe it either. Never

thought she'd pull shit like that."

"No; I mean, I don't see how she could have actually kept Daniel a secret. Surely they have mutual friends."

"Hm," Hellhound said thoughtfully. "Nah, not really. Ya know how it is when a couple breaks up; their friends break up, too. An' John got recruited to join the Department right around then, so he was on trainin' courses mosta the time, an' they set him up with that condo down in the deep south so him an' Lish never crossed paths. She didn't try an' screw him in the divorce; she kept the house but never asked for any support payments, so he let it go with no contest. An' by then he was on active duty so he was gone half the time anyway."

It was my turn to mutter "Hm."

He shook his head. "I can't believe he really quit."

"Yeah. He really did." I frowned. "Well, maybe not officially yet. He hasn't given written notice. Stemp wanted him to come in right away for debriefing, so I hope he's not in trouble over that."

"Huh." Hellhound drove in silence for a few moments before releasing a breath. "Well, I guess everybody's gotta quit sometime. Better to go out this way than tits-up on a slab."

"That's the truth."

He glanced over. "So when're ya gonna quit?"

"Me?" I blinked, shifting mental gears.

"Yeah. You're always sayin' ya hate what you're doin'. So why not quit? Hell, why didn't ya quit long ago?"

"I, um..." I hesitated.

"It's okay if ya can't tell me, darlin'." He squeezed my hand. "I was just askin'."

"No, it's not like it's classified or anything, I just... I

hadn't really thought about it." I yawned, knuckling my aching eyes. "I didn't have a choice in the beginning; I was just trying to stay alive. And now..." I let out a breath and faced the truth. "...it's been four months since anybody tried to kill me, but I don't feel safe without my Glock. If I quit the Department, I'd have to go unarmed."

"Well, darlin'..." His voice softened. "Goin' on more missions ain't the way to get over the feelin' that everybody's tryin' to kill ya."

"I know." I grimaced into the darkness. "But I feel good about the, um..." I searched briefly for the right word to describe my activities without revealing anything classified. "...administrative work I'm doing when I'm not on active duty."

"Think Stemp'll let ya keep doin' it? Usually he's all gung-ho about gettin' agents back in action."

A trickle of fear chilled my backbone but I kept my tone confident. "I think he'll let me keep doing what I do. I've got a few... um... skills... nobody else has..." I trailed off, uncertainty niggling at me.

Stemp had Tammy to do decryptions now. Maybe he didn't need two of us. Oh, God, what if he tried to send me out as a field agent again?

I straightened my spine. I wouldn't go. I'd quit, just like Kane.

Fear closed my throat.

Not 'just like Kane'. Kane was a master of hand-to-hand combat. He could protect himself even without a weapon. I had no skills at all...

Stop it. Don't borrow trouble. So far Stemp hadn't mentioned changing my role.

Too tired to worry over it anymore, I leaned my head

back. "Are we there yet?" I joked, and was rewarded by the sexy rasp of Hellhound's chuckle.

"Have a nap, darlin'," he said. "I'll wake ya when we get there."

The vibration of my waist pouch roused me from my doze, and I struggled upright in Hellhound's passenger seat and extracted my cell phone. After a glance at the call display, I pressed the button. "Hi, John. I'm putting you on speaker."

"Hello," Kane said, the word taut. I exchanged a worried glance with Hellhound as Kane went on, "Where are you?"

Hellhound replied, "Just went through Caroline about ten minutes ago."

Kane uttered a muffled word that might have been an epithet before continuing, "There's a complication. You might want to turn around and stay at Caroline instead. There's some sort of summer festival going on in Rocky Mountain House this weekend, and there's a bike rally, too. I got the last motel room in town, and it's not one of the finer establishments. It's clean and it has two queen beds, but it's definitely not quiet."

Hellhound shrugged, his leather jacket creaking in the darkness. "Hell, I don't give a shit. 'Long's ya don't mind bunkin' together."

He glanced over at me and I gave him a 'whatever' shrug and added, "It's up to you, John. If you'd rather we stayed in Caroline, we can turn around now."

"Keep coming, then," Kane said. "I'll leave word at the office for them to give you a key. Let yourselves in when you get here. I'll probably be in the shower." He gave us the motel name and directions before hanging up.

I stowed my phone in my waist pouch and leaned back in the seat with a yawn.

Hellhound glanced over from the driver's seat and bounced his eyebrows suggestively. "Well, darlin', looks like we're gonna have another threesome. I brought a buncha condoms, an' I hope you're wearin' your little red thong."

"Nngh." I clenched my fists in my hair. "That was probably the most embarrassed I've ever been in my life." Despite the humiliating memory, a smile crept onto my lips at the sight of his devilish grin. "I'm not wearing the red one today," I added. "And your condoms are going to have to remain unused. I'm pretty sure that's more than John wants to know about us."

Hellhound winked. "Hell, darlin', ya never know. Maybe he-"

"Don't even go there," I interrupted.

He chuckled and returned his attention to the road, but he was still watching me out of the corner of his eye as he inquired, "So what about you an' him? The two a' ya still ain't gettin' it on?"

"No."

"How come? Is it..." He hesitated, giving me a sidelong glance before staring through the windshield again. "Is it 'cause a' me?"

"No, of course not."

"'Cause I don't ever wanna come between ya," he went on as if I hadn't spoken. "If the two a' ya wanna try an' make it work together, just say the word an' I'll-"

"Arnie, stop," I interrupted gently. "Nothing's changed between you and me, and you can trust me to tell you if it does. And even if our physical relationship ends, it won't change our friendship. Not for me, anyway."

"Not for me, either." His hand crept over to clasp mine. "Thanks, darlin'." We drove in silence for a few more miles before he spoke again. "So is it that you ain't doin' him or he ain't doin' you?"

I leaned my head back with a sigh. "Both. And... I don't know... Maybe it's better that way." I stared out the windshield at the cone of gray highway revealed by the headlights. "It seems like we get along fine as long as we're not sleeping together, but all the bullshit starts as soon as sex is on the table."

A snicker from the driver's seat made me glance over. Hellhound was grinning again. "Well, darlin', maybe ya oughta stop havin' sex on the table. Try the bed."

I snorted. "Everybody's a friggin' comic."

By the time we pulled up at the motel office, my yawns were threatening to turn me inside-out. "Lucky you're a night owl," I mumbled, rubbing my eyes. "I'd probably have fallen asleep at the wheel by now."

Hellhound grinned. "Yeah, maybe I oughta go see if I can find myself a party." He jerked his chin at the long row of motorcycles in the parking lot. "Gonna be some good times tonight."

I eyed the bar across the street worriedly. Rowdy shouts and the thump of heavy bass were clearly audible even through the closed windows of the SUV.

"Think there'll be trouble?" I asked.

"Nah, probl'y not. Bike rallies are okay. The hardcore guys don't wanna attract attention so they keep their noses clean, an' the weekend warriors just whoop it up a bit an' then go back to their hotel an' sleep it off." He swung out of the driver's seat. "I'll go get our key. Be right back."

A few minutes later we parked in front of our unit and got out. Hellhound extracted his ever-present guitar case and a small duffel bag from the back seat, and shot a grin at the plastic bag containing the few overnight essentials that dangled from my hand. "Ya sure know to travel light, darlin'."

I hefted the bag, smiling. "Well, I didn't think there was much chance you'd take me to a black-tie gala tonight."

He closed the distance between us, wrapping an arm behind my back to pull me against him. His voice dropped to a deep sexy rasp that made my sleepy body wake up and pay attention. "Darlin', I'll take ya anywhere ya wanna go."

"Mmm." I linked my arms around his neck and gave a teasing little wiggle, enjoying the slide of his hard body against mine before regretfully pulling away. "Hold that thought until we have a motel room of our own."

He chuckled and patted my ass as we crossed the sidewalk to the room door. I was pushing the old-fashioned key into the doorknob lock when the door opened from the inside. My gaze made a brief but extremely rewarding traverse of the muscular contours of Kane's naked torso above his jeans before I redirected my attention to his face with an effort.

"Come in," he said, turning away and rubbing his wet hair with the towel around his neck. When Hellhound swung the door closed behind us, Kane gave us a grimace. "Be it ever so humble..." He indicated the worn but still garish orange-and-brown décor with a resigned gesture.

"...there's no place like home," I finished, and dropped onto the nearest bed with a cavernous yawn. "At least the bed feels okay." I nodded toward the inadequate security chain dangling from the door jamb. "And hey, this place is practically Fort Knox."

Kane's face creased with concern as he dug into his pocket and withdrew his keys. "If you don't feel safe here, take the Expedition and go back to Caroline."

"Oh, hell, no." I waved the keys away, embarrassed. "I didn't mean that, I was just joking around." When he continued to eye me worriedly, I patted my ankle holster and grinned up at him. "Seriously, John. I've got you and Arnie and a Glock. I couldn't be safer."

"Ya sure, darlin'?" Hellhound asked. "'Cause I don't mind takin' ya back."

"Jeez, you guys!" I flopped back on the bed. "This is *me*, remember? Not some delicate little flower."

Hellhound chuckled. "Nah, 'delicate flower' ain't the words I woulda used." He leaned his guitar carefully in the corner and dropped his duffel bag beside it. "I gotta take a leak, an' then I'm gonna go grab a beer. Need to wind down a bit. Wanna come?"

I let out a long breath, my eyelids drooping. "Nope, I'm going to be asleep before you go out the door."

"I'll stay, too," Kane said.

Hellhound's shrewd gaze flicked over Kane's expression before darting to me meaningfully. "Well, I'm prob'ly gonna be late, so don't wait up," he said, and headed for the bathroom.

Kane and I avoided each other's gaze as the sound of his peeing transmitted with unfortunate clarity through the thin wall. Kane flicked the TV on and turned up the volume.

When Hellhound emerged and headed for the door with a nonchalant salute, I hurried into the bathroom and took advantage of the relative privacy of the inane television soundtrack to do what needed to be done, too.

Kane muted the TV when I came out with my teeth freshly brushed and awkwardness burning my cheeks. I probably didn't need nightwear. They'd both seen me naked often enough. But still...

"Um..." I didn't quite meet his eyes. "May I borrow a T-shirt for tonight? I didn't realize we'd be bunking together..." I trailed off.

"Of course." Kane's tone was artificially hearty. "No problem. Here you go." He extracted a clean T-shirt from his duffel bag and handed it over.

"Thanks." I shuffled my feet. "Um..." I realized I was still staring at his chest. And his broad shoulders, curving down into the smooth bulges of his biceps. Corrugated abs with that tantalizing strip of hair tracking down from his navel to his-

I jerked my gaze up to his face again. "I'm going to go get some ice," I muttered. Avoiding his gaze, I tossed his T-shirt on the bed, seized the ice bucket, and scurried out the door.

CHAPTER 7

Dodging three large hairy bikers who occupied most of the sidewalk, I speed-walked to the motel office, only to discover that the ice machine was back the way I'd come. When I retraced my steps, the bikers snickered and nudged each other in a way that made me glad I had a Glock strapped to my ankle.

I ducked into the alcove that sheltered the vending machines and filled my ice bucket, then drew a deep breath.

Okay. No need to get awkward with Kane. Nothing had changed between us. We were only going to sleep together...

That thought sent my mind rocketing to a variety of X-rated memories and I shook my head vigorously to dislodge them.

Jeez, no, we weren't sleeping together. We were just sleeping. Together. In the same room, nothing more...

"Hey, babe." The largest and hairiest of the bikers was leaning in the door opening, eyeing me up and down with interest. "Wanna make a little extra pocket money?"

"Nope." I slipped past him, only to pull up short when the other two blocked my way.

Shit.

One biker behind me, two in front. They were

staggering-drunk, but they were each nearly as big as Kane and Hellhound. Not good odds unless I could get to my Glock. It seemed very far away in my ankle holster.

I sidestepped, my heart pattering into a rapid rhythm.

The two in front blocked my path to the sidewalk, but at least I'd gotten my back to the wall. Dammit, the alcove concealed us from both the office and the parking lot. Party noise from the bar would mask any screams or sounds of struggle.

"Come on, babe," the biggest one wheedled. "We're fun guys. You can keep the cash all for yourself. We won't tell your pimp if you don't."

Holding onto my composure and temper with equal determination, I kept my voice level. "I'm not a hooker and I don't have a pimp. You guys need to go look somewhere else for kicks. Excuse me, I have to go."

I attempted another escape, but the three closed ranks and I had to back up or run into a barricade of beer-and-cigarette-reeking leather. I pressed my back to the wall and tried again. "Back off, you guys. I'm warning you."

The ringleader guffawed. "You're warning us? That's rich. Come on, honey, we can do this easy and have a little fun, or we can buy you from your pimp and make you wish you'd been nicer to us when you had the chance."

Fear short-circuited into anger and I jerked forward. "Listen, dipshit, I told you I'm not a hooker! Now get the hell out of my face!"

They drew back, uncertainty flickering in their eyes until the ringleader grinned. "Nice try, babe. I like 'em with a little spunk. But we were sitting right over there when your pimp delivered you to that room." He jerked his bearded chin in the direction of the motorcycles parked across from our room. "So I'm gonna give you one more chance to be nice before I start getting pissed off."

Shit, of course. They'd seen Hellhound fondling me before he 'delivered' me to a room containing a half-dressed Kane, and then minutes later he'd left as though the transaction was complete.

Shit, shit, shit!

The bikers closed in again and I evaluated my chances in an eyeblink, my pulse hammering in my ears.

If they pinned my arms, my gun might as well be on another planet for all the good it would do. They were easily big enough to immobilize me even in their inebriated state. And they were already so close that I didn't have room to bend over and reach my ankle holster.

Time to end this.

I blew out a sigh. "Okay. Fine. How about a nice blowjob for each of you? I'll do you right here."

I dropped to my knees, reaching back to place the ice bucket strategically close to my ankle while I watched their eyes light up.

Right... about...

Now.

Snatching my Glock from its holster, I clamped one hand on the ringleaders' crotch and twisted hard while I jammed my pistol into the nuts of the guy next to him.

"Who wants to get off first?" I snarled.

The ringleader let out a strangled squeak, sweat springing out on his brow. His compatriot froze staring down at the gun buried in his crotch, his legs trembling hard enough to vibrate the Glock. The third man yelped, "Fuck!" and ran, only to crash to the ground when Kane pivoted around the corner and smashed an elbow into his face.

Kane swooped down on the fallen man like some pagan god of vengeance and I shouted, "Don't kill him!"

Kane hesitated, his hands wrapped around the man's head in a grip I knew could snap his neck like a twig.

"Don't kill him," I repeated forcefully. "You quit, remember?"

"Qu-quit...?" the ringleader quavered in a high-pitched voice. Sweat trickled down the sides of his face. "Quit killing guys, like... like quitting smoking or something?"

Kane slammed the unconscious man back to the pavement and straightened, grinding the man's hand under his hiking boot as he stepped over the body with contemptuous disregard.

"Yes," he grated, his glare fixed on the sweating man above me. "It's a habit I've been trying to break. But I'd be pleased to make an exception in your case."

"H-Hey, we don't want any trouble..." the ringleader tried to back away but froze with another squeak when I twisted a little harder. "Jesus, lady, let go of my fuckin' nuts!"

I exerted a few more pounds of pressure.

His pallor turned greenish and he swayed, whimpering, "Fuck, lady, *please!* Look, we didn't mean any harm, it was just a m-misunderstanding..."

The other man had neither moved nor spoken. In fact, I was pretty sure he wasn't even breathing. My surmise was confirmed when he suddenly toppled backward, going down full-length like a tree in a hurricane. His skull struck the pavement with an unpleasantly hollow crack.

Kane smiled. Very slowly, his lips curled into a snarling grin under eyes alight with bloodlust.

I hadn't thought the ringleader could get any paler, but

he did.

He also pissed his pants.

"Ew! You pig!" I snatched my hand away from the warm wetness and wiped it vigorously on his jeans before scrambling to my feet, gun trained on him.

Kane's feral smile widened. "Maybe I can't kill him, but you can," he said softly. "We can bring him back to our room and take our time. I know a lot of ways to make excruciating pain last and last."

I wasn't sure whether Kane was serious or not, but he looked convincing enough to send a chill down my spine. The former ringleader fell to his knees, sobbing out a garbled plea for mercy.

Glowering down at the weeping mess of piss and sweat and tears and snot, I swung my pistol slowly up to point at his head.

"Please, lady, please, no..."

I snapped, "Shut up!" and he fell silent, trembling in the widening pool of urine.

Hiding my quaver of adrenaline in the harshest voice I could summon, I growled, "It's your lucky day. You're so fucking disgusting I don't even want to waste a bullet on you. Take your dumbfuck friends and get on your bikes and get the fuck out of here and don't ever come back. And if I ever see your fucking ugly face again, I'll shoot it off. Got it?"

I didn't wait for a reply, just turned on my heel and strode away before my own trembling knees could give out.

Behind me, Kane added a deadly-quiet warning. "And if you ever mention what happened here, I'll hunt you down and make you wish she'd shot your face off."

As soon as I rounded the corner I ran for the motel room, only to fetch up against it with a thump when the knob didn't turn.

Kane had locked the door.

Of course.

Holding my contaminated hand well away from my body and my Glock out of sight beside my leg, I slumped panting and shaking against the door. The party was in full swing in the bar across the street, but nobody was looking my way yet. Kane still hadn't appeared.

What the hell was he doing?

Oh, God, what if they'd attacked him as soon as I turned my back?

Letting out a whimper, I turned to sprint back the way I'd come, only to cannon into Kane.

"What?" he barked, snapping a wild-eyed gaze around the parking lot.

"Nothing," I quavered. "I just need the room key."

"Oh." He produced it from his pocket and opened the door, pushing me ahead of him into the room.

When the door closed behind us I hurried for the bathroom, where I stuffed my Glock into my waistband and scrubbed my hands with copious amounts of soap and the hottest water I could stand.

At last I shut off the tap and turned to face Kane, who stood leaning against the bathroom door jamb watching me without expression.

"What happened?" he asked.

"They thought I was a hooker."

Kane frowned. "That doesn't give them the right to assault you."

I shrugged. "They thought it did."

"I should have killed them."

The ice-grey of his eyes made me shiver. "No, you

shouldn't have," I said firmly. "Remember, you're a civilian now." He didn't reply, and I laid a hand on his clenched fist and added, "John, you're tired and stressed and you're overreacting. Come on, let's watch some TV and relax a bit, and then you should try to get some sleep."

I nudged him gently out of the doorway, but as we turned the corner into the room, he stopped and gazed down at me, his eyes blazing.

"If they had hurt you, I would have killed them," he said flatly. "Nobody hurts the people I love and lives to tell about it."

I gulped. "Okay, thanks, but you are really overreacting right now. Come on." I guided him to the bed and pushed the television remote into his hand. "Lie down. Do the guy thing and channel-surf."

He obeyed, stuffing the pillow behind his head and thumbing the remote without comment. Turning off the lamp, I sank onto the other bed and eased back on the pillows.

Relax. Breathe.

My tense muscles gradually softened while I took slow rhythmic yoga breaths, willing the adrenaline out of my system. The frenetic flicker of the TV did nothing to aid my relaxation, but at least Kane was lying quietly and not killing anybody. A surreptitious glance revealed a profile that could have been carved from stone. He might be lying down, but he sure as hell wasn't relaxing.

Maybe I should call Hellhound. He'd know how to handle this. And maybe I should tell him to bring a bottle of scotch. Or two...

A tiny sound from the doorknob slammed adrenaline into my veins all over again. I snapped a glance over at

Kane, who was already rolling soundlessly off the bed.

Smooth and silent, he glided forward to take up a combat-ready stance, and I trained my Glock on the door.

The doorknob turned by almost-imperceptible degrees.

I forgot to breathe.

Fighting off the encroaching blackness at the edges of my vision, I let out a trembling breath, then drew another.

Let it out halfway to steady my shaking gun...

The door eased open, the streetlights silhouetting a bulky figure and gleaming on the leather of his jacket.

Some sixth sense must have warned him.

He froze.

"Don't shoot, darlin'," Hellhound said. "It's just me."

"*Shit!*" I collapsed backward on the bed, dropping my gun to clutch at my hammering heart. "Jesus Christ, you scared the living shit out of me!"

Hellhound slipped into the room and closed the door behind him as Kane straightened out of his crouch.

"Christ, we need a secret knock or somethin'," Hellhound said. "I couldn't see a light so I figured you'd gone to bed. I was tryin' not to wake ya."

Massaging my chest with a shaking hand, I managed a completely unconvincing laugh. "Are you kidding? I'm never going to sleep again."

"What are you doing back so early?" Kane inquired, sounding perfectly calm and composed. "I thought you'd be partying it up until dawn."

"Just came back to get my guitar," Hellhound said. "Good crowd over there. Always gotta be a few fuckin' morons, though. Ya shoulda seen the three losers out in the parkin' lot. Fuckin' sad when the wannabes try an' be real bikers."

Kane and I exchanged a glance. "What were they doing?" Kane asked.

Hellhound snorted. "Gettin' into an ambulance. One guy'd done a faceplant an' smashed the shit outta his nose. Bleedin' like a stuck pig. The other guy'd gone over backwards an' knocked himself out. An' their buddy was so fuckin' wasted he pissed himself."

"What was their story?" Kane asked noncommittally.

"No story." Hellhound shrugged. "They were just shit-faced. Ol' Piss-pants was cryin' and tryin' to get in the ambulance an' the EMTs were tryin' to get him offa them so they could look at the guys that actually needed 'em. Fuckin' gong show."

His sixth sense must have kicked in again, because his gaze slid from Kane to me, his eyes narrowing with suspicion. "Ya wouldn't happen to know anythin' about that, would ya?"

"Who, us?" I made big innocent eyes.

Hellhound dropped onto the edge of the bed, grinning. "Okay, spill it."

Kane sank onto the other bed. "Aydan went to get ice. When she seemed to be taking too long, I went after her. When I came around the corner she was on her knees, surrounded by those three men."

Hellhound's brows snapped together. "What the fuck? Aydan, are ya okay?"

"I'm fine," I said at the same time that Kane let out a grim laugh.

"She had everything under control," he assured Hellhound. "She had her gun jammed in one man's crotch and she had Piss-pants by the testicles." The corner of his mouth quirked up. "The third man fled, but he just happened to run face-first into my elbow when I came around the corner."

"Is that so?" Hellhound was grinning again. "An' then what happened?"

"Kane's guy was down for the count," I said. "And the guy I had my gun on passed out and hit his head. That's when Piss-pants pissed his pants."

I wiped my hand on the bedspread compulsively. "Right in my hand. Gross."

"Fuck, I can't leave the two a' ya alone for a second, can I?" Hellhound said. "Maybe I better stay here an' keep ya outta trouble 'stead a' goin' back to the bar." When I gave him a tiny nod and flicked my gaze in Kane's direction, he continued smoothly, "Actually, ya know what? Think I'll call it a night. I'm fuckin' bagged. Early start tomorrow, an' ya know what a bear I am in the mornin'."

"That's a good idea," I agreed gratefully.

CHAPTER 8

Even the warmth of Hellhound's softly-snoring bulk beside me wasn't enough to lull me into a deep sleep. I dozed fitfully, waking at every thump from the adjoining rooms and every voice from the parking lot outside. The air conditioner cycled on and off with roars and asthmatic wheezes punctuated by machine-gun-like rattling.

Kane was visible only as a dark silhouette in the other bed, but from the artificially steady rhythm of his breathing I guessed he wasn't sleeping much, either.

When my phone chirped its alarm at five-thirty AM, I silenced it with a groan. Light already glowed under the bathroom door, so Kane had either woken before the alarm or had never slept. Beside me, Hellhound snored on. I cuddled a little closer, unwilling to leave the comfort of his body heat for the morning chill of the room. He sighed in his sleep and tucked his arm over me, and I was fading into slumber when the bathroom door opened, spilling light into the room.

"Good morning," I said softly, and slid out of bed to head for the bathroom.

"'Morning," Kane agreed in a hoarse rasp that indicated how little sleep he'd had. "I'm going to McDonald's. What can I bring you?"

"Egg-and-sausage McMuffin, milk, orange juice, and a yogurt parfait," I said promptly. "And you'd better bring lots of coffee for Arnie. I don't dare wake him at this hour unless coffee is the first thing he smells."

The tired lines of Kane's face eased into a smile as he regarded his best friend's peaceful slumber. "Right. Back soon." A ghost of humour flickered in his eyes. "Don't shoot me when I come through the door."

"Only if you forget my breakfast," I promised.

By the time I emerged freshly showered, Kane had already returned and Hellhound was propped more or less upright in bed, alternating grumbled profanity with gulps of life-giving caffeine.

As I tore into the deliciously savory grease of the breakfast sandwich, Kane propped his elbows on the other side of the small table. "Mayweather called," he said tightly. "They're organizing the search teams at first light, but I'm not going to join them right away. I want to look at the accident scene first."

I wiped my fingers on the napkin and reached over to squeeze his hand. "Will they let you do that? Will they be done there?"

"They'll let me." His face was grey and grim in the inadequate light, and I spared a moment of sympathy for any hapless police officer who might oppose him.

A short time later we hit the highway, following Kane's Expedition while the eastern sky lightened to dawn behind us.

The sun peeked over the horizon as we turned south on the forestry trunk road, and Hellhound groaned and swung the visor to the side to block its rays. It hadn't seemed wise to initiate conversation earlier, but now I turned to regard his sleepy features.

"Do you want me to drive?" I offered. "You could catch a bit more sleep."

"Nah," he croaked. "Then I'd just hafta wake up all over again."

"How did you ever survive the army? Aren't they all about early mornings?"

He squinted blearily at me before returning his attention to the road. "I *can* wake up early. I just really fuckin' hate it."

After that we drove in silence until Kane's brake lights glowed through the plume of gravel dust we'd been trying to avoid for the past half hour.

"I'm leadin' the way when we go back," Hellhound grumbled. "His turn to eat dust for a while."

Despite his grousing, he looked wide awake and alert when he pulled off on the side of the road and parked behind Kane's SUV. We got out and hurried forward to join Kane where he stood at the edge of an embankment. The road sloped downhill before veering off to the right, and somebody had obviously missed the curve.

The path of Buck Murphy's final ride was marked by crushed undergrowth, gouged earth, and snapped saplings. I held my breath as I leaned over the edge, but it wasn't a sheer cliff. Steep but navigable by foot, the hillside fell away into a small valley. The wrecked truck had been removed, and its destruction was evident in the remaining twisted trim mouldings and glitters of broken glass. Streamers of police tape fluttered from the trees near the road but none stretched across to seal the site, so we moved forward cautiously.

Kane halted at the edge, his gaze sweeping side to side. "I'd like to walk a large perimeter first," he said. "Let's start twenty yards or so outside the damage zone and do a search pattern. Yell if you see anything out of the ordinary."

I eyed the dense forest around us. "We might want to do a bit of yelling anyway. This is bear country."

"Good point," Hellhound said, and unleashed a ringing yodel that would have done an alpine herdsman proud. The echo bounced back on the clear morning air, and he promptly engaged the echoes in an enthusiastic yodelling competition.

When he finished, grinning, Kane squinted at him as though peering through a blinding headache. "Good God. If there were any bears around earlier, they're long gone now. That sounded like Tarzan being slowly roasted over hot coals."

Hellhound feigned injured pride. "What d'ya mean? That was my best Franzl Lang imitation."

Kane shook his head. "I don't know who Franzl Lang is, but I hope I never meet him. Let's get started."

As he turned away, I reached up to give Hellhound a kiss. "You sounded great to me. I've always loved yodelling."

"Really? I didn't know ya were a yodeller, darlin'." He waved an expansive arm over the quiet valley. "Let's hear ya."

"Oh, jeez, no! I didn't mean I love to yodel myself. I meant I love listening to yodelling."

"Aw, go on. Give it a try," Hellhound urged.

"No way. John might have thought you sounded bad, but he'd think somebody was strangling a cat if I got going. Come on." I hurried over the edge of the embankment, but halted when a police car pulled to a stop on the road above, blipping the siren.

Kane emerged from the woods and the three of us trekked up to where the uniformed officer stood beside his car. "This site is part of an active investigation," he informed us. "I'll have to ask you to leave."

"I'm investigating," Kane said shortly, and flashed his badge at the officer. "This is my team." He indicated Hellhound and me.

The officer gave the badge a cursory glance, then nodded and left, obviously focused on wherever he'd been heading before he spotted us.

"Was that, um... a good idea?" I asked hesitantly. "Isn't that kind of like impersonating a police officer?"

Kane just shrugged and turned to plunge into the forest again.

Several hours later, I stretched the sleeve of my T-shirt to mop the sweat off my forehead while I trudged up the embankment for what seemed like the hundredth time. At the top I flopped down to sit on the ground, stretching out my legs.

Crackling in the undergrowth made me jerk to attention but it was only Hellhound emerging from the woods, brushing spruce needles out of his beard.

"Hey, darlin'," he said as he strode over. "How ya doin'?" He glanced at his wristwatch. "I figure you're due to pass out pretty soon if ya don't get some lunch." He lowered himself to the ground beside me and I leaned into him despite our mutual sweatiness.

"I'm starving," I agreed. My stomach let out a rumble of complaint, and I massaged it absently. "But mostly I'm thirsty. I didn't realize we were going to do a marathon hill-climbing session here. I already drank my bottle of water, and I should have brought more."

"Yeah." Hellhound frowned downhill to where Kane was still methodically pacing back and forth across the accident site. "I shoulda known he'd do this. If we don't stop him, he'll spend the rest a' the day here without food or water." He let out a halloo and when Kane looked up, he beckoned and shouted, "Come on up. Time to go back to town. Aydan's gotta eat, an' you do, too. We can come back after lunch."

"You go ahead," Kane called in return. "Just bring me back something when you come."

Hellhound sighed and rose, extending a hand to pull me up. "Come on, darlin'. No point arguin' with him, an' the sooner we go, the sooner we'll get back. It's gonna be stinkin' hot pretty soon so he's gonna need more water."

"It's already stinking hot." I trailed after Hellhound on legs rubbery from exertion and hunger.

A shout from behind made us pause, and a moment later Kane jogged up over the lip of the embankment. Not for the first time, I marvelled at his fitness as he approached, his breathing only slightly accelerated after running up the steep hill.

"Changed my mind," he said. "I don't have a cellular signal out here, so I'll go back to town, too. I want to call Mayweather and see if there are any new developments."

"Okay," Hellhound agreed. "Meet ya at the Burger Baron." He hustled over to his SUV and put it in gear seconds after the passenger door closed behind me. "Ain't gonna eat any dust this trip," he said smugly as we pulled away.

A logging truck surged into view over the crest of the hill.

"Don't be too sure about that," I replied as a giant dust cloud enveloped us.

With a burger and fries nestling comfortably in my stomach, I leaned back in my chair and sipped the remainder of my milkshake while Kane dialled Mayweather's number.

After a terse greeting, Kane asked, "Anything new?"

At Mayweather's response he sat up straight in his chair, his eyes narrowing in concentration while he listened.

Mayweather seemed to be giving him a lengthy report, because Kane sat in silence punctuated only by mutters of acknowledgement. Suddenly the colour drained from his face.

"So... you're searching downstream?" he asked, obviously trying to hold his voice steady and not quite succeeding.

Mayweather's response was short, and Kane cleared his throat and added, "All right. When the forensic team is finished, I'd like to look over the campsite. Then I'll join the search team."

He pressed the disconnect button and leaned his elbows heavily on the table as if holding himself up by sheer will. "They found the campsite uphill about a mile from the accident site," he said. "It was hidden back in the woods. We drove right past it this morning without even seeing it."

Hellhound and I exchanged a worried glance. "And...?" I asked, my stomach clenching.

It had to be bad news. I didn't want to hear it.

"Daniel had definitely been there. They found his toy soldiers in the tent."

We waited in silence while he gathered himself.

"They brought the dogs in, and they picked up Daniel's trail leading away from the campsite." Kane swallowed. "Toward the river." He drew a ragged breath. "They found Murphy's missing boots neatly lined up beside his tent. Tracks matching those boots overlaid Daniel's footprints in the soft soil at the edge of the river. Murphy's prints went down to the river and back again. Daniel's..." He swallowed again. "...went down to the river and ended there."

Sick silence enveloped us.

"Maybe he got tired an' Murphy carried him back," Hellhound offered unconvincingly. "It'd be uphill from the river, right?"

"They have preliminary autopsy results, too," Kane went on, his voice tight. "Murphy was intoxicated. Double the legal limit, but investigators guess he was only going around twenty kilometres per hour when he went over the edge, so there's no way he should have missed the curve unless he either passed out or swerved to avoid something. There were no marks indicating he'd swerved or braked, but that's a well-travelled road so any marks in the gravel might have been obliterated by the time investigators got there."

"That doesn't make sense. What the hell was he doin' drivin' around shit-faced in his sock feet?" Hellhound demanded. "An' I ain't ever known a drunk to drive carefully. He woulda been flyin' down that hill, unless..."

"Unless he was in shock," Kane said tersely. "If he'd just seen Daniel being swept away down the river... he might have gone back to the campsite, tried to drown his sorrows, then driven away in a daze..."

"Nah," Hellhound objected. "He'd a' freaked out an' run for help. He'd a' been drivin' like a bat outta hell. An' why would he take off his boots?"

"Or he killed Daniel in cold blood and threw his body in the river," Kane said grimly. "Then went back to his campsite and got comfortable. Took off his boots and had a few drinks..."

"He wouldn'ta," Hellhound said with certainty. "A murderer woulda gone screamin' outta there an' called the cops to make it look like an accident. An' anyway, why would he take Daniel all the way out here to kill him? He had lotsa other chances that woulda been a helluva lot less trouble."

Desperately clutching at any semblance of hope, I blurted, "Wait, here's a scenario that makes more sense. What if they were just having a nice camping trip? They go down to the river and play around a bit, then Murphy carries Daniel back. Remember, Daniel would be tired after the birthday party, and it would be getting late. So Murphy puts Daniel to bed and then he sits up drinking for a while..."

"The cooler full a' food an' beer," Hellhound said with a nod.

"Right," I agreed. "So he's drunk when he decides to call it a night. Puts the cooler back in the truck so it won't attract bears, takes off his boots, goes into the tent, and then realizes Daniel has wandered off. He panics, jumps in his truck and goes looking for him. Doesn't bother with boots or seatbelt."

"Driving slowly," Kane said, sounding more hopeful. "Maybe calling out the window. But because he's drunk and his attention is divided, he misses the curve and goes over the edge of the embankment. The autopsy showed that he died of a broken neck. He sustained a couple of blunt-force facial injuries just prior to death, but his other injuries were consistent with being ejected from a rolling truck and the examiner believes they occurred post-mortem."

"So he smacked his face as he went over, which broke his neck, and he was dead before the truck ever rolled over him," I translated, and Kane nodded.

"If your scenario is right, they need to send those tracking dogs out again," Kane said, already dialling his phone.

CHAPTER 9

In the passenger seat of Hellhound's SUV again, I stared anxiously out the windshield at the back of Kane's Expedition driving too fast ahead of us on the highway.

"I don't even want to think about a six-year-old out in the woods alone all this time," I muttered. My throat closed and I swallowed hard. "If they find... a body... I don't want to think about what that would do to John."

"Yeah..." Hellhound said absently, and I looked over see him scowling at the road.

"What?" I asked. "What are you thinking?"

He glanced over, his eyes dark. "I'm hopin' your scenario's right an' Daniel's still alive, but I'm thinkin' about why a little kid would run away into the woods in the middle a' the fuckin' night. An' I ain't likin' what I'm comin' up with."

"Oh, God." Nausea clenched my guts. "If Alicia was wrong..."

"If Murphy was a child molester, I'll hunt that fucker all the way to hell," Hellhound grated. "An' when I find him, I'm gonna make him think hell was a fuckin' bible camp." He glanced over again. "Don't mention it to Kane. It's prob'ly already in the back a' his mind, an' he doesn't need to hear it out loud. An' anyway, it's still better than findin' a body."

I nodded, unable to speak.

Kane's brake lights glowed through the dust again. He pulled over to park behind a police car on the shoulder of the road, and Hellhound pulled to a stop behind him. As the dust cleared I could see the long straight slope of road to the accident site nearly a mile farther on.

Flattened tire tracks in the vegetation of the ditch marked the trail that we'd missed when we'd driven by earlier, and as we got out of Hellhound's vehicle a police SUV drove out of the woods. We stepped aside to let it pass, then hurried after Kane as he strode along the trail.

When we caught up to him I reached tentatively for his hand. He gave mine a gentle squeeze but let go almost immediately with a grimace that was probably meant to be a smile.

When we arrived at the campsite, Kane flashed his badge again and conferred briefly with one of the uniformed police officers before waving us over. "Forensics are still working," he said. "So don't touch anything, but we can look from a distance. The dogs are searching in circles around the campsite-"

He broke off as a tech walked by, carrying a pair of hiking boots wrapped in clear plastic.

"Wait," Kane commanded. "May I see the treads on those?"

The tech turned the treads toward him, and Kane whipped out his phone to take a photo, then thanked the tech and returned his attention to us.

"Here, take this," Kane said, holding out his phone. "Watch for any prints that match. I want to take a quick look around here, and then I'll join the search team."

Hellhound glanced at the photo and handed the phone back to Kane. "Got it," Hellhound said, and not for the first time I envied his phenomenal memory. "Come on, let's go look at the prints down by the river," he added.

We stepped carefully single-file where the uniformed officer had directed, well to the side of the markers the forensic team had placed on the way down to the river. At the river's edge we took up cautious positions, trying to get close enough to see the footprints without antagonizing the tech who bristled if we got too close to her painstaking work.

Kane knelt, staring at the small footprints as if willing his son to appear in them. Reaching toward one of the prints, he whispered, "Not even as big as my hand..."

He bowed his head as though struggling to control his emotions, and Hellhound clasped his shoulder in silence. I stood uselessly beside them, sickness coiling in my guts.

"Look!" Hellhound's voice rose with sudden hope. "Murphy's prints are deeper where they lead back to the campsite. He musta been carryin' Daniel like we thought."

Kane shot to his feet, his gaze riveted to the prints Hellhound indicated. "You're right," he said. "I'm sure you're right!" He bounded back up the path without a backward glance, and Hellhound sighed.

"I sure as hell hope I'm right."

I eyed the prints. "I really think you are. Look, where there are two prints side by side, one going and one coming? The one going uphill is definitely deeper."

"Let's go, then, darlin'." Hellhound grabbed my hand and towed me back up the hill at twice the pace we'd come down.

By the time we got back to the campsite Kane was reporting our guesses to the officer in charge, who listened with courteous attention and no expression whatsoever. When Kane was finished, the officer nodded and replied, "I'll be sure to mention that to forensics. Mayweather will be in touch as soon as we have the report."

Kane thanked him, then strode rapidly away as if trying to dissipate pent-up energy. Hellhound and I trotted after him.

When we caught up to him at the edge of the road Kane growled, "They're humouring me. I feel like an idiot. Of course forensics will make a far more accurate evaluation than my half-assed eyeballing and desperate hope. When I was in the RCMP I dealt with people exactly like me dozens of times. People who wouldn't back off and let me do my investigation; who always had to get in the middle of everything. Thought they had some crucial evidence and had to babble out every harebrained theory..."

"Slow down." I grabbed his hand and pulled him to a halt. "Take a breath. I promise, they're listening to you. I bet you listened to those people, too, when you were the officer in charge. They won't blow it off."

His hand clenched around mine and he drew a deep breath, then released me. "Thank you. You're right." He sucked in another breath and let it out in a long slow exhalation. "I'm going to walk this stretch of road. The crash investigators would have checked the area right around the accident site, but they wouldn't have had any reason to look this far away. If Murphy was driving slowly downhill, I want to know why."

"We'll help ya look," Hellhound said immediately. We all

held our breaths as a jacked-up four-by-four roared by, raising another cloud of dust. When it dissipated enough to speak, Hellhound added, "If there's anythin' to find on this road, we better find it fast before any more traffic goes over it. Ya lookin' for anythin' special?"

"Footprints," Kane said tightly. "Especially small ones. Or distinct tire tracks. Skid marks. Disturbances in the vegetation at the side of the road. Anything unusual at all. And call for him. The search parties will be far away from the road by now, but if he's still wandering, he might be close enough to hear us." He raised his voice to a full shout. "Daniel! *Daniel!*"

The echo mocked his call, diminishing quickly into the ever-present sigh of the breeze through spruce trees.

Kane called again, and my heart twisted at the sight of his head raised in hope, his fists clenched by his sides.

When no answer came, he shook his head and cast his gaze down.

"What's that?" he snapped a moment later.

We crowded around the area he indicated.

"Murphy's bootprints," Hellhound said. "Crossin' the road into the campsite."

"Don't let anybody drive over them," Kane barked, and jogged back along the trail to the campsite.

A few minutes later he returned, disappointment telegraphing from the heavy lines of his shoulders. "They already noted them," he said flatly. "Apparently Murphy was a hiker. They found several places where he'd gone for a walk, and they've already been checked for evidence."

I reached over to squeeze his hand. "That's good, right? They're really on top of things."

Kane nodded, but the grim lines of his face didn't ease.

"That's good," he agreed without enthusiasm. "Let's walk the road anyway. Just in case."

We split up to trudge down the road, Hellhound and I on opposite sides while Kane paced slowly down the middle shouting Daniel's name every dozen or so strides. Kane looked utterly focused on the road, and when another plume of dust appeared at the bottom of the hill, I called his name.

"John, there's a car coming."

"I see it," he replied. "Don't worry; I don't intend to get run over."

"That's good. I don't think tire tracks would be a good look for you."

The bleak lines of his face softened into the tiniest hint of a smile as he stepped off the road, and we stood in silent endurance until the vehicle passed and the air cleared enough to breathe. Then we resumed our slow progress, eyes on the road and voices raised in regular calls for Daniel.

The sun blazed down, its heat a searing weight on my shoulders. Sweat mingled with my sunscreen and the ever-present gravel dust to form a gritty layer on my skin. The breeze provided intermittent relief, but as we slowly progressed downhill it diminished to barely a breath. My eyeballs felt broiled in their sockets and the gravel blurred into an interminable line.

I blinked hard and swigged from my water bottle, keeping my attention on the road. Any tiny detail might count...

"Footprints!"

Kane's cry jerked my head up, and I was surprised to see we were only a few hundred yards uphill from the crash site. I placed my water bottle by the side of the road to mark my position before hurrying over. On Kane's other side,

Hellhound did the same.

"Look!" Kane pointed to a patch of boot prints in the middle of the road. Most of them were obscured by the gravel, but some were clearly visible in a softer sandy portion. He pulled out his phone to refer to his photo, but Hellhound was already nodding.

"They match," he said. "Those're Murphy's boots, or else somebody else has a pair exactly the same size an' brand."

"What the hell was he doing?" I asked, studying the pattern of scuffs and overlapping prints. "It looks as though he was just standing in the middle of the road. Taking a smoke break or something?"

"I don't see any butts," Hellhound disagreed.

"Maybe he was walking along the side of the road and somebody he knew drove by," Kane said. "The way the prints are clustered in the middle of the road, he might have walked over to talk to somebody in a vehicle that had pulled to a stop. Stood and visited for a few minutes, and then went back to his campsite." He indicated where the prints turned uphill and headed toward the sparse vegetation on my side of the road.

"Shit, I didn't see any tracks in the ditch," I said in chagrin. "He might have walked alongside the road all the way back to the campsite."

"Ya couldn'ta noticed," Hellhound comforted. "It's just grass an' rocks over there; nothin' that would show a footprint."

"But there might be partial prints..." I began.

"Maybe," Kane said. "But don't try to find them. I want the forensic team to look at this before we contaminate the site any more." He let out a breath. "They've probably already catalogued it, but I don't dare take a chance. I'll run back up. Don't let anybody drive over this. If it's old news, I'll give you a wave from the top of the hill."

He turned and ran uphill and I sighed and wiped the gritty sweat off my forehead. "We'd better make sure he drinks some water when he gets back." I glanced up the road, judging the distance. "Nearly a mile uphill in this heat..."

Hellhound chuckled. "Darlin', the army'd just call that a nice little warm-up jog."

"Fuck the army. I enjoy a run as much as the next person, but I'll do my running in the morning or evening when it's nice and cool, thank you very much." I sighed. "I'm getting sunburned even through my sunblock."

Hellhound sobered and eyed my face and arms. "Shit, ya are, too. You an' that pretty redhead skin a' yours. Here." He peeled off his T-shirt. 'Put this over your head. Sorry it's sweaty, but it's better'n fryin' in the sun."

"No, don't do that," I objected. "You'll get a terrible sunburn if you go shirtless at this altitude."

"Nah, I'll be fine. I was gonna put on some more sunscreen anyway, so ya can do my back for me."

While I tied his T-shirt around my head and centred the knot to cast some shade over my face, he extracted a tube of sunscreen from his pocket and removed the bandanna he'd tied over his shaved skull. Smearing sunscreen over his head, ears, and face with both hands, he rubbed the excess onto his arms and scrubbed the last traces off his beard before handing me the tube.

"Lube me up, darlin'." He winked.

I did my best martyred sigh, grinning. "Well, if I *have* to..."

Gliding my slippery palms over the mountains of his

shoulders, I massaged in small circles, working my way down the ridges of muscle on either side of his spine to the waistband of his jeans. Stepping around to the front, I murmured, "I'd better do your chest, too. I wouldn't want you to miss a spot."

"Mm-hmm." He growled deep in his throat while I worked with leisurely appreciation over his bulky chest and down his hard abs.

Heat gathered in parts of my body I was pretty sure the sun's rays couldn't reach and I circled my hands lower, letting my fingers dip teasingly into his jeans.

"Mmm," I purred. "It's too bad I just smeared sunscreen all over you. You're looking very..." I licked my lips, admiring the glistening swaths of tattooed muscle. "...lickable."

"Damn, darlin'." He grinned. "Maybe I oughta give ya my jeans, too. You could put 'em over your shoulders so your arms don't get burnt. 'Course..." His grin widened. "...then you'd hafta rub sunscreen on a few other places for me."

I wiggled my exploring fingers a little deeper, watching his eyes ignite. "Commando as usual, I see. There might not be enough sunscreen in this little tube."

"Darlin', the way you're heatin' me up, there ain't enough sunscreen in the world."

The blip of a police siren from above made me jerk my hands off him.

Hellhound chuckled. "Guilty conscience?"

"Permanently." I sighed, watching the police car cruise down toward us. "I swear, even now that I work for the Department; even when I haven't done anything wrong; I still think 'What have I done?' every time I see a uniform or a police car."

"Yeah. Me, too." Hellhound grinned. "When Kane wore the RCMP uniform, he used to sneak up behind me every chance he got just so he could watch me twitch when I turned around. Bastard." The epithet was affectionate, and I smiled in return.

"You probably deserved it."

"Well, yeah. I'm usually guilty a' somethin'."

The cruiser pulled to a stop above us, lights flashing, and Kane got out of the passenger side and strode over.

"This was a new discovery," he said. "The traffic investigators checked this area, but they weren't looking for footprints. Now they'll block traffic until they've processed the entire stretch of road." He shot a glance up and down the road. "I don't think there's anything more I can do here. I'll go back up and join the next search party that goes out."

"Okay, Cap," Hellhound agreed. "Let's go."

As we turned to trudge up the road again, Kane glanced at his wristwatch before eyeing Hellhound's bare torso and the sweat-stained T-shirt around my head. "No, you need to take Aydan home..."

Our combined objections drowned out his next words, and he waved a silencing hand and continued, "This is the best way. Aydan can't stay out in the sun any longer, and in any case she has to be at work tomorrow morning-"

"Fuck work," I began, but he shook his head.

"No, you need to go to work."

Something in his voice alerted me, and we walked in silence until we were out of the earshot of the police officer who was placing markers around the footprints in the road.

"Because...?" I prompted when we were at a safe distance.

"Because I need somebody on the inside," Kane said quietly. "Mayweather has been good about sharing his findings so far, but if he finds out I'm not in law enforcement anymore he might dry up. I need to stay on top of everything that's happening in the investigation." He hesitated before adding reluctantly, "If... if you're willing. I realize it will place you in an ambiguous moral position-"

"There's nothing ambiguous about it," I interrupted. "A child is missing. The only moral thing to do is make sure we do everything possible to find him."

Kane sighed. "All right, never mind moral; consider the legal implications. You'd be illegally accessing an active police investigation and leaking information to a civilian. If you get caught, you could go to prison."

My heart rate ticked up in claustrophobic fear at the thought, but I met Kane's gaze squarely and kept my voice light. "Well, hell, it's about time I did something to justify my guilty conscience."

CHAPTER 10

Sitting in the passenger seat of Hellhound's SUV with the vent blasting cool air onto my hot face, I kept my sunbaked eyes closed and continued the argument I'd started before we began driving. "It's a waste of time to go all the way back to Calgary just to pick up John's gun. If we drive straight east from here we can shave at least an hour off the trip and you can get back and join the search party that much sooner."

"Yeah, I know, darlin'," Hellhound agreed from behind the wheel. "But John's already skatin' on thin ice by not goin' in for his debriefin'. Better if everythin' else goes by the book."

"But the gun's perfectly safe at your place. You're the Department's top weapons specialist, so Stemp can't argue that we're being careless. He can just take a chill-pill. We'll get the gun back to him later."

"Sorry, darlin'," Hellhound said regretfully. "This time I'm stickin' to Kane's orders."

I snorted. "That's a first."

"Yeah." I could hear the smile in his voice, but it turned serious as he spoke. "But right now there's nothin' he can do but wait, an' that's the worst feelin' in the world. It'll help if he's in control a' somethin'."

I opened my eyes to gaze over at his homely profile, a lump rising in my throat. "You're such a good friend," I whispered.

When we parked in front of my house at last, I leaned over to kiss Hellhound. "Normally I'd invite you in for a nice long shower, but I guess you'd better get going."

He returned the kiss and held me close for a moment. "Can't believe I'm turnin' down a chance to get ya all wet an' slippery, but..." He smiled and dropped another kiss on my lips. "...I ain't gonna let it happen again. See ya soon."

"Be careful. Call me tonight or as soon as you have news, whichever comes first." I slid out of the SUV and leaned in. "And good luck."

"Thanks, darlin'." The usual twinkle was absent from his eyes. "We're gonna need it."

The heat of the closed-up house enveloped me like a suffocating blanket as soon as I stepped inside. Panting in the airless rooms, I hurried from window to window, throwing them wide open in an attempt to catch even the slightest late-afternoon breeze.

When I returned to the kitchen for a glass of ice water, a folded note in the middle of the kitchen table caught my eye. '*Aydan*' was scrawled across the front of it and I picked it up with smile, anticipating a thank you from one of the guests or possibly a note from Lola, though it didn't look like her usual flamboyant penmanship.

It wasn't a thank you.

I read it through twice, my heart chilling with fear despite the oven-like temperature of the house.

'*Dear Aydan – I'm sorry to have missed you at the*

party. I hope your family emergency wasn't too serious. I'd like to get in touch with you to talk about a mutual acquaintance. Please call me at your earliest convenience.'

It was signed 'Frederick Labelle' and included a sleek business card advertising an investment brokerage.

He could just be some annoying sales guy... but the unnamed 'mutual acquaintance' made small hairs stand up on the back of my neck. And somehow I just knew he was the well-dressed guy who'd set off my alarm bells at the party.

I shook my head vigorously. Get a grip. I was overreacting. He was almost certainly a sales guy. He had probably withheld the name of the acquaintance just to make me curious enough to call him back, and then he'd roll out his sales spiel.

"Yeah, right," I muttered. "But paranoid and alive is better than trusting and dead."

Another thought hit me and I extracted my bug detector from the waist pouch I still wore, my heart pumping a little too hard. The reassuring flash of the green light made me ease out a long breath. Okay, so at least nobody was listening in on me. And my wrist monitor hadn't vibrated since Saturday evening when it had shown Lola locking my gate behind her.

Drawing a deep calming breath, I dialled Lola's number.

She answered with a cheery hello, and I forced a smile onto my face and did my best cheerful voice in return.

"Hi, Lola! I'm back. Thanks for locking up for me."

"Oh, you're welcome, honey." Her tone went grave. "How is Big John? Was the emergency as bad as you thought?"

I swallowed, renewed memory of Kane's haunted eyes

tightening my throat. "Yeah, I'm afraid it might be." I gave her a brief outline, letting her express her concern and sympathy before changing the subject without much finesse. "Hey, Lola, I found a note on my kitchen table..."

"Oh, good, you found it. I figured the kitchen table was best place to leave it."

"Um, yeah... did you see the guy who wrote it?"

"Yes, Fred Labelle." She sounded puzzled. "Did he forget to sign it?"

She knew him. Thank God.

"No, I just didn't get to connect with him at the party and I wondered if he'd left early," I fibbed.

"No, he left right after you." I was beginning to relax when she continued, "He seemed really nice for a salesman."

Shit, she didn't know him.

I kept my tone light with an effort. "I hope he didn't bother you. Were you talking to him for long?"

"Not long; he just said hi and we talked for a few minutes, and he told me about his investment business. He wasn't obnoxious, just an extrovert, you know? I think he introduced himself to everybody. He was worried when you left in such a hurry, and when I explained what had happened he wrote out the note and asked me to give it to you."

A chill skittered down my spine. "Thanks, Lola. Um... was he wearing slacks and a dress shirt?"

Lola laughed. "Yes, he said he felt silly walking around all dressed up while everybody else was in shorts, but he had come straight from the office and didn't have time to change. It was nice of you to invite him. It's too bad you missed each other."

My bullshit meter red-lined, kicking my pulse into high

gear. "Um... yeah, it's too bad..."

I hadn't invited anybody.

"Did he mention our mutual friend?" I asked cautiously.

"Oh, yes, he said Jack Paar had introduced you... no, wait, that's not right. Jack Paar was the Tonight Show host 'way back in the early 60s. Heavens, I used to love him! I'm sorry, I don't remember your friend's first name, but I'm sure the last name was Paar."

I swallowed a hard cold lump of dread. "Nicholas Parr?"

"That's it!" Lola exclaimed.

Shit, shit, shit!

Dropping into a kitchen chair, I focused all my will on keeping my tone nonchalant for the rest of our short conversation, and rang off as soon as I could.

I stared into space, my mind circling frantically. It couldn't be. Parr was dead. We'd convicted and imprisoned all his minions. This nightmare couldn't be starting all over again.

Lola must have gotten the name wrong. I gulped and dialled Spider's parents' number.

His mother answered, and I had to clear my throat before my voice would work. "Hi, Gladys, it's Aydan. How are you? Recovered from the party yet?"

She laughed. "No recovery required. It's easy being the groom's parents. It's such a nice change from marrying off girls!"

"That's great," I said absently. "Um, I have a quick question for you. There was a guy at the shower that you wouldn't have known, but I noticed him talking to you..."

"Oh, yes. I can't remember his name, though. He seemed very nice, but a little absent-minded. Why, is there a problem?"

I cleared my dry throat again. "No, no problem. I just didn't manage to connect with him before I left. He's sometimes a little pushy about his investment business so I was just calling to apologize. I hope he didn't bother you."

"No, of course not! We actually had quite a nice chat once we'd straightened out your name." She giggled.

"Um... what do you mean?"

"Oh, it was funny! He asked if I was a friend of Arlene's, and of course I had no idea who he was talking about. I said so, and when he pointed you out I realized he'd misspoken. When I told him he'd said Arlene instead of Aydan, he laughed and laughed. He'd just come straight from his office where he'd been talking with another client whose name was Arlene, and he said you'd never let him hear the end of it when you found out he'd mixed up your names. He was quite charming."

An icy band of sickness tightened around my stomach. Arlene Widdenback. My cover identity.

I was so screwed.

I forced a laugh. "I'll be sure to give him a hard time when I see him again. Well, I'd better let you go. I just wanted to make sure he hadn't been a pain. Lola said he was glad-handing everybody."

"No, not at all. He was very nice."

I said my goodbyes and pressed the disconnect button before hurrying over to the kitchen drawer to fumble out a secured phone.

Stemp answered on the first ring, as always.

"It's Aydan," I said, fighting the quiver of nerves in my voice. "I've just had a note from one of Nicholas Parr's friends. He showed up at the wedding shower at my place on Saturday looking for Arlene Widdenback..." I trailed off, suddenly realizing Stemp hadn't attended. Had he declined an invitation? Or had Spider deliberately excluded him?

Irrelevant. I shook myself back to the issue at hand and went on, "...but I left before he could introduce himself." I read the note to Stemp and described my conversations with Lola and Gladys.

After a brief pause, he said, "This sounds promising. I wonder whether it's arms smuggling or money laundering."

'Promising' wasn't the word I would have used. More like 'fucking terrifying'. I didn't trust my voice, so I mumbled a non-committal 'hmm' and waited for him to continue.

"Excellent," Stemp said with satisfaction. "I was wondering how long it would take for Parr's former associates to come looking for Arlene Widdenback the arms dealer. We took the backbone out of Fuzzy Bunny; now it's time to gut the rest of their network. I'll assign analysts to run Frederick Labelle through the system right away, and they should have a preliminary report for you by tomorrow morning. I'll leave it up to you as to when you return his call."

Fear paralyzed me. My heart barely quivered in my chest, as if afraid a solid beat would shatter me into pieces. Betrayal curdled my stomach.

All this time I'd been slowly convincing myself I was safe, and Stemp had been using me for bait.

His voice jolted me. "Anything else?"

"No," I croaked.

When the line went dead in my ear with Stemp's usual abruptness I let my hand fall to the table, closely followed by my forehead.

Oh, God, not again.

Four damn months of therapy and unrelenting mental effort, and I was just getting back to almost-normal. I couldn't do this. I'd quit, and to hell with Frederick Labelle and all the rest of them.

If only Stemp would let me keep my gun...

My whole body felt weak and tremulous. Dragging myself up from the table, I tottered to the fridge and ate some cold leftovers without tasting them. After my makeshift supper I picked up the phone, still feeling shaky.

Spider picked up on the second ring, his 'hello' sounding as cheerful as ever.

"Spider! How are you?" I demanded. "Are you okay?"

He laughed. "I'm fine. I don't have a life-threatening allergy to alcohol or anything, I just get really red in the face and really drunk. They checked me out at the hospital and sent me home to sleep it off."

"Thank God," I said. "Do you know who spiked your drink?"

"Tim says it was Tyler Brock, but I don't know. Tim gets a little... over the top sometimes. Anyway, it was no big deal, but I'm sorry it spoiled the party for everybody." His voice went serious. "Lola said Kane had a family emergency and you guys rushed away. What happened? Is... Did somebody... die?"

"No..." I hesitated. "At least I hope not..." I took a deep breath and told him the whole story.

"Oh, Aydan," he said when I was finished, his voice quivering in sympathy. "That's horrible. How can I help?"

"I don't think there's anything you can do right now, but I'll let you know if I think of anything. I'd better get off the phone now in case they're trying to call." I summoned a cheerful tone. "I'm glad you're okay, anyway. I'll see you tomorrow... oh. No, I guess I won't," I amended. "I forgot you're on vacation until after your wedding. Are you getting excited? All ready for the big day?"

"I'm so excited I can hardly sleep," Spider blurted, then gave a self-conscious chuckle. "I guess that's a little silly. I mean, we've been living together for months, but... but..." A laugh burst out of him, so full of joy that I smiled despite my worries. "...I can hardly believe I'll be married to the love of my life on Saturday! And we'll be together for the rest of our lives. I just... I feel like a kid with Christmas coming. Only this is so much better because I already know how good my gift is!"

"I'm so happy for you and Linda," I said, my heart warming. "I feel as though Christmas is coming this weekend, too."

"Thanks, Aydan. It's going to mean a lot to us to have you there to help us celebrate. And maybe..." The smile went out of his voice. "Maybe Kane will have some good news by then, too. I really hope so."

"Yeah. Me, too. Hey, Spider, one more thing. Do you remember talking to a Frederick Labelle at the party?"

"No, should I?"

"No, probably not," I reassured him. "I think he came late, at the same time as Brock..." I trailed off, struck by a sudden thought.

Did that mean anything?

No, it couldn't. Brock had almost as high a security clearance as Spider. He couldn't be in cahoots with any friend of Nicholas Parr's...

"Aydan? Are you still there?" Spider's voice brought me back to the present.

"Yeah. Sorry, I zoned out for a second there. I'd better

hang up before I fall asleep on my feet."

He laughed. "You've had a busy couple of days! Get some rest, and thanks again for hosting our party. 'Bye!"

I hung up and stood irresolutely beside the phone for a few moments. No point in trying to call Kane or Hellhound. Hellhound would still be driving, and Kane would be beyond cellphone range out in the woods.

Nothing to do but wait.

CHAPTER 11

When my phone finally rang at ten-thirty in the evening, I pounced on it.

"Hey, darlin'." Arnie's characteristic rasp sounded weary.

"Hi." I swallowed. "Anything new?"

"Nah." Defeat flattened his voice. "Search parties are in for the night. They can't risk 'em in that rough terrain in the dark. John an' I came in, too, but John's already headed out again, an' I'm gonna follow him right after I get off the phone. We'll keep lookin' through the night 'til the regular search teams start up again in the mornin'."

"Oh." I gulped at the lump in my throat. The urge to try to convince them to quit for the night was strong, but I knew it was futile. They'd be going out with their high-tech infrared and night-vision equipment.

"John figures we'll have a better chance of findin' him at night," Hellhound said into our momentary silence. "I... Hell, I'm just hopin' we're still lookin' for somethin' that'll show up on infrared."

My stomach clenched at the thought of a small lifeless body lying cold and alone in the woods. "Me, too," I choked. "I'm hoping with everything I have. Good luck. Stay alert and take care of each other. Watch out for bears and cougars, and take lots of water-"

Hellhound interrupted gently, "We've done this a time or two before, darlin'. An' this time at least nobody's shootin' at us. Don't worry, we'll be fine."

"I know you will." I sighed. "Just... I just wish I was there."

"Wish ya were, too. Gotta go. Get some sleep, darlin'. 'Bye."

"'Bye," I echoed, and lowered the handset slowly.

I slept uneasily, half-expecting the ring of the telephone at any moment. When my alarm sounded at six-thirty I opened my eyes to red rays of early sunshine fingering through the slats of my blinds and a stubbornly silent phone.

Sighing, I dragged myself out of bed. Halfway to the bathroom the phone rang and I nearly leaped out of my skin, pivoting in midair to dive across the bed and snatch it up.

Kane's tired voice answered my breathless hello.

"Good morning, Aydan. I hope I didn't wake you. Hellhound said you usually get up at six-thirty."

"I was up," I said hurriedly. "Did you... um... how did it go?"

His discouraged exhalation told the story, but his voice was level when he said, "We didn't find any trace. Considering how far we searched last night, along with the area the other searchers covered yesterday, I'm beginning to doubt that we're looking in the right place. I've called in all the favours anybody ever owed me to get more resources on this search, but... he... he's only six. He couldn't have gone that far..." His voice wavered, and he took a breath. When he spoke again his voice was a hoarse rasp. "They're bringing in cadaver dogs to search downstream today."

Sickness closed around my heart. Please God, don't let them find anything...

"Maybe it's good news that you haven't found him," I blurted, grasping at straws. "Maybe you're looking in the wrong place entirely. Maybe... maybe... some Good Samaritan found him and they don't have a cell phone and their car broke down..." My improbable fabrication wasn't helping. "He's okay somewhere, I just know it," I finished lamely, trying to sound positive.

Kane drew a deep breath. "That's what Alicia says, too. She says she'd know if he'd died. That she'd feel it somehow."

"There, see?" I encouraged.

"That's unrealistic, Aydan, and you know it. A six-year-old alone in the wilderness for nearly forty-eight hours? They aren't looking for Daniel anymore. They're looking for his body, and that may never be found. It could be pinned under a log in the river, or dragged off by a wild animal..." His voice went husky and I knew he was fighting for control. "Soon they'll call off the search."

I clenched my fists, the pain in his voice wringing tears from my eyes.

"There's got to be something we've missed," I choked. "This just doesn't make sense. There must be more to it. Maybe Murphy wasn't alone. Maybe..."

I shut up, realizing that the thought of Daniel being taken by a stranger wasn't much more comforting than the thought of him lost in the wilderness.

Kane let out a breath. "I don't know whether to hope for that or not," he said, voicing my own thoughts. "But there's no evidence to support it. I got an updated report from Mayweather. There were other boot prints at the site, but Murphy's overlaid all of them so they were likely from a previous camper. Forensics discovered droplets of Murphy's blood on the toe of his boot, but any minor injury could have caused that. And there was a partial footprint in a patch of soft ground a few yards away from Murphy's campsite. It was leading away from the site, and the imprint was from someone in sock feet."

"From Murphy running around without his boots," I put in.

"Probably," Kane confirmed dispiritedly. "It was his size."

I swallowed hard and held my voice level. "There's more to this, I know it. Why don't you get some sleep..."

"No, I need to-"

"You need to sleep now," I interrupted. "You've been up far too long. You're no help to anyone when you're this tired." He began to protest, but I overrode him. "John, you know I'm right. Find a doctor to prescribe a sleeping pill if you need to, but get some sleep. Now put Arnie on."

Kane grumbled, but a few moments later Hellhound's tired rasp tickled my eardrum. "Hey, darlin'."

"Hi, Arnie. I know you're exhausted so I won't keep you. Just make sure you wrestle John into bed and hit him with a rubber hammer if you have to. And then go to bed yourself."

"Thanks, darlin', I will. I'll call ya this afternoon an' let ya know what's happenin'."

We said our goodbyes and hung up, and I trailed gloomily into the bathroom. Shampooing without my usual vigour, I reluctantly contemplated what would happen if Daniel was found dead. Or never found.

What would Kane do? It had taken four months for him to recover from the trauma of his last mission. Could he ever recover from losing the son he'd so desperately wanted?

And did he even realize what he'd done by quitting the Department? His military and law enforcement career had been his entire life, and now he'd thrown it all away...

I blinked, realizing I'd been staring blankly at the shower wall for several minutes.

Slowly reaching for my conditioner, I considered for the first time what Kane's snap decision would mean to me. He and Spider and I had fallen into a comfortable and efficient routine of decryption and investigation. Who would take his place?

My throat tightened. Nobody could ever take his place.

I shoved my face into the hot spray.

When I walked into the lobby of Sirius Dynamics an hour later, it was an effort to summon my usual smile and banter while the security guard signed me in.

Wandering up the stairs to my office, I dropped into my desk chair and stared at the opposite wall. What the hell was I supposed to do? With my team gone, I couldn't even use the top-secret network key that allowed me to eavesdrop on every digital communication in the world.

I blew out a breath. Well, I *could* use it. I could go down and collect it from Spider's lab in the secured area, and there was nothing stopping me from slipping into the data tunnels of the internet without backup. I hadn't needed Kane to rescue me from the virtual reality network for months, so theoretically I should be safe.

But it had been really good to know he was there if I

needed him.

I shook myself and focused on the computer screen in front of me. Surely the analysts would have a report on Frederick Labelle by now.

My email screen popped up and I let out a breath. A nine AM meeting request from Stemp. At least I only had forty-five minutes to kill.

Forty-five minutes to wonder whether he'd assigned me a new team now that Kane had quit.

Or...

Oh, God. Maybe he expected me to take over Kane's role as a field agent.

Oh, shit.

By the time I walked into Stemp's office on the dot of nine AM, my palms were moist and my throat was dry. He greeted me pleasantly, and I managed an almost-normal-sounding 'good morning' in return.

"Please, sit." He indicated the guest chair in front of his desk. "Do you have Kane's weapon?"

I nodded and lowered myself into the chair, feigning relaxation.

"Thank you," he said. "Please return it to Stores."

"He could really use it right now," I said, trying not to sound accusing. "He's out in the wilderness, and there are bears and cougars..."

I trailed off as Stemp nodded. "Yes. It was unfortunate that he quit."

"Well, you pretty much forced him to," I snapped. "What did you think he was going to do? Say 'yes, sir' and abandon a child he's always wanted but never knew he had?"

"I was hoping he'd retain enough professional detachment to step away from the investigation." Stemp sighed. "I had planned to place him on personal leave, but I wasn't surprised that he quit. It wasn't my ideal scenario, but it's likely best for him in the long run."

"What the... *Best for him?*" I stared at him, anger boiling up in my chest. "How the hell do you figure it's 'best for him' to force him to choose between his child and his career?"

Stemp studied me with his usual reptilian composure. "I wasn't certain that he hadn't already."

"What the hell is that supposed to mean?"

"I've known about Daniel Wyatt Kane since he was born. The ex-Mrs. Kane made no attempt to conceal his existence. His birth and parentage were duly registered. She remained in the family home. The most cursory check would have revealed all of this to Kane. Since he never mentioned a child, I assumed he had reason to pretend the child didn't exist. Since the ex-Mrs. Kane never traced Kane's employment here to demand child support, I surmised he was providing support through discreet channels."

Stemp raised one shoulder a fraction of an inch in what served him for an eloquent shrug. "In our line of work, concealing a child's existence to protect the child is not an unreasonable act."

I gaped open-mouthed, my anger draining away. Of course he would have assumed Kane was concealing his relationship to Daniel. Stemp was doing exactly the same thing with his young daughter overseas.

He spoke into the silence. "Returning to your original question regarding Kane's resignation... under these circumstances, the scope of action available to Kane as an agent and a military officer is... quite restricted. However, as a civilian..." Stemp shrugged again, meeting my gaze meaningfully without completing the sentence.

After a moment I retrieved my jaw from my lap.

Stemp, the quintessential chessmaster. And the fiercely protective father. If his daughter were missing, he would stop at nothing to find her. In fact, I was reasonably certain he'd murdered at least one man to protect the secret of her existence. He understood better than anyone what a father would do to protect his child.

If Kane neglected his official duties to interfere with a kidnapping case outside his jurisdiction, he'd be subject to disciplinary action. And if he injured or killed somebody outside the bounds of one of his assigned cases, he could be dishonourably discharged, losing the pension and benefits accrued over his long years of service. But since he had already resigned...

"You're a fucking genius," I said.

Stemp's emotionless façade dissolved into a completely unexpected bark of laughter, his eyes warming to amber and crinkling at the corners. He sobered rapidly, but his eyes still twinkled. "I was certain you were going to call me a dickhead."

I managed a feeble chuckle. "Not this time. But don't get complacent; the whole week's still ahead of us."

"Indeed." He leaned forward, solemn again. "I've informed the chain of command that Kane is taking personal leave, which does not excuse him from compliance with orders. Nor will it hold up under scrutiny, since Kane hasn't completed the necessary paperwork to apply for leave, either."

"Right. Thank you for covering for him." I met his gaze

uncomfortably. "I'm, um... I'm sorry for all those times I called you a dickhead. You aren't. At least not most of the time... um..."

"Perhaps you should stop now," Stemp advised dryly, but humour warmed his eyes. "Apology accepted; and unnecessary. Sometimes I am a dickhead. Which leads me to my next point..."

I squeezed my eyes shut, waiting for the axe to fall.

Silence hung in the room like a sodden blanket.

"You can open your eyes," he said. "It's not that bad." I was pretty sure I heard a smile in his voice, but by the time I cautiously opened my eyes again he was deadpan as usual. He hesitated. "Or perhaps it is that bad. My parents are here. Visiting me."

"Oh. Uh..." I blinked, trying to catch up to the non sequitur. "Wha... Uh, that's nice. How are they?"

"They are well. Thank you for asking. They are..." He hesitated again, and despite his legendary composure, I was pretty sure he was squirming inside. "They are asking after you. Mother has issued..." He actually gulped, heightening my sense of the world gone awry. "...an invitation," he finished, sounding as though he'd much prefer to be facing a firing squad. "A dinner invitation. Are you available to attend at my home tomorrow night?"

CHAPTER 12

I tried not to gape like a lobotomized goldfish, but I was pretty sure I wasn't succeeding. My mind reeled, clutching at random thoughts in an attempt to stabilize itself. Wait, do goldfish even have frontal lobes...?

Stemp sat waiting, completely expressionless, and I jerked my thoughts back under control. "Uh..." My voice came out in a croak, and I hurriedly cleared my throat and plastered on the closest thing to a smile I could fabricate on short notice. "Thank you, that's, um... very nice. I'd love to come. It'll be great to see your mom and dad again. What time? And what can I bring?"

A faint flush climbed his neck.

Stemp the Unflappable. Blushing. My world cartwheeled out of control.

"Eighteen hundred. And it's not necessary for you to bring anything. Though if you'd like to bring a guest, Mother was particularly hoping to see Helmand again..." I could have sworn I saw pleading in his eyes, and I knew damn well it wasn't desperate hope that Hellhound would come.

Oh, sweet Lord, I could just imagine showing up with Hellhound in tow. His usual moniker for Stemp was 'Asshat', and he'd undoubtedly find some not-so-subtle way express his antipathy. A sudden mental image of Hellhound bellying up to the table in his repulsive Al Hamlin disguise nearly choked me.

I banished the horrific thought and fumbled for an answer. "Um... Arnie won't be able to come; he's out at Rocky Mountain House with John..." Inspiration struck and I straightened with hope. "Would it be all right if I invited Lola Ives? You know, Spider's fiancée's grandmother? I'm sure she and your mom and dad would like each other."

And Lola was an excellent conversationalist, reducing the chances that Stemp and I would have to suffer through any more awkward social interaction than absolutely necessary.

"Yes, of course I remember Mrs. Ives. That's an excellent idea," Stemp agreed with visible relief. "Please invite her, though she won't know me. I made sure she only saw the bomb squad when we rescued her last winter, so please perform the appropriate introductions tomorrow evening."

He leaned forward. "One more thing," he said evenly. "Under no circumstances are you to divulge any details of my work here to my parents. As far as they know I am a middle manager for Sirius's oil and gas research division, and I shall consider it a security breach subject to full disciplinary action if you give them any reason to doubt that. Is that clear?"

"Got it," I agreed, hiding the unpleasant chill that trickled down my spine.

"Good." He leaned back in his chair, his usual impassive expression descending like a merciful curtain. "Please excuse the digression. Let's get back to business."

I drew a breath of relief. After that excruciating exchange, even the possibility of being assigned to a deadly mission didn't seem too alarming. Hell, if I played my cards right, I might even manage to get dead in time to avoid Stemp's dinner party.

"When do you think Kane will return for his debriefing?" Stemp's question interrupted my thoughts.

"Um... I don't know." I hesitated. "If they find Daniel..."

My throat tightened. If they found Daniel alive, the answer would likely be quite a bit different than if they found him dead.

"Sooner would be better," Stemp said slowly, as if choosing his words with care. "Since I don't have his official written resignation, there is some latitude, but... that... is a double-edged sword."

I grasped his meaning without difficulty. As soon as the date of Kane's resignation was officially recorded, he'd be in trouble if he didn't complete his debriefing immediately. But the longer he delayed his official resignation date, the greater the chance that he might lose his pension and benefits if he did something rash.

I sighed, massaging the tension winding up in the back of my neck. "I'll talk to him. But I honestly don't think he cares right now."

"Understood." Stemp nodded, and I was pretty sure he really did understand. "I hope you'll be able to convince him to deal with it promptly." He glanced at his computer screen, then turned it to face me. "This is Frederick Labelle. Is he the man from your party?"

I nodded, and he continued, "The analysts have completed their preliminary report. I'll forward a copy to you, but so far there's nothing definitive. Officially, he owns an investment brokerage in full compliance with all tax laws and financial regulations. But if he's a former associate of Parr's, he's bound to be smart about covering his tracks."

The unwelcome reminder of my current situation made my heart sink. "So, an investment broker..." I ventured. "Probably money-laundering, then?"

At least that sounded safer than gun-running...

Stemp leaned back in his chair. "Perhaps. But he also operates a customs brokerage so arms smuggling is also a possibility."

"Great," I muttered.

Stemp's expressionless façade dissolved into wolfish grin. "Indeed. I've been hoping Parr's former clientele would note the mention of Arlene Widdenback's name at his trial. Combined with your convincing portrayal of an arms dealer when you turned his underlings, you are perfectly positioned to gain their business. Take your time and develop a relationship with Labelle. If he is in fact the first of Parr's former clientele to come searching for a new associate, we want to make sure he goes away satisfied and spreads the word. The more fish we can reel in with this bait, the better."

I licked dry lips. "That, uh... sounds like a long-term assignment."

"Yes. You will become Arlene Widdenback the arms dealer for the foreseeable future. Your initial objective is to get Labelle to trust you enough to initiate negotiations."

"But... I'm not ready to go back in the field," I ventured cautiously.

"Why not?" Stemp's gaze dissected me. "Dr. Rawling informs me that he is satisfied with your progress. According to him, you're sleeping well and your anxiety attacks have ceased. You've successfully completed the anger management program. What is preventing you from returning to active duty?"

"Um..." I swallowed hard to keep the tremor of fear out

of my voice. "Sheer cowardice...?"

Stemp's steely gaze softened. "Hardly. Even if I hadn't read your psych evaluation, your mission reports prove your courage. So... what is the issue?"

"I just... I can't, okay?" I stared at him, willing him to give in.

"So..." His eyebrow raised a fraction. "Am I to understand that you have been perhaps... less than forthcoming with Dr. Rawling?"

My nails were digging into my palms, and I loosened the fists I hadn't realized I'd clenched. "Maybe I tend to, um... underreport... a bit... sometimes..." I admitted, my cold lips barely forming the words.

"He surmised as much," Stemp replied. He studied me in silence for a moment. "Aydan, he can't help you if you won't let him," he said with surprising gentleness.

"I realize that." My words came out stiffer than I'd intended, and Stemp's posture stiffened in return.

"I could order you to cooperate fully with him," he said slowly, "But I know that would be futile, so I will offer you a choice. Go back to Dr. Rawling and cooperate fully and completely. Or report for your requalification testing tomorrow at zero-nine-hundred." His eyes narrowed. "And don't bother intentionally failing the tests. I've been monitoring your usage of the gym and firing range and I know you're capable of passing. Report to my office immediately afterward."

He leaned back in his chair as if everything had been resolved to his satisfaction. "This situation with Labelle is unlikely to escalate quickly," he added. "So that will free you up for other short-term assignments. I need a courier to carry a classified weapon prototype between here and the secured facility in Calgary on Friday. Ordinarily I'd assign Helmand, but I know he'd quit if I tried to force him to abandon Kane. I can't afford to lose my top weapons specialist as well."

"What if I quit, too?" My voice was steady, but cold waves of fear pounded in my belly.

"That would be... unwise." The complete lack of inflection in his tone sent a shiver down my spine. His flat gaze reminded me all over again of a rattlesnake coiled to strike.

Shit, was this even the same man who had laughed aloud and invited me to dinner only a few minutes ago?

"Fucking possessed," I muttered under my breath. If his head started spinning in circles I was so out of here...

His head didn't spin. "I beg your pardon?" he inquired in chilly tones.

"Um..." I squared my shoulders and locked my gaze on those snake-like eyes. "Would you please explain why it would be so... unwise?"

For a moment I thought he was going to start a pissing match, but then his posture eased. "Well, certainly it's your choice," he said reluctantly. "But knowing you the way I do, I suspect you would find the consequences... undesirable."

He massaged the bridge of his nose with a sigh. "As long as you were our only way to do digital surveillance and decryption, the Department was, to some extent, at your mercy. Since Ms. Mellor has come to work for us, that is no longer the case. However, the chain of command believes your skills as an agent mitigate the risk of exposing you and your highly classified knowledge to potential capture by hostile forces."

A few beats of silence gave me enough time to come to

the conclusion he voiced only a moment later: "If you don't prove your worth by reeling in Labelle, the only logical course of action is to relegate you permanently to the secured facility along with Ms. Mellor. If you chose to continue decrypting for us while there, that would be most beneficial, but even if you did not, you would nevertheless remain incarcerated in the interests of national security, and for your own safety."

Claustrophobic terror surged up to choke me.

Jail.

Life sentence with no chance of parole.

With every ounce of control I possessed I held my voice level, though it came out a little shriller than I wanted. "And what happens when I'm too old for active duty? You'll lock me up sooner or later regardless."

He eyed me levelly. "There are many roles available for covert operatives that don't require physical prowess. And mature women are often viewed as non-threatening and above suspicion, so you would likely find yourself much in demand."

"Great." The word stuck in my throat, and I coughed to clear it. My voice came out harsh nonetheless. "Nice to know my life path has been decided."

With sympathy in his eyes, Stemp turned his palms up in a 'take what you can get' gesture.

A blistering tirade burned the back of my throat, but I closed my teeth on it.

Not his fault.

"Thank you for the explanation," I gritted. "I'll call Labelle this afternoon and requalify tomorrow morning. When and where should I pick up the weapon on Friday, and where will I be delivering it?"

If Stemp felt any triumph at my acquiescence, he didn't show it. "You'll pick up the prototype at the Weapons lab Friday at ten hundred hours. The Calgary facility will expect delivery no later than seventeen hundred. I'll provide detailed instructions on Friday at zero-nine."

I frowned. "Why such a long time lapse? It's only a two-hour drive."

He gave one of his inscrutable looks. "It should be an uneventful trip. However, if necessary, the extra time will allow you to deal with any... unforeseen issues that may arise."

Swallowing hard, I nodded. I'd lulled myself into a false sense of security, believing that the true function of Sirius Dynamics was well hidden from the rest of the world. Stupid. If someone had figured out that our innocent petroleum research facility actually housed classified technology, they might be simply biding their time until they could intercept an unwary courier.

Like me.

And if Labelle thought I was a ruthless arms dealer, he might expect me to be carrying secret weapons...

Shit and double-shit...

Stemp was still speaking, and I dragged my attention back to him.

"Report to the lab this morning for a preliminary briefing with Dr. Chow. He'll be the primary resource for your cover as an arms dealer. Send requests through the usual channels if you require the services of the analysts, and if you need any network surveillance or decryptions, you may requisition them directly from Brock until Webb returns from vacation."

He must have detected a flicker of my distaste for Tyler Brock, because he added, "We would prefer to use Brock and

Mellor for the bulk of the surveillance and decryption, but if for some reason you need to enter the network yourself I'll stand in for your support team on an interim basis."

The unspoken addendum, '...but you'd better have a good reason to waste both our time that way' hung in the air, and I nodded.

"Questions?" he inquired. Fighting a sense of impending doom, I shook my head wordlessly, and he added, "Dismissed."

CHAPTER 13

I dragged myself to my feet and stumbled out of Stemp's office. The ladies' room offered a refuge and I locked myself into a cubicle, where I collapsed onto the toilet seat and hunched over with my arms wrapped around myself.

There had to be a way out of this. There just had to be.

No matter how I twisted and turned inside the logic-trap, I couldn't find an escape route. If I quit, they'd lock me up. If I ran away I'd have to run forever, and they'd likely still find me... and then they'd lock me up. But as an agent I'd be in constant danger. At best, I'd suffer the kind of trauma that had driven me to Dr. Rawling's office in the first place. At worst, I'd be captured, tortured, and ultimately killed after the bad guys extracted all my classified knowledge.

My mind raced in circles, my heart rate accelerating.

Trapped...

I straightened. "No, fuck this!" I said aloud, then winced at the sound of my voice bouncing off the hard tiled surfaces around me.

Drawing a deep breath, I brought my thoughts under control. Just the way Dr. Rawling had coached me. Think it through.

No need to panic. If shit happened, I'd deal with it. But

I wouldn't let worry spoil my peace of mind. Not anymore.

And no more bumbling through missions and hoping for the best. If this had to be my new career, I'd damn well get good at it.

My pulse slowed while I drew a few more calming yoga breaths. Then I emerged from the cubicle, washed my hands, and headed back to Stemp's office.

When I tapped on his door frame he looked up with a faint frown. "Something else?"

"Yes." I invited myself into his office and emulated Kane's parade rest in front of his desk. "I need some training courses."

He leaned back in his chair, his frown deepening. "What kind of training courses?"

Hell, I should have looked this up on the internet before I came barging in here. Were there even spy-training courses?

I threw out the first semi-coherent thought that came to mind. "I need to rebuild my confidence. I want to start with the basics and work up."

Stemp nodded slowly. "Very well. Tactical or intelligence?"

Aha. Now I knew the buzzwords.

"Both," I said firmly.

"All right. I'll email you a list of the currently available courses. If you need something that's not listed, send me the course details and we'll discuss it."

"Thanks." Heart thumping, I scurried out.

Shit, it was that easy? Why the hell hadn't I thought of this before?

I hissed out a breath between my teeth. Because I had foolishly thought I'd be able to go back to my 'real' life, that's why. The peaceful rural existence I'd dreamed of for so long...

My throat tightened, and I shook the thought out of my head.

Not an option anymore. Let it go.

I determinedly swallowed the lump in my throat and strode downstairs to tackle my next challenge: the time-delay chamber to the secure underground labs.

"Claustrophobia is irrational," I reminded myself under my breath as I leaned in for the retinal scan.

The heavy steel door released and I stepped into the cramped chamber, holding my spine straight. The door thumped quietly closed behind me, and I stepped forward to trigger the next retinal scan, the profound silence of the small enclosure giving me an eerie sensation of deafness.

Thirty seconds. I could do this. No problem. The walls weren't closing in. The ceiling wasn't lowering to crush me...

I counted down the time, keeping my gaze glued on the door. When the latch released after the longest thirty seconds in human history, I stepped through it with my best imitation of composure before hurrying down the narrow featureless concrete stairs.

Concrete above me, below me, all around me...

Breathe.

I pulled open the door at the bottom and stepped into the sterile coolness of the underground corridor, seeking out the serenity of the white walls and the reassurance of fresh air moving past my face.

Breathe. Just breathe. Perfectly safe down here. Not trapped.

I squared my shoulders and headed for the Weapons lab with a determined stride.

Outside it, I hesitated. I'd never been inside the lab, and I didn't even know if my fob would give me access. Stemp hadn't said anything about it, so maybe he'd already added me to the clearance list...

Shrugging, I waved my fob at the prox pad just as a white-coated bald man with a giant black beard strode up behind me. The door latch released and he gave his fob a cursory swipe over the reader, too, before holding the door for me. I stepped inside only to be confronted by a blank wall and a choice of left or right down a short but featureless corridor.

The bearded man, presumably a researcher, hurried off to the right without a backward glance, and after a moment of hesitation I followed him.

The corridor led into a large open space dotted with counters laden with unrecognizable equipment, and I rounded the corner in time to see the researcher greet a man in a wheelchair.

"Reggie, you lazy bastard, stop lollygagging around in that chair and get on your feet. What the hell's your problem?"

The man in the wheelchair turned toward him and my stomach lurched. Both legs were missing below the knee, the empty beige trousers pinned up neatly. All that remained of his left hand was a misshapen lump of shiny flesh with a pincer of one finger and thumb, and the left side of his head and neck was disfigured by scar tissue puckered around a slit of a mouth, a featureless hole for an ear, and what was obviously a prosthetic eye.

The undamaged side of his mouth twisted into a grin made horrible by the devastation beside it, his remaining eye snapping with wicked humour under shiny black hair. "Fuck you, Sawyer. I ran a half-marathon this weekend and my stumps are hamburger."

Sawyer grinned. "Hope you won at least."

"Goddamn right I did."

Sawyer socked the man on the shoulder in brotherly approval and strode away, and the ravaged face turned toward me. "Well, well, who do we have here?"

Powerful shoulders bulged as the man popped a wheelie in the high-tech chair before jockeying expertly over to screech to a halt inches from my toes.

Thankful for the moment I'd had to recover, I kept my tone casual. "Hi, I'm looking for Dr. Chow..." I trailed off involuntarily as a flicker of movement caught my eye.

A black spot moved on his trousers, a startling contrast against the beige.

A spider.

Crawling up his thigh toward his crotch...

I jerked my gaze back up to his face.

His eye narrowed. "Yeah, so I hit an IED in Afghanistan." His tone was a belligerent challenge. "Lost both legs below the knee. Most of my left hand." He shoved his pincer-like hand at me with an angry gesture. "Half my face. And yes, to answer your *unspoken* question, my cock still works but my left nut is prosthetic. Take a good look. Like what you see?"

Horrified, I gulped, my face fiery and my voice coming out in a papery whisper. "I... I didn't mean... I'm sorry..." Pulling myself together, I added, "I didn't mean to be rude. Thank you for your service and... sacrifice."

I heard the door open behind me, but I couldn't look away from the bitter venom in his gaze.

"Yeah, my *sacrifice*." His remaining black brow drew

down. "What the fuck do you know about this kind of..." His deformed hand described an up-and-down arc from wheels to head and back again. "...*sacrifice*?"

"N-Nothing." I swallowed. "I can't even imagine. And I didn't mean to stare, I just... It's just that, um..."

The spider was still crawling. Unable to help myself, I glanced at it again, half-gesturing toward his crotch.

"You ignorant bitch!" he barked. "You think I'm a fucking sideshow? I went through this shit to protect your lily-white ass. The least you can do is look me in the eye!"

His contempt stung my already-raw emotions and hot anger bubbled up.

"I didn't intend to be rude earlier." My voice was hard and level. "And I'm genuinely grateful for your service. But since you're being such a dickhead about it... which nut did you say was prosthetic?"

His mouth dropped open at my effrontery, then snapped shut. "The left," he ground out.

"Well, that's good, because there's a spider on it."

A dangerous silence swelled between us. Then his gaze flicked sideways, focusing behind me.

"Chuckie," he snapped. "Get this bitch out of my lab."

His lab?

Oh, shit.

Apparently I'd just met Dr. Chow.

Stemp strolled up, halting beside me with a quizzical glance. "Is there a problem?"

"Hell yeah, there's a problem," Chow growled. "I gave this country my legs and blood and suffering and I damn well deserve respect, not gawking and stupid-ass cracks about a spider on my nuts. Get her out of here before I-"

I started to speak, but Stemp silenced us both with an

upraised hand and addressed Chow coolly. "Agent Kelly has given her share of blood and suffering for this country, though her scars are not as visible as yours. I suggest you drop the attitude and offer her the respect you wish for yourself. And there is indeed a spider on your testicles. Or perhaps on your penis, if you happen to be hanging to the left today."

The damaged mouth had slowly fallen open under Stemp's rebuke, and Chow stiffened. "Seriously, Chuckie? You're gonna get in on this fucking grade-school prank, too?" He pitched his voice to a mocking chant. "Hee-hee, made you look! Let's all laugh at the fucking gimp-"

Stemp interrupted, "There is an arachnid on your crotch. I don't care whether you deal with it or not, but Agent Kelly needs her briefing, so stop wasting her time." He gave us a crisp nod. "Excuse me; I have business with Dr. Sawyer."

As he strode away, Chow's gaze bored into me for a long moment before wavering and slowly dipping to his lap as if against his will. Then he let out a yelp and smeared the unfortunate spider across his pants.

"Fuck, I hate spiders!" He scrubbed his hand vigorously against his pant leg as if to wipe off any remains. "Fucking creepy little bastards!"

"Sorry," I offered tentatively. "I just... I couldn't *not* look at it. I really wasn't staring at your..." I trailed off with a vague gesture.

Chow stared up at me open-mouthed for a moment, then burst into laughter. I shuffled awkwardly, not sure whether to laugh with him or try another apology.

He sobered and extended his hand. "Shit. Okay, let's start again. I'm Reggie Chow. Aydan Kelly, I presume?"

"Yeah." I shook his hand.

"Sorry, I was out of line. I'm pissed off because I can't wear my legs today..." He glanced at my carefully neutral expression and elaborated, "I normally wear prosthetics but I'm training for the Paralympics and I pushed too hard yesterday. Now I have to let my stumps heal for a few days, but I hate using the chair because people stare at me like I'm a fucking brainless lump of meat when I'm in it. So I started the day with a chip on my shoulder, and when I thought you were staring..."

"It's okay," I said hurriedly. "You don't need to-"

"Yeah, I do," he interrupted. "I usually do a little orientation with my coworkers. Tell them what happened..." he hesitated, then grinned. "Well, except for the nut. That was a little more information than I usually share. But I like to get it out in the open so people don't feel like they have to pretend I'm not fucked up."

"Well, we're all fucked up somehow," I ventured cautiously. "Yours is just easier to see."

"Huh." He grunted sour amusement. "Yeah. Anyway, here's your orientation, so listen up. I was in a jeep in Afghanistan in a supposedly safe zone when we ran over an IED..." He glanced up. "Improvised Explosive Device. 'Homemade bomb' to you civvies. I was the only survivor. Blew my feet off and that would have been bad enough, but the blast knocked me out and threw me into a fire. That's what happened to my face and hand." The remains of his lips twisted. "Out of the IED into the fire. My nickname should be 'Lucky'. And guess what took out my nut? You're gonna love this."

I shook my head, afraid to say anything.

"One of the shoelace hooks from my boots. Docs took one out of my ass and two out of my guts, too. They must've been flying around like hornets from hell." He snorted. "Everybody bitches about how the army busts their balls; well, they really did bust mine."

I opened my mouth, hoping something tactful or appropriate would come out. Nothing did, so I closed it again.

"But you're right," he said as though I had actually spoken. "It could've been worse. When I woke up in the hospital and found out I still had a cock and a right hand, I just lay there and cried from sheer fucking joy."

He might have been joking, but I wasn't sure how to respond. I kept quiet.

"So I had a bunch of reconstructive surgery," he went on. "They're still working on my face but it probably won't get much better. But I'm getting a prosthetic ear, and they're gradually stretching my scalp so I'll have hair on that side again."

He ran his fingers unconsciously through the thick glossy hair on the right side of his head and continued, "I already had a master's degree before I went over so I worked on my doctorate while I was recovering. When I finished it, I applied here and they damn near tripped over their hard-ons to hire me. Hell, I'm a one-man politically-correct employment demographic. Injured vet, and Asian to boot. The only way I could've made their ratios look better would've been if I'd been an aboriginal female injured vet."

Stemp happened to be passing by on his way to the door in time to overhear the last sentences. "We hired you because your doctoral thesis was outstanding," he corrected. "And you had invaluable practical experience and glowing references from all your senior officers. And we promoted you to head of weapons research because you are far and away the best person for the job."

Chow turned a one-sided smirk on him. "Aw, Chuckie-baby, I didn't know you cared. Does this mean you're gonna invite me to the prom?" But he sketched a salute and I could see his appreciation.

Stemp nodded acknowledgement and continued down the corridor, and Chow turned back to me. "Cat got your tongue?"

I shrugged uncomfortably.

"So what's your story?" His good eye examined me with unnerving intensity. "Where did you serve?"

"I didn't," I mumbled, willing the heat out of my cheeks at the mere thought of comparing my experiences with his. "I've never been in combat."

"Oh, yeah? When Chuckie told me you were coming down for a briefing, I pulled your mission reports-"

"You knew who I was all along," I interrupted indignantly.

"Of course I knew. This is a fucking classified weapons lab. You really think I'd let somebody wander in here without checking them out first?"

At my sheepish 'No, I guess not', he added, "Yeah, I knew who you were, and I figured I'd like you after I read your reports. That's partly why I was so pissed when I thought you were an ignorant bitch."

"Sorry," I mumbled, blushing all over again.

Even though I was studying my toes, I could feel his penetrating scrutiny. "So you were in a firefight with thirty-odd terrorists in the jungle in the middle of the night. That sounds like combat to me."

"No." I nudged my toe at a scuff on the floor. "We only engaged half of them and it was just a rainforest, not a jungle. And I only shot one guy before I fell off a roof-"

"Under fire," he interrupted.

"Well, yeah. But my partner dragged me to safety and it was basically over after that."

"And another time you took out two enemy operatives and rode down in a burning plane..."

"The burning plane was my own stupid fault," I muttered.

"And you infiltrated an enemy installation and blew it up."

"That was just a barn with three old men in it, in the middle of Bumfuck Nowhere, guarded by one pimply-faced rent-a-cop and his dog..."

"Kelly, shut the fuck up."

The unexpected command jerked my head up to meet his one-eyed gaze. "You don't have to apologize for being in one piece," he said. "You served. You're all right by me."

"Thanks," I mumbled, even more embarrassed. "Can we get on with the briefing now?"

"Yeah... but your records said you're not in active service. How'd you pull courier duty?"

I dropped my gaze to my toes again, trying to hide my surge of fear at the thought. "I'm requalifying tomorrow morning."

"You sound pretty sure you'll pass."

"Yeah." I scuffed at the floor again. "I've been doing the tests about once a month. It makes me feel safer to know I'm in top shape. Dr. Rawling suggested it..." I trailed off, cold realization washing over me.

He'd set me up so Stemp could back me into a corner.

A wave of anger stiffened my spine and clenched my fists. "Rawling. That fucking bastard." My voice rasped in my throat. "He played me."

"Well, yeah. Army shrink. Never trust those fuckers." Chow eyed me with sympathy. "They'll help you get better, but you have to remember their ultimate goal is to get you back in action."

I stood seething in silence, and after a moment Chow spoke again.

"Not looking forward to going active?"

I drew a deep shaky breath and told the truth under his steady gaze.

"I'm scared shitless."

CHAPTER 14

"Then don't go back." Chow's good eye burned with intensity. "Tell 'em you've got PTSD. Make shit up if you have to. You've done your time and you owe these bastards fuck-all. Take an honourable discharge and get the hell out."

"I... can't."

"Why the hell not?"

"It's complicated." I sighed. "And classified. Can we just do this briefing?"

He studied me in silence for a moment, then nodded. "Okay. Come on, I'll give you the grand tour." He spun his chair and I stepped over beside him. "Other side," he commanded, gesturing toward his right, and as I moved to obey he added, "I'm blind and deaf on the left, and I hate it when people stand there."

"That must suck," I said without thinking. "It'd drive me nuts to know somebody could sneak up on me-"

I bit off the words, berating myself for my tactlessness, but Chow just grunted agreement. "Tell me about it. But..." He wheeled rapidly away, tossing over his shoulder, "Come look at this."

Screeching to a halt at one of the equipment-laden counters, he snatched up a pair of glasses with fashionable unisex frames. "Check these out," he said proudly. "These are just about ready to go into production. Complete three-sixty-degree real-time audio/video coverage in a heads-up display. For spooks like you it'll be like eyes in the back of your head, but I'm working on a specialized set for myself with an audio feed from my deaf side into my right ear, and the full HUD on one side only."

"Cool!" I leaned close to examine the glasses without touching them. "They're so sleek, you'd never know they had cameras and microphones in them. How do you power them?"

"Power supply is always the tricky part," he agreed. "Let's just say..." He smirked. "We found a way. They're completely self-contained, no external gear at all, and up to twelve hours recording capability between data dumps."

"Wow." I glanced around the lab, spotting the bushy-bearded Sawyer along with another man and woman busy at their respective counters. "So is it just the four of you down here inventing stuff all day long?"

"No, we've got several other-"

His words were cut short by a cry of outrage from the woman. While we'd been talking, she had crossed to stand behind her male counterpart, and now she accompanied another enraged shriek with a smart slap to the back of his head.

"You *pig!* How dare you bring that sick twisted porn in here!"

Chow muttered, "Oh, Jesus, not again."

The man rose and turned, revealing familiar-looking features reminiscent of a basset hound, complete with jowls and mournful eyes. He rubbed the back of his head where she'd struck him and said placatingly, "It's not porn, it's science fiction."

"Science fiction?" The woman planted her fists on her hips, her sleek pageboy bob quivering indignantly. "That's not science fiction, that's, that's..."

She leaned toward the screen he'd been facing, jamming half-glasses onto the end of her nose to scan the screen. "'...*Its hot silky blue tentacles slithered down to tighten around his throbbing cock*'?" She jerked upright, scowling. "'*Spasms of illicit pleasure*'? '*Teasing the cleft of his straining buttocks*'? It's nothing but porn! Alien-porn with butt-sex!"

I had been studying the man's jowly face and trying to figure out how I knew him, and sudden recognition made my jaw drop. "Shit, that's Murray Stout!"

"Oh, Jesus," Chow repeated.

"I recognize his photo from his book covers! One of my friends is a huge fan." I turned to Chow. "Murray Stout is known for his incredibly detailed and accurate science, and his kinky sex scenes. They call him the hard-sci master of soft porn. He wrote that!"

"No, he didn't," Chow said tiredly. "That's not Murray Stout."

"Yes, it-"

"No, it's not," he overrode me. "*That's* Murray Stout." Chow jabbed a finger at the woman still loudly berating the hound-faced man, who stood protesting feebly with his head hanging as if in shame.

When I gaped at Chow, he explained, "They're Melinda and Murray West. She writes the sci-fi. He's just a fan. They met at a convention years ago. She wasn't getting anywhere with her books because a lot of hard-sci readers think women can't write sci-fi. So after they got married she used his first name and made up a new last name, put his picture on the cover, and her books rocketed onto the bestseller list."

"Really?" I stared at the bickering couple. "Murray Stout is a woman?"

"Yep. And this little show's all for you. They've been together nearly fifteen years and I swear this is how they keep the spice in their marriage. Every time they get a fresh audience they pull this shit, and then they fuck like rabbits. It won't be safe to open a supply closet around here for the next week." He raised his voice. "Knock it off, you two!"

"Yeah, really!" the bushy-bearded Sawyer chimed in. "If I have to hear about Captain Mack's tentacle fetish one more time I'm going to lose my lunch."

"I can't imagine how you'd know if you did," Melinda retorted. "You could have three meals piled up in that beard and never know the difference. It looks like a live badger strapped around your neck!"

Sawyer flipped her a cheerful middle finger and they all drifted back to work, casting surreptitious glances my way as if to be sure I'd appreciated the show.

"*Anyway...*" Chow said with long-suffering emphasis. "Welcome to the asylum. Come on, I'll brief you on the prototype you'll be carrying." He wheeled away and I followed, watching Melinda/Murray West/Stout with caution.

"You acquired the original prototype of the fatal ultrasound weapon, right?" Chow inquired as he leaned toward the wall for a retinal scan.

"Um... yeah," I mumbled, still rattled. "John Kane and I did."

A door swished open with a Star-Trek-like sound effect,

and I snickered. Chow gave me his one-sided grin and led the way inside a small room. "Occupational hazard when you work with a bunch of science geeks," he said over his shoulder.

I was still hovering half-in and half-out of the door. From inside the room, the main area of the lab was clearly visible as if through a floor-to-ceiling glass panel, but from the outside it looked like a solid painted wall. I rocked back and forth, craning my neck to examine the panel from both sides.

"Pretty cool, eh?" Chow asked. "That was a byproduct of one of the defense-camouflage technologies we're working on. Unlike regular one-way glass, the light can be as bright as you want in here without compromising the impermeability from the outside. The defense system is still under development and highly classified, but we're gradually phasing these one-way panels into all the labs. They're lightweight and bullet-proof, too."

Grinning, I stepped inside and let the door swoosh shut behind me. "This is so cool. I feel like I'm in a James Bond movie and you're Q."

"I'm much smarter than Q," Chow said matter-of-factly. "So, you saw the original ultrasound weapon in action, right?"

The smile slid off my face at the memory of a handsome, competent young man collapsing into instant death.

"Yeah." My voice came out husky and I cleared my throat, eyeing the deadly bottle-shaped device with trepidation despite the fact that it was locked away under a heavy transparent dome.

"Somebody you cared about?" Chow asked quietly.

"N-no... I didn't know him well. But he was such a nice

young guy..." I shook myself and drew a deep breath. "So I'm transporting this thing again?"

"No. We're still working on it." He patted the dome. "We want more miniaturization and a subtler design. It'll be great for covert close-quarters wet work when it's done, but what you'll be carrying is new technology we've derived from it." He rolled his chair over to another dome housing a black cylinder that looked like a shorter, fatter version of a law-enforcement baton.

Punching a numeric code into the keypad beside the dome, he waved his pincer-hand in a theatrical flourish as the dome rose. "Voilà. The future of non-lethal personnel neutralization."

I backed away a step. "That sounds like a scary euphemism."

"Not as scary as the alternatives." Chow lifted the baton out, hefting it comfortably. "So far all the current non-lethal control methods are pretty unpopular with the bleeding-heart types. We've got microwave guns that'll heat up your skin 'til you run screaming or get second-degree burns, tear gas that'll choke you, rubber bullets that'll knock you out, tasers that'll shoot a hundred feet or more and light you up like a fucking Christmas tree, sonic generators that'll temporarily deafen you, lasers that'll temporarily blind you... it's all technically 'non-lethal'..." he made a one-handed air quote. "...but if you're too close or you get too big a dose you're fucked. This baby, on the other hand..." He hefted the baton again. "...is silent and it can't kill you or cause any permanent damage."

He hesitated. "Well, unless you blow a blood vessel from puking too hard or hit your head when you fall down. It uses focused ultrasound the same as the lethal version, but instead of being tuned to liquefy your brain it's tuned to fuck up your inner ear. Give somebody a one-second burst and they'll fall over and puke their guts out for about ten minutes afterward. It's not too bad if you lie completely still with your eyes closed, but the harder you try to move or focus your eyes, the harder you puke."

"I don't even want to know how you know that," I said.

The undamaged corner of his mouth quirked up. "Yeah, don't mention french fries to Sawyer for a while. I thought it was funny as hell when he horked one up through his nose, but he's still a little sensitive over it." At my grimace, he added, "We needed to know how it would affect different people so we each took a turn, but at least I was smart enough to do mine before lunch. The next-gen testing will happen in Calgary, so that's why you're taking it down."

"What's the range?" I inquired, eyeing it cautiously. "And how do you aim it?"

"There's no real aiming system. It generates a cone that maxes out at about two metres diameter at thirty metres. If your target is closer, the cone is narrower so you need to make sure you're pointing it roughly at their head."

"Doesn't it get lethal at close range?"

"Nope." Chow hesitated, then shrugged. "Well, it didn't do Sawyer any harm, but he's brain-damaged to start with."

"Very funny." I leaned over to examine it. "So this is the business end and that's the trigger?"

"Yep. The rest is battery pack. This thing is good for twelve hours of continuous use."

"Twelve *hours*?" I yelped. "I thought you said a one-second burst would do it!"

"It will, but it's for crowd control. It's strictly line-of-sight so you'd have to sweep it back and forth holding the trigger down, wiping out the front lines until they figured out what was happening and dispersed. It might work in hostage situations, too, but it's not ideal. An asshole with a gun can still do a lot of damage firing blind while he's lying there puking. And this..."

He picked up a ballpoint pen that had been lying under the dome beside the weapon. "This is your covert ops version. Only good for maximum sixty centimetres diameter at three metres, and only enough juice for about ten uses, but if you need to create a diversion at a party, this is your baby."

My mind flashed to Stemp's upcoming dinner party, but I squelched the thought before it was fully formed. The party wouldn't be that bad. Deploying classified weaponry would be overkill. Probably.

Dr. Chow handed over the pen and I held it carefully on the flat of my palm, squinting at the sleek polished cylinder.

"It's a Cross pen," I said blankly. "It's even got the Cross logo on it. Are you kidding me?"

"Nope. It writes, too. Just don't try to write a letter to your mama, 'cause it's only got a few drops of ink. The rest is microminiaturized guts." He pointed to the pocket clip. "If you rotate this ninety degrees it's ready to fire. You squeeze the top of the pen to generate the beam. It scans your thumb and forefinger, so it'll only work if your fingerprint data is coded into the pen in advance."

"Slick! So nobody can fire it accidentally or take it away and use it on you."

"You got it." Chow retrieved the pen and tucked it and the baton back under the dome. "I'll have these packed up for you at ten hundred Friday morning."

I nodded and followed him to the door, which swooshed open as we approached. We were crossing the lab when a shout jerked my head around.

"Goddammit! My flies!"

A buzzing swarm circled Sawyer's head, diving and circling in a choreographed pattern while he swatted ineffectually at them.

Then, as if recognizing the unnaturally perfect formation at the same time I did, his hands dropped to his sides and a grin split his bushy beard as he looked over to where Melinda and Murray stood.

They grinned back, Murray manipulating the joystick on a small handheld box while the swarm of flies swooped up from Sawyer's head and flew a rapid circuit of the room before tumbling into a heap on the table in front of him.

"You did it!" Sawyer bounced up and down with excitement. "It worked!"

"Yes." Melinda was positively glowing. "The genetic modifications were fine; it was the control system that was the problem. We just figured it out last night."

Beside me, Dr. Chow let out a war whoop and wheeled over to the table so fast he laid rubber. I hung back, wary of the buzzing, crawling heap and the crazed light in Murray's eyes as he fondled the joystick.

"Did you see that, Kelly?" Chow demanded. "Fly control!"

"Um... great," I agreed. "Dare I ask?"

"There are so many potential applications for this!" he exulted. "And with a ten-day gestational cycle, we can breed these fucking things as fast as we want, in the field or wherever..."

He broke off, eyeing me speculatively. "Hey, maybe you can help us out."

"Um...?" I took an involuntary step backward.

"No; don't worry, we just want to capture your pheromones." He advanced on me, a fanatical gleam in his eye.

I eyeballed the distance to the door. He could probably peel out in that souped-up wheelchair faster than I could run...

Melinda laid a restraining hand on Chow's shoulder. "Maybe if you explained what you have in mind instead of scaring the life out of her?"

Chow shook himself. "Sorry. It's just that this is one of my pet projects. We're working on a way to differentiate between hostiles and non-combatants. We have imaging systems that can identify any living thing, even through six feet of concrete bunker, but they're bulky and expensive. And when they locate somebody we still don't know whether they're insurgents waiting to blow us to hell or shit-scared non-combatants trying to hide from the fucking insurgents."

He sent a loving glance toward the heap of insects. "Flies are perfect. They can get in anywhere, they're fast manoeuvrable fliers, they're ubiquitous nearly everywhere so nobody pays attention to them, and they have extremely sensitive olfactory processing. Their gestational cycle is so short that even if we lost an entire batch we'd have a whole new one in ten days. And now we can make them fly wherever we want."

"So... how does that help you?" I asked. "Are you going to put little cameras on them?"

"That would be great, too, and we're working on it," he agreed. "But for this application we're using the flies to map personnel locations. They're far cheaper and more portable than an imaging system. And we're also working on isolating the specific pheromones humans excrete in high-adrenaline situations. Our preliminary research indicates that we should be able to differentiate between pheromones released by predator humans and prey humans. Flies would be sensitive enough to smell the pheromones, so once we've pinpointed the specific pheromones the flies will also be able to tell us who our targets are."

"But a predator might also be prey," I argued. "And vice versa. If somebody's hunting me and I turn around and kill him, I'd have both predator and prey pheromones."

"True, but it's not binary; it's more like a spectrum. The necessity of killing in self-defence produces a different blend of pheromones than the intent to kill unprovoked."

"Okay, if you say so. But I can't help you with that," I said, trying to hide my relief. "I don't know a thing about advanced biology or chemistry and I especially don't know anything about flies. And I don't want to."

"No, we need you as a test subject. We've been monitoring our own pheromones in simulated battle scenarios and simulated fear scenarios, but because we know they're simulated, we can't be certain we're getting accurate results. If you're going back on active duty..." Chow picked up a compact black box on a lanyard and advanced on me. "...would you wear this portable pheromone recorder for a while?"

I eyed it with suspicion. "What does it do?"

"When it detects an elevated heart rate it takes an air sample. It's good for ten samples and then it has to be returned and downloaded. So you'd remove it if you were working out to avoid wasting the sample on an artificially elevated heart rate, but other than that you don't have to do anything with it. Just wear it around your neck under your clothes. Completely non-invasive." Chow and the others studied me hopefully.

"If you do this, you could help eliminate a lot of unnecessary suffering," Chow added quietly.

Melinda nudged him. "Way to play the guilt card."

Chow gave me his distorted grin, but his one-eyed gaze met mine with a challenge.

"All right." I took the monitor from him. "But you'll pardon me if I hope it doesn't have any reason to take samples from me."

Chow sobered. "For your sake, I kind of hope it doesn't, too."

CHAPTER 15

I staggered out of the Weapons lab feeling like Alice emerging from the rabbit hole. The sense of unreality persisted during my exit through the time-delay chamber, and when I finally stepped back into the main lobby I stood blinking for a moment. At last I managed to summon my wits, and headed for my office.

As I approached it, Stemp strode out his door, but he halted at the sight of me. "Kelly." He jerked his chin back toward his office, and I sighed and obeyed.

Inside, he eyed me piercingly. "Will there be a problem with Dr. Chow?"

"No, I think we're okay. We just got off on the wrong foot..." I winced. "Oh, God, I didn't mean to mention feet, I just meant..." I drew a deep breath. "We'll get along fine," I said firmly.

Stemp leaned back in his chair. "Good." The hint of a smile tugged at the corner of his mouth. "For once your legendary temper has proved to be an asset. Dr. Chow is abrasive at the best of times, but he has zero tolerance for anyone who patronizes or kowtows to him because of his disability. Calling him a dickhead was probably the best possible way to gain his respect."

I slumped in my chair and massaged my aching temples. "Yay, me. You couldn't have given me a heads-up beforehand?"

"Would it have helped?"

I sighed. "No. It probably would've made things worse." His expression didn't change, but I thought I detected a hint of smugness. "It must be nice to be three steps ahead of everybody else at all times," I added sourly.

"Nice?" Stemp considered that for a moment, one brow raised fractionally. "Not particularly. Necessary? Yes."

I reined in my irritation, releasing a slow breath. Fine. Maybe I could use that annoying trait.

"Are you monitoring the investigation into Daniel's abduction?" I asked.

"No. In the first place, it's outside the Department's mandate. In the second place, there is nothing I could do to expedite the investigation even if I chose to involve myself. And in the third place..." He gave me a wintry smile. "I'm quite sure you're on top of it."

His smile dissolved, leaving the winter-cold behind. "However, for your own good I'm giving you a direct order to stay out of it. If you get caught interfering in a police investigation that's unrelated to any of your ongoing missions, you may be subject to prosecution that even I can't deflect. And I assure you, making the chain of command doubt your discipline as an agent is the fastest possible route to lifelong incarceration."

I rubbed my forehead, my heart aching with futility. "There's nothing to interfere with, even if I wanted to. The man who abducted Daniel was killed in an accident, and it looks as though Daniel wandered away into the woods. If he's been lost all this time..." My throat tightened. "...if they find him at all, he likely won't be alive."

A moment of silence hovered between us.

"I'm very sorry to hear that," Stemp said quietly.

"Yeah." I blew out a breath and hauled myself upright in the chair. "Are we done?"

"Yes."

"Okay." I stood. "There's one more thing I want to mention. I won't be going back to Dr. Rawling. I'm done with him."

Stemp's expressionless façade didn't even twitch. "Very well. Dismissed." As I reached the doorway, he added, "Please let me know as soon as possible if Mrs. Ives will attend tomorrow night."

"Okay. I'll call her right away."

In my office, I hesitated over the phone for a moment before turning back to the corridor. This was going to require some explanations that I didn't want Stemp to overhear.

Fifteen minutes later I poked my head cautiously through the door of Up & Coming. The bell above the door jingled gaily, summoning Lola from the back room.

"Hi, Aydan!" she exclaimed with a smile. "Have you come to get your key back? Here..." She hurried over to retrieve her purse from behind the counter, and handed over my key.

"Thanks. And thanks again for locking up for me," I replied, moving warily into the store and scanning for giant penises.

"You're looking for Big John, aren't you?" Lola teased. "He's over there." She pointed to a shelf containing what I had originally thought were pillar candles.

"What did you do to him?" I demanded, crossing to

inspect the shelf's contents despite my better judgement. "He's... he's mauve and sparkly!"

Lola giggled. "Cute, isn't he?"

"Um... I don't think you can successfully apply that word to a giant silicone dick. Even if it is mauve and sparkly."

"Don't worry." Lola trotted over to pat my arm. "That's not really Big John. That's his brother, Percy."

"Percy?" I choked.

Lola raised a mischievous eyebrow. "I was going to call him Big Jim, but his sparkles were too pretty. And don't worry, Big John is still here." She indicated the black silicone behemoth lurking behind the row of sparkling rainbow-hued dildos of various sizes. "Linda says Big John can be a little intimidating," Lola went on. "She wanted to lighten the mood with some fun new colours."

"Um... good thinking..." I mumbled before dragging my mind back to the issue at hand. "But I'm not here to shop. I have a favour to ask. Are you free tomorrow evening?"

She gave me a wink. "Depends on what you have in mind."

"Free dinner," I coaxed.

"Oh Lordy, it must be bad."

"Probably not for you, but it will be for me," I admitted. "My cold-fish boss has invited me to a dinner party with his parents and I need somebody to run interference."

"Invited you to meet his parents?" Lola chortled. "Oho! Do I sniff a little office hanky-panky?"

"Christ, no!" I shuddered. "No; I'm friends with his parents, and this is his mother's doing. She's trying to play matchmaker, but Stemp and I are equally horrified at the thought."

"Well, jeepers, count me in. I wouldn't miss this for the

world!" Lola's wicked grin made me suddenly reconsider the wisdom of inviting her.

"Remember, you're supposed to be on my side," I reminded her nervously. "Just eat and make polite conversation. Don't do anything evil..." The full realization of what I'd done crashed in on me. "Oh, God, I'm completely doomed."

"Of course you're not." She patted my arm again, doing her best sweet-little-old-lady imitation despite her fuchsia leather hot pants, matching hot-pink hair, and silver-studded stiletto heels. "Everything will be fine. Now, tell me about your boss and his parents so I know what to expect."

I sagged into the nearest chair, then leaped to my feet with a yelp when it began to vibrate and massage my butt. "Jesus! That thing just molested me! You need a warning sign."

"Nice try, honey, but you're smiling."

"Give me strength," I muttered. "Okay. My boss is Charles Stemp. He's basically a robot inside a snake's skin. Don't expect him to act like a human being." A twinge of conscience prompted me to add, "Okay, I'm exaggerating... a bit. He's actually an okay guy most of the time, but..." I made a frustrated gesture, at a loss to describe the enigma that was Stemp without revealing any classified details. "Never mind. You'll see when you meet him. His parents, on the other hand..." I trailed off, a smile creeping onto my lips.

"Go on," Lola prompted eagerly. "I think I like where this is going."

"His parents are completely opposite to him. They're old hippies who live on a commune, and they drive Stemp absolutely bonkers. They call themselves Karma Wolf Song and Moonbeam Meadow Sky and they're into spirit healing and auras and numerology and all that woo-woo stuff..."

I conveniently failed to mention Moonbeam's garrotte and Karma's lethal hand-to-hand combat skills. Even Stemp didn't know about those.

"...and they're both absolute sweethearts," I continued. "I know you'll love them, and I hope you'll be able to tolerate Stemp."

"I'll be there with bells on!" Lola promised. "This is going to be a blast! Where do they live, and what time should we go?"

"Stemp's right here in town. It'll only take a few minutes to get to his house, so I'll pick you up here at five-forty-five."

"Okay. But... are you really going to call your boss by his last name all through the dinner party?"

"I'm hoping not to have to call him anything."

Lola frowned. "What do you usually call him at work?"

I shuffled my feet. "Um... 'Dickhead'...? But I'm trying to quit..."

"Really?" At my shamefaced nod, Lola's wrinkled features split into a wide grin. "Oh, honey, I can hardly wait."

Back at Sirius Dynamics again, I immersed myself in the report on Frederick Labelle in a futile attempt to distract myself from worrying about Daniel.

And Kane.

And the grim portent of the cadaver dogs.

I sighed and refocused my attention on the report.

It didn't make me feel any better. On paper, Labelle was an upstanding businessman with a squeaky-clean reputation. According to Gladys and Lola, he was charming in person.

According to my gut, he was a money-laundering, gun-running scumbag and I didn't have a clue what to do about him. If I had been able to fall back on Kane's experience and Spider's technical expertise I might have had a chance, but without them I was sunk.

I groaned and sank my face into my hands, then hauled myself upright again.

No, dammit, I wouldn't screw this up. I'd get my training courses and do it right. Scowling, I checked the email Stemp had sent me. The earliest course was a few weeks away. The rest were spread out over several months.

Dammit.

But I could get help in the meantime. Stemp had been a top agent before he took over the directorship, so I could depend on his expertise. I didn't mind asking stupid questions if it kept people alive.

But maybe I should start at the beginning.

I dialled Tyler Brock's number.

When his annoying nasal voice snapped, "Brock", I drew a breath and reminded myself to be patient.

"Hi, Tyler, it's Aydan Kelly," I said politely.

"What do you want?"

I held onto my cordial tone. "I'm just calling to ask you a couple of questions about the party at my place."

Wariness shaded his voice. "What about it?"

"You arrived with another guy..."

"No, I brought Tammy," he interrupted. "Are you blind, too?"

"No..." I counted to three and reined in my temper. "I didn't mean you came together; I just meant you arrived at the same time. A well-dressed middle-aged guy..."

"Whatever. So some hilfiger showed up at the same time

as me. So what?"

I briefly considered asking him to define 'hilfiger', but I probably didn't want to know. The derogatory connotation came through loud and clear.

"I just wondered if you knew him," I said mildly.

"No. He tried to talk to me about some midtown investment business and I blew him off."

I already knew 'midtown' meant 'lame' in Brock's language, so I let that one ride, too.

"Had you ever seen him before?" I asked instead.

"No. Are you done wasting my time? I have important work to do here."

Irritation flared. "No doubt," I agreed. "But I'm not done yet. Why did you spike Spider's drink?"

"Stick it, Kelly." The line went dead in my ear.

Teeth grinding, I considered redialling. But he probably wouldn't answer anyway, and since it was physically impossible to reach down the phone line and strangle him, there wasn't much point.

I breathed deeply a few times to dissipate my annoyance, then let it go.

Too bad Brock couldn't provide any extra information on Labelle, but what the hell; I hadn't really expected him to. That would have been too easy.

Squaring my shoulders, I pulled out Labelle's note and reached for the phone.

Finger poised over the keypad, I hesitated.

If I called him from my cell phone, he'd have the number. After that, he'd be able to track my location using any rudimentary tracking system. Was that good or bad? It could work for me if he thought he knew where I was at all times...

Or should I call him from a Sirius Dynamics landline? If I was supposed to be a hotshot arms dealer, surely I'd have staff. If I let him think I had people here working for me...

No. Bad idea. Too close to the truth. I'd let him think I was just a bookkeeper here, and everyone I knew would verify that.

But wouldn't an arms dealer surround herself with bodyguards and hired guns?

I hissed out a breath between my teeth. If Labelle had gotten his information from Parr, he would already know I worked alone.

Stiffening my spine, I drew my lips back in a snarl. Arlene Widdenback the arms dealer was such a badass, she didn't need to surround herself with staff.

I'd just keep telling myself that.

Clinging to my illusions with all my might, I keyed Labelle's number into my phone and hit the Send key.

The line rang once on the other end, and sudden panic seized me. Punching the End button, I stared at my phone, my heart thumping.

Shit, I couldn't even make a simple phone call without almost screwing up. Labelle had come to my farm looking for Arlene Widdenback, and had smoothly covered his slipup when he discovered everyone there knew me as Aydan. And he'd addressed his note to Aydan, under Lola's watchful eye. So was he expecting a call from Aydan or Arlene?

And how much did he know about Arlene's story? Should I play Arlene the petty fraud artist or Arlene the ruthless arms dealer or Arlene the tacky middle-aged porn star? Or should I play Arlene playing Aydan Kelly the clueless bookkeeper?

I groaned aloud. Screw it. He had addressed his note to

Aydan, so he'd get Aydan.

When I dialled the second time he picked up immediately, as if he'd been hovering near the phone waiting for it to ring again.

"Frederick Labelle."   His voice was smooth and reassuring, the kind of radio-announcer voice that inspired instant trust.

It wasn't working for me.

"Hi, it's Aydan Kelly calling," I said in my best bookkeeper voice. "You left a note for me at my farm on Saturday afternoon. I'm sorry I missed you."

"Aydan, so good of you to call," he said warmly. "I was sorry to miss you, too, and I hope your emergency was safely resolved."

"Thanks, that's very kind of you." I avoided any details and went on, "You mentioned some investment opportunities. I'm quite busy this week, but we could set up a short phone meeting..."

"I'd much prefer to meet in person," he demurred. "I'm based in Calgary, but I could come up to Silverside this afternoon."

Not a chance, bucko.

"I'm sorry," I said, sounding amazingly sincere. "I'm booked solid until Wednesday." When he began to make disappointed noises, I talked over him. "As a business owner yourself, I'm sure you understand why I have to make my existing clients a top priority. Would Wednesday at two o'clock work for you? Or I have another opening available on Thursday at ten."

I could tell he wasn't happy about it, but his smooth tone hid it well. "Wednesday at two would be fine. Due to the confidential nature of my business, I'd like to meet somewhere we can have privacy."

Great, because I just fucking love being alone with dangerous criminals.

"Understandable," I agreed, and threw out the first idea that came to mind. Public, but with privacy. "We can get ice cream cones and go for a walk in the park."

"Ice c-" He stifled his incredulous bark and rolled out the warm reassuring voice again. "That sounds delightful. I'll meet you at the ice cream parlour on Main Street at two on Wednesday."

Trembling, I mouthed the usual goodbye pleasantries and disconnected.

I tried to immerse myself in planning, but my mind cycled anxiously between enumerating the many fatal ways I could screw up this new mission and worrying over Kane and Daniel.

It wasn't a productive afternoon.

CHAPTER 16

By five o'clock my head was pounding and my stomach was in knots. I logged out of the network and sat staring at the blank computer screen for a few moments before jitters drove me to my feet.

"Fuck this," I muttered, and headed for the door.

After a short stop at my farm to grab road food and my small backpack, I hit the highway heading west.

When my cell phone rang a few miles past Drumheller, I slammed on the brakes and veered over to stop precariously close to the ditch, heart pounding.

"Hello?" I gasped.

"Hello, Aydan, it's John." His deep baritone was still edged with fatigue, but he sounded a little better than he had earlier.

I hesitated, afraid to ask the question.

"I just wanted to let you know that there's nothing new at this end," he said tiredly. "The cadaver dogs didn't find anything. The search teams have combed everything within a two-mile radius from the campsite, and I'm certain that if Daniel had been in that area, they would have found him." He went silent.

"Oh." The syllable fell from my lips like a stone. "So...

what does that really mean?"

"Nothing. We'll keep looking. It's all we can do."

"Okay. I'm on my way. I should be there in about two and a half hours."

"You don't need to do that," he protested. "It'll be nearly eight by the time you get here. The search teams only stay out until sunset at nine."

"That's okay. I have my gear with me. I'll help you search tonight."

He let out a breath. "Thank you."

"See you soon," I said, and disconnected.

When I pulled into the motel parking lot I cast a wary look around, but apparently the bike rally had moved on. The place was deserted except for Kane's and Hellhound's vehicles and a couple of white half-tons bearing oilfield-service logos.

I parked and shouldered my backpack before crossing to tap on the door of Kane's unit. When he opened it, my heart smote me at the sight of his haggard features and unshaven jaw.

"Oh, John." I stepped inside and drew him into a hug. He sank his face onto my shoulder and I held him close, stroking his hair and wishing I could do something to ease the terrible pain in his eyes.

After a moment he pulled away, squaring his shoulders. "Welcome back to the Ritz," he said with an attempt at a smile. "It's just as ugly as before, but at least it's quieter now."

"Hey, darlin'," Hellhound added from behind him. "Nice to see your pretty face. I'm already sick a' lookin' at Kane's ugly mug."

"Look who's talking," Kane retorted without rancour as I went over to collect a hug from Hellhound. He looked almost as careworn as Kane, but as always his embrace gave more comfort than it took.

"Thank you for coming," Kane added as Hellhound released me. "I was hoping for a chance to communicate over a secure channel, but this is better."

"Really? You have something?" I demanded, trying to hide my hope.

"No, I need something."

"Oh." My heart sank again. "What can I do?"

"Can you get me Murphy's autopsy report?"

I glanced at Hellhound's curious expression and said carefully, "Not this instant, but probably tomorrow."

"Would you please?" Kane hesitated, then added, "If you're still all right with doing that..."

"Of course. Set up a bogus email address tonight and I'll deliver it as soon as I can. It won't be first thing in the morning, though, because I have to do my requalifications at nine AM. Once you get my report, delete the email account."

"Wait, you're going back to active duty? *Tomorrow morning?*" Kane demanded at the same time as Hellhound growled, "Whoa, what the hell?"

"Yes." I answered Kane and avoided Hellhound's frown with a question. "Why do you need the autopsy report? I thought Mayweather already told you what was in it."

"He only gave me the preliminary findings." Kane made a frustrated gesture, his fist clenching before dropping to his side. "And he won't give me the whole thing because I'm not on the case. Privacy Act; open investigation; blah, blah."

"Aydan ain't on the case, either," Hellhound said

suspiciously. "Are ya, darlin'? So how the hell are ya gonna get that report? Are ya some kinda super-hacker or somethin'?"

"Oh, hell, no," I lied with a light laugh that sounded almost convincing. "Spider's the hacker. I'm just-"

"A bookkeeper," Hellhound finished. "Uh-huh."

"Well, no," I conceded. "You know that. But I have my ways."

"That why you're goin' active again?" Hellhound asked. "So ya can get us information?"

"If that's the reason, don't do it," Kane added. "We'll find another way."

"Um..." I eyed the two frowning faces across from me. They didn't need any more worries right now. "No, I just, um... I had to anyway. So it's okay."

"It's okay until you ship out on your next mission," Kane said flatly. "Based on what you told me two days ago, you're not ready. What does Dr. Rawling say?"

"Fuck Rawling and the horse he rode in on," I snapped. "And then bend him over and let the horse fuck him, too. He's an asshole, and I'm done with him."

"Uh, darlin', if he doesn't think you're ready..." Hellhound began worriedly, but I overrode him.

"He's the one who set me up."

"What do you mean, he 'set you up'?" Kane inquired dangerously.

A glance at the fire in his eyes made me backpedal hurriedly. "I didn't really mean that. He was only doing his job, and I shouldn't be so pissed off at him. It was just that I was hoping I wouldn't have to go back to active duty for a while yet..."

Try 'never'.

I bit back the word and continued, "...but this is just how it worked out. No big deal."

"Sure as hell sounds like a big deal," Hellhound observed, his brow still furrowed with concern. "What ain't ya tellin' us, darlin'?"

"The usual classified shit." I waved a dismissing hand, knowing those magic words would prevent him from questioning me any further. "But don't worry," I added. "Stemp promised he wouldn't dump me into the deep end. I've just got a simple courier job on Friday."

"Any mission can turn into 'the deep end' if things go sideways," Kane growled. "And if you're not at a hundred percent..."

"I am," I assured him. "Really. Stop worrying." I changed the subject. "But speaking of worrying, you need to go in for your debriefing. Stemp's getting antsy."

"That will take hours. Maybe days." He brushed the issue away with an impatient gesture. "It can wait. So, you might be able to send me the autopsy report by late tomorrow morning?"

"Probably. Are you looking for anything specific?"

Kane let out a breath of resignation. "I don't know what I'm looking for. At this stage I'm grasping at straws. Maybe..." He hesitated. "According to police statistics, children Daniel's age rarely travel farther than a mile on foot when they're lost. The radius we've searched already exceeds that. There's a diminishing rate of possibility that he went farther, but it seems more likely that we're looking in the wrong place entirely."

He closed his eyes briefly, then went on, "The river is the strongest possibility. If he fell in and was swept away..."

I reached over to squeeze his hand, but he went on, his

voice hard and level. "The cadaver dogs searched downstream a long way today. Using the statistics we have available and knowing the river's flow rate and terrain, it's unlikely that his body would have been carried beyond the area they searched. It's possible, of course, but..."

He shrugged, a tense jerk of his shoulders. "My gut tells me he's not here. Maybe I'm fooling myself because I don't want to believe the truth, but at this point it doesn't matter. If there's more to this situation than Daniel simply wandering off, I need more information and the autopsy report is the place to start. We'll search again tonight, but tomorrow it's time to shift our focus. And... Mayweather as much as told me..." Kane's voice went husky. "...they'll be winding down the search tomorrow. After thirty-six hours..."

His fists clenched.

"Dammit!" he exploded. "This shouldn't have happened! I should have been the one taking him camping! I should have... If I had called Alicia even once in the past six years, I would have found out about him. He wouldn't have needed a loser like Murphy..." His voice choked off.

My heart breaking, I put my arms around him, but he disengaged himself and stepped back, squaring his shoulders. "I'll hire searchers to take over as soon as Mayweather calls off the official search," he said levelly. "Others can do that as well as we can, and our time will be better spent investigating. I'm going to set up that email account now. Aydan, if you have to requalify tomorrow morning, you should go back to Silverside now. It'll be nearly eleven by the time you get home."

"No, I'll help you look," I disagreed. "I brought my night-vision and infrared gear, and three sets of eyes are better than two."

"That's true, but..." I could see he was torn, and after a moment he let out a breath. "All right. If you want to search with us until midnight, that's fine, but then you need to go home."

"Okay." I flopped onto the bed. "After we coordinate the email account, you can lead the way to the site. I'll follow in my car."

By eleven-thirty PM my body was aching from the fatigue of the day compounded by nearly three hours of pushing through dense undergrowth and trudging over uneven ground in the darkness. Kane and Hellhound strode tirelessly a few yards on either side of me, the heat of their bodies glowing in my infrared vision.

We searched in silence, an unspoken surrender to the knowledge that Daniel, if he was here at all, was likely beyond the ability to hear or respond to a call.

I had just switched from full-infrared to night-vision when Kane snapped, "Heat signature, two o'clock!"

Flipping back to full-infrared, I spotted a glowing horizontal blob at approximately chest height. Maybe a child lying on a rock...?

I switched back to night-vision and we crashed through the woods, only to pull up short when we cleared the intervening trees.

"Shit," Hellhound muttered.

My already-racing heart delivered a shock of adrenaline that burned all the way to my toes. "Open your jackets!" I barked. "Make yourselves as big as you can!"

My Glock was already in my hand, though I didn't remember drawing it. One-handed, I fumbled my jacket open and spread it wide, an instinctive growl rumbling in my throat.

On my right, Hellhound's pistol was steady in his hand, his free arm widening his jacket, too. Kane grew dramatically on my left, his arms and jacket widespread.

Obviously unimpressed by our show of dominance, the giant cougar subjected us to an intent inspection, rising slowly from its reclining position on a rock ledge. Its heavy dark-tipped tail swung rhythmically side to side, a furry pendulum counting down the final seconds of its prey.

A snarl ripped from my throat, fading into a keening growl that rattled between my bared teeth. The big cat's eyes widened as if in surprise and it backed away a step, tail twitching.

Hellhound roared, "Fuck off!" at the same time Kane bellowed, "Scat!", and the cougar gave us one last considering glance before turning to glide sinuously into the undergrowth. When the dark tail-tip disappeared into the bushes, Hellhound let out an explosive breath.

"Jesus Christ, Aydan, what the hell? Ya scared me worse'n the fuckin' cougar, growlin' like that."

My laugh came out high and nervous while I turned slowly, scanning a full circle. "Sorry. Habit."

"Habit? What the fuck, darlin'? How often d'ya hafta swear in cougar-language?"

"I used to do it a lot when I was a kid." I flipped to full-infrared, still scanning anxiously around us. "There were some really aggressive feral tomcats around our farm and they used to scare the hell out of me. But once I learned to speak their language, they'd always back down and run. It was pure reflex to let fly with a snarl when I'm shit-scared by a cat."

Hellhound laughed. "Well, it still works like a damn. And I'm glad we didn't hafta shoot it. What a beauty!"

"Our scare tactics might have worked for now." I turned another slow three-sixty. "But cougars will stalk you and attack from behind. I'd rather meet a bear than a cougar any day."

"Yeah," Hellhound agreed. "But it ain't gonna take on the three of us."

"If it does, it'll likely attack you, Aydan," Kane supplied not-too-helpfully. "You're the smallest of us."

"Yeah, but she cussed it out big-time," Hellhound argued. "It prob'ly fucked off for good."

"Well, it doesn't matter," Kane replied. "Aydan, we're going to walk you back to your car now. It's time for you to leave."

"You don't need to-" I began.

"Let's go," Kane said firmly, and turned back toward the road. "I'll take point. Hellhound, follow Aydan and watch our six."

I didn't protest any further. It was nearly midnight anyway. And with the back of my neck tingling at the thought of the cougar stalking us in the darkness, I was pathetically glad of their protection. I stuck close behind Kane's broad back and took comfort from the sound of Hellhound's footsteps behind me.

At my car, I hugged each of them in turn, wishing I could convince them to go back to the safety of the motel and knowing with an ache of pride that they were both too brave. I got into my car amid exhortations to drive carefully and pull over for a nap if I got tired, which I countered with equally forceful instructions to watch each other's backs, stay warm in the chill of the high-country night, and call me as soon as they got back to the motel.

The drive home seemed interminable. In the forested higher elevations I strained my eyes for wildlife at the edges of my headlights' range. Twice I braked hard when deer skittered out beside the road, and once my heart gave a hard thump at the sight of glowing green spots in the ditch. I slowed to a crawl, recognizing the telltale reflection of elk's eyes, but the huge animals made no move to cross the road. I drove on, easing my tense fingers one by one on the wheel.

When I reached the blessedly open grain fields of the east, I relaxed my vigilance at last. The long day and cessation of tension dragged at my eyelids and I stopped repeatedly, getting out of the car to walk around before sliding back into the driver's seat to sing at the top of my lungs while I drove.

CHAPTER 17

After an inadequate four hours of sleep, my alarm sounded only seconds before the phone rang. Eyes still half-closed, I tried to slap the snooze alarm and grab the phone handset simultaneously. I succeeded in knocking the alarm clock off the front of my bedside bureau and dropping the handset behind it.

Cursing, I scrambled out of bed and yanked the bureau aside to snatch the handset out of a fluffy nest of dust.

"Hello-*choo!* Sorry... *Atchoo!* Goddamn dust-bunnies..." I seized a tissue in time to stifle a third sneeze, then used a clean one to whisk the remaining dust off the handset before attempting to speak again. "Sorry. Hello?"

"Gesundheit," Kane said, amusement warming his voice. "Where did you find the feral dust-bunnies? Your house was spotless last weekend."

I mopped my running nose. "Behind my bedside table. Long story. How... How did it go last night?"

He sighed. "The same. I just wanted to let you know we're back at the motel and we're going to bed now. Call me..." He hesitated, obviously unwilling to mention our plan on an unsecured line. "...if you hear anything. I don't want to sleep through it," he added, making it clear that he expected me to call the instant I sent the autopsy report.

"I will," I promised.

I signed in at Sirius Dynamics on the dot of eight AM and headed for the secured area before I could wake up enough to freak out in the time-delay chamber.

It was a good theory, and it almost worked. My heart was pumping a little harder by the time I scooted down the concrete stairs and burst into the cool white corridor below, but I didn't need to take time to gather myself the way I usually did.

Striding toward the Weapons lab, I mentally congratulated myself. I was getting better at this. Maybe with a little more work I could finally overcome my claustrophobia.

I waved my security fob at the prox panel and the door released. Inside, I turned right and headed for the lab, hoping Dr. Chow was in a good mood today.

When I rounded the corner my heart sank. He was in his wheelchair again. Probably cranky as hell.

I drew a deep breath just as he looked up and snapped, "What the hell do you want?"

Yep, cranky.

Shit.

"Hi." Glancing around the abandoned lab, I attempted a joke. "What, no alien-porn today?"

His black brow snapped down and he jerked a thumb in the direction of one of the labs. "They went in there about five minutes ago and they're probably fucking while they watch us through the one-way window. You come down here just to get your jollies?"

"Special delivery," I said cheerfully, and lifted the pheromone detector's small box over my head.

"What, already?" He snatched it out of my hand and wheeled over to the nearest lab counter to connect it to a cable snaking to a computer. "I thought you weren't going active until this morning. You watch a scary movie and piss your pants last night or something?"

"Something," I agreed. "You should have a good 'prey' sample in there. A big cougar was sizing me up for a midnight snack last night."

He spun his chair to face me, his eyebrow going up. "No shit? A cougar? Around here?"

"No, up by Rocky Mountain House."

"What the hell were you doing up there at midnight?" He turned back to the counter and picked up a small screwdriver without waiting for my reply.

"Long story." I watched in silence while he opened the case and extracted two tiny glass vials from the row inside. Then he consulted the computer screen.

"Okay, Sample One corresponds to last night's flag at 23:32. But what the hell were you doing five minutes ago when it took Sample Two?"

"Nothing... oh. Shit." Heat climbed my face. "Just ignore that one. I should've taken the recorder off."

He pivoted to face me, the good side of his mouth twisting sardonically. "What, you really were getting your jollies? You kinky beeyotch."

I snorted. "I wish. No, I'm claustrophobic and that time-delay chamber always freaks me out." An involuntary sigh escaped me. "I thought I'd beaten it this time. Sorry. I'll remember to take off the recorder next time."

His frown softened. "Claustrophic, eh? That's gotta

suck. But it's okay, it'll be a good comparison to the 'prey' sample. Good way to compare a simple heightened adrenaline response with the fear of imminent attack." He turned back to the counter and replaced the two vials with fresh ones, then tapped computer keys for a few seconds before unplugging the detector and closing it up again.

"Here you go." He handed it back. "Don't put it on until you're upstairs this time."

He didn't sound irritated anymore, so I accepted the small box and nodded toward his legs, hoping I was doing the right thing. "You must've really done a number on them on the weekend. How long does it usually take to recover?"

Chow shrugged. "Normally I'd be back on my feet by now, but I got a little fold in the liner when I put the left one on. I realized it about halfway through the race and knew I should stop and smooth it out, but..." He grinned. "I was setting a personal best and I nailed it. I should be walking by tomorrow, and I'll start training again on Thursday."

"When's your next race?"

"Saturday, and it's only a five-K. Easy."

I shook my head. "Easy for you to say. Want to do my fitness requalification for me this morning?"

He snorted. "Nice try, Kelly. Get your lazy ass over to that gym."

I saluted him with middle finger extended and let the sound of his laughter carry me to the door.

Instead of my friend Germain's encouraging presence, the examiner was a dour middle-aged man who looked as though he'd take pleasure in failing me. Despite the knowledge that I had unofficially passed the tests less than a month ago, my palms moistened while I changed into my gym clothes.

Only four hours of sleep last night. God, I was tired. What if I couldn't complete the fitness portion under the time limit? Stemp would have my ass on a platter.

And wouldn't that be a lovely dish for the dinner party tonight? I suppressed a nervous snicker.

Shuffling out into the gym, I shot an apprehensive look at the obstacle course and the examiner's forbidding features, then shook out my arms and legs and bounced up and down a few times to get my blood pumping.

Come on, body, don't fail me now...

It didn't, thank God.

When I collapsed in a gasping heap of sweat and jelly-like muscles at the finish line, the examiner's mouth twisted as though he'd bitten into a lemon. "Congratulations," he said. "You've retained your title as the oldest woman to qualify in the fitness test."

If I'd had any breath to spare, I would have told him to kiss my wrinkly old ass. Fortunately I was too winded to speak, so I just nodded and dragged myself upright to stagger into the changing room.

The firearms qualification was easy by comparison, and when I emerged from the shooting range his nod was slightly less grudging. "Here you go," he said, and handed me copies of the marking sheets before turning his back and striding out.

"Thank you, Mr. Congeniality," I muttered, and followed.

Back in my office, I left the pheromone detector on my desk while I perched on the edge of my chair with a wary eye on the corridor. Stemp was expecting me, but first I needed some plausible reason to access the brainwave-driven virtual reality network in person instead of going through Brock.

Skimming the report on Labelle, I identified a couple of potential leads. Vague was probably best. Less to lie about.

I mustered all my acting skills and headed for Stemp's office.

When I tapped on his door frame, he looked up from his computer with what was almost a smile. "Come in. I see you passed your requalifications." He nodded toward the marking sheets on his desk.

"Yeah..." Stepping into his office, I hesitated at the sight of the high-tech lie detector sitting on the corner of his desk.

"Please sit," he invited.

Or maybe that was a command.

He rose and closed the door as I eased into his guest chair. When he returned and picked up the headband with its crown of electrodes, he answered my unspoken question.

"A new standard for the requalification examinations." He fastened the electrodes around my forehead. "Dr. Travers has completed her testing on this device. She claims it has ninety-nine percent accuracy, but..." His lips quirked as he rounded his desk and resumed his seat. "...you know Dr. Travers. A scientist will never claim one hundred percent. Nevertheless, in all the tests she performed, the device was never wrong. So... is your name Aydan Kelly? Please answer yes or no."

My heart raced while my mind rocketed back over my recent dealings with Stemp. Had I lied to him lately? Shit, I couldn't remember...

"Kelly?" Stemp prompted.

"Oh. Um, sorry, I was just..." I gathered my scattered

wits. "Yes."

The green light flashed, but Stemp shook his head. "Let's try it again. Is your name Aydan Kelly?"

"Yes."

This time there was no doubt about the green light, and Stemp went on with the standard opening questions. Had I ever used any other names; did I work for Sirius Dynamics; did I work for anyone else...

The green light shone its blessing upon my answers, and he continued to questions designed to test my loyalty and adherence to the non-disclosure agreements. None of them were new to me and I fielded them easily, though not confidently.

Damn, even when I was being completely honest I felt guilty. My heartbeat thumped rapidly in my ears.

At last Stemp sat back with a smile. "That concludes the standardized questions we've designed to be part of the annual requalification. We're hoping that this, combined with our upgraded security clearance protocols, will help us identify and eliminate moles or double agents. Are there any other questions you think we should be asking to further that end?"

"Um..." I thought about it for a few moments. "No. But I'll let you know if I think of anything."

"Thank you."

I reached up to loosen the electronic headdress, but Stemp raised a restraining hand. "I'm not quite finished."

"Oh. Sorry." I sat back and waited.

All the expression faded from his face, leaving a cold and clinical mask. His reptilian gaze bored into me as if to expose every lie I'd ever told, and I suddenly realized his right hand was concealed by the desk.

Oh, shit.

Was that a trank pistol trained on me? Or would I get a bullet between the eyes if I answered wrong? I knew how fast he could draw. No hope of escape...

"Before I ask my next questions, I think you should know that I have trusted you a great deal," he said gravely. "More than any other agent, and very likely more than I should have. I hope you won't give me reason to regret that."

I swallowed hard, but my voice came out in a dry croak anyway. "I hope not, too. And I hope you'll ask all your questions before you..." I nodded toward his concealed hand. "...make your final decision."

A tiny quirk of humour disturbed his deadpan façade. "I've never been in the habit of shooting first and asking questions later."

"Good to know."

"These questions are specifically designed for you, Webb, and Brock," Stemp began, and I eased out a small breath of relief. Still standardized questions, then. Maybe I wouldn't get into too much trouble.

"Because we have no way of confirming what information you actually access while you're hacking and decrypting, these questions will address your activities while you are invisible and undetectable inside our internal network and the internet at large," Stemp went on. "First question: Other than as strictly required by the cases you've handled, have you ever accessed our internal restricted, classified, or personnel files?"

"No."

The green light shone steadily, and Stemp blinked.

"No?" He sounded incredulous.

I frowned. "No, of course not. Why would I do that?

The less I know, the safer everybody else is."

He laughed out loud, making me twitch with shock.

"Kelly, you really are the original straight arrow, aren't you?" he said, humour still warming his eyes. "I can't imagine anyone else resisting the temptation."

"It's not hard. All I have to do is think about what would happen if that information fell into the wrong hands."

He sobered. "You're right, of course. But that was not the answer I expected at all. This will considerably shorten my list of questions for you."

"Sounds good to me," I said mildly, still watching his gun hand. Despite his easy posture and laughter, his hand had never wavered under the desk. I felt a moment's pity for any bad guy who'd faced Stemp while he was an agent.

"Next question," he said. "Have you ever falsified or failed to report any information you gathered through your research?"

"No."

Green light.

"Have you ever gathered more information than was strictly required by the cases you've handled?"

I squirmed. "Well, yeah, probably... I mean, I never really know how much information is actually required, and when I'm in the data stream I can't help reading stuff. It's like sitting across from somebody who's reading a newspaper; you can't help but read the headlines."

"Yes or no, please."

Was he trying to frame me?

I scowled, my heart rate kicking up another notch. "Yes."

"Have you ever used information for personal gain or to pursue ideological goals?"

"No."

"Have you ever intentionally avoided reading information to protect yourself or others from suspicion or prosecution?"

"Um..." I thought it over, but my body was pumping adrenaline and my memory wasn't cooperating. "No, I don't think so."

"Yes or no, please."

Tension wound up in my shoulders. "No...?"

The green light shone again, and I managed not to let out a sigh of relief. I was pretty sure I was telling the truth, but I'd been semi-conscious in the network so many times I couldn't be sure.

Did the detector know if I knew whether I was telling the truth...? The convolutions of logic twisted my brain and I rubbed my aching forehead.

"Last question," Stemp said. "Is it in the best interests of the Department and myself personally to continue to trust you?"

"Yes."

The light shone glorious green, and I slumped with relief.

"Thank you." His smile was back, and both his hands were visible again as he rose and rounded the desk to remove the band of electrodes from my forehead. He closed the lie detector's case and added, "Congratulations on your requalification. Dismissed."

I suppressed an overwhelming urge to run far, far away. God, he'd taken that headset off me just in time.

Because I was about to start lying to him.

CHAPTER 18

"Will you have time to spot me in the network for a while today?" I asked, holding my voice level.

Stemp leaned against his desk, arms crossed over his chest, his face impassive. "Why?"

"I want to look into Labelle's business network. I don't really know what I'm looking for so I can't request it from Brock, but..." I refused to let my gaze waver. "I just want to go and look around a bit. I don't think it'll take too long."

Stemp held my gaze for a moment before responding. "Very well. I have time now, as long as you expect to be finished before noon. By the way, have you reminded Kane about his debriefing?"

"Um... yeah." I hesitated. Probably better not to tell him Kane had basically said the Department could go piss up a rope. "He'll be in touch," I said instead.

"It had better be soon."

"I'll tell him." I backed toward the door. "I'll just run down and get the network key from Spider's lab. I'll be right back."

He nodded, and I fled.

Breathing deeply and willing calm with all my might, I braved the time-delay chamber again and retrieved the mote of technology from its safe haven in Spider's secured lab.

Dammit, I hated lying. Would I even be able to pass the lie detector test next year?

I sucked in a breath and let it out slowly. Shut up, conscience. I really was going to check into Labelle. The medical examiner's files would just be a little side trip.

Repeating my rationalizations over and over in my mind, I emerged from the coffin-like depths and trudged back up to Stemp's office.

Inside, I sank into the chair he indicated, and at his nod of readiness I closed my eyes and mentally stepped into the white void of virtual reality.

His avatar popped into existence beside me a moment later, and we made our way to the virtual file repository that served as the home base for my forays into the internet's vast sea of data.

Stemp materialized a desk, chair, and computer terminal from thin air. "I'll continue my work here while you're gone," he said. "I presume you only need me to act as your anchor as usual?"

"Yeah. I'll try to be back before noon, but if it's getting close you could start pulling on my hand. Sometimes I lose track of time. And if I disappear completely, start doing computer searches for, um..." I hesitated, trying to think of something unusual but not suspicious to outside observers.

"I'll search for 'dwarf hardy hibiscus'," Stemp supplied. "I'll rotate my searches through pink, red, white, and yellow, and keep repeating until you respond."

"Perfect." I reached for his hand. "Wish me luck."

He nodded without expression, and I faded into invisibility and seeped into the turbulent data tunnels of the internet. Letting my virtual self stretch from his anchoring grip, I made for the medical examiner's internal network.

Arbuckle Murphy's autopsy report was easy to find. I slid invisibly through the firewalls and stole a copy, encrypting it and temporarily storing it on a convenient public server. Then I traced my route back to the email account Kane had created the previous night, selecting a convoluted path and hiding my tracks.

There would be no incriminating header information in my email. Completely untraceable. And as soon as he removed it and deleted the account, all evidence of this little transaction would be gone.

We'd be fine. Almost no chance of getting caught.

I hesitated.

What if Kane needed something else later? I'd have a hard time convincing Stemp that I needed to poke through the internet on a regular basis. He'd expect to see some results of my so-called case research sooner or later.

I might not get another chance. I should make this count.

Disregarding the prodding of my conscience, I insinuated myself back into the data stream and headed for the police network.

Its security was almost as daunting as Sirius's. Floating in the data tunnel while the busy streams of data packets buffeted me, I sent virtual feelers out to examine their external firewall.

This was going to be ugly. I'd likely lose my connection to Stemp back at Sirius, and he'd have to call me home with his internet searches. And then I'd have to explain what the hell I'd been doing.

If my bodiless self had been capable of sighing, I would have. Instead, I gathered my courage and flung myself at the firewall, thinking of body-surfing with all my might.

The proxy server bounced me, dragging me under and flinging me back time and again like pounding waves with a vicious riptide. My virtual consciousness shredded under the assault and instinctive terror seized me. I flung out frantic tendrils in all directions, completely disoriented. At last I found a grip, and gradually extracted my quivering consciousness from the maelstrom of data.

My connection to Stemp was severed; my sense of Sirius's well-concealed servers long gone.

Lost.

Trapped in the vast interminable tunnels of the internet...

I jerked myself back from the edge of panic. Shut up and get it done. Stemp would be sending his internet searches out, and I still needed this data.

Do it.

I flung myself at the firewall again.

This time I was successful, rocketing through into the peaceful backwater of the internal network.

Thank God.

Vibrating with reaction, I pulled my data bits together and went hunting.

Mayweather's case file fell to my voracious tentacles first. I grabbed everything including the forensic reports from Murphy's truck and campsite before rummaging hurriedly through the rest of the network. The knowledge of time ticking away thrummed tensely in my consciousness.

I was just about to pull out with my treasure when a nagging feeling dragged me to a halt. I took a closer look at the data I'd gathered.

If I'd been capable of breathing, I would have sucked in a

breath.

Oh, shit.

No, that had to be wrong.

But...

Sickness pooling in what would have been my stomach in real life, I gathered every scrap of data before launching myself back into the internet.

It took only a few minutes to pack the files into a single communication and dump it to Kane's bogus email account. Then I returned my consciousness to the internet, watching and listening.

As the stream of '...*hardy dwarf hibiscus, yellow; hardy dwarf hibiscus, pink; hardy dwarf...*' tickled my feelers, I turned to follow it back to Sirius Dynamics.

When I tumbled back into my gasping avatar in the virtual file room, Stemp lunged to his feet and barked, "What happened?"

"Nothing..." I hunched over, elbows on knees, and panted out the last of my fear. "I just... hit a high-security firewall... and got scrambled. Thanks..." I sucked in some more air, trying to calm my rapid breathing. "Thanks for the searches." I straightened slowly. "I have to go back. I didn't get what I wanted."

I suppressed a wince at the profound truth of that statement. If that police data was what I thought it was, I *really* didn't want it.

Stemp eyed me critically. "Is it safe for you to go back?"

"Yeah." I spread my hands. "See, my avatar is fine. You only have to worry if I can't hold my avatar."

"If you can't hold your avatar, it's already too late," Stemp said dryly. "You may recall I've had to drag your mangled remains out of here before."

I blew out a breath, trying to hide my trembling. "You won't have to this time. I'm fine. But I need to go back. I've still got..." I consulted my wristwatch. "...a little over an hour. And I need it."

"Very well." Stemp reached out to grasp my hand again. "Good hunting."

"Thanks." I faded into invisibility again and went to do my real job.

An hour later, I slipped back into my avatar in the virtual file room with a sigh and let go of Stemp's hand.

"That's better," he observed. "Did you find what you were looking for this time?"

I grimaced. "I don't know. I need to go over the data again and give it some more thought."

He nodded, unsurprised. "Very well. Let's go, then."

We abandoned the file repository and strode to the virtual portal together. He stepped through first, leaving me to brace myself for the misery that was to come.

When I stepped through the portal back into reality, the usual pain crashed into my skull. Hissing obscenities through my teeth, I locked my hands around my head and rocked impotently in my chair until the torment subsided enough to open my eyes.

Stemp regarded me expressionlessly across his desk. "That alone convinces me that you wouldn't do this unless it was absolutely necessary."

"You've got that right," I gritted, and dragged myself to my feet. "Thanks. I'll take the key back down to Spider's lab now."

"Leave it with me." Stemp rose, too, extending his hand. "I'm going down anyway."

"Thanks," I repeated with sincere gratitude. I dropped it

into his hand and staggered back to my office to retrieve the pheromone detector, rubbing my still-throbbing temples.

When I stepped out of Sirius Dynamics' air-conditioned chill, the blazing sun was a welcome relief. Sliding into my oven-like car to head for Blue Eddy's for a late and truncated bookkeeping session, I let the heat seep into my tense shoulders and drew a few calming breaths.

I had to be wrong about what I'd found. I was just being paranoid. Kane would go over the data I'd sent and laugh at me for being so silly.

Please let that happen...

Sitting in Eddy's office a few minutes later, I contemplated the free burger he'd supplied along with his usual smile and banter. I knew the burger would be delicious as usual, but my stomach was still clenched with queasy fear. I sighed.

I should call Kane right away.

But I really didn't want to...

My phone vibrated and the sight of Kane's caller ID made my stomach twist.

Shit.

I issued a cautious, "Hello?"

"Aydan!" he growled.

"Um... yeah...?"

"I thought you were going to call me!"

"I was. I just... um... I couldn't call until I got out of Sirius-"

"We need to talk," he interrupted. "We're coming up to Silverside. Come to my house as soon as you're finished work."

My heart sank into the churning acid of my stomach. Oh, no. I hadn't been wrong.

"Um, I can't. I have a... thing... right after work." Stemp probably wouldn't thank me for blabbing about his dinner party. "I don't think it'll run late, though," I added. "I'll come over as soon as it's finished."

"All right. See you then."

"Try to get some more sleep," I urged, but he had already hung up.

Shit.

I managed to force down half the burger before giving up, and the soothing blues music softened the cold stone that seemed lodged in the pit of my stomach. I felt marginally better by the time I left Eddy with a promise to return the next day and finish up.

By the time I got to Up & Coming at one-thirty I had recovered enough to hide my worry from Lola, but I stayed focused on their bookkeeping program and hurried away as soon as my time was up.

Back at Sirius Dynamics, I spent a miserable couple of hours trying and failing to concentrate on Labelle. My dread of Stemp's dinner party mingled with sick fear for Daniel, knotting my stomach and tightening an aching band around my head.

When the clock's hands finally dragged themselves around to five o'clock I stumbled out of my office and hid in the ladies' room, where I gulped a painkiller and an anti-nausea pill in the hope that the combination would see me through Stemp's upcoming social disaster.

CHAPTER 19

At five-forty-five I pulled up in front of Up & Coming again. Before I could get out of my car, a tiny old lady hurried out and slid into my passenger seat. Gaping, I took in her poodle-curled white hair, demurely ruffled pale pink blouse gathered to a cameo pin at the throat, white below-the-knee skirt, and low-heeled white pumps. She even had matching cameo earrings, white gloves, and a conservative clutch purse.

"Who the hell are you, and what did you do with Lola?" I demanded.

Lola grinned. "This is how I looked when you first met me, remember?" Her throaty bigger-than-life voice was even more incongruous coming from the modest church-lady façade.

"Yeah, but..." I swallowed. "But... please tell me you didn't bleach your fabulous pink hair... and... and..." Words failed me for a moment before I managed to sputter, "Cameos and white gloves and kitten heels? Really?"

Lola laughed. "Don't worry, honey, I'm wearing a wig. It's been too long since I did the cute-little-old-lady schtick. Everybody else knows me too well to believe it, but I'll have a fresh audience tonight. This is going to be so much fun!"

Shaking my head, I put the car into gear without further comment. Lola didn't know that Stemp had seen her purple-haired geriatric-pixie-dominatrix persona, and I couldn't tell her without revealing dangerous truths.

Well, whatever. 'Fun' wasn't what I was expecting this evening, but it'd sure as hell be interesting.

It was only a short drive to Stemp's house, but Lola was unnaturally quiet.

I glanced over at her troubled profile. "Lola, what's wrong? If you don't feel like coming tonight, I can take you home and tell them you got sick."

"Huh?" She shook herself. "Oh. No, I'm looking forward to this! I'm sorry, I wasn't going to bring it up before dinner, but... Linda had some bad news today, and I'm upset for her."

A cold hand squeezed my heart. "Oh, no! What's wrong?"

Lola grimaced. "She went for the final fitting for her wedding dress today."

"What's wrong?" I repeated. "Didn't it fit?"

"No, it fit fine." Anger crimped the corners of her mouth. "But somebody had broken into the dressmaker's house and thrown red dye on it."

"*What?*" Slamming on the brakes, I jerked my car over to the curb so I could stare at her. "How could that happen? Who would...?"

"We don't know. The dressmaker works out of her home, and she didn't even realize anyone had been in her house until she went to get Linda's dress out of the closet today and found it was wrecked." Lola blew out a sad breath. "It was so beautiful! Simple lines in a gorgeous white silk, with lace imported from France. And now it's only good for the garbage bin."

"That's... that's just awful. Poor Linda. What is she going to do?"

"Well, she's putting on a brave face for Spider. They'll drive down to Calgary tomorrow and buy something off the rack."

"But she's so tiny, she'll never find anything that fits."

"I know." Lola shrugged, but her shoulders were tight. "The dressmaker was in tears over it, and she promised to alter anything Linda bought in time for the wedding, but..." Her small fists clenched. "Who'd want to hurt Linda? She's an angel!"

"Maybe it wasn't about Linda at all. Maybe somebody was upset with the dressmaker...?" I suggested.

"I doubt it. She grew up here; she's been the only dressmaker in town for nearly forty years; and everybody loves her and her work. And she had several other dresses in the same closet that weren't harmed."

"Has Linda had a problem with anybody lately? Any disgruntled customers at the store, or any personality clashes at the hospital?"

"No." Lola reached over to pat my hand. "Let it go. It's too late to do anything about it now. Let's just try to put it out of our minds and enjoy your dinner party."

"But the dressmaker called the police, right?" I persisted. "That's breaking and entering, and vandalism."

"Yes, but they'll never be able to figure out who it was. She has people coming and going from her house all the time, so none of the neighbours noticed anything unusual and there are fingerprints from so many people in her house..." Lola trailed off. "Never mind, Aydan. As heartbreaking as it is, when all's said and done it's the marriage that matters, not the dress. We'd better get going or we'll be late."

I sighed and put the car back into gear. First Spider's spiked drink, and now Linda's dress.

A sudden thought froze me. Spider's friend Tim had accused Brock of spiking Spider's drink. Surely Brock wouldn't stoop low enough to wreck Linda's dress, too.

No. It just wasn't a 'guy' thing. And it would be far too much trouble for him to make the two-hour trip from Calgary to break into someone's home, wreck a dress, and then drive another two hours back. He was an annoying little shit, but I was pretty sure he wasn't psychotic enough to go to that amount of effort just to spite Spider and Linda...

"Aydan." Lola's anxious voice interrupted my thoughts. "If that steering wheel was somebody's neck, they'd be dead by now. And we're not going to get anywhere unless you take your foot off the brake."

I shook myself and eased my grip on the wheel. "Sorry. I just don't like this. I hope nothing else happens."

"Me, too," Lola agreed as I pulled onto the street.

A few minutes later we pulled up in front of Stemp's house, and I smiled at the sight of the sleek rental car bearing BC plates. Moonbeam and Karma had left the ancient smoke-belching station wagon back at the commune and gone for some modern air-conditioned transportation.

A good choice. I got out of my car and peeled the sweaty T-shirt away from my back.

Over the hood of my car, Lola eyed me with an indulgent smile. "Do you ever dress up?"

Suddenly self-conscious, I glanced down at my clean but faded jeans, snug crew-necked T-shirt, running shoes, and waist pouch. "I never even thought of it. This is what I wear to work..."

I trailed off, connecting the dots. Stemp always wore suits to work. Oh God, maybe I should have asked if this was a formal dinner. What if he'd gone black-tie?

"Come on, it's not that bad," Lola encouraged, and I realized I had groaned aloud.

A rapid survey of the yard showed no place to hide except under my car, and I couldn't fit under there without jack stands.

I squared my shoulders and faced my fate.

A moment after I rang the doorbell, the door opened and Moonbeam's luminous smile warmed me from head to toe. "Storm Cloud Dancer, how wonderful to see you again!" she cried, and drew me into a hug.

"It's great to see you, too!" I said, and returned her hug with affection.

"Storm," Karma rumbled behind her, and I had barely left Moonbeam's embrace before he engulfed me in a bear hug.

I hugged him tightly. "So good to see you, too!" I pulled away to introduce Lola. "And this is my good friend and client, Lola Ives. Lola, Moonbeam Meadow Sky and Karma Wolf Song."

"How nice to meet you..." Moonbeam said, trailing off with the slightly unfocused scrutiny I knew so well. Then she bestowed a brilliant smile on Lola. "You have such a lovely aura! Beautiful oranges and pinks! But... if you'll forgive me..." She eyed Lola's outfit. "Is this your usual appearance?"

Lola's mouth dropped open.

"I'm sorry, I didn't mean to be rude," Moonbeam began hurriedly, but Lola's big-hearted laugh boomed out before she could finish.

"Well, doggone it!" Lola exclaimed. "I haven't even been here ten seconds and already I'm busted!" She whisked her wig off and raked her fingers through her hot-pink hair, standing it up into its usual spikes. Then she unfastened the cameo pin and began to unbutton her blouse.

"Um, Lola..." I began, but she silenced me with an insouciant wave.

"It's okay, honey, I've got a tank top underneath." She peeled off the ruffled blouse and dropped it and the wig unceremoniously in the corner along with her clutch purse and gloves, facing Moonbeam's dancing eyes in a hot pink scoop-necked tank top that matched her hair and revealed abundant wrinkled cleavage.

Moonbeam and Karma's combined laughter pealed out like jubilant bells. "Oh, I like you already!" Moonbeam cried. "And I'm so glad you're not offended. It's just that with an aura like yours, that outfit was just so... not you."

Stemp rounded the corner at that moment, and it was all I could do not to gape open-mouthed.

He was wearing shorts.

Stemp.

Shorts.

No. I must be hallucinating. My mind steadfastly refused to accept the evidence presented by my eyes.

He wore neatly-pressed khakis that grazed his kneecaps, and his legs were actually quite acceptable; moderately haired with muscular calves. Paired with an immaculate collared T-shirt that revealed unexpectedly rippling forearms and smoothly-defined biceps, it was a perfectly appropriate outfit for a casual dinner on a hot summer day.

But...

Shorts...?

As I stood paralyzed, Moonbeam turned, her eyes lighting up at the sight of her son. She linked her arms around him, love and pride glowing in her smile. As if the gesture was unfamiliar to him, Stemp's arm moved tentatively to embrace her in return. His expression never changed, but I thought I detected a softening in his eyes and a slight lean in her direction. My heart warmed. Maybe their long years of estrangement were finally over.

I realized Stemp was eyeing me expectantly, and I gathered my scattered wits and introduced Lola. Or at least I think I did. My lips moved and words came out and they shook hands, so I probably hadn't blurted out anything inappropriate.

"Your dress is beautiful," Lola said, and for a mind-reeling moment I thought she was speaking to Stemp.

My beleaguered brain caught up when Moonbeam responded with a gracious "Thank you."

"It's hand-painted, isn't it?" Lola asked, examining the delicate oriental-style flowers on Moonbeam's filmy caftan.

"Yes, it's one of the crafts I enjoy," Moonbeam replied. "I love playing with colours and textiles, and while I usually wear more practical tie-dyed garments day-to-day, I love to wear my special things when I get the chance. I did the batik for Karma Wolf Song's shirt and sarong, too." She indicated the richly coloured and patterned fabric by running an appreciative hand across one of his broad shoulders and down his barrel chest.

He gently captured her hand to brush a kiss across her knuckles and they smiled at each other, momentarily transported to a private world of their own.

Stemp cleared his throat. "Drinks are served on the

patio..." he began, only to be interrupted by the doorbell. "...Ah. That will be Bud." He crossed to open the door.

His elderly neighbour stood on the doorstep, smiling. "Hiya, Charlie," he said warmly. "Thanks for inviting me to your shindig..."

He trailed off, his gaze travelling over Moonbeam's sweet wrinkled face, long silver braid, and filmy caftan to hesitate at Karma's bare feet, sarong, and neatly bound iron-gray ponytail. He stalled briefly on Lola's cleavage and bright pink hair, but his smile never faltered and he managed to wrench his gaze away from the motley assembly to land on me.

"Miss Kelly." His smile widened. "It's nice to see you again. How have you been keeping?"

"I'm fine, Bud, and remember, it's just Aydan." I went over to shake his hand. "It's great to see you again..." I hesitated, eyeing his emaciated frame. The hands that had been steady on his shotgun eight months ago showed a slight tremor now, and his chest rose and fell with too-rapid wheezy breaths. "How are you?" I finished, hoping he hadn't noticed my pause.

"Ah, well, you know how it goes with the emphysema." He shrugged and grinned, the twinkle undimmed in his eyes. "So far so good, as the optimist said when he fell past the second floor. I'm still buying green bananas, anyway."

"Good to hear." I gave him a smile and moved back so Stemp could perform the introductions.

Apparently Bud had never met Moonbeam and Karma, because Stemp introduced them, too, finishing with, "...and Bud is my neighbour from across the street. He looks after my plants when I'm away, and beats me at cribbage once a week."

Bud pshawed and shuffled his feet modestly, and the conversation stayed general while Stemp ushered us out to his shaded back deck and settled us in comfortable chairs. Moonbeam had given Bud her usual once-over, but refrained from commenting on his aura. It didn't take a seer to read the shadow of serious illness on him.

"I have non-alcoholic margaritas," Stemp offered, indicating a green-tinted pitcher and glasses on the patio table. "Aydan, I know you don't usually drink if you're driving, but if you'd like a beer..."

"No, thanks," I said hurriedly. "The margaritas sound great."

Karma and Moonbeam had already appropriated glasses, and Moonbeam poured an additional one for me and handed it over as Stemp turned to Lola.

"Would you like something alcoholic, Lola?"

She gave him her impish smile. "Not unless you've got Wild Turkey."

Stemp's expression remained grave, but his eyes twinkled. "By an amazing coincidence, I do happen to have a bottle of Wild Turkey."

"No kidding!" Lola sat up, her eyes widening. "I thought I was the only person north of the border who likes Wild Turkey! Thanks, I'd love some!"

As he turned away to pour from a tiny bottle, I caught the satisfaction in his expression. Three steps ahead of everybody, as usual. I knew he didn't keep liquor in his house, so he must have researched Lola using who-knew-what secret methods. And I'd be willing to bet he didn't have any beer at all, even though he'd offered it to me. He'd known damn well I wouldn't drink if I was driving.

He offered a tumbler to Lola, and she beamed up at him

as she accepted it, rattling the two ice cubes gently in the small amount of liquor. "Just the way I like it! Thanks!"

Without questioning Bud about his preferences, Stemp placed a small teapot and cup at his elbow, and the old man nodded his approval.

"Thanks, Charlie." He transferred his smile to us. "I sure do like a hot cup of tea, even when it's warm outside. The heat feels good on these old bones."

Moonbeam smiled and raised her glass. "To comfort and good company."

We raised our glasses and murmured agreement. Stemp busied himself at the barbeque and Moonbeam turned her smile on me. "And how are Blessed Soul Dream and Sunstar Desert Hawk?"

"Um... they're okay..."

I hesitated, my stomach knotting at the thought of facing Kane later, and worry clouded Moonbeam's face.

"Oh, dear. Something's wrong, isn't it?" she asked. "I knew it; I could see the disturbance in your aura."

"No, they're both fine," I hastened to reassure her. "It's just that John's going through a hard time right now, and Arnie and I are both worried about him." I explained the events to date, omitting the fact that her beloved Arnie was only a few blocks away at Kane's place. Stemp would probably throttle me if I let that slip.

Moonbeam sat slowly back in her chair, her expression grave. "What a difficult situation," she murmured. "I will consult the Earth Spirit-"

"Mother!" Stemp interrupted loudly. We all turned to him in surprise, and he added, "Would you like some mango chipotle barbeque sauce on your veggie patty?"

CHAPTER 20

It was a smooth segue and Stemp's expression was as pleasant as it had been when he welcomed us into his home, but his fist clenched around the spatula. As if realizing I'd noticed, he relaxed his grip and the returning circulation eased the whiteness out of his knuckles.

Moonbeam looked startled, but her expression smoothed almost instantly to the same polite mask as Stemp's own. "Yes, dear, mango sauce would be lovely," she said warmly. "Thank you."

He smiled and questioned us each about our burger preferences before returning his attention to the grill, but an awkward silence lingered around the table.

Lola leaned forward. "So, Moonbeam, you called Aydan 'Storm Cloud Dancer' earlier; and you have special names for the menfolk, too? What's the story there?"

"Please call me Moonbeam Meadow Sky," Moonbeam corrected gently. "A person's full name is very important from a numerological standpoint. The numeric vibrations contained in a name influence both personality and destiny."

I hid a wince, expecting another outburst from Stemp, but he said nothing and his posture was relaxed while he applied barbeque sauce to the burgers.

"Oh, that's fascinating!" Lola exclaimed. "How does numerology work?"

Thank God for Lola.

Moonbeam provided a short explanation while Lola encouraged her with avid questions.

"That's so cool!" Lola enthused. "So do you ask everybody for their full name when you meet them and always call them by that? You didn't ask for my middle name."

"No." Moonbeam gave her a smile. "The name you present as your public persona is also numerologically significant; it's just not as personally revealing as your full name. I'll use your regular name as everyone else does, unless you ask me to do otherwise or come to our commune."

"Your commune...? Oh, I get it! You gave Aydan her special name when she was living there." Lola cocked her head inquiringly. "Why do you make up new names for everybody who visits you?"

Uh-oh. Stemp wasn't going to like this...

"You receive your new name when you come under the protection of the commune's Earth Spirit," Moonbeam said quietly. "The names are a symbol of the Earth Spirit's wish for us to live in peace, tolerance, and harmony."

Stemp cleared his throat warningly but didn't turn. His shoulders were stiff as he gathered plates and utensils from a side table, making more clatter than absolutely necessary.

Apparently oblivious, Lola took a leisurely sip of her Wild Turkey and leaned back in her chair, smiling. "What's the Earth Spirit?"

"A fabrication," Stemp said as he turned to distribute the plates and utensils. "An imaginary deity made up for the benefit of those who are unwilling to undertake the intellectual effort required to find meaning in their lives, and who require the crutch of religion to support them."

Hurt flashed across Moonbeam's face, but she said nothing.

"...oh." Lola became suddenly fascinated by swirling the ice cubes around in her glass.

"Come on now, Charlie," Bud spoke up. "If your mama likes her auras and whatnot, where's the harm?" He turned his smile on Moonbeam. "I'm not a religious man myself, but it seems to me it'd be good to have more peace and tolerance and harmony in the world."

Stemp straightened, his dispassionate façade firmly in place, but his telltale hand strangled the spatula again. "You're right, numerology and auras are merely harmless party tricks. But I object to a so-called deity whose arbitrary rules are interpreted solely by self-styled prophets who grant themselves the authority to dictate the behaviour and lifestyle of others."

The air crackled with tension and I gulped my booze-less margarita, wishing it had a healthy slug of alcohol in it.

"Well, I don't know," Bud said mildly. "That pretty well describes most religions, I guess."

Stemp barked out a laugh that did nothing to soften his grip on the spatula. "True. Which is why I have no use for any of them. Lola, may I freshen your drink?"

"Yes, please," she said in a small voice, and handed him her glass. When he returned it, she took a healthy swallow and bravely initiated a topic change. "So what does an aura look like, Moonbeam Meadow Sky?"

Moonbeam glanced at Stemp. "Perhaps Cosmic River Stone would like to tell you." Her voice was as quiet as always, but it cut like finely-edged steel. "He can see them, too."

Stemp reddened. "When I was a child I was subject to flights of imagination, as most children are. Particularly when their elders encourage them in their fantasies," he added cuttingly. Smoke wafted from his ears and I blinked. He must be really pissed off...

No, that was the barbeque.

"Um..." I began, but he and his mother had locked gazes.

"I didn't raise you to deny your personal truth," she said softly, disappointment vibrating in her voice.

"Actually, Mother, you did," he grated.

"Son..." Karma rumbled ominously beside Moonbeam.

I sprang to my feet. "'Scuse me," I muttered as I ducked between them and pried the spatula out of Stemp's fist before hurrying over to rescue the smoking burgers.

"Thank you, Aydan," Stemp said, sounding completely relaxed again. "I'll go and get the potato salad from the fridge, and then we can eat."

As he disappeared into the house, Lola made another valiant attempt. "So, Moonbeam Meadow Sky, can you tell me a bit about your fabric-painting technique? Have you ever worked on silk?"

"Oh, yes." Like her son, Moonbeam instantly banished the tension from her posture and voice, her smile warming us like a benediction. "Silk is perfect for fabric-painting."

"That gives me an idea," Lola said eagerly. "Do you think you'd be able to work a pattern on, say, a white silk dress that had gotten blotches of red dye on it?"

"Of course. Though painting bright red on pure white would be rather... startling. It would be best to lighten the red if possible before proceeding. Natural fibres like silk usually respond well to the application of a gentle bleach solution, but of course it would depend on the dye..."

The conversation revived as Lola described the fate of Linda's wedding dress, and the expressions of concern and brainstorming of patterns carried us safely through the meal. On the opposite side of the table, Karma and Bud and Stemp discussed cribbage strategies and gardening and Bud's long-ago army exploits while I did my best to swallow my slightly charred burger and contribute an occasional polite remark to both sides.

At last everyone's plates were empty, and I rose with what I hoped was a regretful expression. "Well, thanks, this has been..."

I tried to say 'great', but the lie stuck in my throat.

I backtracked. "It's been great to see you all again, but I'm sorry I have to run. I promised John I'd stop by and see him tonight, and I don't want to leave it too late because I know he'll be exhausted."

Understanding nods and sympathetic expressions greeted my announcement and I moved toward the door, hoping my retreat didn't look like the craven flight it was. Lola stuck close behind me.

After a round of warm hugs with Moonbeam, Karma, and Bud and an awkward nod to Stemp, we made our escape.

Half a block down the street, Lola let her head fall back against the seat. "Holy cats! I haven't seen people that tensed up since I went to the wrong address with my Passion Party kit, and it turned out to be a church ladies' retreat."

My strained nerves released in a bark of laughter. "I would've liked to have been a fly on the wall for that!"

Lola giggled. "Oh, it was a hoot. It wouldn't have been so bad if they hadn't been expecting a kitchenware party..."

"No! Seriously?" I stared at her, a grin spreading across

my face.

She nodded, still giggling. "...So I started by laying out my flavoured lubes and gels and they were all tasting them and saying 'oh, very nice, very nice'..." She giggled some more. "...until I brought out Big John..."

We both dissolved into laughter.

"And then..." Her words choked out between guffaws. "And then... one of the ladies... picks him up... by the balls..."

By now we were both howling with laughter, tears rolling down our cheeks.

"And she says..." Lola shook with mirth, clutching her stomach and gasping out the words. "...she says... 'Is this a stick blender?' ...and... and... she hits... the 'on' switch..."

Barely able to see through my tears, I pulled over to the curb so I could fold over the steering wheel and laugh until my sides ached.

"Omigod," I gasped at last. "Omigod. Tell me that didn't really happen."

"It really happened. I swear on my mother's grave."

"Lola..." I dragged myself up by the steering wheel, wiping my eyes. "You light up my life. You really do."

A few more giggles escaped as I steered the car back onto the street, and I wished Lola a fond goodnight when I dropped her off at Up & Coming a few minutes later.

Driving away, my car felt empty without her larger-than-life presence. My worries crashed down again, looming even larger and darker after my brief escape into the light and warmth of Lola's world.

How could I have laughed at a time like this?

It felt like a betrayal in the face of Kane's suffering.

Oh, God, and now I was going to make it worse. Even though I knew I was probably right about what I'd found in the police database, my heart clung to the desperate hope that I'd somehow misinterpreted it.

Laughter was the last thing on my mind by the time I parked in front of Kane's small house. When I got out of my car he was already standing in the doorway, his shoulders stiff and his mouth a grim line.

The door had barely closed behind me when he snapped, "A serial killer. You think it's a serial killer preying on young boys."

I swallowed. "I don't know..."

"Mayweather flagged the possibility in his report. And you wouldn't have sent me all those case files if you didn't agree," he said flatly.

"Well..." I looked to Hellhound for help but he perched in silence on the edge of the couch, gaze downcast, fists braced on knees.

"I really don't know," I said. "I mean, there are similarities, but..."

"Six boys of similar appearance, over the course of two summers, five-year-olds last year and six-year-olds this year," Kane said harshly. "And they all disappeared from camping trips. That's far too much of a coincidence."

"But three different men have already been charged with murder in the three cases from last year. And they're trying to build a case against one of the other men from this year-"

"And yet all the men swore they put the child to bed in the tent and when they came back he was missing," Kane countered. "Don't you think that's odd? And the charges are each based on a small amount of the child's blood found at the scene. Flimsy evidence at best, and again, too similar to be a coincidence. No bodies were ever found. And the boys all had single mothers, and they all vanished from camping trips with the mother's ex-husband or ex-boyfriend."

I sighed. "I know. But Mayweather already tried and failed to make a connection. He went back and interviewed everybody from all the cases again, and he even pulled all the prison and parole records to try to correlate the disappearances with any convicted criminals who'd been released in time to match the abductions."

"Is that why you sent me the files on all those missing women?" Kane asked. "Do you think they're related?"

"Oh. No. I was in a hurry and I just grabbed all the missing-persons cases for the past two years."

"We need to figure out the connection between these boys, and fast," Kane grated. "Sometimes serial killers don't kill their victims right away. Daniel may still be alive. Suffering."

Any parent's worst nightmare. But for Kane...

A glance at his tortured eyes made me hold back a shudder. All the progress he'd made in the past four months was long gone. His body vibrated with tension, his eyes deeply shadowed and his face pale under several days of neglected whiskers. My heart squeezed.

"John..." I tried to put my arms around him, but he pushed me away.

"There's no time for that. Aydan, what are we missing?" he demanded.

"I don't know yet. Have you talked to Mayweather?"

"Yes." His fist clenched. "He's cut me out. Won't say anything except to be patient, they're working on it. Patient! I'd like to see how patient he'd be if he was the one being tortured and praying to be rescued..." His voice broke and he scrubbed his hands angrily over his face.

"Cap," Hellhound said gently. "I know how tough this is,

but ya gotta settle down a bit. Ya can't think straight when you're-"

"WHAT THE HELL DO YOU KNOW?" Kane rounded on him with a full-throated bellow, fists clenched. "DON'T TELL ME HOW TO FEEL, YOU..."

Hellhound didn't move or look up, and despite my sympathy for Kane's torment, my heart broke for Arnie. Just like the bad old days when he had endured his father's repeated attacks without retaliating. His rigid withdrawn posture retold the ugly story.

Bright anger ignited my veins.

"John!" I shoved between them and my voice came out like a whipcrack. *"Stop it!"*

He stopped in mid-yell, his jaw dangling as if I'd slapped him.

"We are your friends," I ground out. "We are here to help you. If you think you can do a better job without us, we'll leave right now. Otherwise, you'll treat us with respect and listen to what we have to say. Which is it going to be?"

CHAPTER 21

Silence blanketed the room. Kane's mouth opened and closed a couple of times. Then he let out a rush of breath and collapsed into the chair, slumping over to hide his face in his hands.

"I'm sorry," he mumbled. When he looked up, his face was haggard. He reached toward Hellhound's immobile bulk. "Arnie, I'm sorry. Aydan's right. You're right, too, and I'm an idiot for taking this out on you."

Arnie raised his head at last, and the pain in his eyes made my throat tighten.

"It's okay, Cap," he rasped, but I knew it wasn't. Too many old ghosts had been reawakened. He'd have to fight them into their graves all over again.

"I'm sorry," Kane repeated. He sank his head into his hands again. "Goddammit. I'm sorry."

"No big deal," Hellhound said firmly. "Don't worry, Cap, we're gonna figure this out."

Kane let out a breath and faced us. "What should we do?"

The childlike question shocked me.

This was Kane. The best agent in the service. Super-cool James Bond.

But tonight he was just the broken-hearted father of a child he'd never known.

Hellhound and I exchanged a glance.

"Aydan an' I are gonna go over these files," Hellhound said. "You're gonna take a sleepin' pill an' get some rest. Ya ain't good for anythin' when ya ain't slept in three days."

Kane's fists clenched, his jaw jutting. "No, I-"

"John..." I interrupted warningly.

The fight went out of him, his body slumping as though every tendon had been cut. "All right," he mumbled.

"Do you have sleeping pills here?" I asked.

"Yes." He dragged himself to his feet, looking so worn out that I hurried over to take his arm.

"Where?"

"Bathroom."

He trudged down the hall, and I flanked him worriedly. In the bathroom, he extracted a small pill bottle from a drawer and handed it to me in silence. The prescription had been issued four months ago, but the bottle was full.

"I never took any," Kane said in a monotone. "I'd rather deal with my issues head-on."

"I know," I comforted, and doled out a couple of pills as per the dosage instructions. "But when you're this tired, you just can't deal with anything effectively."

"I should know that." He swallowed the pills and turned for the bedroom. "But sometimes I need friends to remind me. Thank you."

"You're welcome."

When he was safely under the bedcovers, he said, "I have to call Alicia," and picked up the bedside phone.

I withdrew, leaving the door open a crack, and the quiet rumble of his voice carried me down the hall.

In the living room, Arnie looked up anxiously. "Is he down?"

I sighed and plopped onto the couch beside him. "He's horizontal. Not down for the count yet. He's talking to Alicia, but those pills should kick in pretty soon, especially when he's this tired."

"Good." Hellhound laid an arm across my shoulders and I twisted to wrap my arms around him and press my face against his chest.

"How are you holding up?" I mumbled into his T-shirt.

"Fine."

I pulled away far enough to look into his face. "Liar."

He sighed and sagged back on the couch, pulling me with him into a half-reclining position. "It's rippin' my fuckin' guts out."

"Yeah, I figured." I stroked his cheek. "Do you want to talk about it?"

"Nothin' to talk about. It is what it is." He shifted into a more comfortable position and I tucked my legs up beside him, cuddling close and laying my head on his chest. He lowered his voice. "I hope we find him. Even if he's dead, it's better than not knowin'. Ya never stop wonderin' otherwise."

My heart contracted with sympathy and I slipped my arm over his chest to hold him close, knowing he was thinking of his sister, still missing after thirty years.

He sighed again and stroked my hair. "Ya always make me feel better, though. How 'bout you, darlin'? Ya okay?"

"Yeah. I mean, this whole thing is awful; but I'm okay."

He kissed the top of my head and we lay without speaking, his hand making slow soothing passes over my hair. Kane's voice ceased and the telephone handset clicked into the cradle, followed by silence.

Fatigue dragged at my limbs.

Only four hours of sleep; the physical and mental exertion of my requalification in the morning; the tension of Stemp's disastrous dinner; the emotional toll of worrying about Daniel; all of it pressed down like the weight of an extra atmosphere.

Hellhound's body was blissfully warm, his heartbeat a steady hypnotic rhythm under my ear...

I woke with a start and bolted up, swiping drool off my chin and wincing at the crick in my neck. Hellhound blinked sleepily up at me. "What, darlin'?" he mumbled.

"John." I ran toward the groans and mumbles emanating from the bedroom.

Hellhound caught up with me at the doorway, scooping me aside with a powerful arm. "Stay back." He crossed to the bed in two fast strides in time to deflect a vicious right cross. Kane's fist smacked harmlessly into his palm, and Hellhound parried the jab that followed immediately behind it, calling, "Wake up, Cap, you're dreamin'! It's just a-" He dodged another punch. "...dream. Hey, Cap, wake up!"

"John!" I added my voice to the effort but stayed out of reach. If I'd caught Kane's fist like that, I'd probably have a broken arm. "John, wake up!"

His eyes opened blank and unfocused, his fists still clenched in quivering knots.

"Wake up, Cap," Hellhound repeated softly. "Just a dream."

Kane blinked, then blinked again and pressed the heels of his hands to his eyes. "'M 'wake," he slurred. "Sorry..."

"It's okay," Hellhound assured him. "Go back to sleep. We got your back."

Kane mumbled something inarticulate, his eyelids dropping shut again. A few moments later his breathing slowed and deepened, and Hellhound and I exchanged a glance and tiptoed out.

In the hallway light, I squinted at my watch. "Shit, it's one AM! We were going to go over these files!"

Hellhound yawned and gave a philosophical shrug. "Prob'ly did us more good to grab a nap. We'll be fresher now." He stretched his arms above his head, his back and shoulders emitting a percussive symphony of crackles and pops. "Shit, darlin', I was dead to the fuckin' world."

"Me, too." We trailed back to the sofa and sat side by side, positioning the laptop on the coffee table.

After an hour of scrolling data I sat back, rubbing my aching eyes. "I didn't realize how much there was. We've barely scratched the surface."

Hellhound gave me a quizzical look. "How could ya not realize how much there is? Ya sent it, didn't ya?"

"Yeah..." I sighed. "Long story, and I can't tell it to you." I eyed him enviously. "I suppose you remember everything we've read, down to every date, time, and detail."

He shrugged. "Yeah. An' I skimmed the missin' ladies' cases before ya got here. There's a helluva lot of 'em, but I couldn't see any connection to the boys."

"Yeah. I'm glad you don't think they're connected, because I can't even keep the boys' cases straight." I fell back on the couch. "I can't remember my own name. This isn't going to work unless I start writing stuff down."

"Good plan, darlin'. That way Kane can look at it when he gets up, too. He's got a bulletin board in his office, an' he already got started on some a' the cases while we were waitin' for ya. Let's go put some stuff up."

Two hours later we had tacked up a mosaic of papers and arrows in between trips to the bedroom to soothe Kane's nightmares. When I yawned and rubbed my watering eyes for the umpteenth time, Hellhound put down his pen and drew me into his arms. "Okay, darlin', you're done."

I smothered another yawn. "No, I can keep going."

"Yeah, ya prob'ly can, but if ya do you're gonna miss somethin'. Remember, the cops have been workin' these cases for over a year, an' they ain't stupid. If there's anythin' here, it ain't gonna be obvious. Go home an' get some sleep, an' we'll hit it again in the mornin'."

"But if Daniel's still alive, every second could count..." I began.

Hellhound tilted his head down to rest his forehead tenderly against mine. "I know, darlin'. But you mornin' people are no damn good at this time a' night. I'm still wide awake so I'm gonna keep at it."

He let out a breath and his arms tightened around me. "The best thing ya can do is get some rest so ya can be strong for Kane tomorrow." His gravelly voice held infinite sadness even though he didn't speak aloud the thought that gnawed at my heart: if we found Daniel dead at the hands of a monster, could Kane survive the blow?

I hugged Arnie in silence, seeking comfort that even the warmth of his arms couldn't provide. The thought of my farmhouse lying dark and empty in the night chilled me.

"I'm going to stay," I decided. "I'll just crash on the couch, and then if I wake up early I can do some more reading."

"Why don't ya go crawl in with Kane?" Hellhound suggested. "He's about done punchin' for the night. You'll be more comfortable, an' it'll do him good to have ya there."

"He doesn't want me." I smothered another yawn. "You saw how he pushed me away."

"Sucks, doesn't it? When somebody ya care about shuts ya out?" Arnie asked quietly.

Straightening, I stared him in the eye. "I really hope you're not preaching to me, because I am *so* not in the mood."

"Nah, I ain't preachin'." He pulled me back into the hug. "I'm just hopin' you'll cut him some slack."

"I will." I kissed him and eased reluctantly out of his embrace. "I shut both of you out often enough. Payback's a bitch."

He chuckled. "Ain't that the truth."

I woke to a gentle hand on my shoulder and Hellhound's quiet rasp, even hoarser than usual after his sleepless night. "Hey, Aydan, it's six-thirty. Ya goin' to work today?"

Groaning, I sat up and gingerly stretched my aching neck. "I don't know. Did you find anything last night? Should I stay?"

"Ya should prob'ly go. Like Kane said, we might need ya on the inside. I didn't find anythin' earth-shatterin', but I got a helluva lot a' readin' done an' I filled up another twenty sheets. I'm gonna keep at it 'til Kane gets up, an' then I'll crash while he goes through our notes."

"He's still sleeping?"

"Uh-huh." Hellhound smiled, tired lines bracketing his eyes. "An' he's gonna be pissed that I didn't wake him up, but the longer he sleeps, the better. Get goin', darlin'. Ya got just enough time to go home an' get a change a' clothes an' a shower."

"Okay. Call me if you need anything..." I trailed off with the sudden sick recollection that I had to meet Frederick Labelle at two o'clock. Oh, God...

"What, Aydan?" Hellhound surveyed me with concern. "What's wrong?"

"Nothing." I summoned a smile. "I just remembered I have a meeting this afternoon, so don't worry if you try to call me between two and three and I don't answer."

He eyed me suspiciously. "Okay... What ain't ya tellin' me?"

"Just the usual bullshit." I kissed him and headed for the door under his worried gaze. "Don't forget to nag John to go in for his debriefing when he gets up," I added. "See you later."

When I got to Sirius Dynamics at ten to eight Stemp was crossing the parking lot, and I hopped out of my car and gave him a 'wait-for-me' wave.

He halted, reluctance in every line of his body.

"Good morning," he greeted me with his usual lack of inflection as I hurried up.

"'Morning," I agreed, and got straight to the point. "I just wanted to ask how long your mom and dad will be here. I was hoping to have another visit with them." A visit without Stemp's dampening presence, but I couldn't think of a tactful way to say that.

"They left."

"What?" I gaped at him. "When?"

"Last night."

"But... I thought..."

His stony expression told the story.

My heart sank. "Oh, shit. You fought."

"We did not fight," Stemp said stiffly. "We merely agreed that perhaps close proximity was less than beneficial for all concerned."

"But... but you were getting along so well," I floundered. "You were talking to them regularly on the phone, and last night I thought-"

"You thought wrong," he snapped.

"No, you can still make this work! Call them," I begged. "Ask them to come back-"

"No. If I thought they truly believed in the Earth Spirit, I could tolerate their so-called religion even if I didn't believe in it myself, but..." His shoulders rose and fell in one of his infinitesimal shrugs. "...they created this deity and its rituals solely as a means of controlling the members of their commune. I had good reason to leave them behind when I was eighteen, and nothing has changed since then. They are liars and manipulators of innocent people. We have nothing in common."

He turned away but I grabbed his arm, desperate to change his mind. "They're your parents! You have everything in common!"

Stemp froze, eyeing my hand as if making a mental note to wash his jacket as soon as possible. "What exactly are you implying?" he asked in icy tones.

I let go of his arm. "I'm just... you can't just..." Sucking in breath, I tried again. "Look, sometimes you lie and manipulate people, too, as part of your job."

He let out a bark of mirthless laughter. "Are you implying those charlatans are on the side of justice and national security?"

I clamped my teeth on my tongue so I wouldn't blurt out

'yes'. I couldn't blow their cover, not even with the best of intentions.

"Um... I'm just saying maybe your mom and dad have reasons-" I mumbled lamely.

"No doubt they do," he interrupted. "All to benefit their own agenda. And in any case, they are not my 'mom and dad'. My mother had a..." He hesitated. "...dalliance," he went on in cool clinical tones, "...with Skidmark, which resulted in her pregnancy. My biological father is a wasted stoner and a draft-dodging coward, and my mother duped Karma into claiming parenthood of their bastard child. Me."

My heart wrenched at the hurt in his words. "That's not what happened at all!" I protested. "Skidmark isn't a draft dodger or a coward! He-"

I cut myself off. I couldn't tell him Skidmark had served with distinction in Vietnam, and every day of his life since.

"He's a good guy," I said instead. "Your mom loves him and Karma, and they love her; and they don't care whose biological child you are. In fact, they never even knew for sure..." I trailed off. "So how could you possibly know?"

He stared straight through me. "Whom do I resemble?"

"Oh. Um... well, it's hard to tell... I mean, Skidmark's all hair and beard so you can't really see anything but his eyes..."

I stopped before I dug myself in any deeper. Stemp sure as hell didn't look like Karma or Moonbeam.

"Anyway, it doesn't matter," I insisted. "Lots of kids don't look like either of their parents. And Karma wanted you so much, he and your mom decided to register as your parents to keep it simple because Skidmark is a U.S. citizen..." My words faded into silence at the chill in Stemp's eyes.

"I see you've gotten quite chummy with them," he said quietly. "Very well. If you like them so much, you can have them."

He turned and walked away, a stiff and lonely figure in the empty parking lot.

By the time I signed in at the security wicket and dragged myself upstairs to my office, my head was pounding. A couple of hours of studying Labelle's file and trying to visualize all the possible turns our conversation might take didn't help.

When my desk phone rang at ten-thirty I reached for it with gratitude. I'd welcome any distraction that kept my mind from spinning closer and closer to the conviction that I was about to blow my op before it even got started, and probably sign my own death warrant in the process.

"Aydan Kelly," I said brightly.

Linda's frantic voice lanced icy adrenaline into my veins. "Somebody's trying to kill Spider!"

CHAPTER 22

I lunged to my feet, my chair whizzing back on its casters to crash into the wall. "Where are you? What's happening?"

Tethered helplessly to the land line, I stretched its cord to the limit, heart hammering.

"Nothing. Sorry, I didn't mean somebody's attacking him right this minute," Linda said distractedly. "But this morning..."

"What happened?" I demanded, knotting the phone cord in my sweaty fist. "Did you call the police?"

"Spider won't let me..."

A burst of noise on the line launched my blood pressure into the stratosphere. "Linda! *Linda, what's happening!*"

"Aydan?" Spider's voice made me suck in a gulp of air.

"Spider! What's happening? Are you okay?"

"I'm fine. Everything's fine," he soothed. "Linda's just overreacting..."

"Am not!" a small defiant voice shouted in the background.

"She is so," Spider said firmly. "Stuff happens to cars all the time; it doesn't mean anybody's trying to kill me."

"What kind of stuff?" I barked.

"Well, my brakes failed this morning..."

"Don't get back in your car! Stay indoors, away from any windows! Where are you?"

"We're at home, but Aydan, it's fine..."

"It's not fine until I say it's fine! Stay in your house. I'll be right there!" I slapped the receiver down and ran.

Dashing down the stairs, I flung my security fob into the turntable and jittered while the guard crept through the sign-out procedure at the pace of a crippled snail. Then I pounded to my car at a dead run and laid rubber out of the parking lot.

Minutes later I skidded to a halt in front of their small bungalow. Spider's lime-green Smart car was parked at an odd angle against the opposite curb and Linda's little red Beetle convertible idled in the driveway, its top down in an open invitation to every shitbag assassin from here to Calgary...

Breathe. Evaluate.

I snapped a look around the quiet street, but I was the only visible human being. The spindly trees and small houses bespoke young families with parents at work and children in daycare.

No assassins.

I sprang out of the car, resisting the urge to draw my gun. As I jogged up the walk with my head swivelling in all directions, Spider emerged.

"Get back inside," I snapped.

"Aydan, it's fine," he insisted. "Linda's overreacting. I'm pretty sure it's just a broken brake line because I couldn't stop the car and there's a puddle underneath it..."

"That doesn't just happen for no reason," I growled. "Especially not to a car as new as yours."

"No, I know, but I ran over some metal thing in the street

yesterday. It flipped up and whacked the underside of the car. That's probably what broke the line. I'm really sorry you were scared, but it's no big deal."

"I want to look at it. And you need to get back into the house until I'm finished." When he began to argue again, I added, "*Please?*"

He smiled and shook his head resignedly. "Okay."

When he disappeared through the front door, I relaxed enough to take in the puddle of brake fluid on the driveway and the trail leading to Spider's car on the opposite side of the street. After surveying my surroundings once more for potential threats, I went over and lowered myself to the pavement beside his car, then swore and extracted my reading glasses from my waist pouch to take a better look.

Sure enough, there was an impact mark and a pinhole on the underside of the passenger's side rear brake line.

Hauling myself to my feet, I headed for the house. When I stepped inside Spider and Linda were waiting by the door. Linda clung to Spider's arm, her usual perky smile absent and her smooth dark brows drawn together.

"What do you think?" she demanded as soon as the door closed behind me.

"I don't know." I turned to Spider. "Tell me exactly what happened."

"Well, like I said, I was driving down Main Street yesterday on my way home when I ran over something that flipped up and hit the underside of the car. I didn't think anything of it; just came home and parked in the drive as usual. We haven't been using the garage because we're storing furniture for one of our friends."

"Did the brakes feel mushy when you parked yesterday?" I asked. "Did your brake pedal go down farther than usual?"

"Um... I don't know... a little, maybe."

"But you're not sure, are you?" Linda challenged.

"Not really." He shuffled his feet, flushing. "I'm really not a car guy."

"So what happened today?"

"I started the car, put my foot on the brake and put it into reverse. The pedal went down to the floor and the car started to roll backward so I popped it into neutral and steered it over to the side of the street. It was barely rolling and it stopped when it hit the curb, so no big deal."

"But if you'd been on a hill, you could have been killed!" Linda clutched his arm tighter.

He smiled and kissed the top of her head. "Sweetie, the whole town's flat as a pancake. If somebody wanted to kill me, they'd have a better chance if they attacked me with a spoon."

"What do you think, Aydan?" Linda appealed to me.

"It could have happened yesterday," I said slowly. "If the line got nicked, fluid would squish out every time you braked. Your driveway slopes uphill so you might not have noticed the brakes fading when you parked yesterday."

Linda was frowning and shaking her head, and I added, "Or somebody might have damaged the line in the night. Can you think of anybody who might do that?"

"No, of course not," Spider said.

Linda was silent.

"Linda?" I prompted.

"N-no..." When Spider and I both frowned at her, she added, "But... I don't know... I feel as though somebody has it in for us."

"What do you mean?"

"Well... my dress, for one thing." Her eyes filled with

tears, but she blinked them away and went on with only a slight quaver in her voice. "And last week I went into the post office and when I came out there was a dead bird on the seat of my car."

"What?" Spider yelped. "That's gross! Who would do that?"

"Was your car locked?" I demanded.

"Well, no..." She gave us a wobbly smile. "I had the top down. I thought maybe a bird had hit that big window in the grocery store and bounced off and fallen into my car or something..."

"What kind of bird was it?" I asked. "Was it just lying there, or did it look like it was posed? And was it stiff or floppy when you took it out? Did you notice if it was warm?"

"Ew, Aydan!" Linda attempted a giggle, but it sounded weak. "Lucky I'm a nurse or I'd be totally grossed out." She sobered. "There wasn't any blood, and I picked it out by the tip of its wing feathers so I don't know if it was warm. But it was limp, so either it had just died or else it had been dead long enough that rigor had already passed. And it didn't seem to be posed. I don't know what kind of bird. It was soft gray all over, with some black on its face and bright yellow on the tips of its tailfeathers."

"Cedar waxwing," I diagnosed. "Or maybe a Bohemian waxwing. They're famous for flying into windows, especially if they've been eating fermented berries, but there aren't many fermented berries around in August. So it might have been a coincidence, but it's a hell of a long way for a dead bird to bounce all the way over the sidewalk and into your car. Has anything else happened to make you feel nervous?"

"Not... really..."

When I rotated my hand in a 'keep talking' gesture, she

sighed. "Just some ugly rumours. But it's a small town and everybody has their nose in everybody else's business. If there isn't any juicy gossip they make some up."

"What kind of rumours?"

"Well, one is that I purposely got pregnant to force Spider into marrying me, which is silly, of course, because I'm not pregnant at all." She glanced shyly up at Spider. "Not that I'd mind if I was..."

He flushed and beamed at her. "I wouldn't, either. It would be so cool to have a baby with you!"

Linda cuddled closer, beaming up at him in return. "I can hardly wait! But maybe not for a little while..."

"...until you finish the courses you're taking," he agreed.

Their happiness was so palpable I hated to burst their bubble, but I did.

"Anything else?" I asked.

The joy went out of their faces as if I'd dumped a bucket of cold water over them.

"The only other rumour I've heard is that Spider is secretly gay and in love with Tim but he's marrying me to prove he's straight," Linda said.

Spider chuckled. "That's a new one!" He winked at Linda. "I bet Tim started that one himself."

They both laughed, then sobered and turned back to me.

"So what do you think, Aydan?" Spider asked. "Should Linda take out a bigger life insurance policy on me?"

"That's not funny!" she snapped, then added, "M-maybe if I wasn't so stressed out with all the last-minute wedding stuff I wouldn't be freaking out over this, but... but..." Her lips quivered and she drew a deep shaky breath, blinking rapidly to clear the tears that puddled in her eyes. "I'm scared." She threw her arms around Spider. "I don't want to lose you."

He wrapped his bony arms around her in turn, stooping to pull her closer. "I don't want to lose you, either, Sweetie. And I didn't mean to make light of it. You're right, it is scary."

Linda swiped at her eyes. "And now I'm going to be late to meet Lola and Moonbeam Meadow Sky and I was so looking forward to meeting her, b-but I'm afraid to even leave the house. And I'm afraid to stay here, or drive my car, or... or... anything."

My heart leaped. "Wait, you're meeting Moonbeam?"

"Yes, we were supposed to be at the dressmaker's house ten minutes ago. I called to let them know I'd be late, but..."

Glorious relief flooded me. "Call them back and tell them you're on your way."

"B-but..."

"I'll follow you over and Spider will ride with me," I reassured her before turning a faux-stern frown on Spider. "But he's not allowed to see the dress. It's bad luck."

A few minutes later we pulled to a halt in front of the dressmaker's home, a pale yellow Victorian two-storey with immaculate white gingerbread trim. Moonbeam and Karma's rental car was parked on the street behind Lola's orange Jeep Renegade, and I drew a long thankful breath.

As we got out of our cars I surveyed the quiet street warily, but didn't see any threats. Unlike Spider and Linda's new subdivision, giant elm trees shaded the cracked and overgrown sidewalks. Gracefully-proportioned old houses sat back on their generous lots like serene matrons basking in the late-morning heat. A black cat prowled across the street on some surreptitious errand, its tail trailing low, and an unseen squirrel scolded it vigorously.

Nothing but peace and small-town charm. Too bad I didn't dare believe it.

As we came up the walk, Lola, Moonbeam, and a plump woman with a round cheerful face stepped out on the verandah, obviously engaged in a pleasant conversation. There were smiles all around, but none of them were as broad as the one I felt widening on my own face.

"Moonbeam!" I cried, then belatedly added "...Meadow Sky... I'm so glad you're still here! I thought you'd left."

She threw me a tiny frown and headshake before switching instantly to her usual glowing smile. "Of course not, dear. I promised Lola I'd look at Linda's gown today."

I took her 'shut up' hint. We'd talk later.

"And you must be Linda," Moonbeam went on, fluttering down the verandah stairs like a gaily-coloured butterfly in her gauzy tie-dyed caftan. "How nice to meet you, and don't worry; I think we can salvage your wedding gown."

"Really?" Linda's face lit up.

"Yes, I believe so. We can lighten the red with a gentle bleach solution and make the blotches look planned by repeating them on the rest of the gown to match. Then I can overpaint it to turn the blotches into flowers in a Japanese-style pattern. Your gown is so elegantly simple that the hand-painting will suit it beautifully. And we can soften the effect by dying the background a subtle pink, which would be absolutely lovely with your complexion... if you don't mind pink...?"

Moonbeam's anxious expression dissolved into relief as Linda let out a jubilant laugh. "I'd love a pink wedding dress! I almost went with pink to start with, but then I chickened out and went traditional white at the last minute!"

"Oh, good. It's settled, then." Moonbeam turned to

smile up at the plump woman. "May I take Linda's gown with me? I'll need to drive down to Calgary to get some supplies, and then I'll work on it at our hotel room."

"Of course. I'll go and get it." The dressmaker hurried back into the house, and I made playful shooing motions at Linda, Lola, and Spider.

"You guys go talk among yourselves. Moonbeam and I have secrets to discuss."

They laughed and obligingly turned away as I ushered Moonbeam a few paces down the walk and lowered my voice. "I talked to Ste... um... Ch... Cosmic River Stone this morning."

Moonbeam's sweet features settled into an expressionless façade almost as impenetrable as Stemp's own, but her faded china-blue eyes reflected the depth of her pain. "I'm afraid it's Charles Randall Stemp now," she said softly. "Cosmic River Stone is no more." She sighed. "I was foolish to think otherwise. Cosmic River Stone ceased to exist twenty-five years ago."

"But you're not just going to leave, are you?" I begged. "You can still-"

"Now is not the time, dear," Moonbeam countered with a significant glance at the dressmaker emerging from the house with a zippered garment bag over her arm.

"Okay, we'll talk later," I said hurriedly. "But I have a huge favour to ask. I wouldn't ask at all, but I'm up to my eyeballs in shit right now and-"

"You're wasting time, dear," Moonbeam interrupted with a smile.

"Would you please take Linda to Calgary with you? And Spider? If Karma could go along, too, that would be great."

She frowned. "Of course, but why?"

"I'm afraid somebody might be targeting them."

The fragile butterfly morphed into something considerably steelier. "Report."

I briefed her rapidly while she listened, interrupting occasionally with terse questions. When I was finished, she gave a firm nod. "Karma Wolf Song and I are armed, of course. We'll protect them. What about Lola?"

"Her, too."

"Consider it done."

I threw my arms around her. "Thank you."

"You are most welcome, dear." She hugged me back, deceptively strong under the delicate gauze. "Give us a status update as soon as possible. We're at the Silverside Hotel, room two-ten."

"You could stay at my farm..." I began, but Moonbeam was already shaking her head.

"No, the hotel is closer to Spider and Linda. It's a better choice tactically."

I smiled and deferred to the expert.

CHAPTER 23

Driving back to Sirius Dynamics at eleven-thirty, I practiced a few calming yoga breaths. Relax. Spider and Linda would be safe. Moonbeam and Karma were formidable bodyguards. And as long as they were still here, I might be able to talk Stemp into giving their relationship another chance.

I sighed. So much unnecessary pain between them. If only they could reveal their deepest secrets to each other...

My cell phone vibrated as I pulled into the Sirius Dynamics parking lot, and I swung into the nearest parking space and punched the Talk button.

My hello was greeted by Kane's terse voice. "We're going back to Calgary. Do you have time to meet us at the drive-in? We'll be there in about ten minutes."

I swallowed hard. "See you there."

He disconnected without a goodbye, and I turned my car around to head for the street again, alternating muttered entreaties with obscenities while my heart played a xylophone solo against my ribs.

Please, God, don't let this be bad news.

Fuck, at this point was there likely to be any other kind?

And dammit, in a couple of hours I had to pretend to be

Arlene Widdenback the arms dealer, and how the hell was I going to pull that off when I didn't have time to prepare?

A few minutes later I turned into the drive-in's parking lot, bouncing over the dusty potholed gravel to park far away from the crowd. All the brightly-painted tables were occupied, and the scent of grilled meat and frying oil floated on the warm August air. My stomach managed to flip-flop with queasy nerves and growl with hunger simultaneously.

Kane's Expedition and Hellhound's Forester arrived only seconds after me. We all got out, and I studied Kane's face worriedly. He was still pale and hollow-eyed, but he had shaved and he seemed more composed. I put my arms around him, but he returned my hug only briefly before stepping back.

"We're going to interview the suspects and the mothers of the abducted boys to see if we can uncover any commonalities," he said crisply. "Hellhound will handle the men. They're all in the Calgary area, which seems like too much of a coincidence for my taste."

"But Mayweather tried to connect them and couldn't," I said. "And two of them are in the remand centre, so that doesn't really..."

Kane twitched his shoulders irritably. "Mayweather's missing something. Four of the mothers are down south; Alicia and one other one in Calgary and one in each of Okotoks and Nanton. I'll interview them today. The other three are in Red Deer, Edmonton, and Stony Plain." His fist clenched. "There aren't enough hours in the day. I could phone them, but you always learn more talking to people in person. I'll go up there tomorrow."

"Wait, what about me?" I asked. "I have an appointment at two o'clock that I can't skip, but after that I could take the north loop. As long as they could see me around suppertime or in the evening, there would still be time after I finish my business here."

If I was still alive after I concluded my business with Frederick Labelle; but I didn't mention that.

"Would you?" The furrows eased from Kane's forehead. "That would be excellent. Then we'd have a complete set of interviews by tonight."

"Sure. Give me the names and addresses." I hesitated. "Um... what are we going to tell them?" I glanced around the parking lot to be sure we wouldn't be overheard. "Are you going to get in trouble for impersonating a police officer? Did you hand in your resignation and do your debriefing yet?"

Kane made an impatient gesture. "No time."

"It's okay, darlin'," Hellhound said. "Nobody's gotta impersonate anythin'. I'm a private investigator an' you're both workin' with me. We ain't got as much clout as the cops, but the moms'll be desperate to talk to anybody, an' the guys that're up for murder are gonna help if they figure we might find the real killer."

He gave Kane a sidelong glance as if regretting his use of the word 'killer', but Kane's only reaction was to extract a sheet of paper from his pocket and crease it with his thumbnail before tearing carefully along the fold.

"Here are the three northern contacts," he said, then reached into the cab of the Expedition to extract a small stack of printed pages. "And the police files for the women you're going to see." He handed me the papers, then hesitated as if calculating times. "Aydan, you'll likely be the latest if you're going all the way up to Edmonton, so Hellhound and I will go to my condo in Calgary after we finish and we'll wait for your call there. Of course, if anything important comes up in the interviews, call me immediately. Good luck, both of you."

"Okay, if you can secure your line at the condo, I'll call you from a secured phone..." I began, but he was already swinging into his Expedition. A moment later he pulled out of the parking lot and Hellhound and I watched him drive away.

Hellhound's arm closed around my shoulders. "Don't take it personal, Aydan. He's just-"

"It's okay," I interrupted gently. "You don't have to make excuses for him. I don't even want to imagine what he's going through. If it was my child I'd be going insane."

Hellhound sighed. "He might be, darlin'. He just might be." We stood in glum silence for a moment before he put on a smile that looked almost convincing. "Come on, let's grab a burger. I'm starvin'." His smile vanished into worry. "Shit, I shoulda made John eat, too."

"He'll eat," I said without conviction, then sighed. "You're doing all you can for him. Don't feel badly."

He shook his head, his eyes dark. "I can't feel any other way."

"I know." I slid my arms around him and we held each other in silence for a moment.

After a short wait in the lunch lineup we retreated to the grass at the edge of the adjacent park with our food. I tried to take comfort from the pleasant scent of crushed grass and the sun baking my shoulders, but even its heat couldn't banish the chill of foreboding around my heart.

After a few minutes of silent concentration on his burger, Hellhound popped the last of it into his mouth and reclined on the grass. Tucking his arms behind his head, he lay watching me with sleepy eyes while I nibbled the last of my fries. Moments later, his eyelids slipped closed and the hard lines of his body eased. A small snore escaped him and his eyes popped open.

"Sorry, darlin'. Didn't mean to fall asleep on ya."

"It's okay." I swallowed the last of my fries and wiped my greasy fingers on a napkin before moving over beside him. Leaning back against the heavy wooden post that marked the park's boundaries, I stretched out my legs before tugging gently at his shoulders. He squirmed over to stretch out again with his head on my lap, and I stroked his cheek.

"Did you get any sleep at all?" I asked.

"Yeah, I grabbed a coupla hours after John got up."

"That's not much." I kept stroking with light fingertips. "Have a nap. I don't want you to fall asleep driving to Calgary."

"Mmhm..." he mumbled, his eyes already closing. "Watch my back, darlin'..."

"I will."

His muscles softened into sleep and soon he was snoring gently. Tucking my arm around his head to shade his face, I leaned back and watched the surrounding area for threats while I mapped out my upcoming meeting with Labelle as best I could.

Half an hour later my ass was asleep and my brain was in knots. I hadn't a clue whether Labelle was looking for a buyer or a supplier; or hell, who knew? Maybe he wanted revenge for Nicholas Parr's death and he'd shoot me on sight.

And if Labelle didn't kill me, Stemp probably would when he found out I was working on Daniel's case despite his direct order.

I gulped.

But I wasn't *really* working the case; not as an agent. Just asking a few questions as a civilian, helping a private investigator. So technically I wasn't doing anything wrong...

I'd just keep telling myself that. And keep conveniently ignoring the fact that I'd stolen and disseminated police data...

I shifted uncomfortably and Hellhound grunted and opened bleary eyes.

"Wha' time izzit?" he mumbled.

"Nearly one."

"Shit." He groaned and rolled over, then sat up and brushed the grass off his T-shirt. I joined in, whisking my palm over his bulky shoulders and back, and he grinned. "Givin' me the brush-off?"

I leaned in to kiss him. "Never. Think of it as a hand job."

He laughed. "Bad news, darlin'. You're doin' it wrong." He rose and reached down a hard to pull me up. "I gotta get goin', but I'm gonna grab a milkshake for the road. Want one?"

"No," I said absently. "I'm having ice cream with a gunrunner in an hour."

"You're what-the-*fuck*?" Hellhound demanded.

I blinked. "Damn, I'm getting too comfortable around you. You didn't hear me say that. I'm going for an ice cream cone and a nice walk in the park with a nice man and we're going to talk about his nice legal brokerage and investment business."

"Jesus, Aydan." Hellhound folded me into his arms. "Call me soon's as you're clear so I know you're okay."

"I will. Drive carefully." I reached up for a quick kiss, but he laced his fingers through my hair and turned it into a slow one. Softly, his lips explored mine while he held me against his solid body.

I sighed in bliss and pressed against him while he unhurriedly deepened the kiss, sending tingles to every nerve ending. My hands slid around to knead the muscled ridges of his back and I gave a small moan of appreciation when he did the same. Warm pleasure softened every bone in my body, and when he ended the kiss with a smile and whisker-tickly kisses on my nose, cheeks, and forehead, I tucked my head under his bearded chin to cuddle close for a moment.

"Be safe, darlin'," he whispered into my hair.

"You, too." I stole one last quick kiss before heading for my car.

I was halfway back to Sirius Dynamics before I remembered I'd promised to finish Blue Eddy's bookkeeping today. Goddammit. I had exactly forty-five minutes before my meeting with Labelle, and then I had to hit the road for Edmonton.

Swearing savagely, I headed for the bar.

Despite the almost-irresistible temptation, I managed not to suck back a beer while I entered the last of the bookkeeping data into Eddy's computer. Beer would have been heavenly, but I didn't dare compromise my already-distracted brain. I'd need to be at my best. Not to mention I still had to drive back to Sirius Dynamics.

When I parked in the Sirius lot at five to two, I felt a very long way from my best. Dragging myself out of the car, I hoofed it toward the ice cream shop, smothering yawns of nerves and fatigue. The burger and fries sat in a greasy lump in the pit of my stomach.

A hurried survey of my surroundings revealed no apparent threats, and I stifled a curse as realization hit me.

If I were a real agent I'd have put surveillance cameras on the ice cream shop, with analysts watching the feeds. And if Labelle was the professional I suspected he was, he had probably done exactly that.

Hell, or maybe he just had a sniper hiding in the trees at the park. Because I hadn't been smart enough to arrange backup for myself there, either.

Fuck, I was a moron.

My stride faltered as I seriously considered fleeing into the safety of Sirius Dynamics and calling Labelle to reschedule the meeting for a different time and place. Preferably in about a thousand years, beside the frozen flames of hell.

Too late, dammit. He'd spotted me.

He waved from his seat at one of the small wrought-iron café tables on the sidewalk. I clenched my teeth, sent up a fervent prayer to the patron saint of idiots, and concentrated on looking relaxed.

As I approached, Labelle rose with a smile and offered his hand.

"Aydan, it's nice to see you." The smooth radio-announcer's voice oozed over me like butterscotch and he gazed at me with big brown cow-eyes as if I was the woman he'd been dreaming of all his life.

I wasn't buying it.

"Hi, Frederick. Nice to see you, too," I lied with equal smoothness, and shook his hand. "Have you decided what kind of ice cream you want yet?"

He gave me a charmingly rueful smile. "I'm afraid to commit. A person's favourite ice cream flavour shows their personality, and I want to make a good impression."

I forced a laugh. "Damn, I didn't know that. Now I'm

totally self-conscious, too."

We went inside and the server looked up with a smile. "Hi, Aydan! Do you want your usual?"

I nodded, and Labelle chuckled. "You're a frequent customer, I see." The server was eyeing him expectantly, and he selected a double scoop of butterscotch ripple in a sugar cone.

The thought of all that cloying sweetness made my teeth ache, but what hell, so did Labelle. Perfect choice.

As I accepted my chocolate-and-peanut-butter single scoop on a plain cone, Labelle raised a teasing eyebrow. "Ah, now I know all your secrets. You're nurturing and passionate with a good sense of humour, and you tend to be bossy."

As I nibbled off the uneven edges of the ice cream, he added, "And you bite your ice cream instead of licking it. Aggressive and uninhibited in bed."

Oh, for chrissake.

I bit viciously into my ice cream and smiled through my teeth. "You have the advantage over me. What does your ice cream mean?"

He regarded his cone with smug satisfaction and took a big lick, giving the cone a full rotation against his tongue. "I like sweet things. I'm a wise and traditional leader and a considerate lover, family oriented with a gift for managing money."

And just as full of synthetic shit as that goopy streak of butterscotch in his ice cream.

"That must serve you well in your business," I said in my politest voice. "Shall we walk to the park?"

CHAPTER 24

As we emerged from the ice cream shop I gave our surroundings another quick once-over, but still didn't spot any snipers or surveillance.

Fine. My ice cream was diminishing rapidly under my onslaught, so I'd be finished before we got to the park. Good to have my hands free in case Labelle had some unpleasant surprise planned.

We were only a few paces down the sidewalk when he got to the point.

"So I understand Nick Parr was a mutual friend of ours."

I shrugged. "He wasn't really a friend. I only met him a couple of times."

"Ah."

Labelle took another big lick of ice cream. His tongue was unpleasantly oversized. Cow's tongue. Ew.

He swallowed and gave me a cat-that-ate-the-canary look. "So you were business associates."

"Very briefly. I only worked with his company for a couple of days."

Labelle's eyes narrowed. "And yet a cheque for fifty thousand dollars was issued to you. Your services must have been quite valuable."

My pulse ticked up. Shit, what else did he know?

"That was a settlement for personal damages sustained in a crash on his corporate jet," I said evenly. "I signed a waiver and legal release in exchange. So how do you know what was in Fuzzy Bunny's financial records?"

He smiled and rolled out a smooth explanation in his butterscotch voice. "As I mentioned, I'm an investment broker. I work quite closely with my clients' accounts..."

He began a detailed and boring description of the financial services his company provided and I used the time to adjust my strategy while I smiled and nodded. I'd better assume he knew everything there was to know about Arlene Widdenback's interactions with Parr and his associates. At least I shouldn't have to worry about establishing my cover identity, but I'd still have to play hard-to-get. An arms dealer wasn't likely to admit anything to a brand-new acquaintance...

"...and you're not listening to a thing I'm saying, are you?" he finished, and I nodded and mm-hmmed before my brain caught up to the conversation.

"...oh," I mumbled, fighting the tide of heat rising in my face. "Sorry, I zoned out for a second there. I'm not really big on financial stuff."

"But you're a bookkeeper." His triumphant tone made it sound as if he'd just scored a significant point, and I gave him a blank look in return.

"Yeah. You're a financial guy; I thought you'd know that bookkeepers just keep records of cheques and stuff. I don't deal with investments at all."

"Ah," he repeated, and made another giant tongue-swipe around his ice cream. "So you're only an ignorant peon."

"Yep." I took another bite of my ice cream and savoured

a chunk of frozen peanut butter.

A trace of disappointment flashed across his face. Guess he thought I'd rise to the bait and tell him what an influential arms dealer I was. Nice try, buddy.

He leaned closer. "When Nick and his staff were on trial, they all swore under oath that Arlene Widdenback was an arms dealer."

"You probably shouldn't trust the word of criminals," I said gently, and nibbled the edge off my rapidly-shrinking cone.

"Excellent advice, I'm sure." He gave me a significant look.

There went his disgusting tongue again. God, why had I suggested ice cream cones? I was going to need a gallon of brain bleach to get the memory of that tongue out of my mind.

The tongue mercifully disappeared as he spoke again. "Kevin Barnett had some very unusual lesions on his leg when he was killed."

I held up a restraining hand. "Ew. Do you mind? I'm eating. And I don't have a clue who you're talking about."

"That's interesting, because Barnett claimed you had used a new weapon on him. One that caused excruciating pain without leaving a mark initially, but it caused irreversible damage that resulted in the eventual death of the tissue. It started out as hairless patches on his leg and over the next couple of months the skin gradually rotted away, leaving open ulcers."

Crunching off some more of my cone, I gulped it down along with a wave of nausea. Nothing like the power of suggestion. Barnett must have done it to himself, rubbing at his leg until he wore the skin away. Dammit, even though he'd been a violent killer and sick-minded torturer, I still felt guilty for causing such suffering.

I didn't hide my involuntary shudder. "Unless you want to see my ice cream all over again, you'll shut up now," I warned. "That's gross, and it's nothing to do with me. I thought you wanted to talk about investments, not some disgusting jailhouse skin disease."

Labelle's tongue went into action again, and I looked away. The fucking thing looked even bigger as his ice cream got smaller.

"All right," he said, and the smooth sweetness was completely absent from his voice. "If that's the way you want it, let me be perfectly clear. I know you're not Aydan Kelly, and you're not a bookkeeper. I know you have a couple of large and very... how shall I say it? *Dedicated* bodyguards..."

"Whoa, hang on," I interrupted. "First of all, I *am* a bookkeeper, so why would I need bodyguards? And if they were bodyguards, wouldn't they be here to protect me from whatever you think I need protecting from?"

He smirked. "I doubt if you need protecting. Because I don't know what your business was up in Rocky Mountain House, but I do know you carry a small handgun strapped to your ankle, and I quite enjoyed watching you jam it into that biker's balls."

I stared at him, hoping my silent immobility looked threatening instead of paralyzed.

Shit, he'd followed us.

Lola had said he'd left the party right after Kane and me. I'd never even thought to look for a tail, and of course Kane had been far too distracted. That meant Labelle or one of his hirelings had likely been following me even before the party, and almost certainly ever since...

Nice going, Jane Bond. Way to use your super-spy powers of observation.

I broke the silence with a laugh. "So what? Are you going to call the cops on me? I hope you brought some."

It was his turn to go still. "Excuse me, did you say 'brought'? Or... 'bought'?" he inquired with exaggerated politeness.

"Brought." I waved a hand. "Look around. Do you see any cops here? The nearest detachment is half an hour away."

"Yes..." he said slowly. "Though you certainly managed to avoid their interest during the Fuzzy Bunny trials. Rumour has it that you have a... beneficial relationship with several contacts in law enforcement."

"Rumours. Pfft." I tossed the last of my ice cream cone into my mouth and crunched it rapidly. "You don't want to believe everything you hear."

"Very true." His big gooey eyes had hardened to the consistency of marbles. "In fact, I'm more inclined to believe you're an undercover cop."

My ice cream stuck halfway down, freezing my heart into a motionless lump.

Shit, shit, shit!

I snapped out the first words that came to me. "Watch your mouth, asshole!"

Follow up with some convincing lie. Say something, idiot.

My mind remained stubbornly blank while I glared at him in silence. What the hell could I say? A simple denial wouldn't convince him...

Labelle laughed. "My, that seems like a bit of an overreaction. What have you got against cops?"

Panic nibbled at the edges of my mind. Get the hell out of here and regroup.

I deepened my glare and ground out, "I'm allergic to cops. And I'm allergic to assholes. If you called this meeting just to insult me, we're done here."

I spun and stalked away. When I turned the corner toward Sirius Dynamics, Labelle was still watching me speculatively and licking his ice cream.

God, that tongue was the size of a bathmat.

Safely behind the security of Sirius Dynamics a few minutes later, I tottered up the stairs to my office and fell into my chair. After a few moments of hyperventilation, I calmed down enough to take stock and organize my thoughts.

Labelle or his men would undoubtedly follow me when I left for Edmonton. What if he decided to kidnap and interrogate me? If I didn't file a report, nobody would even know where to start looking for me...

Movement in the hallway made me glance up in time to see Stemp going past my doorway.

"Wait!" I yelped, and he returned to lean into my doorway, raising an inquiring eyebrow.

"Were you speaking to me?"

"Yeah. Sorry to yell at you like that, but... do you have a few minutes?"

"Perhaps," he said warily. "For what?"

I hid a sigh. It was going to be damn tricky to broach the subject of Moonbeam and Karma if he was this prickly. Fortunately that wasn't my goal at the moment.

"I met with Labelle, but I don't have time to file a report," I said, and he relaxed and stepped into my office, closing my door behind him.

"Why not?" he asked. "It's not even fifteen hundred yet."

"I have to leave. Sorry. I'll file my report first thing tomorrow morning, but I wanted to make sure you knew what was going on before I left."

He eyed me narrowly but didn't demand the reason for my unscheduled absence, and I hid my relief and launched into my report, omitting Labelle's disgusting tongue.

"So you've been allowing him to follow you," Stemp said when I was finished.

"Yes."

'Allowing' was a lie since I'd been completely oblivious; but it sounded better than the embarrassing truth.

"If he's been watching me for a while, he must have thought he'd hit paydirt when I went up to Rocky Mountain House," I added. "After weeks of boring trips back and forth to the office, suddenly I take off in Kane's truck, transfer to Arnie's motorcycle, and then transfer again to Arnie's SUV. It must have looked like I was trying to evade a tail." I sighed. "He or his guys will probably keep up their surveillance now."

"Yes. That may complicate your courier assignment on Friday," Stemp pointed out.

"Um... yeah."

Shit, I'd forgotten about that. Too many things on my mind.

Stemp stood staring into middle distance for a moment before speaking. "If he knows of Barnett's injuries, it's unlikely that he truly believes you're law enforcement. He was probably testing you. Playing innocent was the right thing to do at the time, but he's clearly upping the ante by telling you he's been following you."

"Yeah, it felt like a test," I agreed.

"So it's time to command his respect and reassure him that you're not law enforcement. At the very least, you need to elude the tail."

"Okay..." I said slowly.

I hadn't a clue how to do that, but I'd figure something out. At least Stemp was coaching in my corner, three steps ahead of everybody else as usual.

He nodded and turned to leave. "Very well. I'll expect your written report first thing tomorrow morning."

After he left I sat still.

If I were a real agent I wouldn't just rush out the door without a plan and react to whatever blindsided me next. Think it through...

I considered my options for a few minutes before letting out a breath of resolve. I had to get rid of my tail before I visited any of the abducted boys' moms. I wouldn't risk their safety by letting Labelle think they were somehow connected to me.

Three calls confirmed that the moms were all willing to see me, and it seemed like a good omen that I'd reached them all on the first try. After making a quick call to Hellhound to reassure him I'd survived my meeting with Labelle, I headed downstairs.

At the door to the secured area I gathered my courage, unslung the pheromone detector from around my neck, and bent for the retinal scan. I made it through the thirty-second countdown in the cramped chamber without needing to close my eyes, and I mentally congratulated myself while I hurried down the concrete stairs.

At the door to the Weapons lab I stopped to gather myself again. What kind of mood would Chow be in today? Jesus, I hoped he was happy, because I was pretty sure I was about to ask some really stupid questions.

CHAPTER 25

When I rounded the corner into the main area of the Weapons lab, relief buoyed my heart. Chow was standing at a counter working on some unidentifiable device, and his wheelchair was nowhere in sight.

"Nice legs!" I sang out, then winced as The Monks chanted the rest of the title in my memory.

Chow was obviously familiar with the song. "Yeah, shame about my face," he growled, glowering at me from under his remaining eyebrow. "Bite me, Kelly."

"I didn't mean..." I began hurriedly, but his scowl dissolved into a wicked smirk.

"Forget it, I'm just yanking your crank. What can I do-you-for?"

"Well, you'd have to start with a really nice dinner," I joked, grinning.

"You'd do me for a nice dinner? You're such a cheap slut."

"I said '*start* with a nice dinner'," I reminded him. "There's a list of requirements."

He threw up his hands in mock disgust. "Women. Greedy beeyotches, all of you."

I held up my thumb and forefinger and rubbed them

together. "Look, it's the world's tiniest violin, and it's playing just for you."

"Bite me, Kelly."

"Aaaaand we're back where we started." We grinned at each other before I sobered and added, "Can I ask you some dumb questions?"

"Well, that's your first one down," he deadpanned. "Next?"

"Have you got any handy-dandy secret weapons that will take a car off the road?"

His brow drew down. "Armoured car or standard production model?"

"Standard."

"What range?" When I gave him a questioning look he clarified, "Visual range? A few miles away? Or do you need a satellite targeting system that'll pick them off from the other side of the globe?"

"You can do that?"

He made an impatient 'of course' gesture, and I shook off my slightly queasy incredulity and focused on the issue at hand. "Just visual range. I've got somebody following me and I want to get them off my tail. If we were in Calgary I might be able to do it with some fancy driving, but it's a little tricky when we're out on the bald prairie and we can see each other for miles."

"You want to use it on the fly, or set up a fixed weapon for an ambush?"

"On the fly. If I'm being followed inside visual range, I wouldn't be able to set up an ambush."

"Fatal or non-fatal?"

I considered that for a moment. "Non-fatal, I guess. I'd rather be subtle. So, sorry; but throwing a giant fireball from the rear of my car is out."

Chow made a resigned gesture. "Damn. 'Cause I've got this trunk-mounted flamethrower I've been just dying to test in the field."

My jaw dropped. "Seriously?"

"No, you dumb shit, I'm just fucking with you! What the hell use would we have for a flame-throwing car? We're covert ops. *Covert.* As in 'don't attract attention'."

I flipped him the finger. "That's what I just said. So have you got anything?"

"Couple of things that might work. If they're driving right behind you, I've got a laser that would temporarily blind them and make them drive off the road. But if they actually have a brain and they're tailing you a few cars back, you wouldn't be able to use it without taking out all the drivers in between. If you've got a passenger-"

"I don't," I interrupted.

"Hm. Too bad. If you're driving you can't aim at the same time, and if you trigger something generalized it'll wipe out everybody in the vicinity including non-combatant drivers. Can you sneak up on them and disable their car?"

"Maybe... but I was hoping for an easier option. If they left the car I could easily disable it, but I can't see them wandering off so I can do that." I shrugged unhappily. "And if I was going to sneak up on them anyway, I might as well just shoot the driver and solve the whole problem. But that's loud and messy and it attracts too much attention." I gave him a hopeful look. "That ultrasound weapon would be perfect. Silent and unobtrusive."

He snorted. "No way. It's our only prototype. And we don't know what might happen if there was a laminated glass barrier between it and the target. Somehow I can't see you strolling over and asking them to roll their window down so you can liquefy their brains."

"Huh. No." I slumped against the counter. "Shit. So I'm out of luck."

"I didn't say that." He crooked a finger, a conspiratorial gleam in his eye. "I've got a little toy you might like. Come on over here." I trailed him eagerly to one of the lab doors, and he shook his head and leaned down for the retinal scan. "Christ, you're easy. How many times have you fallen for that line? Come on over here and look at my toy, little girl."

As the door swished open, I batted my eyes at him. "Oh, but I feel perfectly safe with you."

He groaned. "Ballbuster."

I followed him across the lab and watched with anticipation while he took a flashlight out of a drawer and laid it on the counter, then extracted what looked like an ordinary taper candle and pressed it into a holder. Just in case the lights were about to go out, I shot a glance around the small room to orient myself and rested my hand on the pocket of my waist pouch that held my tiny LED flashlight.

The lights didn't go out.

Chow leaned an elbow on the counter, watching me with his one-sided smirk. "What do you think?" he asked.

"About what?"

"Where's the weapon?"

I approached the counter cautiously, examining the flashlight and candle without touching them.

"I'm guessing it's the flashlight," I said, fully expecting him to guffaw and magically transform the candle into some kind of guided missile.

"Good guess," he said instead, and picked up the flashlight, flicking the switch on. He let the beam track across the candle and the wall behind it while I held my breath, wondering what was about to happen.

Chow shot me a grin and shone the light on the candle, then thumbed the switch again. Less than two seconds later the middle of the candle disintegrated in a cascade of melted wax. The top flopped over to dangle by the merrily-burning wick for a moment before the wick burned through and dropped the top half of the candle to the counter.

"Oops," Chow said, and blew out the flames before reaching over to rub at a one-inch round scorch mark on the wall behind it. "That burst was a little too long."

"What the hell is that thing?" I demanded.

"A flashlight." He shone the light across the wall again and I flinched involuntarily. He grinned. "And an infrared laser."

"You mean... holy shit, you mean like they use in spy movies to cut through steel doors?"

"It's not a cutting laser. That'd be too dangerous. Steel is reflective to infrared." Chow snorted. "If they tried that in real life they'd probably cut their own damn hands off."

I backed away. "Is, um... does glass reflect it, too, or would it go through and burn something on the other side of the glass?"

"Depends on the glass, but usually it'd go straight through."

"Usually?" I eased a little farther away. "So exactly how and why would I use that thing?"

"Don't be such a pussy." He hefted the flashlight cheerfully and I managed to dampen my flinch down to a small twitch. He shook his head reprovingly. "I told you, it's not a cutting laser. If it was, that single burst would have wrecked several lab walls, a bunch of very expensive equipment, and probably a couple of people. Watch and learn."

He shone the flashlight's beam on the candle again, then thumbed the control. As the candle melted into a flaming puddle and the wall behind it discoloured with an unpleasant smell of singed paint, he passed his pincer-hand in front of the laser.

I gasped and lunged toward him, but he had already clicked the switch off.

"Fuck! Jesus..." I seized his wrist to examine his hand, bracing myself for the blackened skin and nauseating stench of burned flesh...

"Oh... Christ..." I sagged against the counter, his wrist still clenched in my trembling hand while I gasped out my adrenaline overdose. "Christ almighty. I'm going to kill you! As soon as I can walk again, I'm going to fucking kill you, you son of a bitch!"

"Sorry." He tugged gently against my deathgrip on his wrist. "Hey. Kelly. You can let go now."

"Asshole," I growled, and managed to persuade my fingers to loosen.

"Hey, I'm sorry." There was no taunt in his voice and the undamaged side of his face showed concern. "I didn't mean to trigger you. What happened there?"

"Nothing." I swallowed and drew a deep breath, trying to calm my hammering heart.

"Bullshit. You had a flashback. Believe me, I know what they look like. So let's try this again. What happened?"

"Nothing," I repeated. "I just thought you were going to get burned."

Burned. Again. My stomach clenched at the thought of his scarred flesh bubbling and melting.

"So you've got some trauma with burns?" Chow inquired gently.

The sympathy in his fire-ravaged face shamed me.

"It's nothing," I muttered. "Like you said, I'm a fucking pussy. So you were just proving that it won't burn a hole in you if you get in the way, right?"

"Right. If you held your hand in front of it for more than a fraction of a second you'd be in trouble, but it's not going to reflect off something and instantly burn a hole in you. You'd feel it and have time to turn off the beam before you got a serious burn."

"Good to know. So what would I use it for? If it'll reflect off glass and steel, it's not much good for disabling a car, is it? And..." My throat closed and I fought my voice back to normal. "I'd never use it on a person. Never. That's just fucking sick."

"Tires, Kelly. It'll blow out a tire in less than five seconds. And you could still safely burn through a steel body panel. With this large a beam diameter, just about any surface has enough imperfections to harmlessly disperse the reflection. And remember, you'll have time to turn it off if anything goes wrong."

"Okay." I drew a deep breath and let it out slowly. "Thanks. So what's its range?"

He shrugged. "Line of sight. Heat distortions and particulate in the air will disperse the beam over distance, but on a clear day it'd easily work over a mile. So was that a flashback from your plane crash? Or something else?"

Dammit, he wasn't going to let it go.

Okay. Just spit it out.

I straightened my spine. "Both. The young guy who was killed with the ultrasonic weapon... he... burned. During the crash. He was already dead but I thought..." I swallowed. "It doesn't matter. And one time a guy held a butane torch on me a little too long, but it was just a tiny burn. You can hardly see the scar anymore."

"If somebody's holding a butane torch on you, any amount of time is too fucking long," Chow said quietly.

I couldn't look him in the eye so I studied my toes. "It wasn't that big a deal. I just freaked out because..."

I almost said 'I couldn't bear to think of your poor hand getting burned again', but stopped myself in time. He'd be enraged if he thought I was pitying him.

"Anyway, I'm over it," I said determinedly. "I hadn't even thought of it in months."

"Yeah, that's the bitch about flashbacks." He grimaced. "They hit when you least expect them. So if I hand you this flashlight are you going to be okay?"

I squared my shoulders. "Of course. Just tell me how it works first."

"Here's the regular button that controls the visible light beam." He indicated the ordinary-looking flashlight switch and pushed it forward. "You can use this light as your targeting system, or if you want a laser targeting system with longer range..."

He toggled the switch backward and a small red dot appeared on the wall. "It's just a laser sight. No burning or cutting."

"Okay."

"If you want to activate the laser, you have to simultaneously press and hold the main switch down and back while you depress this panel." He turned the flashlight over and showed me a long narrow panel on the underside. "It's designed to fit your fingertips so it's pretty well impossible to activate the beam accidentally. If you just use the main switch without depressing the panel, nothing will happen. Oh, and this..."

He flipped down a cap on the back end of the flashlight and indicated a button. "This is the self-destruct. This isn't highly-classified technology but if somebody's about to take it away from you, press this button to fry everything inside. Don't try to hang onto it after you hit the self-destruct or it'll burn you."

"Okay." I held out my hand gingerly. "I'll give it a try. Where do you want your next scorch mark?"

He grinned and flipped the self-destruct cap closed before placing the flashlight in my palm. "How about right next to that other one?"

"Sounds good to me." I toggled the switch forward to test the flashlight beam, then backward to get the laser dot. Then I sucked in a long slow breath and activated the laser. As the paint darkened, I clenched my teeth and whisked my hand through the beam.

Chow made a sudden move beside me, but I had already released the switch and lowered the flashlight, my pulse pounding in my ears.

"Okay?" he asked cautiously.

"Yeah." I rubbed my tingling palm against my jeans. "No worse than running your finger through a candle flame. We used to do that all the time when we were kids. We thought we were such hot shit."

Chow laughed. "You're still hot shit. Go toast some tires."

CHAPTER 26

With the laser flashlight concealed inside the sweater I usually wore to ward off the chill of air conditioning, I hesitated in the lobby of Sirius Dynamics to gather my composure.

Look casual. Look as though you don't know you're being followed...

Frowning, I considered that. Labelle had told me I was being followed. So wouldn't he be suspicious if I *didn't* look as though I knew I was being followed?

"Fuck it," I muttered, and headed for the door. If my followers didn't already know I was onto them, they soon would.

Driving down the highway toward my farm, I kept a wary eye on the vehicles around me. No way to know if any of them were actually following me. With the long stretches of highway out on the open prairie, it was perfectly plausible that the same vehicle might follow me all the way to one of the major cities.

I slowed and turned onto the gravel road that led to my farm. My followers would know I was headed home, and there was nothing but miles of empty gravel road north of me. If they'd been watching me for a while they'd know I never went that way, so they'd likely wait for me out on the highway.

Unless...

My pulse accelerated as I stopped at my gate. What if they'd tagged my car with some kind of transmitter?

I unlocked the gate, drove through it, and locked it again behind me with my heart thumping. As soon as the garage door rolled down behind me, I pulled the bug detector out of my waist pouch and let out a breath of relief at the sight of its steady green light.

All right, then. As long as I left my cell phone at home to be sure they couldn't track me through it, I'd only have to watch for a physical tail.

Inside my house, I exchanged my smartphone for a couple of secured phones and grabbed some snacks for the road. A few minutes later I locked my gate behind me and turned north.

As I drove up the hill beyond my farm, I spotted the glint of a parked vehicle on the highway. I couldn't make out any details over the two-mile distance, but I didn't need to. The glint moved, and a moment later a distant plume of gravel dust told me my tail was firmly in place.

The crest of the hill hid my pursuers from view as I coasted down the other side, but they'd be able to find me just fine. The warm August air was barely moving, and my dust would hang like a beacon for several minutes after I'd passed.

"Eat my dust, assholes," I muttered, and settled in for a nice drive in the country.

I slowed to a crawl each time a hill hid me from view, and several miles of zigzagging along gravelled roads closed the gap between us enough that I could make out a silver

SUV. It stayed too far away to identify the make, but I memorized the grill pattern and noted that unless there was somebody hiding in the back seat, my original assumption of 'they' was wrong. Only the driver. Good.

I emerged on pavement at last and turned west toward Innisfail, keeping an eye on my rear-view mirror. The silver SUV halted at the stop sign behind me and waited a few seconds despite the lack of oncoming traffic.

Okay, buddy, go ahead and play coy, but you're going to have to cuddle up a little closer in a few minutes...

Sure enough, the SUV closed the gap as I entered Innisfail. The driver kept a couple of vehicles between us at all times, but where I turned, he followed.

Pretending cluelessness, I parked and went into a grocery store. Basket over my arm, I circulated close to the front windows and spotted the SUV parked on the other side of the lot. When I came out with my small sack of groceries and drove down the street, the SUV followed a few cars back as usual.

My heart picked up the pace. So far, so good. Just let him get used to waiting for me in parking lots...

Next stop, a drugstore. I bought a box of cough drops just for the sake of leaving with a purchase, and spotted the SUV parked a few slots over.

When I pulled out, I thought I'd lost him. A steady stream of traffic prevented him from turning out after me, and I was several blocks down the street by the time he tagged onto the tail end of the procession.

Despite the tension of being followed, I breathed a sigh of relief. As long he was sticking to me, it meant he was likely alone. If he had stopped pursuing I would have had to guess whether it was because I'd truly lost him, or somebody else had picked me up.

Time to end this.

I spotted a small fast-food restaurant with a front and back door and pulled in close to the front. Striding to the entrance with my sweater swinging from my hand as if I hadn't a care in the world, I shot a quick glance over my shoulder. The silver SUV was just nosing into a parking spot on the opposite side of the lot.

Perfect.

Inside, I ordered a burger and fries to go and nodded toward the back door. "I'm just going to use the washroom while I wait."

The young server gave a disinterested shrug, and I strolled away. Bypassing the washrooms, I slipped out the back door.

A bit of cautious circling positioned me at the corner of a reeking garbage dumpster, with a clear view of the back of the silver SUV. Hoping his concentration was focused on the restaurant's front door and not on his rear-view mirrors, I pointed the flashlight and steadied my hand against the dumpster.

The red dot wobbled onto one of the rear tires and I drew a slow breath, then depressed the switch and panel. For a couple of long seconds nothing happened.

Then the tire blew like a shotgun blast.

I flung myself back against the dumpster, heart hammering. Holy shit, I hadn't realized it would be so loud. I chanced a peek around the corner, but apparently the driver had thought it sounded like a shotgun blast, too. As I watched, his head appeared briefly above the seat, then disappeared again. A quick peek to see who was shooting at him.

Grinning, I focused on his other tire. Let's just keep him guessing.

The second explosion was even louder than the first, but I didn't stick around to check the results of my handiwork.

Scuttling back into the restaurant, I hurried up to the counter to collect my food, trying to look as though my sweaty fist wasn't clenched around a classified weapon.

I needn't have bothered with my Oscar-winning acting skills. The kid didn't even glance my way, nor did he seem the least bit concerned about two explosions from the parking lot. With the warm greasy bag swinging from my hand, I did my best nonchalant stride out the door to my car.

When I drove away, the SUV driver was standing beside his vehicle with his cell phone pressed to his ear. His scowl followed me out of the parking lot, but I was pretty sure the scowl was all that had followed me.

Just to be cautious, I headed back to the QE2 highway and merged onto its busy northbound lane. A few miles of high-speed driving brought me to a small highway where I turned off and zigzagged west and north. After half an hour with no sign of pursuit, I relaxed into the enjoyment of driving the back roads and reached into the bag for my lukewarm burger.

Soon after I had devoured my food, I was fighting sleep. The relentless sun blazed in the driver's side windows, overwhelming the cool breath of air conditioning on my face.

I blinked hard and patted my cheeks. Wake up and concentrate.

Now that I wasn't distracted by evading Labelle's man, my worries turned to my upcoming interviews.

What should I ask? Dammit, I shouldn't have let Kane drive away without at least giving me some guidelines. There was probably some established technique for interviewing witnesses, and if I were a real agent, I'd know it. Mumbling curses under my breath, I made a mental note to look for a course on that, too. But in the meantime, Daniel's life might depend on my investigative skills.

That disturbing thought held sleep at bay for the rest of the trip while I compiled mental lists of questions only to discard them and start over.

With a few minutes to spare before my first meeting, I pulled into a supermarket parking lot in Stony Plain and read over the police reports, then leaned my aching head against the headrest.

God, I wasn't looking forward to this interview. Contrary to Hellhound's optimistic prediction, Selena Bruner had been reluctant to agree to our meeting. And who could blame her? Over a year after her son had been abducted and presumed murdered, why would she want to revisit the trauma?

When I finally pulled up at the address Kane had given me, my nerves were strung tight.

A little old house sagged dispiritedly in a yard overgrown with weeds. The lawn looked like it hadn't been mowed all summer and a torn screen hung from the front door like a grey flag of despair.

I moved cautiously up the cracked walk and mounted the peeling front steps to rap on the door above a grubby note that stated '*Doorbell broken. Knock.*'

No answer.

Dammit.

I checked my watch. Seven o'clock, as agreed. I knocked again.

After a third attempt I was turning away when the door

opened and a dead-eyed woman in a stained bathrobe regarded me without expression. Even from several feet away the stench of alcohol carried to my nose.

"Hi, Selena? I'm Aydan Kelly," I said, and offered my hand. "We spoke this afternoon..." No comprehension lightened her face, and I added, "About Peter's disappearance...?"

She shrugged and turned away, mumbling something that might have been 'Come in'.

The entrance opened onto a kitchen to the left and a living room to the right, and she shuffled into the living room to drop into a faded recliner. In the corner, the television blared some inane talk show. The sour scent of unwashed dishes emanated from mounds of pots in the kitchen sink.

Selena didn't invite me to sit, but I picked my way around the empty Doritos bags and rolls of fluffy dust on the floor and squeamishly relocated a mound of laundry to perch on the edge of the couch. At least the heap of clothes didn't smell. Probably clean laundry waiting to be folded and put away. I hoped.

I eased out a breath and began, "So Peter disappeared last year in June...?"

"No, he was murdered by my rat-bastard ex last June." Her words came out with weary venom. "I don't know why you're wasting your time talking to me. I don't know a damn thing except my only kid is dead and that asshole isn't convicted yet. I'm going to live exactly long enough to watch him get sentenced and then I'm going to slit my fucking wrists." She gave me a baleful bloodshot glare. "And don't hand me any bullshit about how I've got so much to live for. Without Peter I've got nothing!"

She reached down beside the recliner and extracted a

half-empty vodka bottle from the heap of crumpled fast-food wrappers. Noting the size of her gulp, I decided to ask my questions fast while she was still capable of replying.

"I'm sorry to make you go through it again," I began. "But five other boys his age have been abducted and we think it might be... a serial killer." I hesitated to speak the words, but Selena didn't react.

"I don't give a shit," she mumbled, her words slurred from what had undoubtedly been the first half of the bottle. "Peter's dead. Nothing's going to bring him back."

"But I thought you wanted to see his killer convicted," I argued. "What if it turns out it wasn't your ex at all?"

"Oh, it was him, all right." She slugged more vodka. "They found Peter's blood on his shoe. Him and his bullshit about how I couldn't raise Peter right 'cause I'm only a woman. So he took him away from me. Took him out in the woods and murdered him and got rid of his body so I couldn't even say goodbye..."

Tears leaked down her cheeks and she took another savage swig. "Everything. He took everything I had. Peter. Lost my job 'cause I couldn't get my shit together. Now I'm gonna lose my house. He shoulda jusht... just killed me, too..."

Sickness filled my soul as I looked around at the devastation of her life. Under the patina of dirt and despair, heartbreaking glimpses of a happier time shone through. Delicate watercolours on the walls; a cabinet displaying pieces of fine china through the dusty glass; colourful plant pots that must have once housed cherished greenery instead of the withered sticks that remained. The only clean area was a small table with two candles flanking a framed photo of a grinning freckle-faced child that could only be Peter.

"But Peter loved you," I said softly. "Wouldn't he want you to-"

"Peter doesn't want anything 'cause Peter's fuckin' *dead!*" She lurched to her feet and the vodka bottle described a dangerous arc toward the door, its contents sloshing. "Get out."

"But, Selena..."

"Out! Get the hell outta here." She advanced unsteadily, scowling through the tears that still trickled down her cheeks. Her hand shifted to a white-knuckled grip on the bottle's neck, and I took the hint.

Backing toward the door, I tried again. "But you might be able to help the other boys..."

"I look like I give a shit about any other boys? I only give a shit about Peter, an' he's not coming back!" She swung inaccurately at me with the bottle. "An' don't you come back, either! Jusht leave me... Leeme..." Her arms fell to her sides and her chest heaved with sobs. "Alone..."

My heart breaking, I reached toward her but the threatening bottle swung again.

"Okay, I'm going. I'm so sorry for your loss..." I retreated and closed the door, the broken screen settling behind me with a flat slap of finality.

CHAPTER 27

Drained by the despair I'd left behind at Selena's little house, I steered my car toward Edmonton dreading my next interview. God, I was barely going to make it in time for my eight o'clock appointment. And I'd be lucky to get to Red Deer before ten PM, but at least the woman I'd spoken to there had assured me she'd be willing to talk to me at any time of the day or night.

I had to do better. I'd learned exactly nothing from Selena, and Kane was counting on me. I crossed my fingers for luck. Maybe Leila Hammond would be more help.

When I pressed the security button for her apartment, she answered immediately and buzzed me through the vestibule doors without hesitation.

By the time I had climbed the stairs to her second-floor apartment she was already hovering in her doorway, a thin strained-looking young woman with her ash-blonde hair scraped away from her face into a severe bun at the nape of her neck. The heat in the corridor was stifling, but she wore black leggings with ballet flats and a long-sleeved cotton sweater.

"I'm so glad you're here," she said, taking my hand in her ice-cold one to draw me into her apartment. "When it got past eight o'clock I was so afraid you weren't coming."

I followed her gesture to a wall clock that read precisely eight-oh-five, and apologized, "I'm sorry I'm late. I've had a lot of driving today and I wasn't sure how long it would take me."

"Oh, no, that's okay, it's fine! I didn't mean... I just meant I'm really glad you came..." She knotted her fingers together anxiously. "Would you like a glass of iced tea? Or Coke, I have Coke. Or Seven-Up or..."

She trailed off uncertainly, regarding me with wide hazel eyes, and I put on a smile. "Just a glass of water would be great. Thanks."

"Oh, of course! Please sit down, make yourself comfortable, I'll be right there..."

She hurried into the small kitchen alcove and I shucked off my runners and stepped into a tiny spotless living room. Two chairs and a loveseat, old but clean, were arranged at right angles. All the pictures were inexpensive but precisely level on the walls, the coffee tables worn but gleaming. A plastic bin of brightly-coloured toys was topped with a teddy bear, its arms open as if begging for a little boy's hug. My heartstrings quivered and I looked away.

As I took a seat in one of the chairs, Leila hurried in only to stop, holding the glass up critically to the light. "Oh, I'm sorry, there's a smudge on this one," she said. "I'm so sorry! I'll be right back with a clean one!"

"No, it's okay..." I began, but she had already vanished into the kitchen again, and the sounds of clinking glassware made me wonder if she was sorting through every glass she owned to find one that was pristine.

A few moments later she rounded the corner again, holding out a water glass with a smile. My fingers had almost closed around it when she snatched it back, eyeing me worriedly.

"I'm so sorry, I should have asked if you wanted ice…" she began.

"It's okay, just plain water is great," I soothed, holding out my hand for the glass. "Thank you. Why don't you sit down and let's talk."

"Oh, of course. Here. Sorry." She scurried over to the sofa and sat, drawing up her knees to hug them. That lasted only long enough for me take a sip of water and open my mouth to ask my first question before she sprang off the sofa again. "Oh, I'm sorry, I'll get you a coaster." She whisked off to the kitchen again and returned moments later with a coaster she aligned carefully with the edge of the table beside me.

"Thanks. Leila, what can you tell me about the day Ethan disappeared?" I asked before she could rush off on some other mission.

"I wrote down absolutely everything I could think of!" Off she went again, returning seconds later with several sheets of lined paper covered with neat round handwriting.

I skimmed her organized and detailed narrative while Leila fidgeted on the sofa across from me, picking nonexistent lint off her sweater and springing up to adjust the curtains by a quarter-inch before sitting again. Her written version matched the police report almost exactly, and I suppressed a sigh. Nothing new here.

When I looked up, her knees were clasped to her chest again, her knuckles whitening under the strain. "What do you think, Ms. Kelly? Do you think…" Her knuckles went even whiter and her lips trembled. "You said on the phone that somebody might have… taken… Ethan. Do you think…

there's... still hope?"

God, the poor kid. She was barely more than a child herself. Twenty-two according to the police report, so she'd been only sixteen when she gave birth to Ethan.

My throat tightened. More than anything I wanted to reassure her that everything would be all right, but the lie wouldn't leave my lips.

"I don't know," I said instead. "I guess as long as his body hasn't been found there's always some hope, but... after two and a half months..."

I trailed off as tears filled her eyes.

"I won't give up hope until I know for sure," she said firmly. Then her brave façade shattered and she dropped her forehead onto her knees with a cry so gut-wrenching that my heart stopped in my chest.

"Oh, God!" she cried. "It's all my fault! They were right; they were *all* right; I should have given him up for adoption but I loved him so much and I tried so hard..." She curled tighter into herself and I slid onto the loveseat beside her, wrapping my arms around her and rocking her while sobs tore her body.

"I thought I... c-could do it," she hiccupped between sobs. "I worked so hard... to make a good h-home for my baby boy... b-but I was... so stupid! If I wasn't so stupid... I wouldn't have let Rico take him camping... what kind of h-horrible mother... lets her baby go off alone..."

"Shhh, it's not your fault, you're not a bad mother," I comforted, but she was still weeping and choking out her self-hatred.

"...he was right, I d-didn't deserve Ethan... and I was b-bringing him up all wrong... I'm just a stupid loser... and I didn't know how to b-bring up any child let alone a boy... and

I should have stayed with Rico... then Ethan would have had a f-father... and I would have been there on that camping trip... it's all my f-fault..."

At last my shushing and rocking began to work, or maybe Leila was simply cried out. Trembling, she blotted her face with a tissue.

"I'm s-sorry," she quavered. "I'm such a loser."

"Leila, you're not a loser." I rubbed a soothing circle on her back. "This wasn't your fault. Kids go on camping trips perfectly safely all the time, and you had no way of knowing what would happen." I indicated the obsessively tidy apartment with a wave of my hand. "You've made a good home here. You're doing the best you can and nobody expects you to be perfect."

"B-but it wasn't good enough. I'm never good enough..."

"Who told you that?" I asked gently.

"Rico. My m-mom and dad..." She sniffled and blotted her eyes again. "They kicked me out... wh-when... I got pregnant. They said... I was just a stupid little whore. B-but I'd never even been with a guy before, it was my first time..."

Deep anger filled me, but I managed to keep my voice gentle and reassuring. "You're not stupid, I can tell by the way you write and talk. You're not a loser, and you're certainly not a whore. Those are vicious lies."

Her chin went up. "I never took anything from any of them. I worked two jobs and I got this apartment all by myself and I made a home for my baby... b-but Rico went to court to get access to Ethan because he's his biological father..." Her head fell to her drawn-up knees again. "Oh, God, I should have stayed with Rico; if I'd been camping with them he couldn't have lost Ethan!"

I rubbed more circles on her back. "If Rico was putting

you down all the time, then you did the right thing by making a life without him. That was the right choice for you, and the right choice for Ethan."

Leila shook her head without raising it from her knees, and I kept gently rubbing her back.

"Do you really believe he lost Ethan?" I asked. "He wouldn't... hurt Ethan, would he?"

"Oh, no!" Her head came up again, her reddened eyes wide with sincerity. "No! The police never charged him, and I just know Rico would never hurt Ethan. He was just... just... When he woke up and realized Ethan was gone he nearly went out of his mind, he felt so guilty! But he was so drunk..." She hesitated. "And probably stoned, but I didn't tell the police that. He passed out and when he woke up Ethan was gone."

"If he was a drunk and a stoner, why did the courts grant him access?" I demanded.

"Oh, he wasn't! Isn't. He just... I don't know why he got so drunk that night. I guess he was partying with the guys..."

My heart thudded into my ribs. "There was nothing in the police report about anybody else at the campsite."

"Oh... I thought he'd said some friends dropped by. But I'm probably wrong."

My cynical mind added, '...or if they brought drugs he might not have mentioned them in the police report', but I didn't speak the words aloud.

Leila regarded me uncertainly. "You have the police report? I thought you said you were a private detective."

Shit.

"Uh, no, I'm just helping a private detective. But he's been working with the police," I lied uncomfortably. "So he saw the reports."

"Oh, okay. Sorry, I got that wrong," she said, and then let out a tremulous sigh. "See? I can't even keep simple things straight. I'm such a lo-"

"You're not a loser," I interrupted. "It's normal to have trouble concentrating when you're this stressed. Have you been seeing a psychologist or a counsellor? Or is there somebody you trust that you can talk to?"

"Oh, no, I couldn't afford a psychologist."

She left the second question unanswered, and I filled in the blanks. Her shitbag parents and boyfriend had abandoned her, and worse, made her believe she deserved it.

And there was absolutely nothing I could do to help. That kind of destructive programming went far deeper than a few minutes of encouraging talk could cure.

I glanced at my wristwatch and sighed. "Leila..." I squeezed her shoulder. "I have to go. But you need to know that you're a good person. You're strong and brave and smart, and it was wrong of your parents and Rico to make you believe otherwise."

Pink rose in her pale cheeks, and she cast her gaze down. "Th-thanks. It's nice of you to say that. But-"

"No buts," I interrupted gently. "You're strong and brave and smart, period. I know psychologists are expensive, but you're going through a really tough time and you shouldn't have to do it alone..."

I fought down the urge to tell her to call me if she needed to talk. What number could I give her? And what would happen if she tried to call and I didn't answer because I was undercover as an arms dealer?

"Call the Crisis Line," I said instead. "Just tell them what you're going through and talk to them for a few minutes. Will you do that?"

"Oh, no, I wouldn't want to bother anybody..."

"You're not bothering them. That's what they're there for." I gently raised her chin to look into her eyes. "Leila, will you promise me you'll just give them a call? I don't want you to have to deal with this all alone."

Tears gathered in her eyes and she blinked them away. "Okay. I promise."

"Thanks." I gave her a quick one-armed hug. "You're tough. You're going to get through this."

"Th-thanks."

I rose and she trailed me to the door. When I straightened from tying my shoes, she threw her arms around me.

"Thanks, Ms. Kelly," she whispered. "I'm going to try to be strong."

"It's just Aydan." I hugged her in return. "And you're already strong."

CHAPTER 28

It took nearly the whole ninety-minute drive down to Red Deer for me to regain enough detachment to examine what I'd learned so far. God, those two short interviews had been gut-wrenching, and I was only witnessing the mothers' anguish second-hand. They were living it, twenty-four hours a day with no respite.

And so were Kane and Alicia.

I shuddered and concentrated on following the directions to Willa Buxton's house.

It was after ten PM when I rang the doorbell of a tidy semi-detached two-storey in a neighbourhood where the landscaping featured children's bicycles on the lawns and basketball hoops in the driveways.

The plump thirtyish woman who answered the door greeted me with a smile almost as luminous as Moonbeam's, but her blue eyes were bracketed by lines of patient sorrow. The effect was eerily similar to Jesus's expression in the large painting on the wall behind her.

"Willa Buxton?" I asked at the same time as she inquired, "Aydan Kelly?"

We both laughed, and she reached out a welcoming hand. "Well, now that we know who we are, please come in."

"I'm sorry to bother you so late..." I began as I stepped into the vestibule and shed my shoes.

"No, it's no bother at all." Her smile turned bittersweet. "I rarely go to bed before midnight. I sleep better when I'm exhausted. Please come in and sit down."

She ushered me into a tidy pink living room decorated with articles of faith ranging from needlepointed scripture verses to a large and lugubrious wood carving of a haggard Jesus nailed to the cross. His hollow mournful eyes reproached me, and I looked away with relief when Willa asked, "Would you like a cup of tea?"

"Thank you, that would nice," I agreed, then promptly regretted my choice when she vanished to the kitchen, leaving me in a staring match with Jesus.

He won. By the time Willa returned, my gaze was fixed on my curling toes.

"Now, you said you were investigating the disappearance of several boys the same age as my Noah," she began briskly, saving me the awkwardness of broaching the topic. "How may I help you?"

I sipped the hot tea, wishing I could take comfort from it. "Would you please tell me exactly what happened? Any little detail might be important, so please say anything at all that comes to your mind, no matter how minor it seems."

"Certainly." She leaned back in her chair and took a pensive sip of tea as if gathering her thoughts. Then she laid out a detailed description of everything that had happened when her son disappeared. It all matched the police report, and I sighed. Nothing new here, either.

"So... how long had you and your ex been apart when this happened?" I asked. "Were you on good terms?"

"Oh, yes. We divorced about a year before Noah... went

missing. So almost two years ago now. We..." Willa's gaze wavered. "We... had our differences, but we parted amicably enough." Her chin came up, her blue gaze direct. "Dirk is a good man. An honest man. I was glad he stayed involved with Noah, and the camping trip was my idea. He could never have harmed Noah. The murder charge against him is wrong."

There it was again. The same unshakeable belief that both Leila and Alicia shared.

"How can you be so sure?" I asked. "Didn't the police find Noah's blood on his sleeping bag?"

"Yes, but only a small smear. Noah was subject to nosebleeds, so that's probably what happened. We explained that to the police but they... wouldn't listen." She leaned forward, clasping her teacup in both hands. "And there's more. Dirk believes that he was drugged. He can't remember anything from that night. He remembers putting Noah to bed and then sitting by the campfire for a while..."

"Was he drinking?" I interrupted.

"No. Dirk is AA. He's been clean and sober for nine years. He drank some soda, then began to feel very tired and went into the tent and fell asleep. When he woke up in the morning, Noah was gone. He called the police immediately and began searching, but... a few days later they arrested him. He was so frantic... we both were..."

Her voice trailed off in a quaver and she blinked rapidly for a moment, reaching over to touch her fingertips to the rosary that lay on the table beside her. Then she swallowed some tea and went on, her voice level.

"He was so distraught over Noah that he didn't even think to tell the police about the drugged sensation until after they charged him. Then when he did bring it up, of course it looked as though he was trying to cover himself. The police did a drug test at his request, but it came back negative. According to the internet, drugs like Rohypnol cause similar symptoms to what Dirk experienced, but they are undetectable within a day and he wasn't tested until nearly a week later."

"So he thinks somebody drugged him and took Noah, but he doesn't remember anybody else being there."

"Yes." Willa clutched her teacup. "And that's what I think, too. That's why I was so eager to talk to you when you called. It's..." She swallowed, blinking rapidly. "It's too late for Noah..." She drew a breath and straightened her spine. "It's been a year. Whether he was kidnapped or simply wandered away and got lost in the woods, he's almost certainly dead by now. And I believe he's in a better place. He's safe and loved in the arms of Jesus, far beyond any love Dirk or I could offer. But Dirk doesn't deserve to go to prison. And if a serial killer is preying on young boys, we need to do everything we can to stop him."

"Tell me more about Dirk," I prompted. "What kind of man is he? Does he have a lot of friends? Where does he go and what does he do for recreation? Does he belong to any clubs? Who might want to hurt him? Or hurt you? Tell me everything you can think of."

"Oh..." she said breathlessly. "You... actually believe me?"

"Yes."

"Oh, praise the Lord!" Unshed tears glittered in her eyes. "Thank you, thank you!" She drew a deep breath. "All right. Dirk. He's... stubborn. Set in his ways. He can be... rather... narrow-minded. Very traditional in his views on marriage. That's..." She dropped her gaze to study her teacup. "That's actually what caused our divorce. I was a lapsed Catholic, while he was quite devout. That caused... friction... in a number of areas. Like birth control..."

A tear trickled down her cheek and she wiped it away as though wiping away tears was as much a reflex as breathing.

"If only I hadn't been so stubborn," she whispered. "Noah was our only child. Not that any other child could ever replace him, but..."

She shook herself back to the present and met my gaze again. "Our views on child-rearing and roles within a marriage were different, too. I know..." She raised a guilty gaze to the accusing Jesus. "I know the Bible says wives should submit to their husbands, but... I've never believed that was literal, and I didn't want to raise Noah to believe that, either. Dirk... thought the husband should be head of the household and have the final authority in everything. So... after many, many arguments, I filed for divorce. He was scandalized, of course."

Willa turned the cup around and around in her hands, studying it as though she'd never seen it before. "But in the end he agreed to an annulment and divorce. He's a good man. He is." She shook her head. "But when Noah was taken it was like a punishment from God. I went back to the church. Prayed as I'd never prayed before, shamelessly bargained and pleaded, but..."

She sighed and reached for the rosary. "Every day I do penance."

I swallowed the lump in my throat. "I don't believe God punishes people that way."

She met my gaze with those sad patient eyes. "I didn't used to believe it, either." Then she straightened, visibly putting aside her sorrow. "But you asked about Dirk and his habits and friends, not my crisis of faith. Let me see, where shall I start..."

Half an hour later I knew more about Dirk than I did about myself, and none of it seemed useful. No known enemies, no bad habits, no unusual behaviour before Noah disappeared. Exhaustion dragged at my body and a tension headache thumped spitefully at the base of my skull.

When Willa ran out of information at last, I extracted a promise from her to call if she thought of anything else and staggered back to my car.

Falling into the driver's seat, I checked my watch and groaned. After eleven, and I still had a two-hour drive to get home.

I punched Kane's number into one of the burner phones, pressed the speaker button, and started driving.

Kane answered on the second ring with a terse, "Kane."

"Hi, it's Aydan," I said.

"Thank God." His words came out on a rush of breath, and he added in a muffled voice as if talking over his shoulder to Hellhound, "It's Aydan." Returning to regular volume, he said, "We've been trying to reach you since six."

My heart sank. "Shit, I'm sorry! I couldn't carry my phone because I, um... had a situation..." I got to the point. "What's wrong?"

"Nothing; and what kind of situation? Are you safe?"

"I'm fine. What do you mean, nothing? Why were you trying to call me?"

"Hellhound had some questions for Willa Buxton after he'd finished interviewing her ex."

"Damn. I just left there, but I can turn around. She won't be in bed yet."

An involuntary shudder shook me. She still had an hour

to go under the wooden gaze of her vengeful God.

I braked and took the next right turn. "What were his questions?"

"Has Buxton been clean and sober for nine years; did Noah get nosebleeds frequently; does Mrs. Buxton think he could have harmed Noah; and did she agree to the camping trip?"

"Yes, yes, no, and yes. The camping trip was actually her idea."

"Good, that's all we needed then."

"Oh." I braked again and pulled an illegal U-turn in the middle of the deserted residential street to get back to the main road. "So Buxton told Hellhound the story about how he thought he'd been drugged?"

"Yes. If not for the consistency with all the other ex's stories, I'd say it was a classic case of a guilty man trying to weasel out of charges. But under the circumstances... hold on, I'm going to put you on speaker so Hellhound can hear."

A moment later Hellhound's gravelly voice came faintly over the speaker. "Hey, darlin'. Can ya hear me?"

"Hi, Arnie. Yes, I can hear you fine. So were all the exes drunk when the boys were abducted?"

"Yeah. 'Cept Dirk Buxton. He swears he doesn't drink anymore, an' somebody musta been watchin' him an' drugged his soda when he went to take a leak. An' when I leaned on that little punk Rico he admitted he was stoned fuckin' stupid that night, but I didn't get a killer vibe off him. He was really broken up about losin' Ethan."

"And Murphy was drunk, too," I said thoughtfully.

"Yes." Kane sighed. "There's something else that's been nagging at me about Murphy, though."

"What?" I turned onto the main highway and

accelerated toward home.

"His footprints in the middle of the road."

I stifled a yawn of pure fatigue. "What about them?"

"They went up to his campsite, but there's no trace of them coming down. They started at that spot in the middle of the road. And the autopsy report showed his feet were clean."

"What?" I sat up straighter in my seat, my exhaustion temporarily forgotten. "So... he got out of a vehicle in the middle of the road and then walked back to his campsite? But if somebody else was driving him, why didn't they drop him off at his campsite? And if there was no dirt on his feet, then the shoeless footprint couldn't have been his. But how could his feet be completely clean? If he ran from his tent to his truck without his boots, there should have been dust on his feet."

"That would mean the shoeless footprint definitely belonged to someone else, but I'm not sure that proves anything," Kane agreed. "It might have been someone who camped there earlier. But the footprints in the road definitely imply that someone else was there. Someone Murphy knew."

"So we need to talk to all the exes and get the names of all their friends and see if there's any overlap," I deduced.

"Already done," Hellhound rasped. "No overlaps. All a' them 'cept Dirk Buxton had friends partyin' with 'em that night, but the cops already checked out all the friends an' eliminated 'em as suspects."

"Shit. Even Rico's friends?"

Hellhound chuckled. "He didn't tell the cops about his buddies, but he told me." A smile twitched my lips at the thought of Hellhound's style of persuasion, but my amusement faded quickly as he went on, "I passed their names on to the cops, but I checked 'em out myself an' we're prob'ly barkin' up the wrong tree there. None a' those little shitweasels fit the type."

"Do we have a 'type'?" I asked.

"We have some guesses," Kane replied. "Since no bodies have been found, our killer is likely organized and intelligent. He plans his attacks in advance and removes the victims to kill them and dispose of their bodies elsewhere." His voice wavered slightly on the word 'kill', and he cleared his throat before adding, "That's why there may still be hope for Daniel..."

There was a moment of silence on the line and I imagined him gathering his composure. When he spoke again his voice was flat and emotionless.

"There are two basic types of serial killers. The mission-based type kills his victims almost immediately. If that's the case Daniel is dead, and likely has been since shortly after he was abducted. But..."

He swallowed before continuing, "...the other type gains gratification from power and control, or has some psychosis that motivates him to prolong the lives of his victims, usually while torturing them. He may keep his victims alive for quite some time before ultimately killing them."

Nausea choked me.

Not Daniel. I couldn't think of those chubby cheeks streaked with tears, that innocent laughter shattered into screams and suffering.

I gulped air. In through the mouth, out through the nose...

Don't throw up.

Do *not* throw up.

CHAPTER 29

Somehow Kane was still holding onto his composure. "Female serial killers are relatively rare so that's why I'm using the male pronoun," he went on, his clinical tone almost completely concealing the torment I knew raged beneath his controlled voice. "Though... since the victims are children, our killer might be a woman; maybe someone who gains a sense of power from taking a child away from a man, particularly a man who's an ex-husband or ex-boyfriend rather than a live-in father in a family unit."

I eased my rigid grip on the steering wheel and took another breath to tamp down my nausea. If Kane was managing to hold his emotions together, I had to do the same.

"That makes sense..." I began, but he wasn't finished.

"Or it's a man who's taking a child away from a single woman," he added. "To exert power over her, or cause her suffering, or because he believes she's unworthy-"

"Hang on!" I interrupted. "All three of the women I interviewed said something like, 'he didn't think I was bringing my son up right'. And that's what Alicia said about Murphy, too. In fact, Selena even took it a step farther. She said, 'So he took him away from me'."

Kane's sharp intake of breath sounded clearly through the phone. "You're right. I didn't realize it until you said it, but that's what the mothers I interviewed today said, too."

"Makes sense, but our killer ain't one a' the exes," Hellhound put in. "Two a' them were in jail an' the rest had alibis. So it's gotta be somebody that knows all the exes, or all the moms. An' we've already looked at the friends a' the exes."

"That's it!" Kane exclaimed. "A mutual friend of the mothers. Maybe a woman who can't have children of her own, or who lost a child through death or divorce. She believes these single mothers don't deserve a child if she can't have one..."

"But then why would she grab 'em from the exes?" Hellhound objected. "Why not grab 'em right from the moms?"

"Our killer must have lost access to her own child through divorce," Kane said. "Her son was 'taken away' by her ex, so she 'takes away' these boys from their mothers' exes."

"But why?" I demanded. "If she'd lost her own child, why would she make another woman live through that hell?"

"Remember, serial killers are often disassociated to the point that they don't even consider other people to be human beings. Or she may believe she's rescuing these children from a fate worse than death; that she's doing them a favour by killing them. That might be the case if she or her child had been abused by her ex."

"So we're looking for a woman who lost her child to an abusive ex," I said slowly. "Maybe through divorce, or maybe her ex killed the child. And if her ex was one of those male-supremacy guys, she'd 'rescue' kids who are with a guy like her ex. But why always take them from a camping trip?"

"Shit." Hellhound's rasp took over the line again. "I just realized somethin' else. They were all on campin' trips, but none a' them were in campgrounds. They all disappeared from campsites out on crown land. So there wouldn't be any witnesses."

"Goddammit!" Kane swore again. "So the killer could grab the child and disappear in any direction through the woods!"

"Maybe that's why the boys were all in the five to six age range." My voice came out sounding as hollow as my heart felt. "Easier to carry. They were probably drugged, too."

"Probably..." Kane agreed. "Wait a minute..." His voice trailed off.

He was silent for so long that I asked, "Are you still there?"

"Yes." Sudden intensity blazed into his voice. "Dammit! Murphy was murdered!"

"*What?*" Hellhound and I chorused in unison.

"It's the only thing that makes sense! He caught the killer in the act and fought to save Daniel. And he lost."

"Whoa, whoa, start at the beginnin'!" Hellhound demanded. "How d'ya figure that?"

"Think about it!" Kane urged. "Murphy and Daniel are camping as planned, and Murphy puts Daniel to bed. Then the killer shows up, someone Murphy knows. They drink. The killer encourages Murphy to overindulge, but for some reason he's in a hurry and doesn't wait for Murphy to pass out the way he waited for the others..."

"Hang on, the killer's a 'he' now?" I interrupted.

"Yes, I think so. Murphy realized the killer was trying to take Daniel, and they fought. That's why Murphy's blood was on his boots. The killer hit him a couple of times in the face, then snapped his neck. Daniel must have already been drugged by then, so the killer dragged Murphy's body into the passenger seat of his truck, then removed Murphy's boots and put them on himself. Then he drove Murphy's truck down the hill, put it in park long enough to get out and drag Murphy into the driver's seat..."

"The patch of bootprints in the middle a' the road," Hellhound put in. "That wasn't Murphy talkin' to somebody, it was the killer standin' there while he dragged Murphy's body over behind the wheel. An' then all he hadta do was pop it into drive an' let it coast."

"Yes. Which is why the truck wasn't going very fast when it went over," Kane agreed. "Then the killer walked back up the hill to the campsite and walked over all the other prints and marks in the campsite to make it look as though Murphy had been the only one there..."

"And then took off the boots, left them outside the tent, and left in his sock feet carrying Daniel," I finished. "That's why Murphy's feet were clean; they never touched the ground. And our guy has the same size feet."

"Yes. The killer must have parked nearby, maybe on a quad. There were quad tracks all through that area. Mayweather needs to look at the site again. I'll call him right away..."

"Wait!" I interrupted. "What are you going to tell him? Your scenario is based on Murphy's clean feet in an autopsy report that you've never seen."

"I don't need to mention that," Kane said impatiently. "I'll lay out the scenario as a hunch based on the footprints, and if he's any kind of a cop at all he'll make the connection himself. I'll call you right back. Give me your number."

"Hang on." I pulled over so I could check the number on the secured phone. Seconds after I'd recited it to Kane, the line went dead in my ear.

Parked by the side of the road, I stared anxiously at the phone, willing it to ring. Had Kane simply hung up on me after he had the details he needed, or had something gone wrong?

I punched in his number again, but the line rang busy.

Okay, he was talking to Mayweather.

God, I hoped he was talking to Mayweather.

I was on the verge of dialling Arnie's cell phone when the phone vibrated. When I answered, Kane's voice made me breathe a sigh of relief.

"I talked to Mayweather," he said. "The RCMP will send someone out to the site tonight to make sure no more evidence is destroyed, and tomorrow at first light they'll examine it again."

"Good." Limp with exhaustion, I put the car into gear and pulled back onto the highway. "So now we need to figure out who this guy is. What else did you learn from your interviews?"

Kane, Hellhound, and I hashed over the details of our respective interviews for the next hour and a half while I drove through the moonlit darkness toward home. At last I heaved a deep sigh and scrubbed at my tired eyes.

"Well, guys, I can't think of anything else, can you?" I asked.

After a short hesitation, Hellhound rasped, "Nah," and Kane agreed, "No. So we'll revisit the friends of the suspects and start looking at friends of the mothers tomorrow, looking for a strong man with size ten feet who knows how to kill a man by breaking his neck. Likely military, or a martial artist. That also fits the male-serial-killer profile."

I swallowed hard before replying, "Okay. Do you want me to drive up to see the three moms after work tomorrow?"

"No, that's all right..."

The sound of Hellhound yawning in the background momentarily drowned Kane out, and I glanced at my dashboard clock. God, nearly one AM.

A moment later Kane continued, "We'll phone them. The face-to-face interviews were valuable when we weren't sure what we were looking for, but for specifics like this a phone call is just as good."

"Okay." I stifled a yawn and blinked away the involuntary tears. "Try Selena around ten or eleven in the morning. By then her hangover might not be too bad, but she shouldn't be drunk all over again."

"All right. Talk to you tomorrow," Kane said.

"G'night, darlin'," Hellhound added, and I wished them both a good night and hung up just as the turnoff to my farm came into view in the headlights.

Thank God. At least our brainstorming session had kept me awake for the long drive. Otherwise I'd have fallen asleep by the side of the road, or worse, taken a permanent dirt nap after falling asleep at the wheel.

I turned off toward the farm, the crunch of gravel under my tires sounding comfortingly like home and bed.

Damn, I hoped Kane had taken his sleeping pills along to Calgary. And I hoped he took them.

And I hoped... what the hell?

I squinted at a glint in the vicinity of my driveway, but a dip in the road hid it from view. A mile closer I finally got a clear view and swore as my pulse quickened. Even in the moonlight I recognized that SUV.

Reaching down, I freed my Glock from my ankle holster and tucked it into my waistband, then awkwardly wrestled my sweater on. It fell past my waist, hiding the gun just as I arrived at my driveway and nosed in beside the SUV.

A single dark silhouette sat motionless in the SUV's driver's seat. My heart hitched up into my throat and I drew a deep calming breath. Labelle didn't have any reason to kill me.

At least as far I knew...

I swallowed hard, wishing I had a bulletproof vest.

"Get out of the damn car," I said aloud. "If he was going to shoot you he'd have done it already, dipshit."

Taking another breath so deep my head spun, I eased the car door open and strolled toward my gate. I was Arlene Widdenback, badass arms dealer. Let him think I wasn't the least bit worried by his presence.

The sound of a vehicle door opening made me twitch a glance over my shoulder. In the reflected glow of my headlights, I recognized my follower from Innisfail.

Face and voice expressionless, he said, "Mr. Labelle wants a meeting."

I blew out a breath that was mostly fear, hoping it sounded like annoyance. "It's the middle of the fucking night. Tell him to call me tomorrow and we'll set something up."

"Mr. Labelle tried to call you all day and you didn't return his calls. Mr. Labelle wants a meeting," he repeated. "Now." He swung his hand up from beside his leg and moonlight silvered the gun in his grip.

"Whoa, hang on, take it easy!" I exclaimed, half-turning and throwing out my left hand in a 'stop' gesture that I hoped would distract him from what my right hand was doing.

It worked.

I shot from the hip into the centre of his body mass. He fell backward, his weapon discharging with a hellish bang and bright muzzle flash. A ricochet whined off into the night. Jerking my Glock up, I reflexively pumped a second bullet into his head.

He went still.

I shuddered as queasiness climbed my throat. God, I would never get used to the horrible relaxation of taut muscles into sudden death. It wouldn't be so bad if they went instantly limp like they did in the movies, but that couple of seconds when the brain ceased to provide instructions and the last electrical impulses diminished to nothing...

I shuddered again and turned away, returning my Glock to my waistband and unconsciously wiping my palm on my jeans.

Another day, another nightmare.

At least this time I was prepared, thanks to the admonitions of the cleanup crew a few months ago. And I needed to hide this body, fast. Nobody would normally drive this road at night, but I didn't dare count on that.

Popping my trunk open, I pulled out nitrile gloves, disposable coveralls, and shoe covers. Moments later I was dressed for action, and I sidestepped gingerly past the corpse to reach into the SUV and open the rear hatch. Dragging the floppy body around and hoisting it inside took several minutes of sweat-popping effort and violent swearing, but at last I completed the task, trembling with adrenaline and exertion.

When the body was safely inside, I took off my protective gear and balled it up to wipe the smears of blood off the back bumper, then pitched the clothing in on top of the body and closed the rear hatch.

Tottering back to my own car, I extracted a secured phone and pressed the speed dial button.

CHAPTER 30

Stemp answered on the first ring as always, and I closed my eyes in silent gratitude as I quavered, "It's Aydan. I need a cleanup crew at my gate. A silver SUV, and I put the body in the back. There's blood on the gravel..."

Glancing over at it, I hesitated, then leaned closer to examine my car.

"...Shit. And a bullet hole in my car." I heaved a sigh. "Never mind about that, I'll make it look as though I ran into something. I just need to be rid of this body and vehicle."

A cavernous yawn nearly ripped my face off, and violent shivers of adrenaline and fatigue seized me. The nighttime chill penetrated my sweat-damp clothes, and my shivering intensified.

I added, "I'm going to b-bed. Tell them not to w-wake me."

"What about your neighbour?" Stemp demanded. "Do you need a cover story?"

"Nope." Another yawn escaped and I wrapped my free arm around myself in a futile attempt to stop shivering. "Tom's g-gone for the week. He's up by Camrose doing some custom b-baling and the hired man is only there in the daytime to look after his livestock. Nobody b-but me out here."

"Very well. The cleanup crew is on the way." I was just saying 'thanks' when he added, "Were you working on Kane's case today?"

I was too exhausted to think of a plausible lie, so I quietly pressed the disconnect button and pitched the phone onto the driver's seat of the SUV.

Then I drove through the gate, locked it behind me, and retreated to my garage. A couple of passes with my crowbar generated a realistic-looking scratch and crease leading to the bullet hole in the passenger door. Using the last of the strength in my trembling arms, I wedged the crowbar into the hole to distort it as though I'd run into something sharp. Thank God the bullet had ricocheted off instead of punching through into the passenger compartment.

That accomplished, I quivered into the house. Its stuffy heat enveloped me but my shivering didn't abate. I hurriedly reset my security alarm before tottering to the basement to slide through the concealed panel into my secret room. Stretched out on the narrow cot, I pulled my sleeping bag up around my ears and lay shivering so hard the cot vibrated under me.

Damn, I should have made myself a hot drink. Shock, fatigue, adrenaline. Bad combination. I hugged the sleeping bag tighter around myself, unwilling to leave its warmth even for the temptation of hot chocolate.

When my wrist monitor vibrated I squinted at the glow of the tiny screen in the darkness. A panel van was parked at my gate, and I switched to full-video mode to watch the two bulky figures working at the gravel. Then one climbed into the panel van and the other into the SUV, and a few minutes later they drove away leaving nothing but moonlight and shadows.

Thank you, cleanup crew. I'd better make them some more chocolate chip cookies.

I toggled off the display and curled into a quivering ball, pulling the sleeping bag over my head.

I woke sweaty and disoriented, my heart leaping into a rapid rhythm at the profound darkness that enclosed me. A moment later memory returned, and I pressed the button to illuminate the screen of my wristwatch.

"Shit!"   I sprang off the cot to push through the concealed panel.

Stumbling out into my basement, I hurried for the stairs. At the top I hesitated, my mind lurching groggily from one thought to the next.

I was still wearing my clothes from yesterday. I needed a shower. I needed breakfast. I needed to call Sirius and explain why it was after ten AM and I hadn't showed up or called. I needed... a brain, dammit!

"Come on, get with the program!" I growled. I shook my head vigorously and slapped my cheeks a couple of times, rattling my brain into action.

Okay, call Sirius first.

Hurrying over to the phone, I swore at the sight of my answering machine's blinking light. A glance at my cell phone's voicemail told the same story.

Hell. I'd better listen to my messages first so I knew exactly how big a shitstorm was headed my way.

Vibrating with nerves, I scrolled through my cell phone's missed call records. Three calls from Labelle, two from Kane, one each from Spider and Lola, two from Moonbeam, and a 'call home' text from Stemp last night around one-thirty AM. Right after I'd hung up on him. Shit, he was going to be pissed.

Okay, do the worst first. I grabbed a secured phone and pressed the speed dial, wincing.

When Stemp's brusque answer crackled over the line, I squeezed my eyes closed and said, "It's Aydan. I'm sorry I didn't get your message last night, and I slept in this morning. I'll be in as soon as I can."

"When our call was cut off last night, I was unsure whether to be concerned." If he'd been anybody else, the accusation would have come through loud and clear. Fortunately he was in robot-mode and the words came out as a simple statement.

"Sorry," I apologized again, and crossed my fingers to dilute my imminent lie. "I didn't realize we got cut off last night. I thought we were done so I hung up. And I didn't have my cell phone with me because I was concentrating on losing my tail yesterday and I didn't want Labelle to be able to track me by my phone."

"I see." Before I could analyze his lack of intonation, Stemp added, "What time do you expect to arrive at Sirius today?"

"Um..." I did a rapid mental calculation. "I'll be there in forty-five minutes."

"Report to my office as soon as you arrive." He hung up.

Shit.

Pacing back and forth across my kitchen floor, I listened to the rest of my messages. Labelle wanted a meeting. Urgently.

I snorted. No kidding.

Kane's attempts to reach me were old news, too. Moonbeam's first message advised me in her usual pleasant tones that Spider and Linda had kindly invited Karma and her to stay at their home so I could reach them there. I breathed a thankful sigh. Live-in bodyguards for Spider and Linda. Perfect.

My relief was cut short when Moonbeam's next message played. Its words were benign, but there was no mistaking the edge of tension in her soft voice, and she had called at five AM this morning. "Storm Cloud Dancer, please call me on my cellular at your earliest convenience. I'd like to meet you for lunch today."

Uh-oh.

Spider's message shed an unpleasantly clear light on the reason for Moonbeam's call. His voice trembled, and his attempt at a light tone fell completely flat. "Hey, Aydan, it's Spider. Sorry to bother you, but Linda and I were wondering if we could ask you a huge, huge favour. If... if it's not too much trouble... could we, um... have our wedding reception at your farm? I'm sorry, I know it's really short notice, but, um... the community hall burned down last night..."

My gut clenched while he finished the message with a request to call him as soon as possible. This was far too much coincidence. Somebody was intent on preventing Spider and Linda's wedding, and their tactics had just escalated to arson.

Damn it to hell!

Lola's message echoed the news about the hall and the request to call her as soon as possible.

The messages on my home phone were duplicates of the ones on my cell, and I hurriedly dialled Moonbeam's number. Like her son, she answered on the first ring, and I got straight to the point.

"I'm going to ask Spider and Linda to come and stay at the farm until their wedding. They'll be safer here. If you can come, too..."

"Of course," Moonbeam interrupted.

"Great..." I hesitated, but decided not to go into details over the phone. "We can talk at lunch," I finished. "What time do you want to meet?"

"Whenever you're available, dear. I'm minutes away from everything in town, so just call me with the place and time."

"Thank you," I said with deepest sincerity.

My next call was to Spider, who answered on the first ring, too.

"Hi, Spider," I greeted him. "How are you doing?"

"I... I'm starting to buy into Linda's worries," he admitted hesitantly. "I mean, we don't know yet whether the fire was arson; after all, it was an old building and the wiring might not have been great, but still... Either we're having the worst run of bad luck ever, or..."

"Yeah," I agreed. "I want you and Linda to come and stay at the farm. If anybody asks, tell them it's so you can work on decorating for the reception. But at least with my perimeter cameras we'll have advance warning if any other 'coincidences' are headed your way."

His breath of relief floated over the line. "Thanks, Aydan. That would really be a load off our minds. I'll tell Linda to start packing- ...oh!"

"What?" I snapped, my heart thudding.

"Sorry, nothing bad, I was just thinking of Moonbeam Meadow Sky and Karma Wolf Song. We invited them to stay at our place so we can't really leave..."

"No problem; they're coming, too," I assured him. "I invited them already."

"Perfect. Thanks, Aydan. When do you want us?"

"Whenever you can come. I'll be at Sirius in half an hour, so just stop by the office and I'll give you my spare key."

Spider and I said our goodbyes and hung up, and I hurried to the bathroom for the world's fastest shower, cheerfully ignoring Frederick Labelle's demanding messages.

A few minutes later I was clean, dressed, and chewing a too-large mouthful of cereal bar while I gathered my things together and rolled the laser flashlight into my sweater for its return trip to Sirius Dynamics.

I was halfway out the door when I remembered that Kane and Hellhound might need a private conversation with me today. Ducking back into the house, I grabbed a spare secured phone and noted its number, then dialled Kane.

His line rang busy, and I swore and dialled Arnie's cell instead. It went straight to voicemail.

Of course, they'd both be doing phone interviews today.

I left a brief message, and headed for the door.

The drive to Silverside gave me ample time to worry about my upcoming meeting with Stemp but not quite enough time to come up with satisfactory answers to his potential questions. Lying about yesterday's interviews with the moms seemed like a supremely bad idea. After all, Stemp had that high-tech lie detector.

And maybe he had a built-in lie detector, too. Moonbeam's voice echoed in my mind: 'Cosmic River Stone can see them, too'.

I couldn't quite believe in auras, but *something* made Moonbeam spookily accurate in her 'readings'. If Stemp had any of that talent, whatever it was, that might be why it sometimes seemed as though he was looking right through me. The thought made my skin crawl.

But telling him the truth didn't seem like a much better option, considering I'd been ignoring his direct order.

God, what if the chain of command thought this was a serious enough breach of discipline to warrant locking me up?

I wrestled with my worries all the way to the Sirius parking lot without coming to a satisfactory decision. When I got out of my car, the slam of my door sounded like a drumbeat for my march to the executioner.

CHAPTER 31

When I tapped on the frame of Stemp's office door, my heart tapped an equally rapid rhythm inside my chest.

Stemp looked up from his computer with his usual impenetrable expression and nodded me into the chair in front of his desk. "Close the door," he said as I moved to obey.

Shit.

I turned back and closed the door behind me, then perched nervously on the edge of the chair before gathering my composure and leaning back to fake relaxation.

He eyed me in silence.

Bastard. Trying to make me nervous enough to blurt something out. He needn't have bothered. I was already nervous as hell.

After a few long moments I raised an eyebrow, doing my best emotionless-Spock imitation.

The corner of his mouth quirked in response, but he said nothing.

I hesitated on the verge of breaking the silence, but the mule-stubborn part of my personality stomped its hooves and brayed.

You want to play games? Fine. Asshole.

I gave him a mouth-quirk of my own and leaned back in my chair, pulling my phone out of my waist pouch. Stretching out my legs, I brought up Solitaire and began a game.

With my gaze focused on the small screen, I monitored Stemp's motionless form in my peripheral vision. He likely wouldn't get pissed off and shoot me just for the hell of it.

But I wasn't certain about that.

A few minutes later I ran out of moves and started a new game. The silence was a palpable presence, pressurizing the office until a single whisper would explode it. Nervy pinpricks scuttled down my spine like an army of ants and it took every ounce of my self-control to suppress the need to twitch and squirm.

I was an idiot. Nobody could ever win a battle of wills with Stemp. He'd sit there without moving or speaking for hours if necessary, until I went absolutely screaming batshit or peed my pants. Or both.

As if in response, my bladder gave an anxious twitch.

Goddammit, I wasn't going to let him win.

I finished my Solitaire game and stowed my phone in my waist pouch with unhurried movements, hoping he couldn't see my fingers quivering. Then I yawned, stretched, and rose to head for the door.

I honestly thought he was going to let me leave without saying a single word. My hand was on the doorknob; the door halfway open before he spoke.

"Where are you going?"

I managed not to flinch. Turning with what I hoped was an unreadable expression, I said, "Ladies' room. I need to pee."

"Ah." The glint in his eye might have been humour or

rage. His face was completely impassive. "Please return here when you're finished."

I nodded and went out the door, head high, heart thumping as if I'd just run a mile.

Inside the door of the ladies' room, I gave a head-to-toe shudder and jammed my itchy back against the corner of the wall to gyrate like a bear with fleas. After a few moments of frantic twitching and squirming, helpless giggles overcame me.

That was possibly the stupidest pissing match I'd ever engaged in. Was Stemp secretly twitching and squirming in his office right now, too? The mental image made me giggle even harder, and I clamped a hand over my mouth to stifle myself.

At last both the giggles and the creepy-crawly sensations subsided, and I scooted into a cubicle. Washing my hands a few minutes later, I practiced my deadpan expression in the mirror, but it kept cracking up.

Damn, I'd never be able to face Stemp now. The instant he gave me his robot-face, I was going to fall to the floor and lie there laughing helplessly.

An explosive snicker escaped me, and I clapped a hand over my mouth again. Get it together. You're a secret agent, so show some professionalism...

That thought sobered me.

I had absolutely nothing to laugh about. Daniel could have been suffering horribly while I was wasting time in my sophomoric contest with Stemp. Somebody was trying to spoil Spider and Linda's wedding, and their violence was escalating. And Frederick Labelle was bound to be just a tad cranky over the loss of his henchman. He might kill me out of sheer annoyance. Or hell, if none of those things happened, the chain of command might toss me in jail for getting sidetracked from my official mission.

I heaved a sigh and plodded back to Stemp's office. When I tapped on the doorframe with a sense of déjà vu, he looked up from his computer and said, "Please come in and close the door" in his usual dispassionate tone.

I did as he bade and sat in the chair again, fully prepared to speak first if necessary. Somehow I wasn't in the mood for childish games anymore.

Stemp spoke as though our previous power struggle had never happened. "Dr. Chow tells me you took one of his prototypes for testing yesterday. How did it perform?"

"Great. Blew out a tire in about five seconds, just like he said it would."

"And yet we collected yet another dead body from your farm last night."

I sighed and slouched lower in the chair. "Yeah. Sorry about that. It was the same guy who had been following me earlier in the day. I led him into Innisfail and then blew out his tires and left him there. That was the end of my tail for the day, but he was waiting when I got back to my farm last night. When he pulled a gun on me..." I grimaced. "I probably shouldn't have killed him, but I just reacted."

Stemp gave one of his tiny shrugs. "It's easier to dispose of a dead body than to deal with a wounded prisoner."

"God, this is one seriously fucked-up life."

"Indeed," Stemp agreed. "Have you spoken to Labelle yet?"

"No." I hunched my shoulders moodily. "I figured I'd just let him stew for a little while. I'll call him as soon as we're done here. He must have sent the guy with the gun just to see what I'd do, so he's probably convinced I'm not an undercover cop now. Maybe this will be enough to get him to start negotiations."

Stemp nodded without comment and changed the subject. "Are there any developments on Daniel Kane's case?"

I eyed him in silence for a moment. This was a test.

Well, fuck it.

"They think it might be a serial killer," I said. "I finished up my official business in Innisfail yesterday around suppertime and then drove up on my personal time to interview three women who had also lost sons Daniel's age within the past fifteen months. Sons who looked a whole lot like Daniel. And there were more down south. Six boys in total."

"That's sickening," Stemp said quietly. "As you know, I can't officially sanction you working on the case, but..." Another tiny shrug. "You have some leave time accumulated. If you choose to use it, your activities on your personal time are none of the Department's business." He gave me a look that was clearly a warning. "Nor are they the Department's responsibility should you exceed the bounds of civilian law. And I strongly suggest that you keep your mission to reel in Labelle at the forefront of your priorities."

"Uh... right," I agreed.

Got the message, loud and clear: if I didn't show progress with Labelle, I was going to jail. And I was on my own with Kane's investigation.

"Have you spoken to Kane about debriefing?" Stemp asked.

I slumped back with a sigh. "Yes. He won't take the time."

"That is unfortunate."

Something in the way he said it sent a chill down my spine.

"What... exactly... does that mean?" I asked cautiously.

"Though I have indicated to the chain of command that he is on personal leave, in fact he has neither applied for leave nor completed the mandatory debriefing for resignation." Stemp was back in robot-reptile mode, his expression impassive and his eyes as flat and hard as a rattlesnake's. "When an agent willfully ignores such requirements, the question inevitably rises: Has he gone rogue?"

I jerked upright. "Of course he hasn't! You know damn well he hasn't!"

"Do I?" Stemp stared across the desk, unblinking. "He hasn't reported to me, nor to anyone in the chain of command. I don't know where he is or what he's doing."

"He's at his condo in Calgary, and he's looking for his son! Call him there if you don't believe me!" I glared at him. "You know damn well he hasn't gone rogue!"

"No," Stemp said quietly. "I *believe* he hasn't gone rogue. I have no evidence to support that belief, and very soon my stalling tactics with the chain of command will fail. The risk to Kane is rapidly going beyond the threat of disciplinary action to something considerably more serious."

I swallowed cold fear. Serious; as in 'life-threatening'. The last agent to go rogue had been executed by Kane himself.

"But they have to understand how traumatic this is for him," I argued. "You can't tell me they'd just show up for work like nothing had happened if their own child had been kidnapped."

"Some would," Stemp said. "But that's not the point.

This has gone beyond simply taking a day or two off."

"That's stupid!" I jerked forward in my chair, fists clenching with the need to throttle somebody. "They have to know what this is doing to John. After what he went through on his last mission with that abused child... Can't you get Dr. Rawling to talk to them? Explain-"

"Explain what?" Stemp interrupted quietly. "Explain that an agent with a top-level security clearance and large amounts of classified knowledge is too mentally unbalanced to comply with the most basic administrative protocols? What effect do you think that would have on their confidence?"

Sick dread crawled up my throat. "I'll talk to him," I croaked. "I'll make him come in."

"Please do. I will continue to stall the chain of command to the best of my abilities."

We sat in silence for a moment before Stemp spoke again. "I have the report on your assailant. He was on the payroll for Labelle's company as a 'consultant', and he had a clean record. Either last night was his first foray into the enforcement business, or else he was very discreet in his previous work. I'll forward the report to your email."

I grunted, trying to hide the way my heart was still hammering. "Well, discreet or not, he's very dead. I'll read it over before I call Labelle. Was there anything else?"

"No. Dismissed."

I rose, then hesitated.

I'd never get a better chance.

"One more thing," I said.

His raised eyebrow indicated he was listening, and I drew a deep breath. "I'd like to ask you to reconsider about Moonbeam and Karma..."

His expression closed down.

"I said, 'Dismissed'," he repeated.

"Come on." I dropped back into the chair and hitched it closer to his desk so I could look straight into his eyes. "I understand how much the whole Earth Spirit thing bothers you, and I'm not asking you to compromise your principles. It must have seemed like a huge betrayal when you were a teenager, but that was a long time ago and you're no stranger to moral ambiguity now..."

I might as well have been talking to the wall. He stared through me without a flicker of expression.

I sighed and tried again. "Look, my parents are dead, and I'd give anything to be able to talk to them again. Yours are still alive and you still have a chance..."

He made a small sign of negation, and I leaned closer, willing him to listen. "They *are* your parents, in every way that matters. They love you, and it's tearing them apart to lose you. And you're wasting precious time. Someday they'll die and it'll be too late, but right now you can still make some good memories if you'll just... try."

His fist clenched, and I braced myself for an outburst, an icy dismissal, or a bullet. Or maybe all three, not necessarily in that order.

A moment later his stony façade melted into a heartwrenching mixture of bravado and pain. "I did try," he gritted. "And look what happened. What else can I do?"

"You can try again," I urged. "You can't expect to get it right the first time after twenty-five years apart. It's a process. Screw up, ask forgiveness, try again, screw up again. It's what families do."

"I don't think this one does." His chin came up, his shoulders squaring, but the loss in his eyes belied his determined posture. "And I don't think there can be a compromise. It's not reasonable to expect a person to change their fundamental belief system."

"You're right," I agreed. "So don't expect that." When he shook his head in frustration, I added, "Look, the Earth Spirit thing bothers you because it's a lie and a manipulation, right?"

"Of course." Stemp narrowed his eyes as if to peer through my skull into my brain. "And since I've read your psych evaluations, I fail to see why it doesn't bother you, too."

"Because they aren't manipulating the other commune members for their own personal gain," I said, tiptoeing into the minefield with my pulse pounding. "Think about it. They provide a safe environment and unconditional love and acceptance to all their members. The kids get top-notch schooling. They've got that great gym. They even bring in lecturers regularly for the adults. So if you can just put aside the harmless lie of the Earth Spirit for a minute, you can see how much good they're doing."

He sat slowly back in his chair, still giving me his unsettling scrutiny. After a long moment he asked, "You honestly believe my... parents... are worth the trouble?"

Hope fluttered up under my heart and I held my voice level, afraid to scare him off with too much enthusiasm. "Yes, I absolutely do."

He stared through me for a few more seconds before letting out a long exhalation. "I have learned not to discount your character evaluations, no matter how improbable they may seem. I'll think about it." A wintry smile touched his lips. "Are you finished with your 'one more thing'?"

I nodded, afraid to trust my voice.

"Very well, then. Dismissed. Again."

I fled.

Back in my office, I sank into my chair and breathed slowly. Why the hell was I trying so hard? If Stemp wanted to make himself miserable, why should I care? He sure as hell wasn't going to lie awake at night worrying about me in return.

But the hurt child hiding behind his eyes called to me. And Moonbeam and Karma deserved to have their son in their lives.

Hissing out a breath, I shook off the thoughts. I needed to call Kane. And it was time to deal with Labelle.

The phone rang just as I reached for it, and Lola's number flashed on the call display.

Shit, I'd forgotten to return her call.

Clenching my teeth and wondering how much more bad news I could take, I picked up the phone and offered a fake-cheerful hello.

"Hi, Aydan, it's Lola," she said briskly. "I'm glad I finally caught up with you."

"Uh, yeah, sorry I didn't-" I began, but she was already forging ahead.

"I'm worried about Spider and Linda's wedding on Saturday. With all the things that have happened I think it's time we took matters into our own hands."

"Um... what do you mean?" I asked cautiously.

"Well, we phoned the police and they can't do anything. Other than the damage to Linda's wedding dress they say no crime has been committed, and since there haven't been any overt threats their hands are tied. But-"

"Hang on, Lola," I interrupted gently. "Spider and Linda are going to stay at my place and have the reception there, so don't worry…"

"And shit can happen at your place just as easily as anywhere else," she countered. "That's why we're forming craps."

I blinked. "Uh… you're what?"

"Forming craps." Her voice took on the ringing tones of a proud slogan. "When shit happens, call craps!"

What the hell? No matter how I tried, I couldn't connect the scatological reference with anything that made sense. Or maybe my subconscious was just trying to protect me from another of Lola's dubious schemes.

I squeezed my eyes shut and massaged my temples with my free hand. "Lola, what are you talking about?"

"Citizens Reconnaissance And Protection Services. CRAPS. We're going to make sure the wedding goes off without a hitch. I've got all my friends together and we're going to keep the caterer's house, the deejay's house, and the florist's shop under constant surveillance so nothing can happen to the rest of the wedding things. And we'll put a team on your farm, too. We'll nail these scumbags, whoever they are!"

Oh, Lord help us all.

"Um, Lola…" I began, but she was still bubbling over with enthusiasm.

"We've got my friends from Aquacize and my erotic literature club, and Bud Weems and all his old army buddies; that's twenty people so far, and I bet more will join when they find out…"

"Lola!" I interrupted. "Please tell me you're not forming a vigilante group."

"Oh, fiddlesticks, Aydan!" She gave a light innocent laugh that set off all my alarm bells. "You know me better than that."

Oh God, yes. I knew her all too well. Well enough to know that nothing I could do or say would stop or even slow the juggernaut of crap. CRAPS. Whatever. All I could do was try to inject a note of sanity into the proceedings and hope nobody died.

With only a momentary twinge of conscience, I slung two innocent victims under the bus. "I hope you invited Moonbeam and Karma to join."

Lola laughed. "Oh, it was their idea. They're such pistols!"

Well, shit.

CHAPTER 32

By the time I hung up from Lola's call I felt like a teaspoon of butter scraped over an entire loaf of bread. I didn't even want to think about anything bad happening to Spider and Linda, and my earlier relief at Moonbeam and Karma's presence had dissolved in the fear that Lola or one of her friends would get hurt in an ill-advised attempt to play vigilante hero.

And those weren't the only lives on the line.

Urgency pounded at me; a gut-level intuition that Daniel's time was running out. And when it did, Kane's sanity would go with it. Hell, Kane's time was running out with the chain of command, too.

And as if all that wasn't enough, I had to deal with Smarmy-Butterscotch Labelle.

Muttering under my breath, I dialled Kane's home number. It rang busy. Next, his cell phone. Straight to voicemail.

Goddammit, if anyone from the chain of command tried to call him to verify his whereabouts, they'd think they were getting the runaround and be even more suspicious. I left a message for Kane to call Stemp and/or me, then tried Hellhound's cell phone.

Voicemail, too.

I clenched my teeth and left a message.

Thoroughly edgy, I dialled Labelle. He answered on the second ring, and I got straight to the point. "You wanted a meeting?"

"I wanted a meeting yesterday. And last night."

He didn't sound very butterscotchy at all today. The cold edge in his voice sent a shiver trickling down my backbone, quickly followed by a surge of hot anger at the fact that this pukebucket was the reason I was dodging bullets and skirting jail instead of enjoying a safe and peaceful life.

"Well, tough," I snapped. "I'm busy. What do you want?"

"I want a meeting," he repeated.

"Yeah, I *got* that," I said with exaggerated patience. "Why? Last time all you did was insult me. Tell me what you want and I'll see if it's worth my time to meet you."

"Oh, believe me, it's worth your time."

I blew out an irritable breath. "Fine. If you can meet at two this afternoon at the ice cream shop, be there. Otherwise it'll have to wait until tomorrow."

"It's nearly noon," he growled. "I'm in Calgary. It's a two-hour drive."

"Okay, make it two-thirty, but I can only give you a few minutes then."

"Is this your idea of a joke?" he inquired icily.

"Take it or leave it!" I barked. "And hurry up!"

A pause on the line transmitted only a faint rhythmic hissing, like the sound of a man breathing hard through his nose with his teeth clenched.

"I'll see you at two-thirty," he said in a strangled voice, and disconnected.

I was glaring at the phone and loudly itemizing Labelle's aberrant sexual preferences when a tentative tap at the door interrupted me between 'butt-sucking donkey-licker' and 'goat-fucker'.

Spider leaned cautiously through the opening. "Uh... is this, um... a bad time?"

"Oh. No." Forcing my stiff lips into a smile, I waved him in. "Come on in. What's new?"

"Um... well..." He sidled into the office and lowered his voice. "Have you talked to Lola?"

I sank my head into my hands with a groan. "Yes."

"What are we going to do?" He dropped into the chair across from me, his face drawn with concern. "Linda knows enough about what we do here..." He encompassed Sirius with a vague wave of his hand. "...to be properly scared. But Lola doesn't have a clue. She thinks it's just a big adventure."

"I know." I sighed. "Try not to worry about it, Spider. I've got a few tricks up my sleeve that I can't tell you about, but she's safer than you think."

"Really?" He sat up straighter, hope dawning on his face. At my nod, he sprang to his feet, grinning. "Oh, thank God! You're a lifesaver, Aydan! Literally!" Bounding around my desk in a flurry of lanky legs and awkward elbows, he stooped and threw his arms around me. "Thank you!" he repeated. "I don't know what we'd do without you."

"You're welcome," I muttered, freeing one hand to pat his back and hoping his confidence wasn't as misplaced as it felt. "Here..." I extricated myself from his embrace and dug into my waist pouch for my key. "Take this, too," I added as I handed over the wrist monitor for my cameras.

"Oh, no, Aydan, I can't..." he began, but I grabbed his

wrist and pressed it into his hand.

"Yes, you can. And it's only until I get home. When I can't be there, the panic button will be just as good."

"But, Aydan, that panic button is there to protect you, not me," Spider argued. "I can't justify using Sirius's resources for something like this."

"Sure you can." I grinned. "Or if you can't, just give it to Linda. She won't hesitate."

He laughed uncertainly, but I had a feeling he wouldn't press the panic button even if he needed to. But it wouldn't matter. If any threat showed up on the monitors, Moonbeam and Karma would deal with it long before Sirius could mobilize a rescue anyway.

"Why don't you take Karma out to the farm with you?" I asked innocently. "I'm having lunch with Moonbeam so she'll be along a bit later, but you guys can get started on moving furniture or whatever you need to do for your reception."

"Actually..." Spider hesitated. "We had originally planned a sit-down dinner at the hall, but we've changed to a buffet-style since we don't have any place to sit down anymore... and we thought... if it's okay with you of course..."

Trying not to show my impatience, I smiled and gave him a 'go on' gesture.

"We thought it would be nice to set up the bar and buffet and dance floor in your garage. You've got the fridge out there for the caterers, and we could bring ice chests for the bar. We'll tell people to bring lawn chairs, and with those five big doors open it'll be perfect for people circulating in and out, and your garden's so pretty..."

"That'll be just fine," I interrupted. "My place is yours. Move stuff around, decorate, whatever you want. The keys to all the vehicles are in my kitchen drawer."

"Thanks, Aydan!" He hugged me again. "You're the best!"

"You're welcome." I subtly manoeuvred him toward the door. "I'll see you around suppertime. I'll bring pizza from Fiorenza's."

"Awesome!" He bounced out the door looking like his usual buoyant self.

I breathed a long sigh before tucking the laser flashlight into the concealment of my rolled-up sweater and following him downstairs.

In the lobby, I unslung the pheromone detector from around my neck and braved the time delay chamber to the secured area again. When I let myself into the Weapons lab, the main area was deserted.

Damn, I should have called ahead. I had just assumed somebody would be here.

I wrinkled my nose. Maybe they'd all cleared out after an experiment had gone wrong. It smelled like something had crawled in here and died.

A faint buzzing sound accompanied by a woman's low-pitched giggle made me back toward the door.

Really didn't need to know about Murray and Melinda's sex life...

The buzzing amplified and a sudden swarm of flies descended on me. Swooping around my head, they dive-bombed my face as if making a concerted effort to get into my eyes and up my nose. I let out an involuntary yelp and threshed the air frantically around my head, but they kept up their attack.

When I opened my mouth to yell, one flew into my mouth and my shout came out sounding more like

'*Grrkkphfffbt!*'. I spat out the disgusting bug-morsel and cupped a hand over my nose and mouth while flailing my free hand to keep them out of my eyes.

"*Fuck off with the flies!*" I bellowed through my fingers.

Like gophers in a Saskatchewan pasture, the researchers' heads popped up from behind various counters, their eyes widening in surprise.

"Sorry!" Murray exclaimed, and hastily manipulated the joystick to call off the plague of flying vermin.

I scurried over to the nearest sink to rinse and spit a few times, then moistened a paper towel and thoroughly wiped my face. "If you ever do that again," I growled, "I will hold you down and feed you every last one of those filthy things. Through your nose."

"I'm really sorry," Murray repeated, his basset-hound jowls quivering with sincerity. "We were just doing the final tests on the flies' locating abilities. We weren't expecting anybody else to come in. I thought..." He shot a sheepish glance at Dr. Chow, who was propped against one of the counters laughing uproariously. "I thought I'd found Reggie."

"Asshole," Chow rejoined, still grinning.

"God!" I rinsed and spat a couple more times. "What is it with flies? Why do they always want to get in your eyes and nose and mouth?"

"Well, actually," Melinda said, "These ones are specially bred to do that. We've amped up their attraction to human mucous membranes."

"That's fucking sick." I rinsed and spat again. I could still taste that fly. "Please tell me you don't feed them dogshit or something."

"No, no," Melinda soothed. "We feed them a nutritional

blend that's specially formulated to provide the nutrients they need without spreading disease." She hesitated. "Of course, in the field, they'd fend for themselves, so..."

"So they'd eat dogshit and rotting dead things," I finished, and rinsed and spat one more time. "I really fucking hate flies. And you are truly sick to send them into people's noses and eyes."

"Not really," Chow explained, sobering. "The distraction factor is just a side benefit. The main reason we increased the attraction is to keep the flies more interested in finding people than whatever rotting thing happens to be closest. So far we've had a one-hundred-percent success rate here in the lab."

I sniffed the air, sudden horrid certainty filling me. "*That's* what I smelled when I came in. You've got some gross rotten thing in here to tempt them, haven't you?"

Chow shrugged. "Well, yeah, of course. Wouldn't be much of a test otherwise, would it?"

"But you're driving them with the control box," I argued. "So you'll only find people you know are there."

"No, the control box just stimulates them to move to the next target as soon as the current one is mapped," the black-bearded Sawyer chimed in. "The joystick is an override, in case we want to swarm somebody..." He trailed off at the sight of my expression before adding hurriedly, "...and the control box has a homing beacon to bring the flies back. The discovery and mapping system is working fine now. All we need is the last of the pheromone research and we'll be able to figure out who's hostile and who's not."

"Well, I can pretty much guarantee anybody would be hostile after you sent ten flies up their nose," I retorted. "But I brought you some more pheromone samples anyway." I handed the pheromone detector to Chow.

Chow shot a not-too-intimidating glare at the others. "Get back to work, you fucking slackers." They drifted away with a volley of good-natured abuse in Chow's direction, which he ignored except for a quirk of the undamaged side of his mouth.

"So what have you got for me?" he asked as he connected the pheromone detector to his computer and extracted two vials.

I eyed them uncertainly. "Two? I thought there would only be one."

Chow raised a quizzical eyebrow before consulting his screen. "Yesterday afternoon at two-twenty, and this morning at one-twelve AM."

Yesterday at two-twenty...

Enlightenment dawned. "Oh... I'm not sure how to label that sample. It was just an adrenaline rush. I was undercover and the guy accused me of being a cop. So it would be more prey than predator, I guess, if you have to classify it."

"And the other one?"

"Um... I'm not sure about that one, either. Definitely prey to start with, but then I killed the guy..." I trailed off at the look on his face.

"But then you killed the guy," he echoed. "Okay. Busy day yesterday?"

"Yeah. Oh, and I brought back the laser flashlight. Thanks. It worked really well." I held it out to him.

He absently waved it away. "Hang onto it. Sounds like you need it." He finished downloading the pheromone samples and replaced the vials. "Here you go again." He handed me the unit, frowning. "Sounds like 'active duty' is pretty active for you right now."

I snorted. "Understatement of the century."

Chow gave me a calculating look. "But you're going to be around here for a while, right? You're not getting assigned somewhere else?"

"No, I'll be here as far as I know," I said warily. "Why?"

"I'm just thinking you're a prime candidate to do the final testing for some of our gear." The fanatical gleam was back in his eye. "I'm going to run this up the chain of command and see if I can get clearance to gear you up. Real life is far better than any field testing the Calgary installation can do."

"Um... I don't know..." I began, but he was already talking over me.

"Don't worry, I won't set you up with anything unless I'm positive it'll work. And it'll give you a huge edge, I promise."

Hope seeped in. "I could sure use an edge right now," I agreed tentatively.

Chow thumped me on the shoulder, grinning. "You're gonna be the hottest agent in the whole service."

"Jane Bond," I breathed, my heart lifting.

His grin widened. "Oh, hell, yeah!"

CHAPTER 33

Twenty minutes later Moonbeam and I were tucked into a corner of The Melted Spoon. Only a few tables were still occupied after the lunch rush, but there was enough general conversation to camouflage our words. I leaned closer and spoke softly.

"What possessed you to get Lola and her friends involved in CRAPS?"

Moonbeam winced. "Not my idea, dear." When I raised a skeptical eyebrow, she clarified, "Not the CRAPS part, anyway. Karma Wolf Song and I merely intended to encourage Lola and her friends to be aware of any unusual activity and to report it to the authorities. Instead..."

She made a helpless gesture, and I nodded my sympathy. "Yeah, I should have warned you about Lola. Sorry about that."

"It's quite all right; I should have expected it. With an aura like hers..." She trailed off, smiling, then sobered. "But don't worry, dear. When we realized the inevitability of CRAPS, Karma Wolf Song and I elected ourselves commanders-in-chief and insisted that they bring in a representative from the RCMP to educate them about Neighbourhood Watch programs. And all the members will clear their activities with us prior to proceeding, so we should be able to prevent any injuries. In any case..." She shrugged philosophically. "The extra surveillance will be beneficial. With this many members we'll be able to provide twenty-four-hour coverage of all key wedding personnel."

I swallowed my mouthful of egg salad croissant. "You don't need to put any guards on my farm. I have full surveillance. Motion-sensing cameras that feed to a mobile monitor that looks like a wristwatch."

Moonbeam's face lit up. "Ah, excellent. I noticed you wearing the wristband earlier and wondered if it was simply a watch but..." She broke off, frowning at my wrist. "Where is it?"

I gulped another mouthful. "I gave it to Spider for the afternoon. I'll take it back from him when I get there tonight."

She went still, studying me intently. "Was that... wise? What's your cover story?"

"I don't need one with Spider. He knows what I do. So does Linda, though she doesn't know any details. Everybody else is completely in the dark. That's why Spider and Linda are taking this seriously but Lola thinks it's an adventure."

"Ah." Moonbeam applied herself thoughtfully to her veggie panini. "I wondered," she said after a few mouthfuls. "I thought you must have a support team besides Sunstar Desert Hawk and Blessed Soul Dream, but your young friends seem very..." She hesitated before finishing, "...innocent."

"Spider's an analyst, not an agent," I explained. "He's the most brilliant computer guy I've ever met and the sweetest kid ever, but he has no stomach for anything else. Linda's a nurse at the secured wing of the hospital, and all she knows is that I sometimes show up there with unexplained injuries and nobody asks questions."

"Ah," Moonbeam repeated. "Well, at least your perimeter surveillance should give us enough advance warning to... make arrangements... without compromising our cover. Do you have any suspects yet?"

Shit, what kind of useless agent was I? Figuring out who had it in for Spider and Linda would be a hell of a lot more useful than running around reacting to threats.

"No, that would imply that I actually had a brain and knew how to use it," I said bitterly.

"Oh, Storm Cloud Dancer, don't be hard on yourself." Moonbeam reached over to squeeze my hand. "The kidnapping must be consuming a great deal of your time and energy, and I'm sure you have other official business as well."

"Yeah." I sighed. "But Spider and Linda don't have any idea who might want to cause problems for them, and I don't know their circle of acquaintances well enough to figure it out. The wrecked wedding dress sounds like a jealous woman to me; I can't see a guy doing that kind of thing. But burning down the community hall and sabotaging Spider's car are pretty serious stuff. And not really the kind of thing the average woman would do."

"Perhaps not a jealous woman. Perhaps a jealous gay man," Moonbeam said thoughtfully. "Spider's best man Tim Moorcroft has a tremendous crush on Spider. When I asked Spider about it, he said they've been inseparable since childhood, and when Tim came out of the closet he made a play for Spider. Spider turned him down with no hard feelings and he says they've remained the best of friends, but... perhaps the 'no hard feelings' was only on Spider's side."

"Oh. Shit..." I stared at her, my heart sinking at the memory of Tim's agitation when Spider collapsed at the wedding shower. And Tim had cast suspicion on Tyler Brock for spiking Spider's drink. What if that had just been a ruse to divert attention from himself?

"I hope that's not the case," Moonbeam said. "But we'll keep an eye on him nonetheless. Those closest to someone are the most likely to cause them pain."

"Yeah. Um... speaking of that..." I swallowed a mouthful of tea, hoping it would provide inspiration. "Um... I talked to Cosmic River Stone again this morning. I think he might be willing to try again."

Moonbeam sighed and laid down her panini with a gesture of futility. "To what end? You know we can't budge on the Earth Spirit. It's a fundamental part of our cover, and it's a major stumbling block between us and our son. Perhaps we should simply... let it be." Sadness clouded her eyes. "For the past several months we've been able to maintain cordial conversations over the phone. A long-distance relationship is better than nothing."

"But he might be willing to compromise..." I began.

"There is no compromise, Storm Cloud Dancer, and you know it," she said firmly. "Innocent lives could be at stake, and we simply can't risk it."

Goddammit, just as stubborn as her son. I stared at her in frustration.

"Tell him!" The words burst out of my mouth without obtaining clearance from my brain. "Just tell him the truth. It'll solve everything."

"Absolutely not." The steel was back in her expression, her lips set in a firm line. "He's a civilian. That would be a gross breach of security and a betrayal of everything we've been doing for the past forty years."

"He can keep a secret," I insisted. "I'd trust him with my life."

Moonbeam gave me a level stare that reminded me so forcefully of Stemp that I had to suppress a shudder.

"If it was only Karma Wolf Song's and my lives at stake, I might," she said in a voice as unyielding as stone. "But Charles Randall Stemp made his choice twenty-five years ago, and now my primary responsibility is to the members of our commune. Though I might be willing to gamble with my own life, I cannot and will not gamble with theirs."

"But..."

The truth struggled to escape but I clamped my teeth on it. I was almost certain it was safe for them to know about each other, but 'almost' wasn't good enough. With innocent lives at stake, I couldn't take the chance.

Moonbeam gave me one of her unfocused inspections, her brow furrowing in concentration. "You truly believe in him," she said softly. "You struggle to trust anyone, but yet you trust my son implicitly in this."

I stared at her in hope, feverishly visualizing sincerity billowing into my aura. "Yes, I really do."

Her wistful blue gaze met mine. "I would like to believe in him the way you do, but I'm afraid you're simply blinded by your affection for him."

"What? God, no!" I jerked back, then hurriedly tried to smooth out my expression of revulsion. "I mean, um... I don't... we don't..." I sucked in a deep breath. "Just no. I trust him in a p-" I bit off the telltale phrase 'professional capacity' and substituted, "... pig's eye."

"Oh, my dear." Moonbeam reached over to pat my hand with a motherly gesture while amusement tugged at the corners of her mouth. "Now you're just lying to yourself."

I sighed and gathered my scattered wits. "You're right; I didn't really mean that. I do trust him... in some ways. But we're definitely not interested in each other."

She nodded wisely and began to speak just as my burner phone vibrated.

A wash of relief tempered with worry suffused me, and I held up a hand to stop her. "I'm sorry, I have to take this. It'll be John or Arnie, and I really need to talk to them." I whisked out the phone and punched the button.

"Aydan, do you have time to talk?" Kane's tone would have sounded casual to anyone listening in, but I decoded his question without difficulty. He had secured the line and was checking to be sure I could speak freely.

"I can talk," I replied. "But you have to go in to the Department right away-"

"Later," he said tersely. "We've completed our interviews. Nothing definitive. Serena's ex knew both Buck Murphy and his brother Scot. They belonged to the same archery league but didn't socialize together. Two of the other exes shared a mutual friend, but none of the other exes knew the friend, and in any case Mayweather had cleared him in the initial investigation. None of the mothers had any friends in common."

"Shit." I slumped back in my chair. "Is Mayweather treating Buck Murphy as a homicide?"

"Unknown." Frustration vibrated in Kane's voice. "If he is, it's a separate investigation that he won't share with me. Can you find out?"

I did a rapid mental calculation. "Um... probably. I have a couple of things I can't put off, but I'll get back to you as soon as I can. It'll probably be after three o'clock-"

"The sooner the better," Kane interrupted. "I'll email you a list of the friends' names, too. Hellhound and I will start digging into them right away. They need to be cross-referenced to see if we're missing any connection, and you can probably do that faster and better than we can."

"Um... likely not; I'm good at straight searches, but cross-referencing-"

"Just do your best," he interrupted again. "Call me as soon as you can."

"Okay. But go in right away, it's-" A click sounded in my ear, and I finished, "...urgent..." into dead air.

Blowing out a breath of irritation mixed with worry, I dialled Hellhound's cell phone.

He picked up immediately with his usual gruff, "Helmand."

"Hi, Arnie," I said cautiously, wondering if I'd get the same brusque treatment from him.

"Oh, hey, darlin'." His voice warmed. "How ya doin'?"

In the background, Kane's anxious voice demanded, "Does she have something?"

"How the hell do I know? Lemme get two fuckin' words in, an' I'll ask her." Hellhound sounded uncharacteristically testy, and I could only imagine the pressure-cooker atmosphere at the other end of the line.

"I don't have anything new," I said hurriedly. "Sorry. I just wanted to talk to you."

"Ya don't hafta apologize, darlin'." His voice went muffled as though he'd moved the phone away from his face to speak to Kane. "She ain't got anythin' yet. How 'bout ya get started on that list, an' I'll be right back." Some rustling and a quiet thump signalled his retreat from Kane's condo, and moment later he drew a deep breath. "Okay, darlin', sorry 'bout that. So how ya doin'?"

For a shaky moment the caring in his voice nearly made me pour out all my troubles, but I locked them inside with a deep breath of my own. "I'm okay. Sounds like things are pretty tense there, though."

The click-clang of the outer security door carried to my ear, and the sound of wind rushing over the speaker softened the edges of Hellhound's rasp as he went outdoors, lowering his voice. "He's losin' it, Aydan. I couldn't get him to take any sleepin' pills last night. He's so fuckin' bull-headed he won't listen to me mosta the time anyway, an' now he's so fuckin' sleep-deprived he's even worse. Can ya talk to him? He's gotta get some sleep or he's gonna crack up."

I sighed. "I can try, but he barely let me get a word in edgewise. And he really needs to go in for his debriefing. They're starting to think he's gone rogue."

"Shit! Fuckin' dumbass, I *told* him..." Hellhound broke off and demanded, "How long does he have?"

"I don't know. It's getting dicey. If he won't go in for the debriefing, at least make him email a written request for personal leave."

"I'll try an' get him to do it right away. But he's so fuckin' squirrelly right now..."

Worry squeezed my heart. "What do you mean, 'squirrelly'? He's not taking uppers or something to stay awake, is he?"

"Fuck, I dunno. Never thought a' that..." Hellhound paused, and I imagined him consulting the endless movie-strip of memories that wound through his brain. "I don't think so," he said after a moment. "Usually if a guy's jacked up on somethin' ya can see it in his eyes; the pupils go down to nothin'. He's shakin', but not enough for drugs. It's prob'ly just caffeine. He's suckin' back coffee like it's goin' outta style."

"Great; so he's jittery, irritable as hell, not listening to reason, and not sleeping." I pondered that for a few seconds. "I don't think he'll listen to me if I tell him to sleep, either. Maybe if we were both there, or if I got mad at him again... but I hate to do that in case he shuts us out. Well, more than he has already." Hellhound grunted agreement, and I added, "Can you slip him a couple of sleeping pills in a cup of coffee or something?"

Hellhound let out a bark of mirthless laughter. "Nah. Tried that last night. He could taste 'em, an' he came damn close to kickin' the shit outta me for it."

My heart clutched. "Arnie, are you... safe? Do you think he might get violent with you?"

Across the table from me, Moonbeam sat forward abruptly, concern pinching her face.

"Nah, don't worry, darlin'." Hellhound's voice was full of reassurance that I only partly believed. "Remember, we go back a helluva long way. I've seen him at his worst, an' he'd never raise his hand against a brother. He was just stressed out, was all."

"Okay..." I swallowed hard. "If you're sure..."

"I'm sure."

"Did you get any sleep?" I asked.

"Yeah, I crashed last night. Got a good six hours. How 'bout you?"

I hesitated, but decided not to go into my eventful night. "Yeah. Should I come down there tonight?"

"I dunno," Hellhound said after a moment's thought. "If I thought ya could talk some sense into Kane, I'd say yeah, but I dunno if he'd even listen to ya. An' didn't ya say ya had a job tomorrow? Where d'ya hafta be for that?"

"I have to start here in Silverside. But I'll plan to come down tonight and we can gang up on him then. Maybe he'll listen if he realized I'm worried enough about him to drive four hours round trip."

"Fuck, I hope so." Hellhound's tired exhalation carried clearly over the speaker. "But call me before ya come. No sense drivin' all this way if he ain't gonna listen to ya anyway."

"Try to guilt him into sleeping," I urged. "Make a big deal about all the driving I'll have to do if he won't cooperate." I swallowed a sigh. "But he probably doesn't care."

Hellhound's voice softened. "He cares, darlin'. Lemme talk to him, an' gimme a call tonight before ya leave."

"Okay." I pressed the phone a little closer to my cheek. "Thanks."

"No problem. Well, I better get back up there. Ya gonna have time to look at the names this afternoon?"

"I'll make time. I have a... some stuff to do first, but I'll get started after two-thirty."

"Stuff?" Concern tightened his voice. "How dangerous is this 'stuff'?"

"I wish I knew." I sighed. "Talk to you soon."

"Okay..." he said slowly. "Be safe, darlin'. Love ya."

He disconnected before I could reciprocate, but I knew he didn't need to hear me say it. I lowered the phone slowly, cherishing the brief glow of comfort from our conversation despite my worry for Kane.

"Is Blessed Soul Dream safe?" Moonbeam inquired worriedly. "I have great faith in Sunstar Desert Hawk, but while a clear red aura usually indicates passion and physical energy, it can transmute to anger and violence under extreme stress."

"Arnie says he's okay." I brushed a fingertip over the phone, silently hoping it was true. "I... believe him. I think. But... if John ever attacked him, it would break his heart. And I know Arnie wouldn't fight back. He could; he's a deadly fighter... but he wouldn't. He'd just take it, even if it killed him..." I swallowed hard and squared my shoulders. "But John would never do that."

"I certainly hope you're right."

We applied ourselves to the remains of our lunch with efficiency if not enthusiasm, and a few minutes later I gulped down the last of my croissant and rose. "Okay, I've got to get back to work. Good luck at the farm. If you need anything just rummage around until you find it. I don't have any secrets out there. I'll bring pizza home for supper tonight."

"I don't mind cooking..." Moonbeam began, but I waved her to silence.

"No, that's okay. I've been craving pizza for a while, and I already promised Spider I was bringing it. I'll see you tonight."

"Very well, then." She gave me a once-over with that too-perceptive gaze. "May the Earth Spirit protect you, Storm Cloud Dancer."

"Thanks. You, too," I muttered, and hurried out before I could admit to exactly how much divine intervention I was likely to need.

CHAPTER 34

Back at Sirius Dynamics again, I skimmed the daunting list of names Kane had sent me. God, there were over two hundred. And with only forty-five minutes left before my meeting with Labelle, I didn't dare go into the virtual reality network in case I lost track of time.

Not to mention there was the small issue of using Department time and resources for a case I'd been officially forbidden to tackle.

I contented myself with running the names through the law-enforcement database, which technically wasn't any less illicit but at least it wasn't classified technology and I wasn't using anyone's time but my own. Knowing how feeble an excuse that was, I kept my office door closed and twitched guiltily every time I heard footsteps in the hallway outside.

Finally at a quarter after two I logged out and headed for the lobby, switching to yoga breathing in an effort to calm my pounding pulse. Absently acknowledging the security guard's pleasantries while I signed out, I focused on positive thoughts for all I was worth.

This meeting would go well. Labelle had to believe my cover this time. Not even an undercover cop could make a gunman vanish without a trace. He'd mention weapons or money; I'd respond with wary interest so he didn't get suspicious; and we'd hammer out a deal that would make both him and Stemp happy. The chain of command would be pacified and I'd be able to pour all my effort into helping Kane. And I'd still keep my ass out of jail.

Just keep thinking that...

I sank into one of the wrought-iron chairs outside the ice cream shop and tried to look as though I hadn't a care in the world.

It didn't work.

Despite my best efforts to sit still, my toes wiggled inside my runners and I picked at a ragged cuticle until I caught myself and firmly clasped my hands. That lasted for about thirty seconds, when the breeze wafted a strand of hair across my nose.

I smoothed it back and rubbed the tickle away, but moments later I had to swipe at another tickle on the other side of my face. Then my twitching nerves generated prickles of sensation on my left arm. Moments after I rubbed the spot, more nervy prickles erupted on my leg.

After a few minutes of trying to scratch without looking as though I was infested with a particularly obnoxious case of lice, I sprang to my feet and hurried into the ice cream shop. A nice big scoop of chocolate-peanut-butter ice cream gave me something to do with my hands, and I resumed my seat outside and concentrated on devouring the ice cream before it could melt in the heat.

I had finished the last bite and was beginning to wonder what else I could do to occupy myself when I spotted Labelle approaching across the parking lot.

Showtime.

I drew a deep breath and let it out slowly. Be Arlene

Widdenback, badass arms dealer...

He strode up to my table and jerked his chin impatiently. "Let's walk."

I rose and ambled down the sidewalk, forcing him to shorten his stride. "What's so goddamn important that you had to meet today?" I asked.

"One of my employees was following you yesterday," he ground out.

I shrugged. "Yeah, you can stop doing that anytime. It's pissing me off."

Labelle leaned closer. "Did it piss you off enough to kill him?"

Arlene Widdenback was too smart to admit to murder.

"Get a grip." I put on a suspicious expression. "What are you, a fucking cop?"

"Hardly," he said through his teeth. "But my man's tires mysteriously exploded just as he glimpsed you behind his vehicle. And later he disappeared. Never called in, didn't show up for work, isn't at home."

"So what? Your staffing issues aren't my problem. Maybe you should hire better people." I stared straight ahead, wishing I had another ice cream cone. Didn't know what to do with my hands. My heart vibrated up in the vicinity of my throat.

Hoping I looked casual, I yawned and hooked my thumbs into my back pockets.

Apparently I didn't do casual well. Labelle made a sudden aborted movement.

I shot him an annoyed look. "What's your problem? You think I'm going to wave my magic wand and make you vanish, too? Trust me, if I could, I would."

"About that magic wand of yours..." He leaned into my

personal space again and I stepped away involuntarily, my hands twitching out of my pockets. His hands twitched, too, jolting adrenaline into my system.

Was that a gun tucked under the lightweight summer sport jacket he wore?

Fuck, mine was in my ankle holster, far out of reach. Sweat tickled my backbone.

He was still talking, and I jerked my attention back to his words. "...what did you use?" he asked. "There was no bullet or visible projectile, but the tires exploded. I find that fascinating, because weapons are a bit of a hobby of mine..."

My heart rattled my ribs. He was going for it. He was going to-

"Aydan! Hey, Aydan, wait up!"

Shit!

Teeth clenched, I turned to see Lola trotting across the street behind us, waving and smiling. Labelle turned, too, and Lola's smile widened as she recognized him.

"Oh, hi, Fred!" She hurried up and greeted him with a handshake. "It's nice to see you again. I see you caught up with Aydan."

"Yes." Labelle's big smarmy smile was back and smooth sweetness dripped from his voice. "How nice to see you again, Lola."

"Well, I won't keep you long if you're talking business..." she began, and I fervently hoped she meant it. She went on, "...but I just wanted to let you know we've been in touch with the RCMP."

Labelle made a small movement that wasn't quite a start, and Lola turned to him. "Our community hall burned down last night, and we think it's suspicious," she explained.

"Ah." Labelle regarded her with gooey brown cow-eyes.

"Yes, that certainly does seem like an unusual occurrence in a small town like this."

His voice held an odd intonation, and my blood went cold.

Labelle had been at my party. He had talked to everybody. He would know where and when the wedding was taking place. He knew Spider and Linda were close to me. What if he was instigating their run of 'bad luck' just to keep me off balance? Or worse, what if he was planning to control me by threatening them?

And what else might he have planned?

Pulse pounding in my ears, I tuned back into the conversation just as Lola said, "...no crime in this town anymore. We're going to stop the scumbag who's doing this!"

Oh, no, Lola, don't make yourself a target...

"Well, that's great..." I began, frantically racking my brain for a distraction.

I got one, but it wasn't the kind I wanted.

Lola glanced over and exclaimed, "Oh, hey!" She put her fingers to her lips and let fly with an earsplitting whistle. Then she waved enthusiastically in the direction of the street and called, "Hey, Sandy, over here!"

With a sense of impending doom, I turned slowly to see Officer Peters return a cheery wave and pull her cruiser to a stop beside us.

Fuck.

Labelle was still wearing his genial smile, but it didn't quite fit his face anymore.

Peters got out and strolled over, still smiling. "Hi, Lola. Hi, Aydan."

"Um... hi, Sandra," I croaked. "What's up?"

She flashed a smile down to Lola. "Oh, I just finished up a great orientation with the new Neighbourhood Watch group. There are so many volunteers, and so they're all so keen." Her smile widened. "It's wonderful to see a community dedicated to watching out for each other. Nothing's going to slip by this group."

Shit, shit, shit!

"That's great," I said feebly. "Well, it's been nice talking to you..."

"Oh, yes, and I meant to ask..." She sobered. "How's John holding up? We've been worried about him at the detachment and I meant to call, but..."

Jesus, if she mentioned Kane was an RCMP officer, my cover would be cooked like a bug under a blowtorch.

"He's having a rough time," I said hurriedly. "I'm sure he'd appreciate a call."

Like right now. I mentally bombarded her with psychic messages.

Go. Go away and call Kane. Now. Right-fucking-*now*.

"I'll do that," she agreed. "Well, I'd better get back to work. Nice to see you again, Aydan; and Lola, I'll look forward to our next meeting. Take care, and stay safe."

"You, too," Lola replied cheerfully as she turned away.

Labelle twitched as though he'd been suddenly released from paralysis. "Well, it's been pleasant to see you again, Lola," he said in his smooth voice. He turned to me with a nod that practically dripped sarcasm. "Aydan."

Then he turned and strode away.

"Flaming fuck-monkeys!" I growled under my breath, my heart hammering.

"Sorry, what?" Lola looked up at me with innocent eyes. "Did you say something?"

I unclenched my teeth with an effort and pasted on a smile. "Uh, I just said it's so hot out here it's flaming my undies."

Lola nudged me with a lascivious elbow. "Are you sure you don't just have hot pants for Fred Labelle? He's a good-looking guy. I'd take him for a drive around the block any day."

I managed not to choke. "Nope, I'm pretty sure it's not that."

Worry seized me at the thought of Lola cozying up to Labelle. The last time she'd been unwittingly caught up in one of my ops, it had nearly cost her life.

Never again.

"Hey, Lola," I added, "Stay away from him, okay? He's not nearly as nice as he seems. He's got a mean streak a mile wide."

She sobered, frowning. "How do you know? And why are you even giving him the time of day, then?"

I grimaced. "Business. I don't want to, but he's a financial guy and I'm a bookkeeper. Sometimes our paths cross whether I want them to or not."

"Oh." Her frown deepened. "Well, if you don't trust him, make sure you've always got somebody with you when you meet him. Call me or one of the other CRAPS members, and we'll watch out for you."

My stomach squeezed at the thought of little Lola or frail Bud Weems trying to intervene with a guy like Labelle. When I spoke, my voice came out slightly choked. "Thanks, Lola, but it's financial stuff. Confidential. So you can't sit in on my meetings, but I'll be sure to always meet him in public places."

"You do that, and if you want one of us to watch from

across the street or something, you just give me a call." She patted my arm, smiling up at me. "We'll keep you safe, honey."

I managed not to groan aloud.

Back inside Stemp's office again, I slouched gloomily in the chair while I finished my report. "...so he just gave me this look and walked away. I'm such an idiot. I should have met him somewhere else; somewhere we wouldn't have been interrupted."

And if I'd been a real agent, I would have known enough to do that. I sank my chin onto my chest, waiting for Stemp's well-deserved rebuke.

The silence lengthened, and I dared a glance at him. Was he too furious to even speak?

As usual, his face betrayed no emotion. He stared into middle distance for a few more moments before saying, "Perhaps. Perhaps not. Remember that Nicholas Parr was widely known as a model citizen and generous benefactor of the Police Fund for widows and orphans. Labelle would know that, and very likely expect the same of an arms dealer of Arlene Widdenback's..." He hesitated, humour sparking in his eyes before he finished, "...calibre."

I groaned in acknowledgement of the pun, then said, "Well, let's hope so." Hauling myself upright, I hesitated. "Did, um... did you get an email from John?"

Stemp's lips thinned. "Yes."

Uh-oh.

"That's, um... that's good, right?" I asked cautiously.

"It would have been good on Monday. Today is Thursday." He eyed me as if it was all my fault, which it probably was. "It's too little, too late."

"Wh..." I gulped. "What do you mean?"

"The chain of command met at thirteen hundred today. They are not insensitive to Kane's situation, but..." Stemp's lips twisted. "...neither are they willing to risk a potential security breach. Kane has until end-of-day tomorrow to report to me and undergo the requalification lie-detector test. If he does not comply..."

We stared at each other in bleak silence while I mentally completed his sentence: '...he'll be either in jail or dead by Saturday morning.'

CHAPTER 35

I stared at Stemp, my mind racing. No point in begging him to intercede with the chain of command on Kane's behalf. He had already done as much as he could. But maybe if Kane ran out of names to investigate, he'd take the time to come up here and do the lie detector test.

So I needed to start eliminating names as fast as possible.

Drawing in a deep breath, I met Stemp's reptilian gaze and held my voice steady. "I need to go into the network this afternoon. Do you have time to spot me?"

He pinned me with his expressionless scrutiny. "Why do you need to go in yourself? Why not send your requirements to Brock?"

I started to invent a lie about researching Labelle, but I couldn't force it past my lips.

God, I was so tired of lying to him and evading his questions. And he'd find out that I'd lied anyway; if not now, then next year when I took the lie detector test for my annual requalification.

But if I told him the truth now and he arrested me, I wouldn't be able to help Kane. And if Kane refused to come in because he was still researching names tomorrow...

I sighed. "I can't."

Stemp frowned. "Can't what?"

"I can't use Brock to find out what I need."

Stemp sat eyeing me in silence, and despair dragged my heart into the pit of my stomach. He would demand clarification and I would lie and he would know I was lying. He'd hook me up to the lie detector, and very shortly after that I'd be imprisoned for the rest of my life.

And Kane would go to jail or die because I'd failed him. I might as well have shot him myself.

Stemp spoke, his words like the release of a guillotine blade. "I presume you'll be using some personal leave time..."

We locked eyes and I knew that he knew.

"...to research Daniel Kane's case," he finished expressionlessly.

And there it was.

I envisioned the blade hurtling toward my neck.

"Yes." My voice came out completely flat.

"I see."

Silence balanced precariously on the razor-edge of my approaching doom.

"We're not violating orders," I explained without much hope. "We're not interfering with the police investigation at all. John hired a private investigator, and we're researching names that the moms and exes supplied in our interviews. We informed all of them that we weren't doing this in any official capacity, and everything they told us was completely voluntary."

"A private investigator." Stemp's voice was dangerously mild. "Helmand?"

My heart sank even farther. "Yes."

His upper lip twitched, but I couldn't tell whether it was humour or disgust. "I see," he repeated. His gaze bored into me, his tone completely flat. "Your actions are contrary to the spirit, if not the letter, of your orders. Moreover, I already warned you of the potential consequences of neglecting your assigned mission."

I raised my chin, exposing my throat for the killing blow. "Yes, you did."

We regarded each other without speaking.

After a long moment Stemp sighed and leaned back in his chair, massaging the bridge of his nose before speaking. "Well, it so happens that I have a great deal of personal leave time accumulated, too. Shall we begin in, say..." he consulted his wristwatch. "...ten minutes? I'll retrieve the network key from the secured area and meet you in your office."

For a paralyzed moment I just sat and stared at him. Like a decapitated body. No brain attached.

Then I drew a breath of the sweetest air I'd tasted in a very long time.

"Thank you." My voice trembled, and I swallowed hard to control it. "Ten minutes would be perfect."

I sprang up and hurried out before I could fall apart in front of him.

Several hours later I trickled sluggishly out of the internet's data tunnels and forced my aching avatar into visibility. Stemp looked up from his work in the virtual file repository and released my hand.

"Any luck?" he asked.

"No." I let out a whoosh of breath and slithered down

the wall to sit on the floor, arms limp, head hanging. "I'm no good at this. I can look up information easily; that's only sniffing around and following trails, but cross-referencing..." I dragged my head up to give him a hopeless grimace. "That's just not the way my... talent... or whatever you want to call it... works. That's why I always need Spider to work with me. I've been looking up each name individually but I can't keep all the names in my mind at once, so I could be missing all kinds of potential cross-links."

Stemp gave me a critical scrutiny. "Your avatar is fading at the edges. You need to stop now."

I let my head fall back against the wall, defeated. "Yeah. I'm not getting anywhere, and anyway, I've got hungry people at home expecting me with pizza in half an hour. I'm going to be late already."

He rose and reached down a hand to pull me up. "You have houseguests?"

There might have been a tiny lilt of hope in his voice. Hope lifted my heart in return.

"Yes, Spider and Linda are staying with me, and so are your mom and dad. They didn't leave town because your mom had offered to fix Linda's wedding dress." I hesitated, trying not to sound too eager to push him and his parents together. "Would you like to join us for supper? I'm only picking up pizza, so it would be easy to get a bit more."

Stemp turned away. "Thank you, but no. I have some work to catch up on this evening."

"Oh." I trudged behind him toward the virtual portal, trying not to be disappointed. "Okay. Well, thanks for your help this afternoon. It really meant a lot to me, and I know it will to John, too."

"You're welcome." He stepped through the portal,

leaving me unhappily contemplating the misery to come.

Clenching my teeth, I stepped through after him and jerked into a profanity-spitting ball as the pain exploded inside my head.

When firm fingers began to knead my temples I was so startled I actually stopped swearing.

My initial impulse to pull away from Stemp's ministrations evaporated as his massage worked down to the base of my skull, seeking and extinguishing fiery paths of pain along the way. Eyes closed, I slowly relaxed under his sure touch, the last of the agony diminishing to its usual deep ache.

"Thanks," I mumbled as soon as I was capable of speaking. I dragged my eyes open and focused on him with only a slight effort. "That really helped."

"You're welcome." He hurried out without making eye contact as if afraid to be caught in a compromising position.

Or in an expression of friendship.

I let my head fall back against the sofa to stare at the ceiling. Holy shit, where had that thought come from?

Friendship? With Stemp?

God, I must be more tired than I'd thought.

Hauling myself to my feet, I headed for the door.

An hour and a half later, I pushed my chair back from my kitchen table and began collecting empty plates and pizza boxes. Four satisfied faces smiled back at me, and I carried the plates over to load them into the dishwasher before returning to the table.

"Anybody want tea or coffee?" I inquired.

"Herbal tea would be lovely, dear," Moonbeam agreed

with one of her luminous smiles. The others concurred, and we were soon sipping tea comfortably in the living room.

"So is there any news on the kidnapping case?" Moonbeam asked, tacitly lifting the moratorium on shop-talk she'd imposed at the beginning of our meal.

I sighed and slumped back in my chair. "No. Like I told John, I'm no good at cross-referencing."

"Wait, what?" Spider sat forward abruptly, almost spilling his chamomile tea. "Why didn't you tell me? I can help with that! What are you cross-referencing?"

"Just a bunch of names. And, uh... sorry... I didn't think of passing it on to you. You're on holidays. And you've got all your wedding stuff to think about..."

"Aydan!" Linda shot me a severe look. "A wedding is nowhere near as important as a missing child. Tell Spider what you need, and he can get to work on it right away."

"But... can you get into...?" I hesitated, not sure how much to say with Moonbeam and Karma listening. They knew I'd been back and forth to Sirius Dynamics in my cover as a bookkeeper, but if Spider and I weren't careful with our words they might also guess that Stemp was more than a clueless civilian manager. And he'd been very clear about the consequences of that.

I suppressed a shudder.

Fortunately Spider interrupted. "Of course I can get in; I have my laptop. It's not quite as good as my command centre at home, but I can still do it. 'Course, it'd be better if I could go home..."

The resulting chorus of objections made him smile and raise a placating hand. "Okay, okay, you guys!" He turned back to me. "Give me the list of names. Even without my usual resources, the social media sites are a great place to start. I'll just hack in..."

It was my turn to hold up a restraining hand. "I didn't hear that. All I heard was that you're going to spend the evening messing around on Facebook."

Spider grinned and rose. "Right. Let's get that list."

In only a few minutes he was comfortably ensconced in my office, his laptop and my computer both in use while his fingers flew over the keys. I hovered behind him for a few minutes, but he clearly didn't need anything I could offer.

"Spider?" I asked tentatively.

"Mmhm?" His gaze never left the screen and his fingers didn't cease their rapid tapping on the keyboard.

"Do you need anything from me?"

"Nope," he said without looking up. "Thanks, though."

"Then I think I'll drive down to Calgary tonight. If I go, I'll leave my cell phone here but I'll take a secured phone with me so you can call me if you find anything."

"'Kay," he mumbled, still typing. "Give the number to Linda."

I left him to his work and went back to the living room where Linda, Moonbeam, and Karma were discussing the wedding. They broke off and looked up as I came in.

"I'm probably going to leave for Calgary in a few minutes," I said. "Arnie and I are going to try to convince John to get some sleep."

"But, Aydan..." Linda looked suddenly small and fearful huddled in my big chair. "What if... something happens here? What will we do?"

"You'll be safe here," I reassured her, preventing myself from glancing at Moonbeam and Karma. "The perimeter cameras will catch any movement, and you can call the police right away. They're nearly twenty minutes closer here than to your place in Silverside. And I'll leave you with my shotgun and rifles..."

"Oh, no!" Linda drew up her knees to hug them, beseeching me with the eyes of a frightened child. "I hate guns, and so does Spider! Neither of us has ever fired one, and we'd never, never be able to shoot a *person*. That's just horrible!"

"Don't worry," Karma rumbled in his fatherly bass. "I'm comfortable handling firearms. And I'm sure we can make it through the evening without bloodshed. Nobody knows you're here and there's never been a direct attack on either of you, so there's no reason to believe that will happen now. We'll be perfectly safe."

Linda surveyed him anxiously, her fearful posture slowly relaxing as she took in his powerful build and the serene confidence in his broad seamed face. Reassurance radiated from him, making me wish I could lay all my troubles at his feet and let him protect me, too.

"He's right," I agreed. "You're safe here. And I'll be home by..." I consulted my watch and suppressed a sigh. "Two AM at the latest."

"Moonbeam and I will sit up until you return," Karma promised, then squirmed as Moonbeam prodded his ribs with a playfully remonstrative knuckle. "Moonbeam Meadow Sky," he amended, his eyes twinkling. "We'll keep watch and everything will be fine."

"Okay," Linda said in a small voice. "If you say so."

"Try not to worry," I urged. "I'll just call Arnie now. They may not even need me there."

"Okay," she repeated.

Slipping into the kitchen, I dialled Arnie's cell from my burner phone. He picked up on the first ring, obviously recognizing the number on his call display. Must be nice to have his flawless memory.

"Hey, darlin'," he greeted me. "I'm puttin' ya on speaker now."

"Aydan?" Kane's voice rasped over the speaker a moment later. "Do you have anything?"

"You sound like hell. When did you sleep last?" I chided.

"Never mind that. Do you have anything?" he demanded.

"No, I'm sorry. I spent the afternoon looking but there's nothing yet. Spider's working on it now. If there's anything to find, he'll find it."

"Oh." Kane sounded slightly pacified. "Good. We'll keep digging here, too."

"Okay, but only for another couple of hours," I warned. "I'm leaving now, and when I get there I expect you to take some sleeping pills and go to bed."

"Don't bother coming if that's your only reason," he said flatly.

I swallowed a twinge of hurt and held my voice level. "John, you're being unreasonable again. You know as well as I do that depriving yourself of sleep is a sure-fire way to get sloppy in your investigation. Spider will do more good with those names than all three of us put together. As your friend, and as your colleague, I'm telling you that you need to get some sleep. I'll see you in a couple of hours."

"No, don't come." His sigh carried over the line. "I'm sorry for the way that came out earlier. I just meant you don't need to come all the way down here just for that. I promise I'll go to bed."

"Promise?" I questioned suspiciously. "You promise you'll go to bed in two hours or less?"

"Well..." A conciliatory note slid into his voice. "Not in two hours or less. But I promise I'll go to bed by midnight. Is that good enough, Mom?"

His last sentence was delivered with a slightly sarcastic inflection, followed by a small grunt as though Hellhound had socked him.

Sure enough, in the background Hellhound's voice growled, "Don't be such a fuckin' peckerhead. She's lookin' out for ya 'cause she loves ya. Christ only knows why."

"I was just teasing, for God's sake!" Kane snapped. The long slow hiss of a controlled breath floated over the line before he spoke again, his tone softer. "I'm sorry. I'm being a jerk again. Thank you for your concern, both of you. And Aydan, thank you for offering to come down, but it really isn't necessary. I give you my word that I'll be in bed before midnight."

"Okay, if you promise," I relented. "Arnie, can you act as the jailer there? Or should I come down with a trank gun just in case?"

His gravelly chuckle tickled my ear. "We'll be fine, darlin'. Get some sleep, an' we'll see ya tomorrow. 'Bout what time d'ya think you'll get here?"

I did a rapid mental calculation. If I picked up the weapon from Dr. Chow at ten and everything went smoothly...

"Sometime after lunch," I said. "I don't know exactly where I'm going yet, but I could probably make it down to the condo between one and one-thirty if everything goes well. If not..." I shivered and swallowed hard to keep my voice level. "Well, if there are any complications, I'll see you when I see you. I'll give you a call tomorrow when I'm closer."

"Okay." Hellhound didn't sound happy. "Be safe, darlin'."

"Call us if you need help," Kane put in. "Take care."

"Thanks. You, too." I put on a scolding-mother voice. "And get to bed, you rotten kid!"

Their laughter warmed me as I disconnected.

CHAPTER 36

As I laid down the phone, Linda peeked around the corner. When she saw I had finished my call, she came in carrying her empty mug.

"Sorry, I didn't want to interrupt anything," she apologized. "I just wanted a refill." She crossed to the counter to and picked up the kettle.

"It's okay, you weren't interrupting." I motioned her toward the tea drawer. "And I guess I don't have to go down to Calgary tonight after all."

"Oh." Her word came out on a little gust of breath and she steadied herself against the counter. "Oh, I'm so glad," she said breathlessly. "I mean, Karma Wolf Song is wonderful, but... I feel so much safer knowing you're here to protect us."

Moonbeam drifted into the kitchen with her mug, saving me from a reply, and the three of us stood waiting for the kettle to boil in silence. When our mugs had been refilled I turned to go, but Linda reached out to touch my arm.

Pink rose on her cheeks and she studied her toes briefly before raising a guilty gaze to mine. "I feel like such a hypocrite," she confessed. "Criticizing firearms one minute and then hiding behind you and expecting you to protect me the next."

My heart squeezed. "It's all right. I don't ever want you to be the kind of person who thinks it's okay to shoot people. Here." I handed her the kettle. "Go and see if Spider needs a refill, too."

She departed with a shaky smile, and I propped myself against the counter and morosely swirled the tea infuser inside my mug.

Moonbeam's slender arm slid around me in a gentle hug. "That's what we work for," she said softly. "If we do our jobs right, all our citizens will have the luxury of condemning what we do."

I sighed and rested my head briefly against hers. "I guess you're right. Thanks."

As Linda returned with the kettle Moonbeam stepped away and put on her usual smile. "So, there are four of us. Shall we play some euchre?"

Our card game was an exercise in futility. I was so tired I couldn't keep the rules of the game straight, and Linda was too distracted by her worries to concentrate. When a faint buzzing sound emanated from Moonbeam's caftan and she withdrew a cell phone, I laid down my cards gratefully.

My relief was short-lived. Moonbeam's spine straightened, her dreamy blue eyes sharpening as she listened to the phone. "Have they arrived yet?" she asked crisply. "...You did? And?"

She listened for a moment, her lips pressing into a grim line. "I see. Well, you should have waited for the police to arrive. If you see anything else, don't investigate on your own." The corners of her mouth twitched when the caller spoke again, but Moonbeam's voice was grave as she replied, "Nevertheless, if it happens again, leave it to the police. Old Bessie with a rock salt load might have been all right seventy years ago, but these days you could be convicted and imprisoned for that. Please don't take the chance."

After a few more admonitions, she disconnected and sank her face into her hands, her shoulders shaking.

Alarm tightened Karma's face and he leaned in, closing a protective arm around her shoulders. "My love! What's the matter?"

"Oh..." Moonbeam looked up, wiping tears away, but her body still vibrated with mirth. "Oh, Spirit save us all!" She lay back in her chair and laughed until she was limp. "That was Lola's friend Pearl, from the erotic literature club. She's ninety-three years old and utterly fails to understand why it's not a good idea to pull out her shotgun and fire a load of rock salt at an intruder."

Karma sank back in his chair, grinning. "Pearl is a formidable lady."

"Yes, indeed," Moonbeam agreed feebly, still dabbing her eyes.

"But..." Linda perched on the edge of her seat, her eyes wide. "There was an intruder? Where? What happened?"

Moonbeam sobered, sympathy softening her face. "Yes, dear. I'm sorry. Pearl and her patrol partner were watching your house." At Linda's gasp of fear, she hastened to add, "It was just a shadowy figure that hurried up to your front step, dropped an object, and then fled. There was no attempt to break in."

I reflected that a stinging load of rock salt from Old Bessie would tend to take the fun out of breaking and entering, but I kept that opinion to myself and instead asked,

"What did the intruder drop? It sounded as though Pearl went to check it out herself instead of waiting for the police."

"Yes, she did." Moonbeam grimaced. "I do hope she'll heed my warning next time. But it turned out to be harmless."

"What was it?" Linda whispered through trembling lips.

"Roses painted black."

"Oh..." Tears filled Linda's eyes and she wrapped her arms around herself.

I knelt beside her chair and enclosed her in a hug. "Don't worry, you're safe here. We'll keep you and Spider safe."

She pressed her lips tightly together, somehow preventing her tears from falling. "I know you will, Aydan," she said tremulously. "But maybe we should just cancel the wedding. Somebody really doesn't want us to get married, and I'm scared. If it was just Spider and me, that would be one thing, but what if somebody hurts one of our guests... or... or worse? I'd never forgive myself."

"No, you're going to get married right on schedule," I said firmly. "We're going to get Spider out here and we're going to brainstorm about who might be doing this, and then you're going to get on the phone and tell your guests that both the wedding and the reception will be held here at my farm. The weather's supposed to stay nice, and you can have an outdoor wedding under that rose arbour that's in full bloom. It'll be beautiful, and more to the point, it'll be safe."

Moonbeam and Karma were already nodding approval. "Perfect," Karma agreed. "The gate provides a choke point so we can control traffic to the yard. Vehicles can be parked on the road to keep them away from the guests..." He trailed off at Linda's wide-eyed expression and coughed uncomfortably.

"Sorry," he mumbled. "Bit of an armchair strategist."

Linda nodded slowly, and I nudged her in the direction of my office. "Go and get Spider, and let's figure this out."

"Okay..." she said uncertainly, and headed down the hall.

"Do you have any imaging systems for weapons or explosives?" Karma asked quietly. "A wrapped wedding gift is the perfect cover for a bomb. And one person with a weapon could turn it into a massacre."

I sighed. "I know. I don't have anything like that in place, but I'll see what I can do. If we keep all the vehicles outside the yard and limit it to foot traffic through the gate; maybe set up an arbour or something to hold the detection gear and funnel everybody through it..."

I broke off as Spider and Linda returned, their arms wrapped around each other.

"Okay, let's figure this out," I said as they took seats at the table. I shot a questioning look at Moonbeam. "I forgot to ask, did Pearl or her partner get a good look at the intruder?"

"No, he or she was masked and wearing dark-coloured clothing," Moonbeam replied. "But Pearl did say that it could have been a woman or a slightly-built man. Definitely not tall or bulky."

"Okay, there's our starting point." I turned back to Spider and Linda. "Think of absolutely everybody that might have been upset by the idea of you getting married. You've been living together since last fall, so it has to have been the wedding that triggered this."

Both of them shook their heads. "I can't think of anybody," Spider said. "Who would care if we got married? But..." He paused and regarded Linda thoughtfully. "If it was somebody who was jealous, they'd have to be connected to you, Sweetie." A flush rose on his cheeks. "It's not like there was any lineup to get married to me."

Moonbeam reached across the table to pat his hand. "Don't sell yourself short, dear. You're a marvelous person and any girl would be lucky to have you." She hesitated, then went on, "Or any man, if you happened to be gay. Could your friend Tim be jealous?"

Spider's mouth dropped open. "No! No, of course not! Tim's my best friend and he loves Linda like a sister. He'd never do anything like this!"

"Are you quite sure?" Karma prodded. "The fact that Tim is completely off your radar makes it possible that if he does have feelings for you, he might be hurt enough by your disregard to act on his jealousy."

"No! Absolutely not!" Spider insisted. "Even if he was feeling that way... he just wouldn't. He's so anti-violence he won't even watch a movie unless it's a romantic comedy."

"Did you ever resolve your hostilities with Tyler Brock?" I asked. "He swore he was going to get revenge four months ago, and this would be a perfect opportunity for him."

"I talked to him," Spider said uncertainly. "I apologized for the discord we'd had and asked him if we could start over. He..." Pink rose in his cheeks. "He, um... was his usual self over it..."

"An obnoxious little shithead," I filled in.

"Well, yeah, kind of, but don't tell him I said so." Spider gave me a beseeching look. "I know you don't get along with him and I don't blame you, but as his supervisor, I need to. So anyway, after he got his digs in he settled down and we've been working together all right since then." He gave me a slightly sheepish look. "It helps that he's in Calgary two hundred kilometres away. Anyway, I can't see him doing this."

"I can," I muttered darkly.

Spider sighed. "Well, maybe we can eliminate him from the suspect pool. Hang on." He got up and hurried down the hall, returning a few moments later with his laptop. After a short interval of typing at light-speed, he let out a breath. "Nope, it's not Tyler."

"How do you know?" Karma demanded.

"Um... I tracked his cell phone," Spider admitted.

My heart rose. "You've been monitoring him since April?"

"Well, no, not really. I haven't looked at the logs since then, but..." Spider gave me a look that was equal parts shame and triumph. "It was just too good an opportunity to test my skills. So I left the hack in place. And he's been in Calgary ever since Saturday. It couldn't have been him."

"What about any ex-girlfriends?" Moonbeam asked. "I'm sensing a feminine energy around this somehow."

Spider blushed scarlet. "I... never really had a girlfriend before Linda. I mean, I went out a few times in university, and I've got lots of friends who are girls, but..."

"What about one of your female friends, then?" I prompted. "Maybe somebody who wanted to be more than friends...?"

His face went so red that even the tips of his ears glowed. "Um, I really don't think so. They're all married or in relationships. And even if they weren't..." He made an awkward gesture. "Well, I mean... I was single. They could've just asked me. It's not like I ever turned anybody down."

"What about you, dear?" Moonbeam inquired, turning tactfully to Linda. "Who might be jealous if you got married?"

Linda went pink, too. "I don't know. I can't really see any of my ex-boyfriends throwing dye on my wedding dress."

"That's true; it does seem more like a feminine attack," Moonbeam agreed. "Would any of your female friends be jealous that you were getting married? Or perhaps an ex-friend who might be harbouring a grudge and see this as a convenient way to hurt you?"

"I... don't know." Linda frowned. "I wouldn't like to think so, but..."

We sat in silence until she shook her head. "I'm sorry, I just can't think of anyone. I haven't broken up with a friend since high school. We just all grew out of that kind of pettiness. I mean..." She hesitated. "Most of us did. It's a small town so it can still be a little cliquish, you know?"

"Yeah," I agreed. "So who's in the opposite clique from you?"

After some more prompting and prodding we extracted a few names from Linda, but she seemed doubtful that any of them could be suspects. A perusal of the guest list for the wedding was equally unrewarding. At last we abandoned the discussion and I dragged myself to my feet, barely able to keep my eyes open.

"Go to bed, Storm Cloud Dancer," Moonbeam urged. "You look exhausted. Karma Wolf Song and I will sit up for a while."

"Thanks," I mumbled, and made sure everybody had towels and bedding before staggering toward my bedroom. Moonbeam's soft call stopped me just as I reached the door.

"Storm Cloud Dancer..." She hurried down the hall, casting a cautious glance over her shoulder. Leaning close, she murmured, "What is our emergency response protocol?"

Blinking stupidly, I attempted to boot my brain into some semblance of thought. "Um... I've got the monitor back from Spider..." I lifted my wrist to show it. "If I see anything incoming, I'll wake you. If it's only one person, I'll deal with it and you can stay in the house to defend Spider and Linda. That'll maintain your cover and provide an extra layer of protection just in case. If there's more than one attacker, I have a secret room in the basement where we can put the kids while we take care of business. And if it's an army, I'll hit the panic button and we'll all hide out in the basement and let my backup team deal with it."

She brightened. "You have a backup team?"

"Yep." I hid a wry smile. The chain of command wouldn't risk losing me, and I was pretty sure Stemp would use that as an excuse to unleash holy hell on anybody who attacked while his parents were here.

"We only have to survive for twenty minutes or so to give them a chance to get here," I added. "But I'm not expecting a major frontal attack. So far it's all been sneaking around in the shadows."

Moonbeam unleashed a predatory smile, her soft façade dropping to reveal the lethal agent behind it. "And it just so happens we're very *good* at that. Sweet dreams, dear."

"You, too," I mumbled, hiding the shiver that brushed my spine like icy cobwebs.

Of course the deer had to pick this night to traipse all over my yard. Twice I woke to the vibration of the monitor, my heart pounding. The first time, around two AM, I could still see the soft glow of my office lights under the door. Spider was obviously hard at work.

When I bolted up in bed the second time at three forty-five, the rest of the house was dark and quiet. Easing myself back onto the pillow, I switched to full-video and watched the doe and half-grown fawn nibbling the lawn and looking longingly through the page-wire fence at my garden.

Once I might have enjoyed watching them, or even envied their freedom. Now I noted every twitch of their ears, every wary survey of their surroundings, every quiver of taut muscles ready to flee at the slightest threat.

I knew exactly how they felt. Poor little bastards.

CHAPTER 37

The buzzing of my alarm clock at six-thirty was an affront to decency. Groaning, I slapped the snooze button and buried my face in the pillow.

My eyes finally opened after I'd stumbled through the shower, and by the time I made it to the kitchen they actually focused in the same direction. That seemed like a good start.

Karma and Moonbeam drifted in on silent bare feet as I was eating my second piece of toast, and Karma waved me back to my chair when I began to rise.

"Don't worry, we know where everything is," he assured me, and they helped themselves to yogurt and cereal before joining me at the table.

"How did you sleep?" I asked.

"Oh, very well, thank you." Moonbeam looked fresh and bright, and I envied her with every cell in my body. "How did you sleep, dear?" she added.

"Okay. Deer triggered the cameras a couple of times, but other than that everything was quiet." I gulped another mouthful of toast and peanut butter and passed over my wrist monitor. "Here, I'll leave this with you. I don't know if I'll be back tonight, but I'll be here tomorrow morning by eleven at the latest. If the wedding is at two, guests might be arriving as early as one." I crammed the last bite of toast into my mouth and rose with my dishes. "I'll see what I can do for weapons detection," I mumbled through peanut butter. "I'll call you as soon as I know."

"Very well, dear. How may we contact you if necessary?"

"Hang on..." I read off the number from the burner phone I'd been using, then appropriated another from the drawer and gave them that number, too.

"Excellent. Good luck with your day, and don't worry about a thing here," Moonbeam said, and I nodded my thanks and headed for the door carrying my small backpack.

On the way to the office I watched my rear-view mirror anxiously, but there was no sign of pursuit. The parking lot at Sirius Dynamics held the usual vehicles and I didn't spot anybody watching while I walked up to the entrance doors.

Maybe Labelle had been permanently scared off yesterday.

The thought filled me with a queasy mixture of relief and fear. If he spread the word that I wasn't to be trusted I could drop the arms-dealer charade, but that likely meant I'd be assigned to another, possibly more dangerous mission.

Or consigned to prison.

I swallowed hard and pasted on a smile for the security guard while I signed in.

Plodding up the stairs, I attempted to look at the bright side. At least if Labelle wasn't following me today, my courier mission to Calgary should go smoothly.

But somehow I had a feeling it wasn't going to be that easy.

I tossed my backpack onto the sofa in my office and dropped into my desk chair to check my email. I was wading through the usual administrative crap when my desk phone rang, displaying Reggie Chow's caller ID.

Picking up with a quiver of anxiety, I kept my greeting down to a brief 'Kelly' to hide my nerves.

"Hey, Kelly, good news," he said cheerfully. "I got the approval to gear you up. If you can get down here before ten we'll have time to do it before you leave for your assignment."

Some of the weight eased from my shoulders. A technological advantage. Exactly the kind of confidence-booster I needed right now.

"Okay," I replied. "It'll depend on how long my nine o'clock meeting with Stemp goes, but I'll be down as soon after that as I can."

"See you then."

He hung up and I leaned back in my chair, letting my mind drift to fantasies of some cutting-edge spy gear or performance-enhancing drug that would miraculously make me ten feet tall, bulletproof, and competent. And maybe even confident.

Imagining the glorious possibilities, I saw myself engaging guys like Labelle in conversation without a single surge of adrenaline or droplet of sweat. Boldly striding through ambushes, effortlessly identifying and eliminating the bad guys even though I was outnumbered. Somehow I had become a martial arts master, too...

The 'ding' of my meeting reminder jolted me awake, and I jerked upright from my slouch and wiped a bit of drool from the corner of my mouth.

Shit.

So much for the half-hour of work I'd planned to get done before my meeting with Stemp. I had exactly enough time to use the washroom and get to his office.

Suppressing a groan, I hauled myself out of my chair and headed down the hall.

Stemp's agenda was mercifully brief. He supplied me with the address of the Calgary facility and the protocols for accessing it, then asked, "Anything else?"

"Um, no... I can't think of anything else I'll need for today... but..." I shifted uncomfortably in my chair. "I was wondering..."

His expression smoothed to watchful waiting.

"Um, I didn't mention this to you before, but, um... Spider and Linda's wedding is tomorrow and they've been having problems..."

He frowned. "I'm sorry to hear that, but their personal issues are really none of my business."

"Oh, no, I didn't mean that. I meant... well, you heard about Linda's wedding dress, but there have been other things as well. Some damage to the brakes on Spider's car; and the hall where they'd planned to hold their reception burned down; and they've had things like dead birds and black roses showing up on their doorstep. Somebody doesn't want them to get married, and I'm afraid it'll escalate to a bomb or a weapon attack at the wedding." I eyed him imploringly. "Do you think... would the Department maybe lend them a weapons detection system for a few hours on Saturday... as a wedding present?"

For a moment I was treated to the unprecedented sight of a speechless Stemp.

After a brief silence his lips twitched. "Well, that is certainly the most unexpected request I've ever received. But as much as I'd like to help, I can't justify the deployment of a classified system and a tech to operate it simply because of a damaged dress and a dead bird."

"No, those aren't the things that are worrying me," I argued. "I'm worried about the hole in Spider's brake line and the community hall burning down. Labelle was at their wedding shower, and he could very well be threatening them to get to me."

"But why would he?" Stemp objected. "Other than the gunman, who was likely only a test, why would Labelle want to coerce you? If he's looking for a business associate, antagonizing you would be a poor way to start. And if he is doing these things to coerce you, he would have given you some indication of what he wants by now."

"I don't know why he'd be doing this stuff." I stared at him in frustration. "If I knew, I'd just solve the problem. And in the meantime, you could lose your top analyst if somebody slips a bomb into a wedding gift."

Stemp blew out a breath. "True. I simply doubt the likelihood of that happening."

"And you might lose more than just Spider," I argued. "Remember, your mom and dad will be at the wedding, too."

He stared at me, his face hardening. "That was a low blow," he said stiffly.

"I didn't mean it as a blow at all. It's a simple fact. I'll be there, too, along with John and Arnie."

Hellhound actually braving any wedding was unlikely at best and I couldn't imagine Kane being in any condition to celebrate, but I ignored that and pressed my advantage. "You were invited, too. Top analyst, top decryption asset, top agent, top weapons specialist, and the director of operations. All of us could be gone in a second. Can you justify the detection system now?"

His mouth twisted as if he'd bitten into something sour. "Perhaps. If you seriously consider Labelle a threat, I could theoretically justify the expense against your current mission. But I still doubt the connection."

"Doubt it all you want," I snapped, and jerked to my feet. "But you'd better be right."

Stemp sighed. "Indeed. The story of my career."

For a moment he looked so tired and dispirited that my heart smote me. "I'm sorry," I muttered. "I know you're doing the best you can."

"Always." His lips crimped into what was likely meant to be a smile, but it looked more like a grimace of pain. "Dismissed."

I trailed out of his office and down the hall to collect my backpack, deep in thought. Stemp was right; I couldn't think of any reason why Labelle would want to coerce me. Was I just letting my paranoia run away with me?

But it isn't paranoia if they really *are* out to get you...

Blowing out a breath, I headed for the Weapons lab.

When I rounded the corner into the main area of the lab, Chow looked happier than I'd ever seen him. Grinning, he beckoned me over to his counter.

"This is great," he exulted. "I've never had an agent with a high enough security clearance to use all my toys without them being deployed 'way the hell-and-gone out to where I can't get the prototypes back easily. Here."

He handed me the fashionable glasses I'd seen on my first trip to the lab. "We put tinted lenses in, since it's summer," he said. "Designer sunglasses, just for you. Put 'em on; see what you think."

I slipped them cautiously onto my face.

"Where's your phone?" he went on. "I'll load up an app so you can control the heads-up display zoom and brightness and the audio volume remotely, for when you can't get caught fiddling with the sunglasses."

"Um... I'm just carrying burner phones right now." I held one out to him. "Sorry, normally I'd carry my smartphone, but-"

"No problem; I'll load it onto as many phones as you've got. The app isn't classified. It looks like a cheap useless audio player, and if anybody picks up your burner phone after you ditch it, they'll think it's shit and chuck it. But everybody's always got their phones in their hands these days, so it's the perfect cover for when you're listening in or watching somebody. Just stand there staring at your phone like the rest of the fucking zombies."

While he loaded the software I walked around the lab, getting used to the distraction of the heads-up display showing objects receding behind me and the whisper of the enhanced audio in my ears. Two tiny pressure-sensitive pads on the side provided a visual zoom that was good enough to identify fine details even at the far end of the lab, while two pads on the opposite side adjusted the sound amplification and balancing. I played with the control, fading out the ambient noises in the room and boosting the murmur of voices from inside one of the sealed labs.

By the time Chow had loaded and demonstrated the app, I had heard every detail of the modifications Sawyer and Melinda were planning for some unspecified piece of equipment, and I was sold.

"This is fabulous!" I exclaimed, grinning. "No more trying to sneak peeks over my shoulder and into plate-glass windows to see who's following me! And I love the way I can isolate and amplify voices!"

"And you can turn up the amplification as loud as you want," he agreed. "There's a limiter circuit so if there's a sudden loud noise in the frequency range you're amplifying, it'll automatically suppress it to a bearable level. Okay. Next." He guided me over to Murray and Melinda's counter. "We're giving you the flies and the control box."

"Uh..." I shrank back from the small but furiously buzzing box he extended. "Thanks, but I'll pass."

"Don't be such a fucking pussy," he said without heat. "Take it. You don't have to carry it for long. We just want to try the location system in a larger crowd than what we can test here. You're going to be in Calgary today so you'll have a better chance of finding a crowd than we will."

"And then what?" I griped, still avoiding the box. "Don't you think people are going to wonder when a swarm of flies suddenly comes out of my backpack? And what if somebody kills them all? Sprays them with Raid or something?"

"Then we breed another batch and try again in ten days. Take it, Kelly." He glared. "Or I won't let you play with the rest of the toys."

I eyed his lopsided scowl and sighed. "Okay. Fine. Give me the damn flies. How does the control box work?"

A brief demonstration left me feeling slightly more confident. There wasn't much to it other than pressing one button to move the flies to the next target and another button to call them back into their box. I didn't even need to use the joystick unless I wanted to. Still, I suppressed a shudder as I stowed the buzzing box inside my backpack.

I gave Chow a glower of my own. "You'd better have something good for me. You owe me for putting up with these disgusting flies."

He returned a smug smile, lifting a lightweight black jacket from the back of a chair. "How about this?"

"*That's* supposed to be good?" I grimaced at the

garment. "I may have all the fashion sense of a blind troglodyte, but I do know that is one fugly jacket."

"Fugly?" Chow inquired, his remaining eyebrow rising.

"Fucking ugly," I enunciated clearly.

He snorted. "You're right, you have no fucking fashion sense. This is a knockoff of some big fancy-ass designer."

"What big fancy-ass designer?"

"How the hell should I know?" Chow gave me an irritable glare. "Do I look like I give a rat's ass about designer clothes?" He glanced over as Sawyer strode in. "Hey, Sawyer, what designer did we knock this off of?"

"No idea." Sawyer's brow furrowed. "Prada?"

"Did you just make that up?" Chow demanded.

Colour rose through Sawyer's beard. "Yeah," he admitted. "That's the only designer name I know. Does it matter?"

I shrugged. "Not to me. I still say it's fugly. What's so good about it?"

"It keeps you from getting shot or stabbed, you ungrateful beeyotch." Chow shook out the jacket by its shoulders and handed it to me. "Lightweight, flexible, discreet, and it'll stop bullets and edged weapons."

"Really?" I examined it with new interest. "But it's so light. The impact from the bullet would kill you even if it didn't penetrate."

"Well, it'll knock you on your ass all right, same as a regular bullet-proof vest," he agreed. "No way to completely counteract the force transfer, but it'll leave you with less of a bruise than a conventional vest. The fabric is woven from nanotubes containing a non-Newtonian colloidal fluid. The higher the mass and velocity of the projectile that hits it, the harder and faster it stiffens up."

"Non-Newtonian..." I stared at him for a moment before comprehension dawned. "Oh, you mean like cornstarch and water. You can mix up a pourable solution, but if you slam your finger into it, it goes solid."

"Yeah. And it's got steel nanothreads woven into it, too, so an edged weapon can't cut it." He shrugged. "You'll still feel the impact, but it'll distribute the force over a larger area."

"But... um..." I whisked the sleeve experimentally through the air a couple of times. "If it reacts like cornstarch, wouldn't it stiffen up if you tried to move fast?"

"Ah..." Chow's eye contact wavered. "Well, we're working on that. It does stiffen up a bit, but a human being can't really move fast enough to activate its top resistance level. We've tested it in the lab and it seemed okay to us, but we need somebody to field-test it."

"So it's not quite ready for production yet," I said dryly.

"Not quite. But we know the protection is good, and with the long sleeves and hood it's 'way better coverage than a vest."

"I'll take that," I agreed. "I was lucky the one time I got shot wearing a vest, but a couple of inches over would have been a whole different story."

Amusement glinted in his eye. "Well, then take your fugly jacket and shut up about it. Speaking of nanothreads, do you have the new hand restraints yet?"

"Um... what new hand restraints?"

"Jesus, Kelly." He shot me a disgusted scowl. "Don't you read your interoffice memos? The next-gen restraints with nanothread reinforcement are available for everybody from Stores. Pick some up on your way out, and make sure you get the special cutter for them, too."

"That'll be good," I said, trying to cover my embarrassment. "I wasn't feeling too confident about nylon hand restraints after I broke out of them a few months ago."

Chow's eyebrow went up. "You broke out of law-enforcement hand restraints? That's pretty tough to do."

"Oh." Shit, now I was even more embarrassed. "Um, no, they were just ordinary nylon zip-ties," I mumbled.

"Well, duh." He gave me a look as if rethinking his decision to trust me with his high-tech toys. "Come and get the crowd-control weapons and then you can get going."

Face flaming, I followed him. A few minutes later I slunk out of the lab wearing the ugly jacket, with the fancy sunglasses perched on top of my head and the ultrasound weapons safely stowed in my backpack.

CHAPTER 38

I had just emerged from the time-delay chamber and was standing in the lobby drawing a few deep breaths to dispel the claustrophobia when Stemp arrived from the direction of the offices.

"Ah, Kelly, you haven't left yet. Good." He inclined his head toward the direction he'd come, and I followed him back up to his office. When we were safely inside with the door closed, he said, "There are no large-scale weapons-detection units available on such short notice. However, we could lend you one of the small portable units."

I sat forward in my chair, my heart lifting. "That would be great, but I've never used one before. How big are they, and how do they work?"

"They're about the size of a laptop computer, and they detect both concealed weapons and explosives. Their imaging works on a similar principle to ultrasound, detecting the difference between rigid dense materials and human tissue. It works through clothing, from a distance of up to six feet, and it will find everything from a firearm to a ceramic knife to an explosive vest..." He trailed off with a rueful grimace. "Also leg braces, lingerie stiffeners, and whatever other dense material is on the body. It's programmed to alarm if it detects the outline of a knife or gun, but its output needs to be monitored for other potential threats and to eliminate false positives. And it detects explosive residue using a wireless wand."

"Oh." My elation ebbed. "So all the gifts would have to be swabbed, and each guest would have to be checked over. I suppose its detection system is line-of-sight."

Stemp nodded. "Yes, you'd have to walk around each guest or get them to turn three hundred and sixty degrees."

"Shit. I can't do that and watch for threats at the same time. And I don't want to turn Spider and Linda's wedding into an airport-security experience for all their guests. But..." I frowned. "Is there..."

"No techs are available," Stemp answered my question before I'd asked it.

"Shit. And we'll need somebody with a high enough security clearance to use it." I pondered for a moment. "Could you...?"

"No." His expression was completely unreadable. "I won't be attending the wedding. And in any case, I wouldn't risk compromising my cover, especially with my parents there."

My heart sank. Moonbeam and Karma would be leaving after the wedding. This might be my last chance to arrange a reconciliation.

"But... Spider invited you. He'll be hurt if you don't come," I argued.

"I promised Webb I would attend the reception," Stemp said stiffly. "And I shall. But I will not be present for the wedding ceremony."

"God, don't tell me you've got a wedding phobia, too."

He blinked, his hand twitching up to adjust his tie.

"Not... exactly a phobia, no..." When I stared at him, he actually squirmed and dropped his gaze. "I'm simply not comfortable with..." he mumbled, then apparently got a grip on the situation and donned his usual impenetrable façade. "Irrelevant. I will not be attending the wedding."

"Okay." I tamped down an involuntary grin and concentrated on the issue at hand. "So who has clearance to operate the detector?"

"The techs, any agent in active service, top-level analysts, Dr. Chow, and I."

I opened my mouth, but he beat me to the question.

"All active agents are currently deployed. Webb and Brock are the only analysts with sufficient clearance."

"Shit." I slumped in the chair. "Reggie is running a 5K race this weekend. Spider's going to be a little busy getting married. John's not in active service..."

"No, and he needs to come in today," Stemp interrupted. "Or he'll never be in active service again."

I swallowed hard. "I'll bring him back with me from Calgary. Tranked, if necessary. You said 'end of day'? So technically that's midnight, right?"

Stemp gave me a severe look. "Technically that's seventeen hundred hours."

"But it's already after ten..." I began frantically.

He made a 'calm down' gesture. "I think I can successfully argue the technicality with the chain of command. I will make myself available until midnight."

My relief whooshed out on a long breath. "Thank you." New hope rose as a thought occurred to me. "How about Arnie? Could he operate the weapons detection system?"

"No. He's not an agent."

"But he's a weapons specialist..." I began, but gave it up

at the look on Stemp's face. "Shit. So that leaves me again."

Stemp's mouth twitched. "Or Brock."

I didn't dignify that with a reply. "Okay. When can I pick up the unit?"

"It will be available from Stores tomorrow morning by zero nine hundred."

"Thanks." I rose. "I guess I'll see you tomorrow at the reception, then."

After a quick stop at Stores to pick up a few sets of the new hand restraints and the special cutter, I signed out, then walked slowly toward the exit doors. The laser flashlight and ultrasound baton dragged down my backpack far beyond their actual weight, and the sunglasses felt heavy on my forehead. The faint buzzing in my ears might have been the flies in my backpack, but more likely it was sheer nerves.

What if Labelle had just been biding his time? What if he had somehow discovered I'd be making this courier run today? If he ambushed me on a desolate stretch of the highway, he could walk away with all my classified technology and sell it to the highest bidder.

My leaden feet moved closer to the doors. My Glock weighed down one ankle; a trank pistol the other. God, I was carrying so much hardware that Labelle could just drop me in the nearest lake and I'd sink like a stone.

The urge to draw my Glock was strong, but I couldn't exactly burst out onto the sidewalk waving a firearm.

Get it together, chickenshit. You've been through these doors hundreds of times and never been ambushed yet.

Okay; only once...

Maybe I should go down through the secured area and come out the secret bowling alley exit.

I trailed to a halt, staring out the glass doors.

No, dammit, if Labelle was watching and he'd seen me go in the front doors with my backpack, he'd expect me to come out the front doors with my backpack. Showing up from the opposite direction would arouse far too much suspicion.

Just act like everything's normal...

"Aydan?" The security guard's voice made me jump. "Everything okay?"

"Oh... um, yeah." I smacked my forehead lightly and tried for a grin. "Zoned out for a second there. Too much on my mind."

So much for acting normal. Way to go, Jane Bond.

I gave the security guard a cheery salute and stepped out the doors, holding my breath.

Nobody gave me a second glance. I slid the sunglasses into place and attempted a casual stroll over to the parking lot. The sun blazed onto the black jacket like a branding iron. Perspiration dampened my brow and prickled my back and armpits.

Yeah, it was the heat making me sweat, not fear...

Swinging my backpack off my shoulder, I slid into my oven-like car and cranked on the air conditioning. After one more suspicious survey of my surroundings, I hit the road.

For the first thirty miles I remained hyperaware of all the vehicles around me, but after half an hour with no sign of pursuit I relaxed unless I was approaching a blind corner or hill.

Driving gave me entirely too much time to think. My mind circled anxiously through all the things that could go wrong in the next twenty-four hours.

I hadn't asked Spider about his progress, but since he hadn't woken me last night or called me today, I assumed he had nothing to report. Was that good or bad? If he eliminated all the names on the list without finding a connection, would Kane admit defeat long enough to come to Silverside for the lie detector test?

Dammit, I didn't care whether he admitted defeat or not. I'd drag him back to Silverside myself, even if I had to trank him and get Arnie to load his unconscious body into my car. I did a rapid mental calculation. I was carrying two magazines of ten trank darts each. At about twenty minutes of sedation per dart...

No problem. One way or another, he was coming back to Silverside tonight. He'd be angry, but he'd be alive.

But would he ever forgive me for taking precious time away from his search?

A memory-flash of Daniel's smiling face made my chest ache. Please let him be dead, killed quickly and mercifully nearly a week ago. If he was still alive in the hands of a monster, finding him would be the worst thing that could happen to Kane. My throat tightened with nausea and emotion. With an effort, I blinked away the burning behind my eyes and wrenched my attention back to the road and my other worries.

I hadn't considered all the ramifications of being Chow's guinea pig, either. I had been looking forward to the relief of completing my delivery of the ultrasound baton, but as long as I was carrying the rest of the classified technology I'd have to be constantly on guard.

And shit, how was I going to scan for weapons and bombs at the wedding tomorrow? There was no way I could scan each of a hundred or so guests along with the wedding gifts, all while dealing with the myriad distractions and complications of playing both hostess and bodyguard.

I briefly considered handing the scanning duties over to

Moonbeam and Karma. Since we'd discussed a weapons detection system, I'd have to tell them about it.

But telling them about it and actually handing it over to them were two different things. If Stemp showed up unexpectedly, he'd instantly recognize the unit and know I'd given it to them, and I'd be in jail so fast it'd make my head spin. And if I tried to save myself by revealing that Moonbeam and Karma were active agents, their cover would be blown all to hell and so would our friendship.

Dammit.

As the miles slipped by outside my car, the revolting truth became clearer and clearer.

I was going to have to ask a favour of Tyler Brock.

It took another half an hour of driving before I could bring myself to pull over and dial his number. I could have used the hands-free, but being behind the wheel while infuriated would probably break the distracted-driving laws.

After a few deep breaths, I hit Talk.

"Brock." His unpleasant nasal voice made my teeth clench.

With an effort I unclenched them and said, "Hi, Tyler. It's Aydan Kelly calling."

"What do you want this time?" he snapped.

Breathe. Count to three.

"Actually, I'm not calling for myself. I was hoping you might be able to help Spider out."

"If he wants help, he can ask me himself." The line went dead in my ear.

After some loud swearing followed by a couple of minutes of deep breathing, I dialled again.

"Don't hang up," I said hurriedly as soon as he answered. "This is important."

"Oh, yeah?"

"Yeah, life-or-death."

"Oh." He didn't sound quite so snotty, and I drew a breath of hope when he asked, "What is it?"

"Well, you know Spider and Linda are getting married tomorrow..."

"Yeah, so what?"

"So they invited you..."

He interrupted with a sharp braying laugh. "Like I'd go. Weddings are so fin."

I didn't bother asking for a translation. "Maybe, but they could really use your help, and you're the only one that can do it."

"*My* help? For what?"

"Well, I told you earlier that somebody had spiked Spider's drink and he had a bad allergic reaction, and since then somebody's been leaving them creepy presents like dead birds and black-painted roses, and Spider's brakes failed and the community hall where they were going to have the reception burned down. I'm worried about them, and Linda is beside herself."

"Oh."

I couldn't quite interpret his intonation, but at least he hadn't hung up yet. I went on, "They're going to have their wedding and reception at my place so we'll have perimeter security, but I want to run weapons and bomb checks on everybody as they come in."

"Uh..." He hesitated, and when he spoke again his voice had a wheedling quality that set my teeth on edge. "Listen, Kelly, it's probably not as bad as you think. Um..."

He hesitated again, and I waited him out in silence.

A moment later he blew out a short breath. "I spiked

Webb's drink. It was an accident."

"An *accident?*"

I didn't quite manage to keep the incredulous note out of my voice, and he blew out another huffy breath. "The groom's supposed to get shellacked at his party. How was I supposed to know he had some stupid allergy?"

Teeth clamped hard on my tongue, I waited until the urge to yell subsided enough that I could speak normally again. "Okay, but did you have anything to do with the other things?"

"No! Jeez, you're such a bitch! Why would you automatically assume it was me?"

I drew a deep breath and prayed for patience before answering, "I wasn't assuming, I was just asking. A spiked drink isn't really a big deal, but the other stuff is downright threatening."

"So what are you calling me for?" he demanded, snotty attitude firmly back in place.

I drew another deep breath, willing my blood pressure down. Cut to the chase before you lose your temper...

"I was hoping you'd be able to discreetly scan the guests with a portable weapons scanner and check the wedding gifts for explosives," I said levelly. "Nobody else is available except me, and I need to be ready to react in case something happens."

"Oh, so you want me to risk *my* life," he snapped. "I don't think so."

"You wouldn't be risking your life, but you might be saving theirs," I retorted. "Or are you too much of a selfish coward?"

"Listen, you bitch-"

"Wait, I'm sorry," I blurted. "Look, I'm worried sick

about them and I can't do it alone. I know you wouldn't give me a sack of rotting shit even if I begged for it, and that's okay, but will you please help Spider? And Linda?"

His silence spurred me to desperation. "Look, Brock, I'll pay you. Whatever your day's salary is, I'll pay it."

"Overtime pay," he sniffed. "Time and a half."

"Bullshit! Salaried workers don't get overtime."

"I do now. If you want me to do this you'll pay me time and a half." The supercilious sneer in his voice made my fist clench involuntarily, searching for his throat.

"Fine," I growled. "I'll pay you time and a half. You can pick up the detector from Stores tomorrow morning at nine-"

"Hang on, I didn't say I'd do it yet," he taunted.

"What now?" I barked, at the extremities of my patience. "What else do you want? Peeled grapes? A trailer with a star on the door? An autograph from the master of the fucking universe?"

"Language, Kelly." He sniffed. "You certainly couldn't get any autograph I'd want-"

"What? What autograph do you want?" I demanded. I didn't care if he wanted Shakespeare's autograph from beyond the grave; I'd find somebody to forge it.

"Never mind," he drawled as if he were a nobleman granting a boon to a particularly unprepossessing peasant. "I'll be at your farm at one o'clock tomorrow with the detector. Have my cheque ready. And you're going to owe me a favour. Whatever I want, whenever I want it."

My blood pressure surged to the point where I could hear the blood swishing through my brain. "You know I can't promise that, Brock," I said, holding my voice as level as I could. "And I need you there at noon just in case people start arriving early."

"Fine." I imagined his petulant flounce on the other end of the line. "A favour of my choice, then, within the bounds of legality and national security. Take it or leave it."

"I'll take it," I ground out between my teeth. "See you tomorrow."

Then I disconnected and spent the next several minutes in a concerted effort to melt every plastic part in my car with the heat of my invective.

By the time I neared the outskirts of Calgary, I had reined in my fury at Brock enough that I was no longer in danger of biting the steering wheel. At least my outrage had made the drive go quickly, and I still hadn't spotted a tail despite my constant vigilance.

I was beginning to think my trip was going to be uneventful when my burner phone rang and my home number came up on the call display.

Shit, that's right. I'd forgotten to call Moonbeam and Karma about the weapon detection system.

When I activated the hands-free and answered, Spider's excited voice made my heart leap in a mixture of hope and dread.

"Aydan, I think I found something!"

CHAPTER 39

"What?" I demanded, braking hard and pulling over to the shoulder of the highway.

"A connection. Through Facebook, just like we were joking about last night!"

"Who? What's the connection?"

"Penobscot Salinger Murphy, Buck Murphy's brother. He knew Selena Bruner's ex-husband-"

"Yeah, we knew that," I interrupted. "But they weren't close friends, and he didn't know any of the other exes. He didn't even know any of the friends of the exes."

"No, I know, but listen. He knew friends of friends of the exes. He and some of the friends of friends belong to a male supremacy group, and in each case one of his friends from the group is friends with one of the exes. He has a connection twice removed to all of them. And get this, Aydan, he has a son who looks a lot like Daniel! Matthew Mark Murphy."

My heart gave a giant thump. "Is it Daniel? Or one of the other kidnapped boys?"

"No, but there's something weird with Scot Murphy's Facebook posts. Up until fifteen months ago he was posting regularly, lots of pictures with Matthew camping and fishing and stuff. Then there's a hiatus right around the time when Peter Bruner was abducted. After that Murphy's posts pick up again, but more sporadically, and there's a gap around the time of each boy's abduction."

"So what does that mean?" I demanded.

"Well, I was thinking maybe he was just trying to be kind to the Bruners, you know, not rubbing it in that he still had his son and they didn't."

"But what about the others? If he didn't know them..."

"Well, he was connected through friends of friends, so he'd still have been able to see posts from them. Most people aren't careful enough about their Facebook security settings to limit their posts only to friends. And when the boys were abducted their parents put up all kinds of pleas and offers for rewards on Facebook that got shared everywhere. Maybe Murphy just didn't want to make them feel bad."

"That seems awfully sensitive and thoughtful," I said suspiciously. "Especially for a misogynistic pig."

"Or maybe he figured out that the boys all looked like Matthew and he was afraid Matthew might be next," Spider suggested.

Fear closed an icy fist around my stomach. "Shit, we need to call the police right away! If whoever's stalking these boys is finding them through Facebook..."

"I don't think it would help to call the police," he said uncertainly. "They can't put a security detail on every boy in the province with dark hair and grey eyes. And anyway, how are you going to say you found out? Hacking Facebook is illegal and you can't blow your cover unless it's an emergency."

"Shit!" I pounded a fist on the steering wheel. "And Stemp already told me he can't give me any legal protection on this case. I'm sorry, Spider, I shouldn't have involved you..."

"It's okay," he interrupted. "I won't get caught. I'm too good a hacker for that..." His voice wavered into uncertainty again. "...unless you tell the police..." His tone firmed, and I imagined his cheeks flushing and his shoulders squaring. "Matthew's life might be at stake. You have to tell them."

"No, Spider, I'm not going to get you in trouble over this. I'll find another way. And you're right, they couldn't protect Matthew even if I did tell them. We can contact Murphy ourselves and warn him if he doesn't already know." I put the car in gear and accelerated back onto the highway. "Email everything you've got to John, and tell him I'll be there in twenty minutes."

"Okay, Aydan. Good luck."

Exactly twenty minutes later I parked in one of the visitor parking slots at Kane's condo building and ran for the door. The lock released as soon as I pressed his call button, and I took the stairs two at a time to the third floor.

By the time I arrived panting at the top, Hellhound was already framed in Kane's open doorway.

"Hey, darlin'." He enclosed me in a brief hug and drew me inside, closing the door behind us.

My first look at Kane stopped me in my tracks. Thick stubble coated his jaw and his hands trembled finely. Haunted eyes sunken in deeply-shadowed sockets were the only trace of colour in his face.

"John...?" I asked cautiously. "Didn't you go to bed last night?"

"Of course I did. I gave you my word," he snapped,

returning his attention to the laptop screen in front of him. "Have you seen this new data from Webb?"

"Um, no, but he told me a bit about it."

I threw a 'what-the-fuck?' look at Hellhound and he leaned down to murmur in my ear. "He went to bed at midnight an' told me he was takin' his pills, but I think he lied. Soon's he was down I crashed, too, an' when I got up this mornin' he was already up. Doubt if he slept more'n a coupla hours, if he slept at all. Prob'ly just lay there waitin' 'til I fell asleep-"

"Do you mind?" Kane demanded. "Can you stop whispering sweet nothings to each other long enough to focus on saving my son's life?"

A sharp retort rose to my lips, but Hellhound shot me a warning look and replied, "Sorry, Cap." He led me over to the table where we peered over Kane's shoulder at the name diagram Spider had sent. "I dunno if that means what ya think it means, though," Hellhound added as though rejoining an argument that had been in progress before I arrived.

"Of course it does!" Kane barked. "Look!" He traced an impatient finger over the network of lines that connected Scot Murphy through friends of friends to each of the exes. "And the Facebook posts prove it!" He flipped to a view of Murphy's Facebook feed and began to scroll.

In the photos from two years ago, Matthew Mark Murphy displayed a wide grin for the camera, posing with a fishing rod and a jackfish nearly as big as himself, or perched on a motorized quad wearing child-sized camo fatigues. He resembled Daniel, but there was no confusing the two.

Then came the gap when Peter Bruner had disappeared, and when the photos resumed there were no more closeups of Matthew. Instead, he appeared as a small figure in the distance, or turned away so the camera didn't capture his face.

"Scot Murphy was scared," I surmised. "He realized Matthew looked like the disappearing boys and he didn't want to display a full-face picture in case Matthew was targeted."

"No, Scot Murphy is the killer," Kane growled. "Look at these children. They're not Matthew. They're not even the same child in all the photos. Something happened to Matthew, and Murphy has been stalking these children on Facebook, abducting them and dressing them up to look like Matthew, and then killing them and taking another. He's probably trying to replace his own son. Classic psychosis."

"I dunno, Cap," Hellhound soothed. "I don't see how ya figure these are all different kids. Ya can't see enough of their faces to know."

"Dammit, you can see it in their body language!" Kane jabbed a finger at the screen. "Look! They're frightened! Cringing and turning away!"

"Or lookin' at somethin' on the ground," Hellhound corrected gently. "If we had video we'd know, but ya can't really tell for sure from a still shot. But like I said, ya gotta call Mayweather. Pass it over-"

"No!" Kane surged to his feet, fists clenched. "Scot Murphy murdered his brother and took Daniel and all these other boys. If Mayweather starts investigating, Murphy will kill Daniel and hide every trace!"

"How do you know Scot killed Buck?" I asked mildly, hoping to calm the wild look in his eyes.

"Scot's fingerprints were in Buck's truck," Kane said. "And we know Buck knew his attacker because they were drinking together. And Scot is the same size and build as Buck, so they likely wore the same shoe size. Scot would have known Daniel if Buck had been dating Alicia, and he would have known about Buck and Daniel's camping trip, too. It's got to be him!"

"That's a lotta circumstantial evidence," Hellhound began. "An' they were brothers, so Scot prob'ly rode in Buck's truck lotsa times..."

"I know, but dammit, I feel it in my gut!" Kane appealed to us with both hands outstretched. "It's Murphy, I know it is! And your argument doesn't hold water, Aydan. Peter Bruner was the first to be abducted. Murphy wouldn't have had any reason to suspect a serial killer or fear for his son's life then."

"That's true..." I agreed reluctantly.

"We've got to get to Murphy before the police come to the same conclusion and start questioning him," Kane urged. "If Mayweather doesn't get a warrant right away and tips his hand with too many questions to Murphy..." He trailed off, his fists clenching all over again. "...or even if Mayweather does get the warrant, if Murphy isn't hiding Daniel at his home Mayweather will never find anything. And Murphy will kill Daniel and go under the radar until the heat is off!"

"Yeah, but if we confront Murphy, the same thing could happen," I argued. "What can we do that the police..."

I trailed off at the feral gleam in Kane's eyes.

"Cap," Hellhound warned. "We gotta think this through. What if you're wrong?"

"I'm not wrong!" Kane glared at us.

"Okay, I believe ya," Hellhound said in pacifying tones. "So let's think it through. You're gonna grab Scot Murphy, an' then what?"

"And then I'll make him tell me where Daniel is." Kane's words were simple, flat, and utterly terrifying.

"Okay, but that's messy an' it's gonna take a bit a' time," Hellhound argued. "An' what'll ya do if he won't tell ya?"

"He'll tell me."

I shuddered involuntarily.

"What if he can't tell ya 'cause he didn't do it?" Hellhound asked quietly. "Ya gonna kill him to keep him quiet an' hide the body? Keep on huntin' an' torturin' an' killin' innocent guys 'til ya find the right one? That's startin' to sound about as sick as a serial killer to me."

"I'll know," Kane argued. "I'll know as soon as I talk to him. I'm a trained agent. I've staked my life over and over on my ability to read people. If he's innocent, he's perfectly safe."

"Yes, you're a top agent, but you're not at your best right now," I objected. "You're exhausted and overstressed and reacting to your past trauma as well as this one. You know as well as I do that now's not the time to be jumping to conclusions. You can't afford to be wrong about this."

Kane hissed out an impatient breath and strode over to the kitchen island as if unable to stand still any longer. "I'm telling you, I'm right! I know it!" He jerked out a drawer and rummaged momentarily in it, his back to us. Then his movements stilled. "But you're right," he said in a softer tone. His shoulders eased.

"You're right," he repeated. "It's dangerous and illegal, and it's wrong of me to even consider involving you in it." He turned again to face us, and I barely glimpsed the gun in his hand before he added, "I'm sorry," and fired.

CHAPTER 40

I woke to an insistent hand patting my cheek and the sound of some truly inventive swearing.

"Wha...?" I mumbled.

"Wake up, darlin'." The annoying hand patted my cheek again. "Come on, Aydan, wake up."

"'M 'wake..." My eyes wouldn't open and my tongue didn't seem to be cooperating. But my arm hurt like hell. "Ow," I added.

"Sorry, darlin'." A strong arm closed around my body and pulled me farther up on the pillows.

Pillows?

What the hell?

I managed to pry one eye open to focus on Hellhound's anxious face inches away.

"Wake up, Aydan," he urged. "He tranked us an' took off. We gotta get loose an' stop him."

"Uh...?" I shook my head vigorously and got my other eye open. "Oh, f'r shit-sake," I mumbled. "Again?"

"Yeah. Again." Hellhound directed a scowl up at our wrists, handcuffed together over our heads and looped through the headboard of Kane's bed.

"Fuckin' dumbass bastard," Hellhound ground out.

"When I find him I'm gonna kick his fuckin' ass from here to hell an' back."

With the help of a massive adrenaline surge, the tranquilizer receded to a fuzzy sensation in the back of my brain and a foul taste in my mouth. I bolted up as far as I could without ripping my arm out of its socket.

"Fuck! He's gone to torture Scot Murphy! We have to stop him!"

"Is there an echo in here?" Hellhound inquired wryly. "If ya got any ideas, darlin', now'd be a good time. The only other person with a key to this condo is Dad Kane in Winnipeg, so we're either gonna hafta bust outta here on our own or call the cops. He left us the phone."

My vision cleared enough to squint at a small object on the low chest of drawers. "He left us the handcuff key, too. Out of reach. So he wants us to call 911 and get them to break in and unlock us…"

"…but then we'll hafta explain why we were locked together in the first place," Hellhound finished with disgust. "He's buyin' time. Stallin' us. He knows we won't rat him out to the cops. If we call 'em, we're gonna hafta tell 'em we were gettin' kinky an' were too fuckin' dumb to keep the key in reach. An' that'll be a low-priority call so they'll take their time gettin' to us…"

"…and then there will be paperwork and more time wasted before we can follow him." I grabbed the centre post of the headboard and jerked fruitlessly at it. "Goddammit!"

"Already tried that, darlin'. It's solid. An' he took away everythin' we coulda used to shim the cuffs open." He jerked his chin toward the bureau where my waist pouch lay out of reach as well.

I gave the post one more jerk from pure temper.

"Dammit! Don't you know anybody who can pick the door lock and get us out?" Inspiration struck. "Weasel! He's a car thief! He has to know how to pick locks!"

"He does, darlin', but car locks are different than house locks, and anyway, nobody's gonna pick this one," Hellhound said ruefully. "Kane replaced it with a high-security one. Even Weasel couldn't pick it."

"What about the management company or the cleaning staff?"

Hellhound was already shaking his head. "Nah, no such luck. If they need to get in an' Kane ain't around I gotta come down here with my key."

"Shit! We've got to get to that handcuff key!" I squirmed up toward the headboard so I could scramble to my knees. "Your arms are longer than mine. If we shuffle the bed across the floor, I can push my arm between the slats to give you more reach..." I grabbed the headboard and jerked, driving my weight backward.

The bed moved a fraction of an inch, and I swore. "Goddammit, why do you big guys always have such fucking heavy beds?"

Hellhound chuckled. "Why d'ya think? Nothin' worse'n havin' the bed let go when you're in the middle a' gettin' busy." He lurched up to his knees beside me as I tried again.

"Hang on, darlin', let's not let the phone get outta reach." He grabbed the cordless handset and placed it safely between us before gripping the headboard on his side. "Okay, let's show this bed some action. Ready? An' *push... push... push...*"

In short order we had shuffled the bed across the hardwood floor. Under Hellhound's greater weight and strength, his corner had taken the lead and wedged itself firmly against the bureau, and my side refused to get any closer despite my best efforts.

"Stop, darlin', we're stuck," Hellhound said as I jerked at the bed again, swearing with all the breath I had left.

Panting and sweating, I slumped against the headboard and stared at the mocking glint of the handcuff key beyond the foot of the bed.

"Fuck." I blew out a breath and tried to stop panting. "Okay, I'll push my arm through the headboard. See if you can reach."

I crammed my arm through the slats, gritting my teeth. Elbow and wrist contorted to allow Hellhound as much chain as possible, I panted, "Go."

On his knees and bent at the waist, he stretched his arms wide, his fingertips straining toward the foot of the bed. The chain tightened and I let out a hiss of pain.

He jerked back toward me, slackening the pull. "Sorry, darlin'. Ya okay?"

"Yeah," I said through my teeth. "Try again."

"No." He gently eased my arm back through the slats. "I wasn't anywhere close, an' I ain't gonna hurt ya. Time to call the cops."

"Wait," I panted as he reached for the phone. "I have another idea."

"Okay, but if it doesn't work we gotta call. It's been half an hour since he tranked us, an' who knows how long it'll take the cops to get here an' spring us. If they're busy today..."

"Yeah, I know." I untied my running shoe and jerked it off with my free hand, followed by my sock. "Okay, your turn to give me as much slack as you can."

"'Kay..." He crammed his hand against the headboard.

"Sorry, darlin', my arm won't fit through." He eyed the slats with frustration. "If I could get far enough away I could kick the fuckin' thing to pieces, but I ain't that much of a contortionist."

I eyed his bulky frame fondly and dropped a kiss on his lips. "You're flexible enough for what I need. Lie on your back."

He complied, grinning up at me. "This's gettin' good," he teased as I turned to face the foot of the bed, my handcuffed arm behind me while I knelt astride him. "I'm likin' your kink. But I hate to say it, darlin', we ain't got time for this right now."

I gave him a playful fondle in a place that made him purr. "You've got a one-track mind. Put your knees up. No, a little lower. Lower... Good, there," I said when his knees were at the same level as the footboard. "Now hold your arm up and bend your elbow so your forearm is across your body and parallel to the bed. That's where I'm going to put my shoulders."

"Good thinkin', darlin'," he agreed as I leaned into his arm and arched my back to carefully position the backs of my thighs on his knees. "But be careful," he added. "If ya fall, you'll rip your fuckin' arm off."

"So don't let me fall," I panted, wobbling precariously while I squirmed toward the foot of the bed, my handcuffed arm stretched above my head. His knees bruised the backs of my legs and his forearm felt like an iron bar across my shoulders. "Thank God you're strong," I added, and drew a breath of relief when my heels touched the footboard.

Momentarily stabilized, I panted a few breaths. His arm was still a rock-solid support for my upper body, and I sent up brief but fervent thanks.

"Okay," I said. "This is it. Give me as much chain as you've got."

He grunted assent, and I squirmed carefully and painfully toward the dresser, the handcuff tightening on my wrist, my bare toes reaching for the key.

"Stretch me!" I hissed, and his knees dug into my ass in response. I inched forward, my shoulder pulling almost out of its socket.

My breath came in sharp gasps of pain and effort. Under my back, his supporting arm vibrated with strain. My toes reached, squirmed, curled...

"Got it!" I cried, and jerked my foot back. "...Whoa-*shit!*"

Toppling off Hellhound's knees, I fell for a horrifying instant before his powerful arm snagged me from the air and body-slammed me onto the bed. I lay gasping for a moment, braced for the agony of a dislocated shoulder, but it didn't come.

"Ya okay, Aydan?" He rolled onto his knees beside me, wincing.

"Yeah." I let relief seep in until I realized his face had a faint greenish tinge and sweat beaded his brow. I bolted up to sitting position. "You're hurt! What's wrong? Is it your arm?"

"Nah." He managed a strangled chuckle. "Ya nutted me. I ain't likin' your kink quite so much anymore."

"Oh, shit, I'm sorry!" I reached involuntarily for the injured area before drawing my hand back and stroking his arm instead. "Um... how bad is it?"

"I'll live." He flashed me a grin. "Ya can kiss it better later. Let's get outta these cuffs."

"I dropped the key. It should be at the foot of the bed."

"Okay, gimme some chain, darlin'."

I complied and he reached, coming up a moment later with a grunt of triumph and the key.

Free at last, I strapped on my waist pouch and hurried for the door. "Do you know where Scot Murphy lives?" I asked over my shoulder.

"Yeah, he's on an acreage south a' town, but slow down, darlin'," Hellhound admonished. "First lemme try phonin' Kane. He might pick up now that he knows we're damn near forty-five minutes behind him. An' go grab some food from the fridge. Might be a long day an' we can't have ya passin' out."

"Right..." I headed for the kitchen, only to turn aside. "And I need a bathroom break. I needed to pee when I got here and now my back teeth are floating."

Hellhound threw me a grin, phone pressed to his ear. "Really glad ya managed to hold it, darlin'. Golden showers ain't my thing."

"Ew." I hurried into the bathroom.

When I returned, Hellhound was scowling at the phone.

"No luck?" I inquired, my heart sinking.

"Nah. Come on, we'll take my SUV an' head for Murphy's place. Ya can call Webb on the way an' see if he can track Kane's cell phone."

We hurried out, and as soon as I was settled in Hellhound's passenger seat I dialled Spider.

He answered on the first ring, and I rapped out, "John ran off on us. Can you track his cell phone and find out where he is?"

"Ran off...?"

"Long story. Can you find him?"

"Um, probably, but it'll take me longer than if I was at work..."

"Do it," I snapped. "We think he's headed for Scot Murphy's place. John thinks Matthew died last year and Scot has been trying to replace him by abducting children who look like him."

"Oh, no!" Spider's voice rose in consternation. "Aydan, that's all wrong! Matthew isn't dead. Scot Murphy's children are home-schooled, and I just found out that Matthew completed his academic equivalence test for Grade One two weeks ago!"

I allowed myself a single heartfelt bellow of '*FUCK!*' before adding, "Find him, Spider! ASAP!"

"I will, I will! I'll call you as soon as I have something!"

I disconnected and turned to face Hellhound's worried frown. "Matthew isn't dead. Spider just found his school records from two weeks ago."

"Fuck!" He stepped on the gas and the SUV leaped forward. "Shit, darlin', I coulda sworn Kane was right about those kids on the Facebook page."

"What?" I stared over at him. "But you said..."

"I was just tryin' to keep him from goin' off half-cocked. Those kids..." He shook his head. "They *were* different. Different builds. An' he was right, they looked scared."

"But..." I clutched my pounding head. "Why..."

"I dunno, but we better catch Kane, an' fast."

"But, Arnie, he's an agent. If he doesn't want to be found, we won't be able to find him."

Hellhound reached over to pat my leg. "Yeah, but I think he'll let us find him." When I gaped open-mouthed, he explained, "He was just protectin' us. Makin' sure we can't be charged as accessories." He glanced at his watch, his face grim. "By now he'll have snatched Murphy, an' he's prob'ly already got answers. Soon's he finds Daniel an' makes sure he's safe, he'll prob'ly call the cops an' make it look like we turned him in for roughin' up Murphy."

"But..."   My heart sank all the way to my toes and I turned an imploring look at Hellhound.   "But he can't get arrested! He'll lose all his pension and benefits..."

"Little late to worry 'bout that," Hellhound said grimly. "Soon's he lays a hand on Murphy, he's goin' to jail. The only question is whether it's for assault or murder."

CHAPTER 41

Hurtling south on Highway 2 well above the speed limit, I stared out the windshield half-paralyzed with fear while Hellhound wove in and out of traffic with grim concentration. When my burner phone vibrated it took an effort to unlock my grip on the Jesus bar above the window.

"Kelly," I said faintly.

"It's Spider. I've got Kane's phone northbound on Highway 2, just north of DeWinton."

"*Northbound?*" I squawked. "Fuck, we just passed him! Turn around, turn around!"

Hellhound slammed on the brakes and careened over to the side of the highway where a turnoff loomed impossibly close. By the time I pried my eyes open and restarted my heart we were already accelerating northbound, leaving behind a chorus of honking horns.

"Where is he?" Hellhound rasped.

"Spider, where is he now?" I activated the speaker on my phone so we could both hear his reply.

"Still northbound. It looks like... yes, he's taking Deerfoot."

"Lemme know if he turns off," Hellhound commanded. "Aydan, keep your eyes peeled."

In the heavier traffic as we approached the city, Hellhound's speed was even more terrifying. If not for the need to watch for Kane's black Expedition, I would have squeezed my eyes shut and prayed. As it was, I clung to every ounce of trust I had in Hellhound's driving skills and concentrated on the traffic ahead of us.

"Fuck, how fast is he goin'?" Hellhound growled. "We shoulda caught up to him by now."

"He's going at the speed limit," Spider replied. "Oh, wait, hang on... he's turning off. He's taking the Glenmore exit."

"What the *fuck!*" Hellhound snarled, and made another suicidal dive across three lanes of traffic to take the Memorial Drive exit. "We passed him! How the hell did we miss him?"

"I'm s-sorry," I quavered, my heart rattling in my throat. "I must have c-closed my eyes for a second..."

"It ain't your fault, darlin', I didn't see him, either. Webb, where is he?"

"Westbound on Glenmore."

Hellhound slowed to a decorous fifteen kilometres over the speed limit. "I bet he's gonna take Glenmore north to Sarcee. He's headin' up to the forestry reserve. If Murphy talked..."

I glanced over at his grim profile, my heart breaking for Kane. "Murphy confessed that he killed Daniel and hid his body right near where he abducted him. Oh, no. Poor John."

Hellhound slowed to the speed limit. "Webb, can ya pick up my cell on your GPS, too? Watch an' make sure we don't overshoot him again. I'm gonna take Memorial to Crowchild an' from there I can hook up with the TransCanada or 1A, whichever he decides to take. If he changes course, lemme know, but I'm bettin' I'm right."

"It looks like it," Spider said in a small voice. "He's just following Glenmore onto Sarcee now." He fell silent for a moment before adding, "This is awful. I know it was stupid, but..." His swallow came clearly over the speaker and when he spoke again his voice was choked. "I was really hoping for a happy ending."

"Me, too," I said softly, grief bowing my shoulders. "But... it might be best this way. If he didn't suffer long."

"Keep your head in the game 'til it's over, darlin'," Hellhound rasped. "Even if we can't help Daniel anymore, we gotta look out for Kane."

"You're right." I swallowed the lump in my throat and straightened under the weight of despair. "How are we doing, Spider? Are we still converging?"

"Yes."

We rode in silence until we had merged onto Crowchild Trail.

"He's westbound on the TransCanada now," Spider reported. A few minutes later he added, "Now he's merging onto Stoney Trail."

"Awright, he's headin' for 1A," Hellhound said, and accelerated slightly above the speed limit again. "Tell me when I'm gettin' close."

Several more minutes passed before Spider spoke again. "You're coming up behind him now. You should be in visual range."

Hellhound and I both scanned for a black Expedition.

"I can't see him," I said. "Are you sure we're close?"

Spider sounded puzzled. "You're practically on top of him."

Fear seized my heart. "Oh, God, what if Murphy killed him and he's going to dump his body-"

"What does Murphy drive?" Hellhound barked.

Spider's voice rose in anxiety. "I don't know; hang on!" The frantic clicking of computer keys filtered over the speaker while we stared at the vehicles around us.

Approximately an eternity later, Spider spoke again. "A two-tone brown Dodge Ram 3500-"

"There!" I jabbed my finger at a jacked-up dually truck with knobby tires and a quad tied into the box a few cars ahead of us. "Got him!"

"Can't see the driver," Hellhound muttered and accelerated.

As we drew abreast of the truck I stared in the window and my heart gave a sharp contraction of relief. "He's okay!"

"Thank God!" Spider breathed. "Is he driving?"

"No."

Scot Murphy didn't look much like the cocky redneck from his Facebook photos anymore. In the driver's seat, he stared rigidly ahead, hands on the wheel at ten o'clock and two o'clock positions. His face was shock-white, and even from several feet away I could see him trembling.

On the passenger's side, Kane's gaze flicked away from Murphy for an instant. He acknowledged our presence with a tiny jerk of his chin to the rear, then returned his attention to Murphy. His hands weren't visible, but I could guess what at least one of them was doing.

"He's got a weapon on Murphy and he wants us to follow," I said just as Hellhound slackened his speed.

"Got it, darlin'," he said, and drifted back to pull in behind the big truck. "Makes sense," he added. "Kane wouldn't just believe him. He'll make him take us right to

Daniel."

The words, '...and then kill him' hung unspoken in the air.

I nodded, and we drove on in silence.

When we turned north on the forestry trunk road, Spider's voice came through the speaker in a staticky crackle. "I'm losing your cell phone signal. I can still track you by GPS but we might not be able to communicate."

"Okay, thanks, Spider. I'll hang up now. Just keep watching us, and I'll call you when I can."

I disconnected, and Hellhound sent a glance my way. "Didn't wanna say anythin' while Webb was listenin', but..." He stared out the windshield into the choking cloud of Murphy's dust. "We gonna let Kane kill him?"

Letting my head fall back onto the headrest, I stared at the ceiling. "If he's a sicko who's been murdering little boys?" I swallowed red-hot anger, but it still choked my voice when I spoke again. "The world would be a better place without him. But..."

Hellhound sighed. "Yeah. But. We can't let Kane kill him. Right now he's on the hook for assault an' kidnappin', an' prob'ly forcible confinement an' a weapons charge or two, but I still think a judge would go easy on him. But if he kills that fuckin' waste a' skin it'll be a different story. He'll go down for premeditated murder."

"Do you think we'll actually be able to stop him?"

My question hung between us like a portent.

Hellhound's mouth flattened into a grim line. "I dunno."

After nearly forty minutes of driving north, Murphy's truck turned off the main road and began to wind through heavier forest on increasingly narrower byways.

"Fuck." Hellhound broke the silence that had filled the

SUV. "If he's gonna use that quad..."

"Damn. If I'd only known, I could have brought my truck and my dirt bike." I glared into the dust cloud. "What will we do? John can probably make Murphy drive the quad and ride behind him..."

"Don't think he'd do that," Hellhound objected. "Too easy to flip a quad, an' the passenger always gets the worst of it. Better if Kane ties Murphy onto the back an' makes him give directions."

"Yeah, I guess," I agreed. "But then he'd have to turn his back on Murphy. And either way, that leaves us on foot and far behind. We can't protect either of them from each other. Dammit!"

Hellhound growled agreement, then added, "But Kane's smart. He's prob'ly got a plan."

"When he's not sleep-deprived and suffering from PTSD he's smart," I said doubtfully.

"Even so, I trust him more'n any other fresh an' rested guy," Hellhound said with certainty. "Ya got your Glock? We can't go much farther before we run outta road so we better be ready."

"I've got it." Delving into my backpack, I extracted my shoulder holster and strapped it on, then transferred my Glock into it and wriggled into the ugly jacket. "Are you armed?" I asked.

"Nah. Left my sidearm back home when we got back from Rocky Mountain House, an' I been at Kane's ever since."

"Well, take this, then." I freed the trank pistol from my other ankle and handed it over along with the spare magazine.

"Thanks, darlin'." He stuffed the weapon into the back

of his jeans and tugged his T-shirt over top, concealing absolutely nothing. He gave my jacket a humorous sidelong glance. "Chilly?"

I winked. "Something like that."

A few minutes later Murphy's truck turned onto a crossing that led into a small clearing where a few other trucks were parked. Murphy nosed in beside them and stopped, and Hellhound did the same.

"Awright, darlin'," he said. "Let's go give Murphy a welcomin' committee."

We both jumped out of the SUV and I shouldered my pack before hurrying after his long strides. God, I didn't even want to imagine the depth of shit I'd be in if I left classified technology lying around in the woods.

As we reached Murphy's truck the driver's door swung open and Murphy slithered slowly out, grimacing. Behind him, Kane kept a fist clenched on his collar and a dangerous-looking knife pressed against his back as he followed.

Up close Murphy looked even worse. He was still trembling and white to the lips and he didn't seem to be able to stand up straight. Dark moisture stains on the inner legs of his jeans looked like watery blood, and sweat soaked his T-shirt and trickled down the sides of his face.

My mind served up an unwelcome memory of Kane's cold voice: 'I know a lot of ways to make excruciating pain last and last'.

A shudder shook me.

Kane's eyes were completely devoid of emotion, the blank soulless grey of a shark. "Don't come any closer or I'll kill him," he said as Hellhound stepped forward.

Hellhound stopped, his hands rising slowly in a placating gesture. "Okay, Cap. It's okay, I ain't comin' any closer.

Nobody's gotta die."

"John..." I began.

"Shut up."

His flat words hit me like a slap, but the tiniest quiver of Kane's eyelid made me hope he wasn't as far gone as he looked. Maybe he was still protecting us. When the police came, we could honestly say we couldn't have stopped him.

Hellhound took a slow step back. "Okay, so what's goin' on?" he said conversationally.

"We're going for a walk in the woods," Kane snapped. "Move." He shoved Murphy forward.

Murphy limped a couple of paces. "We have to take the quad," he whispered. "It's over half a mile. I can't walk that far. And there are bears-"

Kane's knife hand flashed back and forward so quickly that for an instant I thought he'd stabbed Murphy. Murphy let out a wrenching cry and fell, writhing in agony.

Hellhound winced. "Don't worry, Kane didn't really let him have it," he muttered out the side of his mouth. "He'll piss blood for a week, but he'll live."

So that's what a kidney punch looked like. I made a mental note to avoid receiving one at all costs.

"Looks like he's already pissing blood," I whispered back, nodding toward the stains on Murphy's jeans.

"Get up," Kane said coldly. "Whine like that again and I'll give you something to really whine about." He jerked Murphy to his feet and pushed the knife against his back again. "Walk."

Doubled over gasping and whimpering, Murphy tottered toward a quad trail that disappeared into the woods next to a sign stating, 'Private Sporting Club. Members Only. No Hunting. No Trespassing'.

"Not on the trail." Kane steered him roughly by the back of the neck into the forest.

We hiked more or less in silence. Murphy emitted quiet groans and whimpers whenever the uneven ground jarred his body or he had to step over a log. He and Kane went first, and Hellhound and I followed.

Sweat trickled under my hair and down my spine.

Should I take off the jacket?

No. If I got shot while carrying a state-of-the-art bulletproof jacket in my backpack, I deserved to die. I compromised by leaving it open and flapping it back and forth in an attempt to gather the slightest cooling breeze.

After about ten minutes of walking, Hellhound moved closer to mutter, "This feels like an ambush to me. We're still beside that quad trail. What d'ya wanna bet he's got a buncha buddies at the end waitin' for us?"

"No bet," I murmured back. "Sporting club, my ass. Bunch of rednecks with hunting bows is my guess. Guns if we're really unlucky. Do you think John knows?"

Hellhound shot a doubtful look at Kane's rigid back. "Hope so. Problem is, we won't know if they're innocent or not 'til they make a move."

I sighed. "Well, I might be able to level the playing field a bit." I donned the special sunglasses, toggling up the amplification until the ambient sounds of the forest and our shoes crunching through the undergrowth was nearly uncomfortable. Then I pulled the crowd-control baton out of my backpack.

Hellhound eyed it with interest. "That ain't standard-issue."

I shouldered the pack again and kept walking, baton in hand. "Nope."

Our whispers reverberated inside my head as though we were shouting, and I suppressed a wince. Chow had better be right about that sound-limiter circuit, or if somebody sneezed nearby my head would explode.

"Cool," Hellhound whispered. "How does it-"

I jerked up a silencing hand at the sound of a slow silvery hiss I'd heard a thousand times before.

An arrow sliding stealthily along an arrow-rest. Adrenaline punched into my veins and I scanned wildly.

Camo-clad archer in a tree-stand coming up to full draw.

Too late, I swung up the ultrasound baton.

CHAPTER 42

Launching myself between Kane and the archer, I hit the trigger on the baton an instant before a hard blow to my shoulder knocked me out of the air and spun me to land facedown on the ground.

Thumps and violent rustlings.

A quickly-aborted yelp of pain.

The sound of vomiting.

Footsteps crashed through the undergrowth and I rolled fast, swinging up the baton only to jerk it aside at the sight of Hellhound's wild-eyed face. He dove to his knees beside me, his hands rapidly exploring my body.

"Where ya hit, darlin'?" he demanded.

"I'm okay." I flexed my shoulder slowly.

"No fuckin' way." He continued his careful examination. "Broadhead'll go right through ya. You're in shock..."

"No, really." I grasped his hands and sat up. "It bounced off. This jacket is bulletproof and blade-proof."

"Fuck... off." Hellhound sat back on his heels, staring. "Nothin' stops a broadhead, not even Kevlar."

I shrugged and stretched out the neck of my T-shirt so he could see the reddening mark on my shoulder. "Ta-da. It hurts like hell, but it's not as bad as getting shot in a bulletproof vest."

"Well, fuck me." Hellhound traced the edge of the bruise with a feather-light fingertip.

"Later," I promised, and he rewarded me with a grin.

We both rose and regarded Kane staring empty-eyed at Murphy's sprawled body. My already-racing heart doubled its pace.

"Is he... dead?" I whispered.

"No. He tried to run and I knocked him out."

The archer was still vomiting behind us, and a memory niggled.

Reggie Chow saying, 'the harder you try to move or focus your eyes, the harder you puke'.

I whirled in time to see a throwing knife flash from the archer's hand, but spasms wracked his body and the knife bounced harmlessly off a log to land at my feet.

Glancing up at Hellhound, I froze as the personality I had secretly named 'The Killer' emptied his face of all emotion. In a couple of quick strides he crossed to the archer. Seizing one of the scattered arrows, he crouched beside the man, who tried to struggle away and only succeeded in retching harder.

Hellhound reached out to clinically palpate the man's inner thigh while I watched uncomprehending. Then he wedged the nock of the arrow into the soft ground and in a single fast motion lifted the man and dropped his thigh on the upturned point of the arrow.

The blades sliced home as his body fell. Bright blood fountained.

Gurgling on vomit and strangled screams, the man thrashed helplessly while his lifeblood squirted from a severed femoral artery. His struggles grew feebler, then ceased as the rhythmic spurting weakened and slowed to a dribble.

Stunned, I stood staring, my stomach twisting.

"Oughta wear a safety harness in a tree-stand," Hellhound said dispassionately. "Pretty dangerous if ya fall on your arrows."

Kane nodded and crouched beside Murphy, fingering his pulse. "Still out," he grunted. "Damn, I shouldn't have hit him so hard. I wonder how many more of those there are." He jerked his chin toward the blood-soaked heap of camo.

I was still staring at Hellhound. Did the gentle, good-natured musician step back willingly when The Killer surfaced? Or did The Killer imprison the true Arnie against his will, crushing him even while he fought to escape?

My gentle Arnie was back, his face creased with concern. "Aydan?" he asked softly. He reached toward me, but lowered his hand without touching me, self-loathing rising in his eyes as he took in my expression.

In another moment he'd be lost to me; hating himself too much to let me in...

"Damn, I hope that guy wasn't a member of our archery association," I said shakily. "Or our insurance premiums are going to go through the roof."

Shock chased across Arnie's face, followed by relief. I held out my arms and he came into them in a short fierce hug.

"Thanks, darlin'," he whispered into my hair, then pulled away and faced Kane. "Awright, ya fuckin' dumbass," he said gently. "Spill it."

"Daniel's here." Kane's eyes burned with intensity. "Murphy said he'd take me to him."

"Okay," Hellhound said. "So let's call the cops an'-"

"No! He might be lying. We'll only get one chance. Once the police are involved he could clam up and refuse to tell them anything."

"I get it, but, Cap..." Hellhound jerked his chin at the crumpled body of the archer. "Murphy's leadin' us into an ambush. Let's take him back, wake him up, an' make him tell us exactly where-"

"I don't think so," Kane interrupted. "I took Murphy by surprise so he wouldn't have had a chance to arrange an ambush. That man..." He nodded at the fallen archer. "...had cause to shoot at me, especially if he knew Murphy. And he probably did, if they both belong to this sporting club. He saw me pushing his friend along at knifepoint and correctly guessed that it was a life-threatening situation. Even if he'd killed me, he likely would have been acquitted in court."

"He tried to kill Aydan," Hellhound said in The Killer's flat voice. "An' we dunno how many more there are."

"I can find out." I swung my backpack down and pulled out the control unit and the box of flies whose buzzing had been driving me slowly insane in the enhanced audio. "Here we go."

Sliding open the box's cover, I recoiled as the swarm of insects boiled up toward my face. A quick press of the button transferred them to Hellhound, then to Kane, Murphy, and the downed archer before a final button press sent them on their way.

"What the fuck was that!" Hellhound exploded.

"Tracking and mapping system." I tilted the control panel toward them and pointed out the clustered dots that indicated our position. "Now we just have to wait." I shouldered my pack again and watched the screen.

Hellhound stared open-mouthed, and even Kane managed a quirk of his mouth that looked almost like a smile. "Looks like somebody's been making friends with Reggie Chow."

I grinned. "I'm his new favourite."

Hellhound grunted. "His only favourite, I'd say. He's as warm an' fuzzy as a fuckin' alligator."

"Actually, I kind of like him," I began, then broke off as another dot appeared on the screen. I pressed the button, and another dot formed immediately beside the first. Then another and another.

"Aw, fuck," Hellhound muttered as more dots crowded the screen.

A few minutes later I stared at the screen, my heart sinking. "Seventeen people. All clustered just over that rise. And it looks as though this one's another sentry." I tapped the outlying dot between us and the cluster. "John, I think Arnie's right, we should-"

"Aydan..." Hellhound interrupted quietly, and something in his voice sent icy shivers down my spine. "Does your puke-stick work on bears?"

Heart jackhammering my ribcage, I turned slowly.

"Back away," Kane whispered. "Nice and easy."

He hoisted Murphy's flaccid body up into a fireman's carry and we all followed his lead, stepping cautiously.

"Is that a grizzly?" Kane breathed as the giant bear moved closer, its glistening black nose twitching while it scented the air.

"Yep, that's a grizzly," I babbled in a high-pitched breathy whisper. "Little round ears, dished face, big hump on its back, big fucking claws, that's a grizzly all right, yep, yep, yep..."

My Glock was trembling in my hand, but I couldn't imagine nine-millimetre bullets doing anything but annoying the huge animal.

My pulse rocketed up into heart-attack range as crashing in the woods to our left resolved into a second grizzly triangulating toward us.

"Fuck-fuck-fuck-fuck-fuckety-fuck..." I forced my trembling legs to keep backing away slowly. The audio amplification in my sunglasses was no damn comfort at all. Behind me and to my left I could hear Kane's and Hellhound's accelerated breathing and the rapid percussive duet of their heartbeats.

The bears didn't even look our way. Their attention was riveted on the sour smell of vomit, still detectable even to my inadequate human nose. To the bears it must have smelled like a glorious buffet. As we backed over a rise, my last sight was of their muzzles dipping down toward the archer's body.

But the sound of tearing cloth and flesh and the nauseating pop of bones was all too clear in my ears.

Hands shaking violently, I muted the audio.

"Well, I vote to go forward instead of back the way we came," Kane whispered.

Hellhound and I nodded in fervent silence as a third grizzly ambled by about fifteen yards away, nose twitching in the direction of the buffet.

"How many a' these fuckin' things are there?" Hellhound demanded in a whisper. "I thought they were supposed to be fuckin' endangered."

"I don't know." I unmuted my audio, trying to ignore the slurping and crunching from over the rise. There was no more crackling of large bodies moving through the woods, but I caught the not-too-distant sound of buzzing and frantically rustling cloth.

"Shit, I forgot about my flies!" I pressed the homing button on the control box I was still clutching with nerveless fingers, then slid open the storage box. A breath of relief and some brushing sounds carried to my ears, and I kept my voice low. "The other sentry is right beside us. He must be just far enough down the hill that he can't see us."

"How d'ya know, darlin'?" Hellhound inquired. "Ya got some other gear we don't know about?"

"Yep." I tapped the sunglasses. "Massive audio boost. I just heard a squirrel fart three trees away."

He snickered, then sobered, his eyes widening. "You're serious."

"Yeah. Well, not about the squirrel, but that's how I knew the archer was there. I heard his arrow sliding on the arrow rest."

"Fuckin' cool!"

The swarm of flies returned to their box and I closed it with a shudder and stowed everything in my backpack again.

"So I wonder..."

"What they're guardin'?" Hellhound finished. "Prob'ly that."

I followed the direction of his pointing finger without comprehension for a moment. Then the forest of tree trunks resolved itself into a stockade wall.

"Holy shit." I moved downhill a few paces, trying to get a sense of the size of the structure. A row of timbers with the bark still on them soared about twenty feet tall, the tips tapered to points. The wall marched off into the distance a good fifty yards or so, and by ducking my head I spotted the opposite corner that formed a roughly square enclosure. A large and forbidding iron door was centred on the wall, its heavy latch and welded cross-banding looking like the entrance to a medieval castle.

"I think that's where the other sentry is," I murmured. "Guarding the gate."

"Man, what are these guys doin' out here?" Hellhound asked.

"Daniel must be inside," Kane growled. "They're guarding the gate so he can't escape." Sweat stained his T-shirt, and I finally brained up to the fact that he'd been holding Murphy over his shoulders all this time.

"Why don't you put him down?" I suggested.

"Right." He shook his head as if waking up and lowered Murphy to the ground, then crouched beside him. "He's still out. Dammit."

Hellhound and I exchanged a glance, sharing the worry that Murphy might not wake up ever again.

"We'll go circle the perimeter an' see..." Hellhound began, but a slow shiver of realization made me hold up a restraining hand.

"What?" Kane demanded.

Oh, God. This was bad.

"Remember how I said I could hear a squirrel fart?" I asked faintly. They both nodded, worry rising on their faces at the sight of my expression. "Well, I just realized I can't hear anything else. Just ambient forest noise."

When they didn't respond right away, I added, "There are seventeen people inside that stockade and I should be able to hear normal conversation. But not a single one of them is saying a word. And..."

I didn't want to say it, but I had to. "I can hear whimpering."

Kane went chalk-white. "Let me see the mapping again,"

he hissed.

When I handed over the control box he jabbed a shaking finger at the dots that were separated from the others. "Here's the sentry outside the gate. This must be a guard directly inside the gate. And here are three other guards off at angles. Surrounding that cluster of people." He looked up, the muscles in his jaw standing out like cables. "It's a hostage situation. They're holding the children in there!"

"We gotta call the cops," Hellhound said, and pulled out his cell phone.

"No!" Kane's hand shot out to stop him. "It's a fortified structure. One entrance, guarded. You know how this goes. Negotiations. Hostages dying." His eyes burned with feverish intensity. "And you know how it ends. I won't take that chance."

"John," I said gently. "You're reacting to an old trauma here-"

"No, I'm reacting to what I've learned," he snapped. "I've been there, done that. Learned my lesson. No more negotiating while innocent people die. Especially not my son. I'm going in."

He turned toward the sentry and Hellhound seized his arm. Kane went deadly still, glaring at Hellhound. Suppressed violence crackled in the air.

"I ain't gonna stop ya," Hellhound said firmly. "But we gotta have a plan if we're gonna make this work."

Kane drew a deep breath, visibly fighting his need to batter his way inside, through a solid log wall if necessary. "You're right. I'll circle around the back of the structure so I can avoid the bears and get back to the quad trail. Then I'll walk up the quad trail in plain sight. When they challenge me, I'll tell them I'm a new member and I was supposed to meet Scot. His truck is in the parking lot, but I can't find him. That should get me through the gate."

"Maybe. But then what?" I demanded. "You don't have a clue what you're getting into. Even if you take my gun, one of those guards can probably take you out before you can drop all of them. Here, take the ultrasound baton-"

"No. I won't take a weapon." When I began to protest, Kane shook his head forcefully. "No. In the first place, I don't want to leave you without it, and in the second place I don't want to look like a threat. If they feel threatened, they'll kill the hostages. You can listen in with your super-hearing so you'll know what's happening, and if things go sour you can call the police then. They'll be able to react much more effectively if they know what's going on inside."

"But it'll take them at least an hour to get here. And we don't know for sure that all the people in that cluster are hostages; and what if more club members arrive in the meantime?" I demanded.

Kane grinned, a deaths-head grimace that chilled me to my toes despite the heat. "Then we'll have a party."

He turned and slipped away into the forest.

CHAPTER 43

"Fuck," Hellhound said, and we stared at each other for a moment.

"I know John doesn't want us to, but we should call the police now," I said. "We can tell them to stay out at the road and wait for our signal."

Hellhound already had his phone out, but a moment later he repeated, "Fuck." He pocketed his phone with a defeated air. "Woulda been a good idea, but I got no signal at all out here. How 'bout you?"

I checked my phone and shook my head, my heart sinking.

He sighed. "Ya think the kids are even still alive? The flies mapped that dead guy."

"He was really fresh," I countered uncertainly. "They're attracted to mucous membranes, so once those dried up..." I let out a breath of frustration and fear. "I don't know."

Hellhound grimaced and nudged the still-unconscious Murphy with an ungentle toe. "Well, come on then, darlin'. Let's go." He knelt and slung Murphy over his shoulders. "We gotta get into range to take out that sentry in the tree-stand before Kane gets there."

"We'd better not," I argued. "If this is their normal

setup, the guy inside will be expecting to hear the guy outside. Hell, maybe they have a secret password or something. We have to let the sentry challenge John first."

Hellhound nodded impatiently. "Yeah, that's fine, but we gotta be close enough so we can see if he's drawin'. If he does, ya gotta hit him with the puke-stick before he can get a shot off. What kinda range d'ya get with that thing?"

"Reggie says up to thirty metres, but it's line-of-sight. It seemed to work okay through a few leaves, but we were closer to that other guy."

We eyed each other in dismay for a long moment.

Then Hellhound heaved a sigh. "Shit. So we're gonna hafta go back the way we came. Can ya tell if the bears are still there?"

I shuddered at the juicy sounds emanating from my earpieces. "Yep. Let's see if we can stay on this side of the rise. I really don't want them to think we're inviting ourselves to dinner."

Creeping cautiously, we moved closer. To my relief, the rise provided natural concealment from the bears until we were nearly behind the sentry's position. From there I could glimpse the quad path through the trees, so the sentry's tree-stand was perfectly positioned to guard both the gate and the path.

Hellhound had barely lowered Murphy's limp form to the ground when I spotted Kane striding along the quad path toward the stockade. I nudged Hellhound and he nodded, then jerked his chin toward the sentry. Aiming the ultrasound baton at the tree-stand, I waited.

A moment later Kane rounded the corner of the quad path, nearly under the sentry's nose. The archer in the tree slowly raised his bow with an arrow nocked, but he didn't draw.

Kane didn't even glance in his direction. Striding up to the iron door, he thumped his fist on it a couple of times. "Hey, Scot, are you in there?" he shouted. "Open up!"

"It's open, dipshit!"

Hellhound and I exchanged a puzzled glance. Not the response we were expecting.

Kane unhesitatingly lifted the latch and swung the door open. As he stood framed in the opening, a camo-clad man with a hunting bow turned to frown at him. Beyond, I could see the corner of a small building, but no sign of the cluster of people the flies had mapped.

"Who the hell are you?" Camo-man snapped.

"New member," Kane replied. "Where's Scot? He told me to meet him here."

"How the hell would I know?" the man replied irritably. "And if you're a new member, where's your bitch?"

Kane evaded the question. "Well, his truck's parked out at the road. He has to be around here somewhere. Maybe he came in when you weren't looking. Mind if I look around for him?"

He advanced a few steps, and Camo-man gave him a rough shove to the chest. "Yeah, I fucking mind! You bring a bitch, or you don't get in." He squinted theatrically out the gate. "And I don't see any pussy, so buh-bye New Member. Go wait for Scot somewhere else."

"I brought one, she's around here somewhere..." Kane began.

"Well, when you find her, you come right on back." Camo-man pushed him out and slammed the gate in his face.

Handing the ultrasound baton to Hellhound, I shrugged off my backpack and unfastened my holsters.

"Aydan, don't," he hissed. "You're goin' in there blind, an' I know what these guys are like. You're a piece a' meat to 'em, nothin' more. At least take your gun."

"I can't." I handed him my Glock and the spare magazine. "John said no weapons."

Kane let out a piercing whistle and shouted, "Hey, Arlene, where are you?" He began to walk back along the quad path as if looking for someone.

"And anyway, he already saw inside. He wouldn't be calling me if he thought it was dangerous," I added hurriedly. "His cover will be blown if I don't go, and then you know he'll get desperate and do something stupid."

"He's already desperate an' doin' somethin' stupid," Hellhound growled. "An' I fuckin' guarantee it's dangerous."

"Maybe, but if Daniel's a hostage and I carry a weapon in there against John's wishes and something happens..." I swallowed hard. "I can't risk it. Here." I handed him my glasses, feeling suddenly deaf without the amplified sounds. "You can listen in just in case."

"Don't, Aydan, this is a really bad idea..." Hellhound began, but I dropped a kiss on his lips as Kane whistled and called again.

"Wish me luck," I said, and hurried toward the quad path as quickly and quietly as possible.

When I emerged from the forest, Kane strode over and seized me by the back of the neck, giving me a shake. "Where the hell were you? I told you to keep up."

"Sorry," I mumbled, keeping my gaze on the ground. "I stopped to pee."

Kane made a noise of disgust and marched me back toward the gate. When we reached it, he lifted the heavy iron latch without knocking and pushed me ahead of him into the stockade.

Camo-man spun, his bow rising, but his frown faded into a nasty grin at the sight of me. "Huh. So you did have a bitch after all." He circled me, his gaze like dirty hands running up and down my body. "Nice. Haven't had fresh meat in a while." He jerked his chin toward the small building I'd glimpsed through the gate. "Put her with the others and we'll break her in later. Not enough guys here yet, but they'll be here for the weekend pretty soon."

A shiver of primal fear coursed down my spine as Kane nodded and pushed me toward the shed. I glanced up at him, but his gaze was darting around, cataloguing the enclosure.

Six quads were parked along the wall next to the iron gate. To our left was a large roofed structure with open walls containing picnic tables and a forty-five gallon drum cut open to form a barbeque grill. A few small cabins dotted the grounds, along with a large open firepit, some archery butts against the far wall, and an outhouse. The shed ahead of us was about eight by sixteen feet, with vertical slits in the walls only a few inches wide. The iron latch on its door looked disturbingly sturdy, but the door itself was ajar.

I swallowed hard, my mouth going dry.

A man came out of the shed, hitching up his pants. He bolted the door behind him, then turned and noticed us approaching. He grinned and strolled closer, giving me an up-and-down scrutiny out of piggy eyes and wiping his hand across his chin.

As he lowered his hand, I spotted a large smear of blood on the palm.

But his mouth didn't look injured.

My legs began to tremble and Kane's grip tightened on

my neck.

"So fresh she's still got her teeth," the man said appreciatively. "Shit, if I'd known, I wouldn'ta wasted my time on that bitch." He cocked a thumb back toward the shed. "Well..." he shrugged philosophically. "Let's prep her. I'll go get the pliers." He seized my face roughly, his fingers digging into my cheeks. "Dibs on that mouth as soon as her teeth are gone."

Kane's fingers closed convulsively on my neck, making me wince. "This one's mine," he growled.

The other man snorted. "Nice try, newbie. If she survives the gang-bang, you can have her afterwards." He grinned and shoved his hand down my jeans, his fingers probing. "'Course she won't be quite so tight by then."

Kane reacted so fast I only felt the wind of his blows. In seconds the man was sprawled on the ground. Unconscious or dead; I didn't know or care.

"This one's mine!" Kane raised his voice and turned in a challenging circle, staring down Camo-man and two other men who had emerged, one from a cabin and the other from the outhouse.

Camo-man's bow came up, an arrow nocked in a single fast motion. "Don't think so. Put her in the shed and settle down, or I'll plug you and give you to the bears. Haven't fed them yet today, so they're nice and hungry."

My heart thudded against my ribs so hard my head went light.

Kane stood still, apparently calculating the odds, but I already knew he didn't have a chance. Camo-man was at full draw and the other two were approaching fast, knives in hand.

"Okay, sorry," Kane mumbled. "I didn't know. Scot was

supposed to meet me here and give me the lowdown." He moved slowly toward the shed, dragging me along not because I was actively trying to resist but because my legs had stopped working.

"Where's Scot?" Kane asked, obviously stalling. "If I'd known I had to share her I would've done her myself first. Can I do her now? She'll still be good for the gang-bang afterward, I promise."

"Too late," Camo-man sneered. "Put her in the shed, and hurry the hell up."

As Kane lifted the latch and swung the door open, my mind went blank with horror.

Naked women were crammed into the small space. Some were still lucid enough to cower away but others slumped catatonic, their eyes vacant. Nearest the door, the pig-man's latest victim dragged herself slowly across the rough wooden floor, leaving a trail of blood.

Unable to move or think, I stood frozen by the monstrous abuse evident in their toothless mouths and the horrific wounds on their bodies.

"Hey, help! Scot's hurt, come quick!" The urgent call in a familiar raspy voice broke my paralysis and I turned to see Hellhound shouldering through the gate with Murphy's body in his arms. As everyone spun, Hellhound let go of Murphy and fired a trank dart into Camo-man.

Kane shoved me to the ground and dropped on top of me as Hellhound fired twice more, bringing down the two men behind us.

Snapping a fast glance around the enclosure, Hellhound charged across the intervening space and skidded to a halt as Kane rolled off me.

"Ya okay?" he demanded, and when I nodded he pulled

me to my feet and pressed my Glock into my hand. "Here..."
He glanced into the shed and recoiled a step, his face
blanching. "Jesus Christ," he choked, then shook himself
and jerked his chin at Kane and me. "Clear the buildin's," he
rasped, slapping the ultrasound baton into Kane's hand.

Together we rapidly checked the small cabins and
outhouse, finding nobody else. We were turning back toward
the main gate when a *swish-thunk* made us dive for the dirt.
An arrow vibrated in the wall of the outhouse only inches
away.

My Glock was halfway up, my finger already on the
trigger when Kane roared, "NO!" and swung up the
ultrasound baton.

Another arrow zipped by so close I could hear the fletch
feathers hissing through the air, but the baton had done its
work. Scot Murphy hit the ground hard, vomiting while he
struggled to draw the bow again.

Kane was already on his feet and pounding across the
stockade. Hellhound and I scrambled up and followed as he
jumped on Murphy, ripping the bow away from him and
pinning his hands behind his back.

"Where is he?" Kane bellowed. "Where's Daniel?"

Murphy said something and choked, his words
unintelligible from retching.

"WHERE?" Kane jerked Murphy's arms up behind him
and Murphy screamed as his muscles parted with a tearing
pop that was audible even from where I stood a few feet
away.

"In the pit!" Murphy shrieked, a fresh flood of bloody
urine sparkling around him in the dusty grass.

I sucked in a breath of air that seemed devoid of oxygen
and staggered back a step as my heart stopped in my chest.

Hellhound's arm came around me from behind, tight enough to stab daggers of pain through my ribs.

Kane went stock-still, all the blood draining from his face. "The pit..." His voice was barely a breath of sound. "...where?"

Murphy vomited again, his face falling into the mess as if he was too weak to hold it up.

Kane jerked his head up by the hair. *"Which pit? Where?"*

Murphy's voice was faint but intelligible. "The outhouse pit. There."

In a single violent twist, Kane snapped his neck.

CHAPTER 44

"NO!"

Hellhound's shout came too late. Murphy's body twitched and spasmed, but it lay on its stomach while his vomit-streaked face gazed emptily at the sky.

I sucked in an inadequate breath through my nose, afraid to open my mouth in case I vomited, too.

Kane rose slowly, his eyes dark wells of torment in the bone-white of his face. He stood staring at the outhouse, fine vibrations coursing through his body while his fingers clenched and unclenched.

"Cap..." Hellhound said cautiously.

"It was a long shot." Kane's voice was bleak and lifeless. "I was hoping, but..." He choked into silence and turned away.

Chills rippled through me as he went on after a moment, "Matthew is dead, too. Murphy told me he didn't realize Matthew was playing behind his truck, and he accidentally ran him over and killed him fifteen months ago. He didn't report the death; just buried Matthew's body..." He swallowed audibly. "...in his back yard... in the outhouse pit."

Hellhound's arm slackened around me and fell to his

side. "Jesus, Cap," he rasped. "I'm sorry. I'm so fuckin' sorry."

After a moment of silence, he went over to lay an arm across Kane's shoulders. "Let's call the cops," he said quietly. "Come on. Time to go home."

Kane shook him off. "No. I have to..." He shook his head wordlessly and tried again. "Have to..." He turned toward the outhouse.

I found my voice at last, a bare and trembling ghost of itself. "John, leave it. Please. Forensics will have to excavate..."

I stopped. He wasn't hearing me. Plodding like a robot toward the outhouse, he kept walking even when Hellhound planted himself in his path.

"Cap," Hellhound said gently. "Come on, we gotta get outta here before any more guys show up..."

He trailed off as Kane detoured silently around him. We followed while he walked around the outhouse to where a shovel stood upright in a pile of fresh dirt next to a sheet of plywood on the ground.

He had just pulled the shovel loose when Hellhound flung out a hand and barked, "Stop!"

There was such urgency in his voice that Kane went still, staring at him as if momentarily jolted out of his trance. Hellhound stood with his head flung up as though listening, and I suddenly realized he must still have the sound amplification activated in the sunglasses. He drew the trank gun and moved slowly and smoothly, placing his feet like a hunting tiger while his head turned slightly this way and that.

Listening.

Stalking.

I drew my Glock, staring around but unable to detect the threat.

Hellhound glanced over at me and jerked his chin toward the plywood, then took the shovel from Kane. Glock at the ready, I sucked in a breath, trying to slow my hammering heart.

I gave a sharp nod and Hellhound flipped the plywood with the shovel, jumping away from my line of fire and levelling the trank pistol in a single movement.

A squeak emanated from the pit and two huge grey eyes stared up at me from a mud-streaked face. I swung my Glock away so fast I nearly dropped it.

"*Daniel?*"

He cowered against the wall of the pit, tears tracking through the dirt on his cheeks. Clutching a single toy soldier to his chest like a lifeline, he stared up at us without a sound.

Kane fell to his knees as if his legs had broken, the sudden movement snapping us out of our immobility.

"The new outhouse pit..." he muttered blankly. "Not the old one..."

Hellhound and I crouched. "Hey, Daniel," I said softly. "It's okay, you're safe now. We're going to take you home to your mommy."

I moved forward but he plastered himself against the wall of the pit, his bare feet scrabbling in the dirt as if to burrow to safety. Hellhound eyed his panicked expression and backed away without speaking, delegating the role of comforter to someone whose face didn't tend to frighten grown men.

"It's okay, Daniel," I tried again. "Come on, let's get you out of there." When I moved forward, he let out another squeak of terror and cringed into the corner, making himself as small as possible.

At last Kane's paralysis broke and he dragged himself to his feet to lay a trembling hand on my shoulder. "Let me try."

Moving slowly, he handed me the ultrasound baton and then stretched out on the ground beside the pit, pillowing his head on his arm. "Hi, Daniel," he said in his deep calming cop voice. "My name is John. I see you've got a soldier for a friend. Does he have a name?"

Big grey eyes blinked fearfully, tears still sliding down Daniel's cheeks, but he didn't try to burrow away again. Kane said nothing else, just lay quietly waiting.

After a long moment, Daniel whispered, "John."

"Yes, I'm John," Kane confirmed patiently. "What's your soldier's name?"

Daniel straightened just a bit. "John. His name is John."

A quiver of tension zipped through Kane's body, quickly banished. He managed a chuckle that sounded genuine. "Well, that's funny, because I'm a soldier and my name's John, too."

"A soldier?" The big grey eyes got wider and Daniel wiped a grubby hand across his cheeks, smearing away the tears. "I wasn't crying," he said defiantly.

"I can tell you're a very brave boy," Kane assured him. "But it's okay to cry."

Daniel sniffled and stood up straight, clutching his soldier to his chest. "Men don't cry. Only girly-boys cry."

"No, Daniel," Kane said huskily, his voice the sound of a heart breaking. "That's not true. Even soldiers cry sometimes."

Daniel advanced a couple of paces, peering inquisitively

up at Kane. "Are you crying?"

"Yes."

"Why?"

"Because I thought something bad had happened to you and I was scared."

"Why?"

"Because..." Kane swallowed. "I always wanted a son like you."

"Really?" Daniel was standing on tiptoe at the edge of the pit now, gazing up at Kane. "My daddy was a soldier. But he died..." His voice quavered, tears puddling in his eyes again. "And the mean man that hit Uncle Buck, he said Mommy and Uncle Buck died, too, so he's my daddy now, but he's m-mean..." Sudden terror froze his face and he backed away, his chest heaving with hiccupping sobs that he tried to muffle with a grubby hand over his mouth. "He t-told me to s-stay in the c-cabin b-but the b-bad man pushed m-me in here and s-said to b-be quiet, he's g-going to b-be so m-mad..."

"No, he's not," Kane said firmly. "I won't let anybody hurt you. The mean man isn't your daddy, and your mommy isn't dead. That was a lie. Your mommy is fine and she's very worried about you. Will you let me take you to her now?"

"B-But..." Daniel darted a frightened glance at me. "That lady's mean, too."

"No, she's not mean, I promise." Kane reached out. "She and that other big man are soldiers, too. Here, take my hand, and I'll introduce you."

"*She's* not a soldier." Daniel's chin came up with the certainty possessed only by six-year-olds and misogynistic assholes. "Ladies can't be soldiers."

"Yes, they can," Kane countered. "This lady is a brave soldier and that's why she has a gun. But..." He lowered his voice to a confidential whisper. "Can I trust you to keep a very, very big secret?"

Daniel nodded, his eyes wide.

"This lady is a secret soldier so nobody can know she carries a gun. Can you be a secret soldier, too, and never tell anybody no matter what?"

Daniel nodded vigorously, staring up at me. "Can I look at your gun?" he whispered.

"Maybe later," Kane said. "Will you be brave enough to come with us now?"

Nodding again, Daniel stretched his arms up, trust shining in his eyes.

"You're a brave boy," Kane complimented him. "I need you to follow my orders just like a soldier. Can you do that?"

"Uh-huh."

"Okay, when I lift you up I want you to wrap your arms and legs around me and hang on tight no matter what, and put your face right here..." Kane patted his shoulder. "...and don't look around, don't even peek until I say it's okay. Will you do that?"

"Uh-huh!"

Kane knelt and lifted Daniel effortlessly out of the pit, tucking him close as he gently guided the boy's face into the crook of his neck. For a moment he stood still with his cheek on Daniel's dusty hair, a father cradling his most precious burden.

"Let's go," he said.

I had been so absorbed in their exchange that I hadn't realized Hellhound had been hard at work. When I turned, all the bodies were gone and he was hesitating by the shed door, visibly bracing himself to face the hellish sight within.

I hurried over just as he swung the door open, and whimpers rose from the women who were still capable of reacting. Pressing into a knot against the far wall, they regarded him with terror-filled eyes.

"It's okay, I ain't gonna hurt ya," he said softly, but they were far beyond the point where they'd ever believe that again.

Laying a hand on his arm, I tugged him gently away from the door. "Go and cover John while he gets Daniel out."

He frowned down at me. "Are ya fuckin' nuts? I ain't leavin' ya. More a' those assholes might show up."

"Let me try." I stepped back to the doorway, generating a fresh wave of whimpers before they realized it wasn't Hellhound returning. "Hey," I said quietly. "Let's get out of here."

They only bunched together tighter.

"The gate's open. All the guys are gone. Come on, hurry up, let's go," I urged.

One of the women detached herself a pace from the group, daring to look me in the eye. "No. They'll kill us."

Her speech was distorted by missing teeth, but her fear came through loud and clear.

"They won't. They're gone."

"It's a trick. They're just waiting to see who tries it, and then..." She shuddered. "Go if you want. We're staying here where it's safe."

"*Safe?*" I stared, words failing me.

"Come on, darlin'," Hellhound muttered from outside the door. "Leave 'em. We gotta go."

I jerked back to face him. "I'm not leaving them! What if more guys come? They'll take it out on them-"

Hellhound laid a finger on my lips, silencing me. "Aydan, ya gotta trust me on this. I'll explain later. Lock 'em in an' let's go."

"Goddammit, I *won't-*"

"Please." From inside the shed, the woman's voice vibrated with terror. "Please lock us in."

Gently detaching my grip on the door, Hellhound swung it shut and slid the bolt home. "Come on, darlin', the sooner we get outta here an' call the cops, the sooner they'll be safe."

He turned me toward the gate, where Kane waited with Daniel in his arms.

I dug in my heels with a furious whisper. "If any of those guys come back and find out what's happened before the police get here, they will make those women suffer in ways I can't even think about without puking! There's no way it's *safer* for them-"

"Aydan," Hellhound interrupted. "These assholes've been feedin' the bears to keep 'em around. I counted seven fuckin' bears so far. An' if one a' the ladies pisses 'em off, they feed her to the bears, too. Ya don't wanna know what I found in the woods. They really are safer here for now."

When I stared at him, my stomach churning, he added, "Come on, let's get outta here before the bears finish chowin' down on Murphy an' his asshole buddies an' start lookin' for their next meal."

"You threw them to the bears?" I whispered.

The Killer stared down at me from Arnie's eyes. "Just takin' out the trash. Come on."

While we talked, Kane had slid onto the seat of one of the quads that still had keys dangling from the ignition. Daniel perched on his knee, his arms and legs wrapped around Kane and his face still obediently buried in Kane's shoulder.

Hellhound gave an approving nod. "Good plan. Come on, let's see if there are a couple more with keys. If we stick together an' move fast we oughta get by the bears okay."

We each selected one, and after a wary peek through the iron door, we fired up the quads and drove outside. I got off to close the door and hesitated.

Hellhound swung off his quad and strode over to mutter in my ear, "Hurry up, darlin'. I dunno how many more bears there are, but Kane's got Murphy's puke on him, an' I got some on me, too. We're walkin' bear bait."

His urgency made my pounding heart hammer even harder, but every fibre of my being rebelled at the thought of leaving those women to be brutalized again if more men showed up before the police arrived.

"Come on, Aydan, move it!" Hellhound growled.

Inspiration struck. "Hang on, I have an idea. Here, hold this and give me my backpack."

He accepted the ultrasound baton and swung the backpack down off his shoulder, anxiously eyeing the woods around us.

"Go!" I waved a shooing gesture at him and Kane. "Get to the SUV. I'll be right behind you."

Kane shook his head. "No, we stick together. Hurry up! What are you waiting for?"

Rummaging through the backpack, I drew a breath of relief when my fingers closed around the laser flashlight. Making sure the gate latch was fully engaged, I trained the laser on it and tried not to flinch with the fear that it would reflect at me.

"What're ya doin'?" Hellhound demanded, frowning at the flashlight. "It ain't lightin' up. Your batteries are dead."

I grinned as the latch took on a dark cherry hue. "No,

they aren't."

"What the…" His mouth dropped open. "Okay, I gotta start suckin' up to Chow. I want one a' those."

A few seconds later the latch was glowing bright orange and I stepped back from the scorching heat. In a moment the metal sagged, and I flicked off the flashlight and stowed it away again.

"Okay, now they're safe," I said, and shouldered the backpack. Hellhound handed back the ultrasound baton, and I added with satisfaction, "Nobody's getting in here without a cutting torch-"

A volley of gunshots from the woods slammed icy adrenaline into my veins. Hellhound seized my arm and practically flung me onto my quad.

"*Ride!*" he bellowed, and we all goosed our throttles.

CHAPTER 45

Our quads sprang forward, roaring and kicking up dust. Ahead of us, Kane drove one-handed with his other arm holding Daniel tightly to him. Hellhound half-stood on his quad beside me, his head snapping right and left in search of the source of the gunshots. I struggled to control my handlebars with one hand, but I wasn't about to stop and stow the ultrasound baton I still clutched in my left-handed deathgrip.

Just past the bend in the path, a flicker of movement caught my eye. A man burst out of the woods and sprinted across in front of my quad, his expensive dress shoes sliding on the gravel.

A shock of recognition jolted me but I didn't have time to dwell on it. Everything clicked into slow motion when I spotted the grizzly bear charging after him, teeth bared.

Charging directly at us.

I saw everything as if in a chaotic freeze-frame. Flinging up the ultrasound baton and punching the trigger, I felt the bulletproof jacket resisting me and wondered crazily if it would protect me from bear teeth.

Labelle ran directly into Hellhound's path. Hellhound swerved too late and two bodies tumbled through the air.

His quad snarled to a rocking halt.

The bear was nearly on us when its muzzle dipped, its stride faltering. A moment later its snout plowed into the ground and the momentum of the huge furry body carried it into an ungainly somersault. Its hind claws sliced the air only inches away and I cracked the quad's throttle, launching myself forward several feet before slamming on the brakes again.

Hellhound was rolling to his feet, thank God. Labelle was scrambling up, too, and I let out a mindless shout.

"Stop him!"

Hellhound whipped out the trank pistol and fired. Labelle dropped with a moan.

No, that wasn't Labelle moaning.

Another groan yanked my attention back to the bear. Bleeding from several bullet wounds, the animal rocked halfway up onto its front paws only to vomit and collapse back to the ground. It emitted another anguished groan and pressed both front paws over its face, a gesture so human that my heart wrenched.

"Ya okay, darlin'?" Hellhound barked.

"Yeah, you?"

"Fine." He absently brushed some gravel out of a bloody abrasion on his arm, staring at the downed and bleeding bear. "Poor damn thing. Put it outta its misery an' let's haul ass. Ya want me to load up Dumbfuck?" He cocked a thumb at Labelle's unconscious body.

"Yes, please."

A few yards ahead, Kane held Daniel's face clamped to his shoulder, both arms wrapped around him as if his embrace alone could stave off all the bears in the world. Kane looked shell-shocked, white and wild-eyed.

How much longer could he hold it together?

I dismounted and walked a few paces closer to the bear. Afraid to relinquish the ultrasound baton, I tucked it between my knees so I could use both shaking hands to steady my Glock. My tremors increased when I noticed something that looked very much like a human hand in the pile of vomit in front of the bear.

Taking careful aim, I put a bullet in its brain before holstering my gun and retrieving the ultrasound baton. Hellhound had already searched Labelle for weapons and dumped him across the back of his quad before mounting up, and I clambered gracelessly onto the seat of my quad, too, my rubbery legs barely cooperating.

The remaining half-mile drive to the parking area was an exercise in nervous tension. Every time the breeze ruffled the leaves beside the trail my heart lurched up into my throat until I was sure it wasn't another bear.

And what if more club members arrived?

I shook myself and concentrated on the trail. Keep your head in the game. They'd be expecting the sound of quad traffic so they wouldn't have any reason to arm themselves until they spotted us, and by then it would be too late. There were no innocent men here. My Glock would deal whatever justice was necessary.

To my surprise, we encountered no more threats. Hellhound's SUV still waited unscathed in the parking area, and he wasted no time in clicking the electric door locks open and motioning Kane into the back seat.

Driving around to the rear of the SUV, he dismounted and opened the hatch to stow Labelle's unconscious body, but I stopped him with a hand on his arm.

"I'm not putting that sack of shit anywhere near us," I

muttered.

Hellhound scowled down at me, tension vibrating in his shoulders. "Well, what the hell d'ya wanna do with him?"

I only had to think about that for a second. "Strap him to the roof rack."

Hellhound barked out a laugh. "Ya got it, darlin'. Gimme a hand."

Even with Hellhound's considerable strength, hoisting Labelle's flaccid body on top of the SUV left us both sweating. Whipping out my brand-new steel reinforced hand restraints, I cinched his wrists and ankles to the roof rack, then tottered around to the passenger's side. A moment later Hellhound slid behind the wheel and we were on our way.

Kane had at last released his hold on Daniel and belted him into the centre seat, and the child was taking in everything with wide eyes while chattering ceaselessly to Kane.

Hellhound lowered his voice and muttered, "So who's your guy up top?"

"Remember the gunrunner I was meeting for ice cream?" I replied quietly, and nodded toward the roof.

"That's him?" Hellhound shot me an incredulous glance. "What the hell's he doin' out here?"

"I don't know, but I'm going to find out."

By the time thumping from the SUV's roof indicated Labelle's return to consciousness about fifteen minutes later, I had almost stopped trembling. Daniel gaped up at the roof while Kane attempted to distract him with a story.

"Pull in at this next crossing," I instructed Hellhound, and he complied. Thanking my lucky stars that we were still well off the main roads and hadn't spotted another vehicle yet, I turned to face Kane. "It's time for you two to play a game."

Kane gave a nod of understanding and turned to Daniel. "Game time, Daniel.   I want you to cover your eyes up tight..."

Daniel obeyed, grinning with anticipation.

"...and let's see what you remember about where you are," Kane went on as Hellhound and I slid out of the SUV. "Without peeking, can you tell me what colour the seats are?"

I permitted myself a small smile.   Daniel would soon be as good at instantly cataloguing his surroundings as Kane.

Handing Hellhound the cutter for the hand restraints, I stood back while he freed Labelle.   When Labelle sat up shakily, I trained my Glock on him.

"Get down."

"What the..."

"Get down before I put you down permanently."

Labelle slid awkwardly off the roof, landing with a wince behind the vehicle.

"Move."   I jutted my chin in the direction of the woods beside the road.   "Over the fence and into the woods."

"Wait, we can talk about this-"

"Or I could just shoot you now," I suggested.

"Don't kill me!   I've got..." he eyed Hellhound nervously. "...something to tell you..."

"Then step into my office and tell me," I grated, inclining my head toward the woods again.   "You've been a giant pain in my ass for far too long."

Sweat glistening on his forehead, Labelle stood in silence for a moment before limping toward the fence.   Hellhound leaned down to mutter, "Want me to come with ya?"

"No.   Stay in the SUV and get ready to drive."

He pressed his lips together as though he was about to

argue, but stepped back reluctantly and let me pass.

Labelle hesitated at the barbed-wire fence and I snarled, "Hurry up, asshole."

He stooped and tried to step through the strands, succeeding in snagging his expensive-looking pants on the lower strand and his nice shirt on the upper one. Caught by his clothes, he gave me an imploring look.

Hellhound strode over and planted a foot on Labelle's hip, shoving him through the fence. Labelle's clothing tore loose and he tumbled onto the ground on the other side. Handing my Glock to Hellhound, I stepped up onto the middle strand next to a fencepost and swung my leg over, then reversed my feet and swung down on the other side while he kept Labelle covered. Retrieving my gun from him, I turned back to Labelle.

"Now get up and walk."

"But there might be bears…" he began anxiously.

"Yeah, and there might be bullets," I countered, sighting on him and wishing I could just pull the trigger and rid myself of him once and for all. "Move it. Hands on your head."

He dragged himself to his feet and limped toward the trees, tags of torn fabric flapping from his shirt and pants. Begrimed and grass-stained, with spruce needles in his dishevelled hair and spots of blood staining his shirt where the barbed wire had scratched his skin, he didn't look much like the smooth businessman who had taunted me only yesterday.

When we were far enough into the woods that Hellhound's SUV was only visible as a few sparkles through the trees, I snapped, "Stop."

Labelle turned slowly, hands still locked on top of his

head. "Look, I have a deal for you..."

"Yeah, I've heard that before," I snarled. "Why have you been following me?"

"Because I have a client who's interested in your services."

"If they want a bookkeeper they can call me directly."

Labelle hissed out a frustrated breath. "Would you drop the bookkeeper bullshit? You're holding me at gunpoint in the middle of nowhere and you just took down a bear, and me, with weapons I've never seen before."

"Which still doesn't answer my question." I let my gun track downward. "Next time you evade a question, it's going to cost you a knee. Why are you following me?"

"I'm sorry!" His voice rose frantically. "I've been following you because my client told me to make absolutely sure you weren't an undercover cop! He would have killed me if I was wrong!"

"Well, how's that for irony?" I drawled. "'Cause now I'm going to kill you just for fun."

"No, please!" Labelle actually dropped to his knees. "Look, it's worth a lot of money to you! You've got designer weapons; I've got clients. I was Nick Parr's weapons broker and I can do that for you, too!"

"Yeah, and stab me in the back the first chance you get. I don't think so. You're more trouble than you're worth. And I hate your tongue," I added in what might have been a slight non sequitur. I sighted at his head again.

God, I was exhausted. I could hardly hold my gun steady.

Maybe I should just shoot him. Tell Stemp he'd attacked me and I'd had to react in self-defense...

Labelle was babbling something and I yanked my

attention back to him. Hell, I really was tired. Zoning out while holding a man at gunpoint. Not a good sign.

"Okay, fine," I interrupted whatever he was saying. "Give me the name of your client and I'll have my people look into him. If he comes up clean you can set up a meeting for us. If he's a cop..." I gave him a hard-eyed glare. "You're going to wish I'd let the bear eat you."

"Okay, no, he's legit, I swear! His name is Benoit Riel, and he and Nick did business for years!"

"We'll see." I backed away, keeping him covered. "Stay here until we drive away. If I even catch a glimpse of you I'll shoot you on the spot."

"Don't leave me here!" He lurched forward, hands outstretched in supplication, but stopped with a jerk when I slipped my finger onto the trigger. "I lost my gun in the woods! I haven't seen another vehicle the whole time I've been out here and there are bears..." His voice rose in a tearful tremolo, and I showed him my teeth.

"Don't worry, pretty soon there are going to be more vehicles than you can shake a stick at. Stay on the road and you'll be fine." I continued to back away. "And if you're smart, you'll tell them you went into the woods to take a piss and saw a bear. You ran scared, and you got lost. If you're not smart..." I trailed off with a shrug and left him kneeling there staring fearfully around him and snivelling.

When I emerged from the woods, Hellhound shot a look behind me. "Did ya kill him?" Then he shook his head. "Shit, sorry, forget I asked that."

I handed him my Glock and swung over the fence again. "I didn't kill him." He returned my gun and I sighed and headed for his Forester. "Wanted to, though." I extracted my bug detector from my waist pouch and sighed again at the sight of the flashing red light. "He must have tagged you in Rocky Mountain House. He probably tagged John's truck, too."

Moving closer to the SUV, I watched the detector's cadence speed up until it led me to the rear of the vehicle. There I detached a small device from under the bumper and pitched it into the ditch.

Looking up at Hellhound's thunderous scowl, I said, "Okay, let's go."

"Fuck!" He glared at the bumper. "I shoulda checked it. I been so wrapped up in this thing with Daniel..." He trailed off, his shoulders squaring into parade rest and chin rising as if bracing for a reprimand. "Sorry, Aydan, no excuse. I led him right to ya."

"It wasn't your fault, and it worked out fine. I got what I wanted from him." I reached up to kiss him. "Let's go."

CHAPTER 46

Back on the road again, we drove in silence except for the soft rumble of Kane's voice in the back seat while he told a delighted Daniel one of the stories from his unfinished children's book.

As soon as my phone picked up a signal, I hit the speed dial for Stemp.

"It's Aydan," I said after his brusque greeting. "I had an issue with the delivery, but it's solved now. I'm going to be about an hour late getting there, so could you please let them know? And John will be in Silverside to meet with you by ten PM at the latest."

"Very well." He hesitated. "Am I to deduce that there has been a development in the kidnapping case?"

My lips creaked into a smile as though they'd almost forgotten how. "Yes. We found Daniel and he's safe."

"Oh..." Stemp said nothing for a moment, and when he spoke again his voice was deep with emotion. "That is excellent news."

"And there's more," I said eagerly. "I had a break in my official case because of my work on Daniel's case. So you can tell the chain of command I've achieved the objective."

This time I could hear the smile in his voice. "That is

excellent news indeed. I will look forward to your report."

My next call was to Spider. He answered on the first ring, sounding anxious. "Aydan, are you okay? What's happening?"

"I'm okay." I glanced around the car, my heart swelling with slow relief. "We're all okay. Including Daniel."

"*What?*" I imagined his smile dawning like a sunrise and he let out a triumphant whoop. "You've got him? He's okay after all?"

"Yes, and yes!" The cold armour around my emotions melted under the warmth of his enthusiasm and I grinned wide enough to make the stiffened muscles of my jaw crack. "We're taking him home. I just wanted to let you know I'll probably be back around ten tonight, or maybe a little earlier." My joy dampened a little. "Oh, and Tyler Brock will do the security scans at your wedding tomorrow."

My happiness trickled away, leaving an anxious void. Shit, I should have forced Labelle to tell me whether he'd been behind the attacks on Spider and Linda.

And now I'd threatened and humiliated him and abandoned him out in the woods. And he'd have a ride back to his vehicle as soon the police arrived, so he'd be less than two hours behind me.

If he decided to seek revenge...

"...Sorry, what...?" I asked as Spider's voice filtered through my unpleasant thoughts.

"I said, would you be able to do a really big favour for me while you're in Calgary?" he repeated. "It won't take long, but-"

"Sure, what is it?" I interrupted, still contemplating the many ways Labelle could wreak havoc.

And if it wasn't Labelle after all, Spider and Linda's

enemy was still at large. Shit, shit, shit.

"Could you stop by a bookstore and pick up a hardcover copy of Murray Stout's new book, '*Mack Force, Objective: Blue Star*'?" Spider asked. "Brock is a huge fan, so I'd like to get it for him as a thank-you."

I nearly choked. "Seriously?"

When he began to apologize, I interrupted, "No, I didn't mean... I meant, I don't mind at all. I'm just shocked he actually admits to liking something. I'll grab it on my way out of town. See you soon."

When I disconnected, Kane leaned forward from the back seat. "We'll need to call the police soon."

"Okay..." I eyed him anxiously, but Daniel was still absorbing the conversation and I didn't dare say anything he might repeat.

Kane gave me a significant nod and leaned back in the seat again, tucking his arm around Daniel. "Would you like another story, Daniel?"

Daniel snuggled close, his eyes shining with hero worship. "Uh-huh." Then he corrected himself with a small frown of concentration followed by a proud gap-toothed grin. "Please."

We drove in silence while Kane spun out another tale, his voice blurring into a soothing rumble that threatened to sink my eyelids shut despite my worries.

By the time the rumble stopped I was fighting sleep, and Kane's touch on my shoulder startled me into a violent twitch.

"Sorry," he murmured, leaning forward and keeping his voice low. A glance into the back seat showed Daniel fast asleep, slumped sideways in the boneless repose only children can sustain without waking up crippled.

"So what are we going to tell the police?" I asked softly.

"The truth," Hellhound said. "We were investigatin' the exes' friends, an' when Kane questioned Murphy he panicked an' said he'd take us to Daniel if we didn't call the cops. He brought us out here an' the bears attacked so we ran for the fort. When we got inside we found the ladies in the shed, grabbed Daniel, an' barely got outta there alive. We dunno whether the bears got Murphy an' his buddies or not an' we didn't dare go back, so we drove out to where we could get a phone signal an' called the cops."

Kane and I parsed his edited version of the truth in silence. "That should work," Kane agreed after a few moments' thought. "I'll tell Mayweather I rode with Murphy in his truck so there won't be any suspicion if they find my fingerprints or any other physical evidence in there. After that, the chewed-up corpses in the woods should clear us of any suspicion." He hesitated. "...As long as they don't do any drug tests during the autopsies. Because three of those men will likely still have traces of tranquilizer in their bodies."

"Four," Hellhound corrected. "I tranked the sentry outside the gate, too. But the trank'll be gone. They were already startin' to wake up by the time I got 'em dragged outside."

I swallowed rising fear. "So they might still be alive. What if-"

"Nah," The Killer said in emotionless tones. "I found the dog food they'd been feedin' the bears an' stuffed their pants full of it."

I stared at him, not sure whether to laugh or throw up. "So even if they managed to empty it all out..."

"They'd still be reekin' like bear bait," he finished. "An'

they ain't gettin' back inside that fort."

Realization dawned. "But... you handled the dog food. The smell would be all over your hands. The bears could have just as easily torn you apart."

He shrugged, staring impassively through the windshield.

Throat tightening, I laid a hand on his muscular thigh to reassure myself of his presence. Kane reached forward to thump an affectionate fist on his shoulder.

"Thank you," he said softly. "Both of you. I can't tell you how good it is to know you've got my back."

"Always do, Cap," Hellhound said.

I seconded that with a murmur of agreement and Kane gently squeezed my shoulder before leaning back to punch a number into his phone.

After providing his report, he disconnected and leaned forward again. "RCMP and emergency vehicles are on their way to the compound, and Mayweather says to take Daniel directly home. He'll want a statement from each of us so he'll meet us there."

Hellhound nodded, and Kane subsided into his seat again with a long exhausted sigh.

A few minutes of silent driving later, I peeked back to see his eyes closed, his arm cuddling Daniel close to his side while his chest rose and fell in a slow steady rhythm.

"Finally down," Hellhound murmured. "About fuckin' time."

The hypnotic sound of tires on pavement changed as our speed slackened. I lurched upright, blinking the sleep out of my eyes and wiping the corner of my mouth in case of drool.

"'Mornin', Sunshine," Hellhound teased as I yawned cavernously and eased the kinks out of my neck.

"I'm sorry, I didn't mean to fall asleep on you," I apologized, but he reached over to pat my leg.

"It's okay, darlin', ya needed it." A smile softened the corners of his mouth. "Not as much as him, though." He nodded toward the back seat, where Kane and Daniel still slumbered peacefully.

"Yeah, it's a pity to wake him," I agreed. "But I guess we'll have to soon."

"Mmhm." The smile slid off his face.

I wasn't feeling much like smiling myself. There were still so many things that could go wrong...

A few minutes later we pulled up in front of Alicia's house. The Forester had barely stopped moving before she flung herself at the back door, jerking fruitlessly on the handle until Hellhound punched the lock release.

The sound woke Kane, who started violently and tightened a protective arm around Daniel, his free hand clenching into a fist.

"It's okay, we're in Calgary," I said hurriedly, hoping to God he'd wake up enough to realize Alicia wasn't a threat.

A second later she was in the back seat, smothering a sleepy Daniel with frantic kisses and tears. He blinked, then blinked again, his eyes widening.

"Mommy!" He threw chubby arms around her neck. "The bad man said you died!"

"Oh, sweetheart..." She buried her face in his dirty hair, running her hands over and over him as if to reassure herself that he was truly there. "Come on, let's get you in the house and cleaned up." She spared a glance for Kane at last. "Thank you." Her tears began afresh. "Thank you, all of you."

Behind her, a white-haired man and woman clung to each other, tears trickling into their smiles. Mayweather stood back in a formal-looking parade rest, but he was smiling widely and his eyes were soft.

Hellhound let out a breath. "Well, let's go do it."

"Do what?" Alicia gave him a suspicious glance.

"We need to give our statements," I explained in my best non-confrontational voice. "Is it all right if we come in and do that?"

"Oh, of course! Yes, of course, I'm sorry..." She shook her head, still clutching Daniel, who was beginning to squirm in her embrace. "Please come in."

We trooped up the walk behind the little cluster of Daniel and his mother and grandparents, who reached to touch him every few steps. A glance at Kane showed he had his cop face on, but his eyes looked bereft.

Our reports didn't take long. While we filled out the forms Mayweather received a couple of calls, and when he hung up from the last one he was grinning from ear to ear.

"That was the RCMP," he announced. "They just found the other boys alive."

"Wh... what...?" Gasping around the expanding bubble of hope in my chest, I stared at him. "Alive? Are they... okay?"

Mayweather's expression darkened. "Traumatized, of course, neglected and undernourished, but overall in good health. Murphy had locked them in a root cellar in his basement. He rotated through them, pretending each was his son until they displeased him somehow, and then he'd put them back in the root cellar and try the next one. It was actually Peter Bruner who completed the Grade One equivalency exam in Matthew's place."

I swallowed hard. "Thank God. I thought they'd be dead for sure."

Mayweather shook his head. "Fortunately Murphy was obsessed with having replacements for his dead son, so he kept them all. His wife knew what was going on, but she lived in fear of Murphy so she kept quiet. She and their two daughters have basically been captives on that acreage for the past eight years."

"Are they..." A memory of haunted eyes and toothless mouths rose, twisting my guts. "Are they... injured?"

"Physically nothing serious; just some bruises. Mentally..." Mayweather sighed and tilted his hand back and forth in an equivocating gesture. "They're still interviewing Mrs. Murphy, but it looks as though Murphy was targeting sons of single mothers because he believed women were unworthy to bring up boys. And he pushed Buck into arranging the camping trip so he could abduct Daniel and frame Buck for it."

Despite the twisted wrongness of Murphy's actions, suddenly I couldn't stop smiling. "So all the moms will get their sons back."

"Yes." Mayweather smiled back. "Yes, they will. We're calling them now."

"All except Mrs. Murphy," Kane said quietly. "Have they found Matthew's remains yet?"

Mayweather sobered and shook his head. "They'll bring in forensics to excavate the pit as soon as possible."

"Did Mrs. Murphy have any idea why Daniel wasn't put in with the rest of the boys?" Kane asked.

"He was, originally." Mayweather frowned. "I suspect our investigation prompted Murphy to move Daniel, and he likely intended to move the other boys as well. When Arbuckle Murphy's death was declared a homicide, the RCMP contacted Scot to notify him since he was the next of kin. He likely figured we were getting too close to the truth." He eyed Kane gravely. "It's lucky he was obsessed enough to simply relocate Daniel."

The words, 'instead of killing him' hung chilling but unspoken in the air.

Mayweather departed soon afterward with our written statements, and after a few strained pleasantries with Alicia we moved toward the door, too. Daniel, cleaned up and fed, had been absorbed in his toy soldiers on the living room floor, but he looked up at the movement of bodies.

His eyes widened, fear paling his cheeks.

"Don't go!" He flung himself at Kane, wrapping both arms around his leg.

"Daniel, sweetheart, these people have to leave now," Alicia said gently. "Come on-"

"No, no! What if the bad man comes?" He clung tighter to Kane's leg.

Kane bent to enfold him in a hug. "It's all right, Daniel, the bad man won't come."

"H-how do you know?" Alicia asked, suddenly pale herself. "Officer Mayweather said they hadn't found him yet. What if..."

Kane, Hellhound and I exchanged a glance, but we couldn't tell her the real reason why we knew Murphy wasn't coming back.

Daniel was still sobbing and clinging frantically to Kane. "You p-promised!" he cried. "You p-promised you wouldn't let the b-bad man get me! Don't go!"

Kane knelt and Daniel locked his arms and legs around

him, still crying hysterically.

"Shhh," Kane soothed, standing up and rocking the child in his arms. "Shhh, Daniel, it's all right..."

"Don't go, don't go, don't go..." Daniel wept.

Kane met Alicia's eyes over Daniel's head. "Daniel," he coaxed. "Hey, Daniel, would you feel safer if you came with me?"

Alicia stiffened, her fists clenching and her gaze shooting sparks. "Don't you dare..." she began in deadly tones.

"No, don't worry," Kane assured her. "I'm not trying to take Daniel away from you. I want you to come, too. I have to leave right away to go back to Silverside for a meeting, but if you both come with me you'll be safe until Murphy is in custody."

She took a step back as though his lack of resistance had left her off-balance. "But... That's all fine and good, but... What about Mom and Dad?"

"They can come, too," Kane replied, but Alicia's father shook his head.

"No, we'll be fine here. Ally, you and Daniel go with John. We'll hold down the fort until you get back." He gave her a gentle squeeze. "Run and pack a bag for yourself and Daniel, lovey. We'll feel better knowing you're safe."

"But..." Alicia gazed around as though searching for another argument. "Where will we stay? We can't afford to stay in a hotel for days..."

Kane patted Daniel's back, still rocking rhythmically as the child's sobs quieted. "I'm sure it won't be days. They'll likely have him by tomorrow. They've already got his truck. He's running out of places to hide."

"You can all stay at my place," I offered. "I've got a houseful of company, so there will be safety in numbers." I didn't bother to add that there would also be enough people and distractions to keep them from each other's throats.

Kane gave me a grateful glance.

"So it's settled," Alicia's father said comfortably. "Go pack your bags, lovey."

CHAPTER 47

On the front steps of Alicia's house, her luggage in hand, Kane turned to Hellhound. "If you'll drive me down to my truck-" he began.

"No," Hellhound interrupted.

Kane blinked. "Please," he said stiffly.

"No, Cap. Sorry." Hellhound shook his head as Kane began to protest. "I ain't tryin' to be a shi-" He bit off the word with a glance at Daniel and began again. "I ain't tryin' to be a pain, it's just that you're too bagged to be drivin' ten minutes, let alone two hours. I'll drive ya."

"No, I'll be fine," Kane argued. "I had a nap on the way down here-"

"An' you're still about eighteen hours short of bein' caught up," Hellhound countered. "An' ya got a pretty good reason not to take a chance on fallin' asleep at the wheel." He cast a pointed glance at Daniel, still nestled in Kane's arms with his head on Kane's broad shoulder.

Kane's face softened. "You're right. Thank you."

"Come on, Aydan." Hellhound turned to me. "I'll drop ya off at your car an' then Kane an' I'll grab our stuff from his condo. Ya can do whatever ya gotta do here, an' we'll meet ya in Silverside."

We trooped down to Hellhound's Forester and piled in, Kane and Alicia in the back with Daniel between them. When we were under way, I glanced back, smiling at the sight of Daniel's happy face while he clutched Kane's hand on one side and Alicia's on the other.

As I watched, Daniel turned an adoring gaze up to Kane. "Will you be my daddy?"

Kane and Alicia both went still.

"Yes," Kane said without hesitation. "Will you be my son?"

"Uh-huh." Content, Daniel cuddled back between them, but a moment later fear shadowed his face. "Will you go away to war like my other daddy?"

"No, I won't go away," Kane said softly. "I'll be your daddy for as long as you want."

"Forever and ever?" Daniel pressed.

Kane cleared his throat, blinking rapidly. "Forever and ever," he agreed huskily, and offered his hand. "Let's shake on it."

Daniel shook, his small hand engulfed in Kane's large one. Then he settled back with a happy sigh, leaving Kane and Alicia regarding each other warily over his head.

In the parking lot at Kane's condo, I pulled out my bug detector and eyed the flashing red light with resignation mingled with self-disgust. Add another protocol to the Spy Manual: Check the car *every* time you drive it.

Circling the vehicle, I found the locator device under my rear bumper. After a moment's consideration, I pulled it off and stuck it under the bumper of the car beside me.

Have fun tracking that, asshole.

Then I headed for the testing facility, doubling back a few times and taking a circuitous route to be sure I wasn't being followed. With the ultrasound baton and its covert pen counterpart safely delivered, I stopped in at a bookstore and then at a fast-food place. Worry about Spider and Linda nagged at me, and I got my dinner to go.

On the highway at last, I gobbled the food one-handed without tasting it. By now Labelle would be on the road, possibly even ahead of me. I took small comfort from the knowledge that Kane and Hellhound would be at my farm before I was.

Everything would be fine. Spider and Linda would be safe.

I wished I could believe that.

Two hours later I turned off toward my farm, slightly reassured by the fact that all looked quiet and no columns of smoke billowed up on the horizon.

God, I felt as though I'd been away for days, not just fourteen hours. The trees around my creek glowed green and gold in the long rays of the setting sun.

When I turned in the lane, my heart rose at the sight of Hellhound's Forester parked in front of my house along with Moonbeam and Karma's rental car and Linda's little red Beetle.

Inside the house pandemonium reigned. Wedding things were spread around the living room while seven adults and one overstimulated child tried to dodge each other. As the eighth adult, I considered the house full beyond capacity.

Kane and Alicia both looked exhausted, Hellhound

looked tense, and Daniel zoomed up and down the hallway winding himself up into a frenzy of activity. Spider and Linda converged on me with wedding-planning questions while Moonbeam and Karma hovered together in the background, a much-needed oasis of serenity in the chaos.

I had planned to give Alicia and Daniel my bedroom, but Daniel staged another hysterical meltdown at the prospect of being separated from Kane, so I crammed an inflatable bed into the room as well and Daniel was appeased.

After supplying the final set of blankets, pillows, and towels, I met Hellhound's desperate look with an equally desperate one of my own.

"Well," I said with false cheer, "I still have to go into town and there are no beds left here, so Arnie and I will stay at the hotel. If you need us, you know where to find us."

Hellhound's look of relief was so comical I almost cracked a smile, but I managed appropriate seriousness while I fielded the last of my guests' questions and managed a more-or-less graceful withdrawal, clutching my backpack.

"I'll drive, darlin'," Hellhound said, striding toward the Forester as if afraid the madness inside the house would reach out and drag him back.

Sliding into his passenger seat with relief, I let my head fall back against the headrest, and he accelerated with slightly more vigour than necessary.

We let out simultaneous sighs of relief when we reached the highway, but tension reclaimed me a moment later.

"I'm going to have to go back after I finish at Sirius," I said. "If that gunrunner decides to get revenge tonight..."

Hellhound reached over to squeeze my hand. "I didn't get that kinda vibe from him. I think he's just a middleman. He's the kinda guy who'd rat ya out to somebody bigger in a heartbeat, but he ain't got the balls to do anythin' himself."

I tried not to gape at him. Dammit, would I ever develop the kind of instincts he and Kane had?

"You're probably right," I admitted.

"So ya don't hafta go back unless ya want to," he went on. "Webb's got the monitor for your perimeter cameras, an' Kane's there if anythin' goes wrong. He slept all the way here, so he'll be fresh enough to handle it."

"So..." I gave him a hesitant look. "Did he... did you..."

"I took him straight into Sirius," Hellhound confirmed. "An' he passed the lie detector test no problem. I was afraid Stemp might ask about what we did today, but he just stuck with the standard requalification questions. Kane answered 'em, and we were outta there in about fifteen minutes."

"How do you know what Stemp asked?"

Hellhound chuckled. "I was listenin' in with your fancy glasses. That reminds me, ya better take 'em. I meant to give 'em back before we left Calgary." He passed them over. "But the whole thing was a fuckin' gong show. Daniel went batshit when Kane tried to leave him an' Lish in the lobby, so they ended up havin' to get visitor passes for both of 'em. I stood with 'em out in the hallway so Daniel could see Kane the whole time he was doin' the test. That kid is gonna have serious issues for a while."

"I think they all are," I agreed. "It'll be a rocky road."

Hellhound glanced over. "Did ya really hafta go in to Sirius, or were ya just blowin' smoke to get outta the house?"

"Um..." I hesitated. "A bit of both. I'd like to file a quick report on what I got from questioning my gunrunner today. And I need to drop off a couple of things at the Weapons lab, but everybody will be gone for the weekend so I shouldn't be long."

"Okay, I'll wait for ya in the lobby, then."

We made the rest of the trip in blessed silence.

At Sirius I filed a quick report on Labelle and sent the name he'd given me to the analysts for research. Drooping with exhaustion, I made my way through the time-delay chamber with barely an uptick of my pulse and plodded down the hall to the Weapons lab.

When I turned the corner into the main lab, I backpedalled with a yelp of surprise.

"What the hell are you doing here?" Chow demanded. "Isn't it time for good little agents to be in their beddy-byes?"

"Long past time," I agreed, ignoring his sarcasm and offering a tired salute to Melinda and Murray at the next counter. "What are you guys doing here this late on a Friday night?"

Melinda smiled. "This is what we do for fun."

"And it's not like I'm going to hit the bars trolling for chicks," Chow added sourly. "There are no beer goggles thick enough to make this look good." He made a bitter up-and-down gesture with his pincer-hand.

"Oh..." Swallowing hard, I racked my exhausted brain for a tactful reply, failed to find one, and went with an insult instead. "Well, I don't know; maybe you should try that Goth chick that tends bar at the Silverside Hotel. She's into spiders so she'd probably like to get up close and personal with your left nut."

"Fuck off, Kelly," he growled, but the undamaged corner of his mouth quirked up. "So did you come down here just to indulge your unhealthy fascination with my balls?"

"Yep," I agreed. "Your balls are constantly on my mind. Oh, and I was also going to drop off the pheromone collector. I'm pretty sure it's full."

He gave me a piercing scrutiny. "So that's why you look like you've been chewed up and shit out. Tough day?"

The accumulated terror of the day suddenly dropped on me with the force of a boulder and I fought to keep my knees from buckling.

"Yeah." My voice came out in a dry whisper.

"Shit, Kelly." He stepped forward, his good eye darkening with concern. "Are you gonna hit the deck?"

"No." I summoned a joke with the last of my strength. "That would be too much like lying down, and you know there's no rest for the wicked. Here."

I handed him the pheromone detector and propped myself against the counter. He accepted it with a frown and carried it over to connect it to the computer.

"Yep, they're all full," he said. "You want to give me a rundown?"

Abandoning pride, I slid down the counter to sit on the floor, propping my head on my drawn-up knees. "Not really. But I will anyway." I leaned my head back to stare at the ceiling. "Okay, in order: Two near-death experiences at the mercy of somebody else's driving. You can classify that as 'prey'. Then a couple of hours later, a guy shot me with a broadhead. Prey. Thanks for the jacket, by the way; it worked like a damn. But it does hold me back a bit when I try to move really fast."

Chow's eye narrowed. "Where did he hit you?"

"Shoulder." I pulled back the neck of my T-shirt to show him the tender spot, which was now an unflattering shade of mauve. "The way he was working to pull that bow, I'd figure about a seventy-pound draw weight, and he got me from about fifteen yards away."

"With a broadhead?"

I nodded and he grinned. "Sweet! That normally would have gone right through and killed whatever was behind you."

"Yeah." I tugged my T-shirt back into place and let my hand fall to the floor, too tired to hold it up. "That would be the grizzly bear that nearly ate me a few minutes later. I'm going to go with 'prey' on that one, too."

"Shit." Chow's eye narrowed. "But that's only four. There are ten samples in here."

"Oh, that was just the warmup," I said bitterly. "So then I had to go around the grizzly while he was eating the guy that shot me. Prey. And then I came within a hair of having all my teeth pulled out and getting gang-raped. That would be prey. After that..."

My gorge rose and I gulped down hot bile. "After that... I... saw something I... can't even think about right now. I don't know how to classify that one. It was..." My head felt suddenly too heavy for my neck and I let it fall forward onto my knees. "I don't know," I mumbled. "Classify it however you want."

Silence reigned while I took a few long slow breaths before adding, "Then I watched a guy get his head twisted off. I didn't give a shit about him, so I don't know how you want to classify that one, either."

"Seeing a guy's head twisted off didn't bother you?" Melinda inquired in a strangled voice, and I looked up to see I'd acquired an audience. Chow, Melinda, and Murray stood in a semi-circle looking down at me. For a moment I considered standing up again in a show of bravado, but it was too damn much effort.

"I don't even want to know about the other thing you saw, then," Murray put in quietly.

"Neither do I, believe me." I sighed. "Then there was another grizzly. Charging. I definitely felt like prey. Then I nailed it with the ultrasound baton and had to shoot it."

The memory of the poor bear's anguished groans made me swallow hard. "I didn't feel like a predator. I just felt like shit."

"One left," Chow prompted.

"Yeah. That was when I really, really wanted to shoot a guy. But I didn't. That one's probably pure predator, but I was so damn tired by then I don't know how good the sample will be. Oh, and..." I dragged my backpack over and extracted the flies and the control box. "Here are your flies. They worked great on a group of twenty-two, but they also map freshly dead people. Just so you know."

"Thanks," Murray said faintly as he accepted the items.

The weight of the backpack jogged my memory. "Oh. Right." I pulled out the hardcover copy of '*Mack Force, Objective: Blue Star*' and held it out to Melinda. "May I ask you a huge favour? Would you please autograph this?"

She recoiled from the book as if I'd offered her a snake and turned to glare at Chow. "You told her!"

Chow shrugged. "She's an agent. She can keep a secret."

"Please?" I gave Melinda an imploring look. "I'd get down on my knees, but I'm already on my butt and I'm too tired to move. And this might get me out of a really tight spot."

"Murray Stout only autographs three books per release," Melinda said stiffly. "And two autographed copies of '*Mack Force, Objective: Blue Star*' have already been issued."

"Please," I repeated. "I tested your flies. And your pheromones. And your glasses and your jacket and your ultrasound baton and your laser flashlight..."

Melinda was already holding up her hands in surrender. "All right, fine, but this doesn't go beyond the three of us. Ever. Agreed?"

"Agreed."

She pulled a black marker from the pocket of her lab coat and scrawled Murray Stout's iconic signature across the inside front page of the book.

"Thank you," I said fervently. "You might have just saved my ass."

CHAPTER 48

When I emerged from the tomb of the secured area, Hellhound rose from one of the chairs in the lobby.

"Come on, darlin'." He laid a gentle arm over my shoulders. "Ya look like you're done."

"Done like dinner," I agreed, and dragged myself over to the security wicket to sign out.

In his SUV, I laid my head back while he drove the few minutes to the hotel. Anxiety nagged at me. I should be back at the farm, protecting Spider and Linda as well as Alicia and Daniel. What kind of lousy hostess leaves her guests at home and goes to a hotel? Especially when her guests might be in danger...

"Aydan?" Hellhound's quiet voice broke into my thoughts. "You're worryin' about not bein' at the farm, ain't ya?"

I sighed. "Yeah. I feel like I should be there. What if something happens?"

"Well, darlin'..." He pulled into a slot in the hotel parking lot and turned to face me. "Ya know how ya told Kane he was too tired to think straight an' he oughta listen to his friends?"

I nodded slowly, knowing what was coming.

"Well, this is your friend tellin' ya that ya ain't thinkin' straight. After what ya went through today, ya need some time. You're gonna be wakin' up screamin' tonight, an' that ain't gonna do your company any good. An' Kane got nearly four hours a' sleep in the car, so he's in better shape than you anyway."

"But, Arnie, he's not expecting any trouble. And somebody's trying to stop the wedding tomorrow, and they've been threatening Spider and Linda. I don't know whether it's the guy I left in the woods or somebody else... or..." I groaned and clutched my aching head. "Hell, maybe it's both."

He frowned. "That's bad, darlin', but whoever it is, I can't see 'em attackin' a houseful a' people tonight. They'd wanna take out just the bride an' groom; or else they'd wanna take 'em out plus hurt as many a' their friends as they can. Either way I'd put my money on an attack at the weddin' tomorrow."

I let my face fall into my hands. "Is this supposed to be making me feel better?"

"Nah." He reached over to stroke my hair. "It's supposed to be makin' ya go in the hotel an' get some sleep. I don't think anythin's gonna happen at the farm tonight, an' if it does, Kane'll handle it. Ya know what his reflexes are like, 'specially after this week. An' he's got Daniel to protect. Trust me, nobody's gonna get by him." He coaxed my hands away from my face. "Come on, darlin', let's go check in."

Hesitating, I forced my tired brain to follow his logic. I wasn't sure if it really made sense, but I was too exhausted to figure it out. And if he was confident Kane could handle anything, surely Kane and Moonbeam and Karma together would be unstoppable.

Hellhound was still waiting patiently, and I sighed and nodded. We slid out of the SUV and he retrieved his duffel bag and guitar from the rear hatch while I shouldered my backpack.

When we closed the hotel room door behind us a few minutes later, it felt like an escape to a safe haven despite the steady muffled thump of bass from the bar below. Lowering my backpack to the floor, I stepped into Arnie's arms, my battered soul yearning for his comfort.

He kissed me slowly and gently and I let my body soften and mold to his, pressing closer to tease him with my tongue.

He pulled away a few inches, stroking my hair back from my face, and I eyed his troubled expression.

"What's wrong?" I asked.

"I..." He stepped back, taking his warmth with him. "I need a bit a' space. Sorry."

"Oh." Confusion and disappointment chilled me, and I fought the urge to wrap my arms around myself. "Okay. I'll get a separate room."

"No, stay."

When I frowned up at him he made a frustrated gesture, his hands closing as if to grasp thin air. "I... I'm kinda fucked up right now. I just need a bit a' time. Go to bed, darlin'. I'm gonna play for a while. Or..." He hesitated. "If you'd rather get a separate room, it's okay..."

"No, I like to hear you play, and I want to stay with you."

Relief softened his face. "Thanks, Aydan." He nodded toward the bathroom. "You're up first."

The notes of his guitar started while I was brushing my teeth, and by the time I slipped out into the room again he was locked away in his world of music. His expression brooding, he stared into nothingness while his gifted fingers coaxed a haunting melody from the strings. The minor key made me shiver, and I undressed rapidly and slipped into bed without disturbing him.

I tried to listen for a while but my eyelids were too heavy, and the dark current of music carried me into equally dark dreams. Several times I half-woke from nightmares to Arnie's soothing voice and hands, but each time the music started again and carried me back to a cold black place where I fought the brutal grasp of unseen enemies.

The cessation of music roused me. Moving quietly for such a big man, Hellhound shed his T-shirt and turned off the lamp before sliding in beside me still wearing his jeans.

Cuddling close, I laid an arm over his chest and whispered, "Better?"

He stiffened. "Sorry, darlin', I thought ya were sleepin'."

I reached across him to click on the lamp again so I could look down at him on the pillow. "Hoped I was sleeping, you mean."

He stared up at me expressionlessly for a moment before his face softened into resignation and he sighed. "Yeah."

I stroked his cheek. "Your music usually helps. It didn't this time?"

"Nah." He blew out a short breath. "It happens. Go back to sleep, darlin'."

"No, talk to me. What's bothering you?"

"I'm fine. Just bagged." He turned off the lamp. "G'night."

I clicked it on again. "You promised not to lie to me."

"For shit's sake, Aydan, let it be!" He locked his fingers together, knuckles whitening. "I..." He drew a couple of ragged breaths, then lurched out of bed. "I gotta go."

Springing up, I leaped across the room and pressed my

back to the door, arms and legs wide to block his path. "You're not leaving here until you tell me what's wrong. After that I'll let you go if that's what you really want."

"Aydan..." His fists balled into hard knots, his expression tortured. "Ya can't stop me." He opened his fists again, holding his hands away from his body as if to divorce himself from them. "Don't ya get it? Ya can't stop me. I could... I could... do anythin' to ya, an' ya couldn't stop me. I could hurt ya so bad..."

Sudden comprehension flooded me. The women in the shed.

"But you wouldn't," I said softly. "You'd never hurt me like that."

"Ya don't know that, Aydan. How can ya know that? My ol' man was like that, so why wouldn't I be?" He stood in the centre of the room, a mountain of deadly muscle utterly helpless to defend himself against his own torment. "If I snapped... Aydan, I can hit somebody so fast an' hard they can't even fight back. It doesn't matter how brave ya are or how hard ya try; your body just shuts down when ya get hit like that. An' then..." He threw an anguished glance at my Glock on the nightstand. "You're standin' there naked sayin' you'd stop me, but ya couldn't even get to your gun. You'd just... suffer. For as long as I wanted."

"But, Arnie..." I moved toward him and he backed away, locking his hands behind his back as if afraid they would attack me of their own volition. "Arnie, listen to me. You don't want to. You'd never do that. I saw how you reacted when you opened that shed door. You weren't aroused, you were sickened."

"I damn near puked," he said quietly. "But what if I didn't? What if I looked in there an'... an'..."

"But you didn't. And you wouldn't," I soothed. "And even if you did get aroused, you'd still be in control of yourself. You have more self-control than any guy I've ever known."

"Yeah, until I lost it," he said hollowly. "An' then I killed a guy."

"No, you defended yourself against a man who'd tortured you your entire life and who had just told you he was going to beat you to death," I corrected. "That's not the same. I'm talking about when you're with me. Even when we're in bed together and you're really enjoying yourself, there's always some little piece of you that's holding back. You never lose yourself. You're always watching to see what I want; how you can make it better for me." I tried for a joke. "I swear if we were going at it and you were one stroke away from coming your brains out, you'd still quit on the spot if I said 'stop'."

Hellhound gave me an affronted scowl. "What kinda fuckin' asshole would I be if I didn't?"

"You'd be a pretty normal guy," I said gently.

"No, I'd be a fuckin' asshole." He glared at me, but his anger was all for himself. "So it's okay to keep goin' for one stroke after ya say stop? How about two? How about ten? How about forcin' ya even when ya say no? How about rippin' out all your goddam teeth so I can fuck your face in comfort..."

His voice broke and he scrubbed his hands roughly over his face. "An' ya know what the worst part is?" he choked out. "You'd forgive me. 'It's okay, Arnie, it was just a flashback. It's okay, Arnie, ya didn't mean to do it'." He jerked his hands down to face me, his eyes glittering with unshed tears. "It ain't okay! It ain't *ever* okay!"

"But you believe that right to the bottom of your soul," I said softly. "So why would you think you'd ever act differently?"

He stood in silence, his chest heaving with emotion.

"And I wouldn't forgive you," I added. "I'd shoot you, just like I promised."

"You're lyin'," he said quietly. "I know ya wouldn't."

"I'm not lying," I lied with all the sincerity I could muster. "I promised I'd shoot you if you ever lost control, and you know I keep my promises."

"Ya wouldn't keep that one." He drew a deep shuddering breath. "An' even if ya tried, I could stop ya."

"You could, but you wouldn't."

His head drooped. "You're right," he whispered. "If I ever hurt ya I'd wanna die."

I crept a little closer, but he didn't back away this time.

Closer still.

When I reached up to caress his cheek with my fingertips he flinched as though I'd slapped him.

"I can't do this, Aydan," he rasped. "Ya gotta let me go."

"Not yet." Reaching for his hand, I stroked his clenched fingers until they relaxed, then pressed a kiss into his palm.

He jerked away. "Don't."

"Arnie..." I began, but he was staring at his hands with loathing.

"Aydan, ya watched me kill a guy in cold blood today. After that I dragged those guys out to the bears an' loaded 'em down with bait. Judge, jury, an' executioner. These hands..." He held them away from himself. "They've killed so many people..."

"And they've created such magic, too," I countered softly. "Today you did what you had to do. We all did."

"Ya didn't kill anybody," he disagreed. "Ya ain't like me."

"You're right, I didn't." I gently captured his hand again. "But you expected me to. The first thing you said when I came out of the woods alone was 'did you kill him'. You know we're more alike than you want to admit. Hate yourself if you want, but then you need to hate me, too."

"Ya didn't kill anybody," he repeated stubbornly.

I sighed and let my forehead fall against his chest. "No, I did that a few days ago. I double-tapped a guy, got out my disposable coveralls and cleaned up the mess, dumped his body in the back of his SUV, and then went to bed and slept like a baby. No nightmares, nothing. The only thing I felt was pissed off that he'd left a bullet hole in my car."

Hellhound went still, and when I looked up he was staring down at me. "When was that?"

I did a mental count, my brain sluggish with fatigue. "Wednesday night, after I got home from Edmonton. God, that seems like years ago."

"Ya didn't say anythin' about it when I talked to ya yesterday."

I shrugged. "I couldn't talk freely. And anyway, it was just part of my job. Same as yours."

"But..." He frowned down at me. "It damn near broke your heart to shoot that poor fuckin' bear. I could see it in your face."

"Just like it would have broken yours," I said softly. "So we're more alike than you want to admit. And we aren't our jobs."

"But, darlin'..." He took my hands in his and we stood looking down at them together. "Don't ya ever worry that... someday... ya just... won't feel anythin' at all anymore?"

"Yeah." The word came out on a shaky breath. "Every

time. Every time, I feel like... a little piece of my soul dies. But..." I brought our clasped hands to my lips and brushed a kiss across his knuckles. "Today, when you killed that guy... it had to be done. You didn't hesitate, but you didn't enjoy it, either. You're still a good person. If you weren't, you wouldn't be trying so hard to push me away."

I reached up to kiss him. "It's not going to work, by the way. Just so you know."

Some of the tension went out of him at last. "I dunno why ya like me," he whispered. "But I'm glad ya do."

"Of course I do." I gave him a smile. "What's not to like? Come to bed." I tugged him in that direction, but he moved a reluctant couple of steps before stopping again.

"I better not, darlin'. I'm gonna have nightmares like ya wouldn't believe. I might hurt ya in my sleep."

"Arnie, we've been through this before." I cupped his face in my hands so I could look into his eyes. "Even after you killed your da- ...old man, we slept in the same bed and you were fine."

"I was shit-faced," he countered. "Passed-out drunk. I'm sober tonight."

Letting my hands fall to my sides, I fought the urge to curl into a ball and cry. "So go down to the bar and get drunk..."

"Bar's closed, darlin'," he reminded me, and I realized there was no thumping bass anymore, only the silence of a sleeping hotel at three o'clock in the morning.

"Arnie, please!" I couldn't quite keep the tears of desperation from my eyes. "I need you tonight. Please just come to bed."

His face softened. "Okay, darlin'. Tell ya what. Ya put those new steel-reinforced hand restraints on me, an' I'll come to bed. At least it'll give ya a fightin' chance if I can't swing at ya in my sleep."

Too tired to argue, I delved into my backpack. "Do you need a bathroom break first?"

"Nah, I'm good."

"Okay, I'll leave the cutters on the table beside you in case you need to get loose in the night."

He nodded agreement, and a few minutes later I was cuddled close to his warmth, my mind already drifting toward slumber.

"Aydan?" His quiet rasp roused me just before sleep claimed me.

"Mm?"

"How d'ya do it? How d'ya stay sane?"

"Uh?" I struggled back to wakefulness. "You think this is what sanity looks like? You're more fucked up than I thought."

He chuckled. "That ain't what I meant. I meant..." He hesitated for so long I was almost asleep when he spoke again in reflective tones. "I been in combat zones where ya don't know who the hostiles are. Ya never trust anybody an' you're never safe. But that's what it's like all the time, bein' a woman, ain't it? Ya never know when some asshole's gonna hurt ya just 'cause he can. How can ya ever trust any guy enough to fall asleep next to him?"

I sighed and laid my head on his shoulder. "Good instincts and cautiousness help. But sometimes you're just in the wrong place at the wrong time and there's nothing you can do. You just have to live with the risk."

"That's fucked up. Nobody should hafta live like that."

"Well..." I snuggled closer. "It helps to know that there are only a few bugfuck crazies who really like hurting women, and there are a hell of a lot of good guys who treat women well. And there are lots of guys who'd put their lives on the line to protect a woman. And..."

I trailed a row of kisses up to his lips. "...there's one guy who'll go to bed wearing hand restraints because the thought of hurting a woman, even accidentally, makes him sick. I keep those ratios in mind when I'm walking down the street."

"Huh." I felt him shake his head on the pillow. "I still say it's fucked up." He placed a gentle whiskery kiss on my forehead. "G'night, darlin'. Sleep tight."

"As long as you're here, I will."

CHAPTER 49

Bladder nearly bursting, I rolled away from Hellhound's warmth and slipped out of bed to hurry to the bathroom. When I returned he was awake, his hands free of the restraints and a smile on his lips.

"'Mornin', darlin'," he greeted me, and I slid under the covers and into his arms.

"Good morning." I gave him a kiss. "How did you sleep?"

He shrugged. "Not as bad as I thought."

"Good." I snuggled closer, then sighed and pulled back when my conscience twinged. "I guess I'd better get back to the farm."

"What's your hurry?" He slid a persuasive hand up my arm, then around my shoulder to stroke languorously down my back. "Take a bit a' time, darlin'."

"Mmmm." My eyelids dipped to half-mast as my muscles softened against his palm. "No... I'd better not..."

I didn't sound convincing even to myself, and he chuckled. "Why not?"

"Because..." I shook myself out of the seductive relaxation and sat up. "Because, assassins."

"I don't think so, darlin'." His hand glided up my back.

"If nothin' happened last night, nothin's gonna happen this mornin'. You'll wanna be there a couple hours early to make sure everythin's secure, but ya got time to relax a bit first." His fingers twined into my hair, massaging my scalp and coaxing me down toward him. "Come on an' relax with me a while."

"Ohmigod, that feels so good..." I collapsed onto his chest, squeezing my eyes shut in sheer bliss. "Mmmm..." With a supreme effort of will, I tried again. "But... Are you sure? What if..."

"Aydan." He stopped massaging, and I opened my eyes to see him regarding me seriously. "Webb's a good kid, an' I like him. If I thought there was gonna be a problem, I'd already be there."

"Oh." Relief melted me, and I relaxed into his kiss. "Okay. Thanks."

A few increasingly hungry kisses later, I pulled away to eye him seriously, my pulse picking up at the thought of what I was about to suggest.

He gave me a half-smile, his gaze searching mine. "What, darlin'? Ya look like ya got somethin' on your mind."

"I... do..." I hesitated. "I'm going to suggest something, and feel free to say no."

His smile widened. "Gettin' your kink on, darlin'? Sounds interestin'. Lay it on me."

"Well..." I propped my chin on his chest. "You know how last night I said that when we're in bed together I feel like you're always holding back?"

His smile dimmed, wariness lurking in his eyes. "Yeah..."

"I was wondering what it would be like for you if you didn't have to hold back. If you could just... let go. Full strength."

"No." He tensed, his expression closing down. "Ya don't know how strong I really am, Aydan. Ya don't know... what I might do."

"No, calm down." I sprinkled kisses over his cheeks. "I have a pretty damn good idea of how strong you are, and I don't even want to think about you letting loose on me. That's not what I'm suggesting."

"Oh..." He drew a deep hitching breath and let it out slowly, the tension receding from his body. "Okay. Sorry, darlin', that... pushed a few buttons. Go ahead, I'm listenin'.'"

"What if... I tied you down? Not to hurt you or dominate you; you'd still be in control and I'd do whatever you wanted. Just... so you could react without being afraid you'd hurt me. So you could just let go."

When he said nothing, I added softly, "I know what it's like to feel like you're constantly holding back. To feel like... like... you'll burst out of your skin if you can't do something full force, full strength. That's why I work out so hard."

He blinked, looking surprised. "Ya feel that way, too?"

"Yeah."

"I... I dunno, Aydan. It sounds... great, but..."

"Don't feel you need to do it because I asked." I leaned down to kiss him. "It's not a turn-on for me, and I don't want to try it unless you think you'll like it. And of course I'd make sure you could get free in case anything went wrong. I don't want to take your control away."

"But..." Hellhound swallowed, his gaze locked on mine in a mixture of fear and hunger. "But, Aydan... what if..." He swallowed again and looked away. "What if I like it?" he whispered, his words barely audible.

"That's the whole point." I kissed him again. "If you like

it, great, we'll do it some more. If you don't, we'll stop. You're calling the shots here."

He blinked, then laughed. "Fuck, you're right, darlin'. Guess I got hung up on the tyin'-up part. I was thinkin' about BDSM."

"Oh. No." I shuddered. "No, that whole domination-and-pain thing just... just no. I don't think I could do that even if you wanted it."

He grinned, mischief sparkling in his eyes. "So basically you're offerin' to do whatever I want, an' all I gotta do is lie back an' enjoy it."

I mirrored his grin. "That about covers it."

"Well, shit, darlin', get out the ropes. I'm all yours."

"Oh. Ropes. Well, that might put a crimp in it." I frowned at the featureless hotel bed. Only a mattress with a solid headboard glued to the wall. "No place to attach any tie-downs."

"No problem." Hellhound rolled out of bed and delved into his duffel bag, coming up with a couple of coils of climbing rope. "Had this with me when we were searchin' the woods up at Rocky Mountain House. We can just run the ropes under the mattress an' tie me down to that."

"Okay, that'll work." I took the ropes and hesitated. "If you're sure..."

He grinned and lifted the mattress. "Get those ropes under here, darlin'. I got good times waitin' for me."

A few minutes later the bedcovers were in a heap on the floor and Hellhound lay spread-eagled on the bed, wrists and ankles tethered securely but with enough slack to reach the nightstand where the cutters lay.

Smiling down at him, I circled the bed. "Okay, I guess I lied about the turn-on part." Eyeing the delicious tattooed muscles laid out for my gratification, I shivered as heat flooded me. "I didn't think it would, but this is totally turning me on."

"Same here, darlin'."

His growl made me shiver again, and I ran a slow hand up the inside of his thigh, enjoying the hard evidence of his arousal. "Yeah, I can see that." Caressing him teasingly, I leaned closer. "What do you want me to do?"

He let out a raspy purr, his eyes half-closing in the sleepy-eyed smile I knew so well. "Touch yourself, darlin'."

Kneeling onto the bed between his legs, I circled my hands slowly over my breasts. "Like this? Or..." I slid my hand down my stomach, then lower. "Like this?"

"Yeah, darlin'. Oh, yeah..."

"Or..." I bent forward, squeezing my breasts together around his erection and rocking back and forth. "Like this?"

"Christ, Aydan..." He pulsed hard against me once; twice; three times, his breath accelerating. Then he went still and rasped, "Stop."

I sat up, worry lancing through me. "Are you okay? Should I untie you?"

"Nah, I'm good." He squeezed his eyes briefly shut, his chest rising and falling with his rapid breathing. "But this ain't gonna work. These ropes ain't enough to hold me down." He bounced his hips a couple of times in demonstration. "I could still really hurt ya."

"I'll be careful," I began, but he interrupted.

"No. It ain't safe. Just gimme a hand job. I got some lube in my duffel."

"Okay." I swung off the bed and located the bottle in question, then turned back to the bed. Slicking my palms, I grinned. "Any last requests, soldier?"

He grinned back, muscles flexing against the ropes. "Yeah. Polish my flagpole, recruit. An' watch me... ahhhh..." He sucked in a breath as I knelt beside him and went to work. "Watch me... salute... the flag..."

Stroking him slowly, I watched his muscles tighten, his eyes closing and fists clenching.

"Faster," he rasped, and when I complied his hips bucked with my rhythm. The ropes tightened on his arms and legs, massive muscles bulging.

"Both... hands... Tighter!" His voice came out raw between laboured gasps. Slamming up into my grip over and over, his body strained against the ropes. "*Harder!*"

As if the single harsh command had shattered the last of his control, he fought his bonds, snarling and battering himself up into my hands. The hard slap of flesh on flesh recalled memories better forgotten, and fear arrowed into my veins as his thrusts grew even more savage.

God, what if I had ignored his warnings? I'd be bleeding by now...

His contorted face was almost unrecognizable, consumed by the beast within. Heart hammering, I fought for balance against the violent jerking of the bed. The ropes scored the edges of the mattress and it curled inward, no match for his immense strength.

My trickle of fear gushed into an icy torrent. What had I unleashed?

Suddenly he went still, panting. His muscles slowly relaxed, and he opened his eyes and spoke in normal tones.

"Ya can untie me now, darlin'."

Trembling, I backed off the bed.

Frenzy to serenity in an instant. Could I trust the change?

Or had I freed the brutal animal he had warned me about?

"Ya can hold your gun on me if ya want," he said quietly, sadness shadowing his face.

I wiped my hands on the sheet and approached cautiously to look down at him. "Do I need to?"

"Nah, but do it if it'll make ya feel safer."

Looking deeply into his eyes, I could see only my own gentle Arnie. I drew a breath and went to work on the knots with shaking fingers.

When he was free, he lay without moving and fear prickled the back of my neck again.

"Arnie, are you okay?" I knelt cautiously beside him, taking his hand in both of mine and shivering at the angry rope burn around his wrist.

"I'm okay, darlin'. I just didn't wanna make any sudden moves 'til ya were feelin' a little safer." He brought my hand to his lips and brushed soft whiskery kisses over my knuckles. "I scared ya. I'm sorry."

"You don't need to apologize." I stretched out beside him, cuddling close. "You did scare me a bit. What happened?" I nodded downward, where he was still hard despite the reddened marks where my hands had struck his belly over and over. "You didn't get off. Why did you stop?"

He moved at last, closing his arms gently around me. I laid my head on his chest and he pressed a kiss to the top of my head. "I didn't get off 'cause I wasn't... gettin' off. If ya know what I mean."

"Not really."

"I thought I was gonna like it," he said slowly. "An' I did, at first. An' then The Animal came out..." He hesitated, then explained, "I call him The Animal. He's different than The

Killer. The Killer comes out when I'm snipin'..."

"And yesterday, when you killed that archer," I agreed. "I call him The Killer, too."

"Ya saw him?" Hellhound stiffened. "What... how can ya tell?"

"I can see him in your eyes and hear him in your voice. He's completely emotionless. He does whatever he has to do without hesitation. Without remorse." I stroked his rigid arm. "Does he... Does it bother you when he comes out?"

"I... no, I..." He leaned up onto one elbow, frowning down at me. "Shit, Aydan, ya knew that shit was inside me, an' ya still..." He waved an inarticulate gesture at our naked bodies.

"I've known for a long time," I said softly. "But I've never been afraid of you because I know you're always in control. I thought..." I looked deep into his eyes. "I thought it might be the only way you can protect yourself. The real, true you; the gentle guy I know. The Killer protects you from the awful stuff you have to do."

Hellhound sagged back again and lay staring at the ceiling. "Yeah... I guess. Never thought of it that way. I always thought he was in there fightin' to get out. An' that's what I thought about The Animal, too. I hated havin' him inside me. Whenever I thought about him, he had my ol' man's face. But..." He stared fixedly at the ceiling, tensing as if to brace for my reaction. "I... I need him, too. Sometimes... in combat... The Killer ain't enough by himself."

"I get it." I traced slow fingertip-circles on his chest until he relaxed again. "So The Animal came out, but then you stopped him. Why? Was he scaring you?"

"Nah, he only scares me when I think he might get out

an' hurt somebody I care about. An' I knew he couldn't get to ya 'cause a' the ropes." He pressed another gentle kiss to my forehead, sorrow darkening his eyes. "An' I knew ya were scared enough that if he did get loose, you'd do what ya hadta do."

I didn't deny it. "So why did you stop?"

He smiled, the darkness lifting. "'Cause I found out somethin' about The Animal I never knew before. I never worry about The Killer 'cause he's always under control, but The Animal... I'm always holdin' onto him for all I'm worth. Afraid to let up even for a second. But..."

His smile widened, and for the first time I saw peace in his eyes. "Even when I totally let him go, he wasn't thinkin' of how he could get loose and hurt ya. He was just..." he shrugged. "...doin' what he does. He ain't my ol' man after all. He doesn't get off on hurtin' people, even though he has to sometimes."

My throat tightened and my voice came out choked with emotion. "I'm so glad you're finally free of your old man. Good riddance to that asshole."

Arnie's arms tightened around me. "An' that's why I stopped, 'cause I don't need to get off that way. It's 'way more fun when we're playin' together." His voice softened. "An' the best thing is, now I know there ain't any part a' me that wants to hurt ya."

Realization dawned and I sat up, staring down at him. "That's what you meant. When you said, 'What if I like it'. It wasn't anything to do with BDSM. You were afraid if you let The Animal out, he'd be excited by the thought of hurting me."

He turned his face away, but not before I saw the truth in his eyes.

"Oh, Arnie, I'm sorry!" I clutched his hand, my heart breaking for him. "I'm so, so sorry. I didn't mean to push you past your limits. I thought I was doing something you'd like."

"Shhh." He pulled me back down to his chest, stroking my hair. "Ya didn't push me, darlin'. I went there 'cause I wanted to." His chest rose and fell in a heavy sigh. "Needed to. After ya trusted me so much last night, I hadta know if it was time to push ya away once an' for all." He kissed the top of my head again. "Or if I could trust myself enough to let ya trust me."

"But... what do you mean?" I leaned up on one elbow and frowned down at him. "I didn't do anything special last night. Nothing I didn't do when you killed your da- ...your old man, anyway."

"Yeah, ya did." He smoothed the hair back from my cheek with gentle fingertips. "An' ya didn't even notice."

"What are you talking about?"

He smiled. "When we first got together ya told me ya didn't need me an' you'd never need anybody ever again. You've said 'I need ya' to me lotsa times, but only when you're wantin' one part a' me real bad." He gave me a wicked wink and bounced his hips suggestively before sobering again. "But last night, ya trusted me enough to say ya needed me outside of bed. Just askin' for comfort. For the very first time."

"Oh." A peculiar mixture of warmth and fear swamped my heart. "What does... Does that mean one of us needs to run for the hills?"

Hellhound chuckled. "Nah, I think we're good, darlin'. You're lookin' panicked enough for both of us." He sobered. "An' I never thought I'd say this, but I'm okay with ya needin' me a bit every now an' then. Just don't do it too often or I'll freak the fuck out."

I let out a long breath of relief, slumping back into his arms. "Thanks, Arnie."

CHAPTER 50

"So, darlin'..." Hellhound's hand coasted down my side and up the curve of my hip. "What time d'ya wanna get back to the farm?"

I craned my neck to peek at the clock-radio on the nightstand. "It's only nine..." Reluctance warring with duty, I pressed my forehead against his shoulder. "I should go back now. What kind of hostess lets her guests fend for themselves for breakfast? I should be there to make sure everybody gets fed..."

"That's a lotta 'shoulds'," he murmured against my neck, his whiskers sending a cascade of delicious shivers through my body. "What d'ya really wanna do?"

"Honestly?" I raised my head to meet his gaze. "All that chaos last night, and Daniel running around? I just want to stay here in this hotel room until they all go away."

He chuckled. "How 'bout we compromise? I'll make it all go away for ya for a little while..." His hand rounded my hip in a feather-light caress. "...an' then I'll come with ya to the farm an' help ya sort things out."

"Would you really?" I stared at him. "I thought you were allergic to weddings."

He twitched. "Stop sayin' that word. I ain't goin' to a

weddin'. I'm gonna be workin' security for a big backyard party."

"Okay, that works for me," I agreed. "But first..." I let my hand drift downward. "I seem to recall I have some unfinished business here."

He rumbled satisfaction as my palm bumped over his abs, my fingertips circling down through the rough hair below his belly button.

"Ahh, that's what I'm talkin' about," he breathed as I reached my goal. Then he twitched again. "Just go easy there, darlin'. I got some tender spots for some reason."

"Gee, I wonder why?" I agreed. "You'd better talk to that Animal of yours."

He chuckled and eased me onto my back. "I'd rather talk to your animal." Blazing a trail of kisses down my throat, he teased, "Now lemme see, where did I see it last? Was it... here?"

Gently capturing my hand, he kissed his way up the tender inside of my wrist, smooth lips and rough whiskers playing a symphony of shivery pleasure on my skin.

"Mmmm..." My body melted, my eyes half-closing.

His kisses turned to teasing nibbles as he worked up my arm and around my shoulder to unerringly find the magic spot at my collarbone.

"Ohmigod, Arnie..." Riding the tide of rising heat, I ran greedy hands over his hard shoulders, then down his back to grip the ridges of muscle and pull him closer.

The sexy rasp of his chuckle against my throat turned into a purr as he traced a line of heat up to my lips. Slow tantalizing kisses gradually deepened, alternately teasing and urging with the sensual artistry of a gifted blues musician.

When his kisses wandered down my throat to explore the

sensitive skin of my cleavage, I lost my breath. A whimper of need choked from my throat, my body begging for his touch.

Lips and whiskers traced closer.

Paused for an exquisite instant...

His hot mouth closed over my nipple, his dexterous tongue flicking. Gasping, I arched into him only to writhe in pleasure as he cupped my other breast at the same time, gently rolling its nipple between his fingertips. Sensation jolted downward, igniting the liquid heat between my legs.

When he relinquished my nipple to trail kisses down my body I moaned at the loss, but a moment later his hand took its place. His kisses marched lower, then lower still while his hands worked their magic on my breasts.

"Hmmm." His deep rumble vibrated an extremely sensitive spot, making me catch my breath in hungry anticipation. "Look what I found."

The first delicate touch of his tongue wrung a cry from my throat, every nerve ending pleading for more.

He chuckled. "Little sensitive yourself, darlin'?"

"It's been..." Another gasp stole my breath as his tongue did something that should have been anatomically impossible. "...too long," I managed before my eyes rolled back in my head and I ceased to think.

Luxuriating in the safety of trust, I gave myself utterly to his hands and mouth. Sparkles of delicious sensation swirled and gathered fast. Tingles sizzled inward, coalescing in my centre only to explode like fireworks.

Bucking mindlessly in the grip of ecstasy, I floated for endless moments before returning slowly to a deeper ache of hunger.

"Arnie..." I panted. "I need you..."

His chuckle was full of joy. "Got ya covered, darlin'. Just

wait'll I get covered..."

The sound of a condom wrapper promised the reward I craved. A moment later strong arms lifted my hips and my eyelids fluttered half-open to see him kneeling between my legs, his hot gaze stroking my body.

"*Please...*" The word wrenched out of me.

Holding my lower body off the bed, he slid into me. Slow, easy strokes filled me while he adjusted the height and angle of my hips until I cried out in sudden bliss.

"There! Ohmigod, there! Yes... *harder... ohmigod... Arnie...!*" My words blurred into inarticulate cries while he increased his tempo, thrusting home again and again until my mind shattered into brilliant points of ecstasy and my body spasmed out of control. In the last bare moments of awareness I heard his deep-throated groan as he reached his own climax, and then there was nothing but hot sensation and glorious release.

Sometime later I eased out of his embrace, my body rubbery with satisfaction.

"Goin' so soon?" he mumbled, his eyes half-closed.

"Yeah. I need a shower, and we can still make it to the farm by ten-thirty."

"Mm." He rolled over and sat up, grinning. "Seems to me I still owe ya a nice long hot shower."

I eyed him appreciatively, taking note of an outstanding portion of his anatomy. "Okay, as long as we're at the farm by eleven."

We made it by eleven-fifteen. Chagrin gripped me as I surveyed the numerous cars already parked in front of the house.

"Shit, what...?" I began, only to slap my forehead. "Oh shit! I forgot all the bridesmaids and groomsmen would be coming here, and there's probably a hairdresser and a florist and God only knows what else..."

In the driver's seat of the Forester, Hellhound shifted nervously. "I'm, uh... gonna go check the perimeter."

"Good plan. I'll come with you."

He shook his head, grinning. "Sorry, darlin'. Ya gotta go in there. This's your show."

"Not my circus; not my monkeys," I objected. "I'm just the security detail."

"Nice try." He leaned over and kissed me. "Go on. I'll be out here if ya need me."

Heart thumping, I trudged toward the front door.

Dammit, I should have told Brock to arrive earlier with the security scanner. Karma's plan to keep vehicles away from the house had already gone down in flames, and any number of bombs or weapons could have been smuggled inside under the cover of gifts or wedding paraphernalia.

Inside, it was just as bad as I'd expected. Far too many bodies; all of them in a state of nervous anticipation. Over in a corner of the kitchen I spotted Karma and Moonbeam, even their massive equanimity looking frayed around the edges. Daniel was whooping and running up and down the hall again, dodging young men in boxer shorts and tuxedo shirts and young women in dressing gowns, full makeup, and curlers.

Alicia emerged from my bedroom, turning to say something to Kane behind her. He nodded and scooped Daniel up and the three of them went out the back door, lowering the decibel level only slightly.

I was sidling toward Karma and Moonbeam when Lola

popped out of one of the bedrooms and hurried over to buttonhole me, her eyes sparkling with unholy glee.

"What?" I asked warily as she tugged me out onto the front porch.

She pulled the door closed behind us, mercifully cutting off the bedlam within, and motioned me down to her level.

"It was awesome!" she chortled. "You should have seen it! It was a triumph of CRAPS! Our finest moment!"

"What are you talking about?" I asked, trepidation coiling into a squirmy ball in my stomach.

"We caught the saboteur! Oh, Aydan, it was so *badass*!"

"What?" Worry and relief fought for ascendancy. "Please tell me you didn't go vigilante on somebody's ass."

"Oh, we did, we *absolutely* did!" She was practically vibrating with glee.

"Oh, shit." I tottered over to the nearest patio chair and sank into it, visions of arrests and lawsuits dancing in my head. "Tell me what happened. Don't leave anything out."

She plopped into the chair beside me, her eyes sparkling. "It was Claire!" When I gave her a 'who-the-hell-are-you-talking-about' look, she added impatiently, "Claire! You know, the second bridesmaid."

I had no idea who the second bridesmaid was, but I nodded anyway. "Are you sure it was her? Why did she do it? Did she set the hall on fire and sabotage Spider's brakes, too?"

"No, we just found out this morning that the fire was caused by faulty wiring. And Spider swears he wrecked the brakes himself." Lola waved both away as irrelevant. "But it was Claire who threw the dye on Linda's dress and put the dead bird in her car and left the black roses on their doorstep. She said Linda had spoiled her wedding so she was paying her back."

"*Linda* spoiled her wedding?" I frowned. "I find that hard to believe."

"Oh, Claire's crazy," Lola said airily. "Her wedding was a couple of years ago and apparently she's been harbouring a grudge ever since."

"Because... why?" I inquired, massaging my temples. Less than five minutes, and I had a headache already.

"Well, there was a contagious bug going around the hospital at the time," Lola explained. "I can't remember what it was, but it gave people really bad diarrhea. Somehow the whole wedding party ended up with it. It was so bad they had to postpone the wedding for two weeks, and then the groom got it again on their honeymoon, and then to top it all off he decided he was in love with somebody else and ran off three weeks later."

"I'm still not seeing how that was Linda's fault," I said.

"Linda was a bridesmaid. Claire blamed her for carrying the bug back from the hospital, but Linda's a good nurse and I'm pretty sure she wouldn't have. And anyway, Claire was the first to get sick after she'd been visiting her grandmother in the hospital."

I began to speak, but Lola held up a restraining hand. "But wait, there's more. The girl the groom ran off with was a friend of Linda's, and she had introduced the two of them at Claire's wedding shower."

"Ouch," I agreed. "But how did you find out all of this? She just stood up and confessed?"

"Oh, she confessed, all right." Lola's eyes lit with an evil gleam. "After Moonbeam and I waterboarded her."

"YOU DID WHAT?" I bellowed. "ARE YOU ABSOLUTELY FUCKING NUTS?"

Across the yard Hellhound glanced over, alarm in every line of his body. I waved a reassuring hand at him and managed to bring my voice under control. "You do realize that's illegal and you'll probably go to jail for it," I said in my most reasonable tones. "She's probably reporting it to the police right now. Unless..."

My heart skipped a beat and sank into the pit of my stomach. If Moonbeam was involved...

"You didn't kill her and hide the body, did you?" I whispered.

Lola's big laugh burst out. "No, of course not. And she won't go to the police. We told her she could go to jail for what she did, so she won't say anything because she knows we've got something on her."

"Lola..." I massaged my aching head again. "Dropping a dead bird in somebody's car is not on the same level of criminal activity as waterboarding."

"But breaking and entering is illegal," Lola countered eagerly. "And then there's the vandalism to Linda's dress, too."

"Except for the small issue of *no evidence*."

"Yep, and she has no evidence, either," Lola said smugly. "She never saw our faces so she can't say for sure that it was us, and nobody else knows what happened. Well, except Karma, and he won't blab."

I pressed my eyes shut, deciding for the sake of my blood pressure not to inquire about the details. "So how did you figure it out?" I asked instead.

"We caught her this morning. All the bridesmaids and groomsmen came to the house, and Claire said she was making a special cocktail for the wedding party. I thought it was pretty early for drinks, but..." She shrugged. "It was sheer luck that Karma walked through the kitchen just as she was mixing it up, and he recognized Citro-Mag." She gave me an accusing look. "You didn't tell me he's a doctor."

"What's Citro-Mag?" My pulse quickened. "Is it poisonous?"

"No, it's a super-strength laxative. Claire was planning to re-enact her wedding woes." Lola snickered. "And she did. Or she will, very soon."

I stared at her, slow comprehension dawning. "You made her drink the Citro-Mag, didn't you?"

Wicked satisfaction glinted in Lola's eyes. "Oh, yes, indeedy! That's what we used for the waterboarding. Karma said it was the same dose people would normally take for a colonoscopy prep." Her smile widened. "She's going to shit herself cross-eyed."

The next forty-five minutes were a chaotic whirl. To my surprise, Brock actually arrived on time at noon, looking just as petulant and annoying as usual. I met him in the driveway, glancing over my shoulder to make sure we couldn't be overheard. "Thanks for coming. Have you got...?"

He hefted his man-purse, exactly the right size to hold a laptop. "Of course. There wouldn't be much point in me coming otherwise, would there?"

His snotty tone ratcheted my already high blood pressure up another notch, but I managed to keep my voice level as I handed him his cheque. "Okay, that's great. It's pretty crazy inside the house, but check the vehicles out here first and then just do the best you can with the wedding party and everybody in the house. The rest of the guests shouldn't be arriving for at least another hour or so. Oh, and..." I slipped the book out of its bag and handed it to him. "This is from Spider and Linda, to say thank you."

Actual pleasure warmed his eyes. Then he opened the cover and his mouth fell open at the sight of the signature.

"The autograph is a gift from me," I said quietly. "In exchange for the favour which I'll now consider discharged."

His pierced brows snapped together. "Nice try, Kelly. This is fake. Everybody knows Murray Stout doesn't autograph more than three books from each release."

"It's authentic. I know Murray Stout personally."

He snorted. "Nobody knows Murray Stout personally. He's a recluse. That isn't even his picture on the cover of the book; it's just some random guy who won a contest at one of the conferences." His lip curled. "And before you try to feed me any more crap, yes, I know the guy in the picture is one of our researchers at Sirius, and I know he's *not* Murray Stout. I've run an analysis on his reports and he couldn't write his way out of a paper bag. This is bogus."

"That guy didn't sign it," I said, holding onto my temper for all I was worth. "Look closer. If you're that big a fan, you know what his autograph looks like. And it's an original signature. You can still smell the ink. He just signed it last night."

Hesitantly, as though expecting me to laugh at him, Brock brought the book to his nose and sniffed. His eyes widened.

"Original," I repeated. "The third of three autographed books."

"But..." His voice wavered, then firmed into his usual irritating nasal drawl. "Fine. Thanks, Kelly. But you still owe me a favour."

Channelling Kane's lightning-fast reactions, I snatched the book from his grasp. "Okay. I'll return this to Murray and replace it with an unsigned hardcover from Spider and Linda. See you later."

I turned and walked away.

I had only taken a couple of steps when Brock bleated, "Wait!"

When I turned, his mouth worked for a few moments as if struggling to form words. With a tremendous effort of will, I managed not to taunt him.

"Do we have a deal?" I asked instead, holding out the book.

"Yes!" He snatched it back and held it against his chest with both hands. For a moment we stood looking at each other, then he said, "I'll get started now," and strode toward the house, slipping the book reverently into his man-purse.

I drew a deep breath and let it out slowly.

So far, so good.

At least after Lola's revelation, I was less concerned about guests with weapons, but if Labelle decided to strike today...

I eyed the rolling hills around my farm with a shiver. Outdoor wedding. Perfect opportunity for a sniper.

CHAPTER 51

Forty minutes later I was thoroughly impressed with Brock. Whether due to euphoria induced by the autographed book or through supreme acting talent, he had managed not only to act like a normal human being, but also to discreetly scan everyone in the house.

Circulating with his phone on video, he encouraged everyone to hold the explosives-detection wand like a microphone while recording good wishes and bad karaoke for Spider and Linda. He even managed to scan a full three-sixty of each person by swooping around them like a hyperactive cameraman.

At last he faded back to the corner of the kitchen where I was trying to stay out of the way and nibbling on the platter of cold cuts and cheese someone had thoughtfully provided.

"I got everybody except the old lady in the nightgown and that cross-dressed old fart," he muttered, nodding toward Moonbeam and Karma. "I can't get near them."

Shit, that hadn't even occurred to me. Of course they were both armed, so they'd use all their spy-skills to avoid triggering his scan. And knowing Moonbeam, she probably had residue from explosives on her hands, too.

"Don't worry about them," I whispered back. "They're

harmless. You're doing a great job. Did you get something to eat? Help yourself to that platter if you want."

He stared. "Why are you being so nice to me? What do you want?"

I sighed and told the truth. "All I want is one day with no hostilities or bloodshed. I've seen so much scary awful shit in the last twenty-four hours, I just can't take any more."

"Oh..." His nonplussed expression might have been funny if I hadn't been so stressed. He nodded. "I'll go and start setting up by the gate so I can catch all the guests." Scooping up a few crackers and cold cuts, he made for the door, leaving me staring after him and wondering what benevolent aliens had snatched the real Tyler Brock and deposited this stranger in his place.

An hour later the guests had all been discreetly scanned and ushered to my lawn, where they unfolded their lawn chairs and took seats. Touring my garden for a last-minute inspection, I noticed that someone, probably Karma, had deadheaded my flowers and lightly watered everything so the blooms glowed fresh and radiant in the afternoon sun.

Then tinny strains of music from a portable boom-box produced a flutter of anticipation among the seated guests. Spider and his groomsmen marched down a makeshift aisle between the lawn chairs to take their places beside the justice of the peace who waited under the rose arbour.

A suspenseful moment later, the wedding march filled the air and the first of the bridesmaids came down the steps of the house. When Linda emerged, her eyes sparkling and her delicate pink hand-painted gown floating on the warm summer air, murmurs of appreciation rose from the guests as they stood to greet her.

As she joined Spider at the front and the words of the

simple but meaningful ceremony began, I stood at the back of the assembly surveying my yard and the rolling fields beyond.

No sign of trouble. No weapons on the guests; no bombs in the gifts; no snipers on the hills.

To the side, Moonbeam and Karma stood watching, too, and we exchanged a nod.

Hellhound had been circling the perimeter, but as the vows began he drifted closer to stand behind me and slip an arm around my waist. "All clear so far, darlin'," he rasped in my ear.

I leaned back against his solid warmth, hugging his arm to me and letting my vigilance relax for a moment. All eyes were riveted on the couple under the cascade of roses. Linda said her vows in a clear voice ringing with joy. Spider choked up and muddled through his vows, dabbing at his eyes. Watching them, my throat tightened and I had to blink rapidly to clear my vision.

A movement made me glance back in time to see Hellhound gazing at the sky and blinking rapidly, too. "Fuckin' bug flew in my eye," he muttered.

Then the justice of the peace pronounced Spider and Linda husband and wife, and peals of joyous music accompanied them down the aisle in a shower of rose petals flung by a pair of enthusiastic little girls in ruffled white dresses.

My yard erupted in cheers as everyone converged on the happy couple to offer their good wishes.

Later, after the buffet had been eaten and the toasts had been drunk and the evening sun had mellowed to warm gold,

I leaned against the side of my garage dividing my attention between watching the happy crowd and scanning for potential threats.

Still uninformed of our worries, Kane was doing his best to visit with the other guests but his gaze kept straying to Alicia and Daniel, his eyes soft and a smile hovering on his lips. Spider and Linda circulated, laughing and beaming and holding onto each other as though they'd never let go, and I sent up a brief but fervent prayer that they'd never have to.

On the other side of the garage, Moonbeam and Karma kept a close eye on the proceedings, too, and Hellhound still prowled watchfully around the buildings.

Shepherds guarding our happily oblivious sheep.

I sighed. Stemp hadn't shown up. I had expected better of him, and the depth of my disappointment surprised me. When had I started thinking of him as one of the good guys?

Sighing again, I straightened, trying to ease the ache in my tired muscles. I probably shouldn't blame him. Good people sometimes made bad personal decisions, and he had more reason to do so than most.

The vibration of my phone startled me, and I snatched it out of my waist pouch and answered before it could go to voicemail.

Labelle's unwelcome voice sent a shiver down my spine. "Good evening, Ms. Widdenback; it's Frederick Labelle."

"Hi," I said flatly, my heart rate picking up.

"I just wanted to let you know I've been researching that investment we discussed, and it looks as though everything will go ahead smoothly."

"Oh. Good." I glanced around, but nobody was within earshot. "I'll check into it a bit more at my end, then," I said, holding up our pretense of being congenial business associates. "I hope to have everything I need within the next few days."

"That will be fine. I'll wait to hear from you," he replied. "And... I also wanted to apologize. I'm afraid we started off on the wrong foot and I wanted to let you know there are no hard feelings. I'm hoping we'll be able to enjoy a long and profitable business relationship."

I almost gagged, but managed an affable reply. "Me, too. I'll be in touch. 'Bye."

Then I stowed my phone back in my waist pouch and went to find a much-needed beer.

Grabbing two bottles, I walked out to meet Hellhound, letting my strides lengthen and my muscles relax at last. He gave me a quizzical glance as I handed him an ice-cold bottle.

"Come on in," I said. "I just had a call from you-know-who, and you were right, he's sucking up now. I think we're safe."

He let out a breath and tipped up the bottle for a long, long swallow. "Damn, darlin', that's good," he said hoarsely. "I'm gonna go grab my guitar, then. Webb an' Linda have been buggin' me about playin' a few tunes for 'em." He shrugged. "Dunno why; they've got the music man, but whatever. If it'll make 'em happy..."

He shrugged again, but I could tell he was secretly pleased.

I reached up for a kiss. "Go get your guitar. You're officially off-duty."

He headed for his SUV and I walked back to the garage. Moonbeam and Karma had spotted our exchange, and they wove through the chattering guests to meet me at the edge of the crowd.

"Update?" Moonbeam inquired.

"Yes. I just had a call, and we can stand down now." I nodded toward the music and light spilling out the open doors of the garage. "It's all over but the party."

"Aydan?" Kane's deep voice made me turn.

"What, you managed to escape your keeper for a few seconds?" I teased, glancing over to where Daniel stood with one hand on his mother while his anxious gaze tracked Kane's location.

Kane chuckled. "Yes. Briefly." He sobered. "I just got a call from Glen Birch." Glancing at Moonbeam and Karma, he elaborated, "One of the RCMP officers who was working on Daniel's case." They nodded and he went on, "He was just letting me know they found Scot Murphy's body. He and several of the other club members had been mauled to death by bears. Apparently they had been feeding the bears and it backfired."

"Oh." I didn't dare say anything else.

"What will become of the bears?" Moonbeam inquired.

Kane shrugged. "Fish and Wildlife officers trapped them, but they'll likely have to be euthanized. They're too habituated to human contact."

"That's sickening," Moonbeam said quietly. "I understand that it's necessary, but..."

Kane nodded and went on, "On a happier note, the other boys have all been reunited with their families, and Mrs. Murphy and her daughters are receiving aid and counselling from Social Services. Matthew's remains have been retrieved, so they'll be able to give him a proper burial as soon as the autopsy is complete."

"What about the rest of the so-called club members?" I asked, anger rising all over again. "Did they nail those assholes?"

"They're working on it." At my gesture of frustration, Kane added, "It will take a while. It seems there were two tiers of membership in the group. Most of the members were unaware of the atrocities being perpetrated by the inner circle. The main group is innocent of everything except general wrong-headedness."

"You can say that again," I muttered.

Kane went on, "The inner circle evaluated the regular members through general conversation, and if they were amenable they completed their initiation by supplying a woman to the club. After that their solidarity was enforced on pain of death."

I shuddered. "And nobody would ever have known if you hadn't been so determined to find Daniel."

"How many victims were there?" Karma rumbled, anger hardening his eyes.

Kane sighed. "We'll likely never know. They were homeless women and prostitutes abducted off the streets, so although some matched up to unsolved missing persons cases, there were likely many more who were never reported missing in the first place. And the firepit inside the stockade was full of charred bones and ashes. Apparently after the bears were finished the members retrieved any remains and burned them, and judging by the depth of the ashes they had been doing so for quite some time."

"Those poor women," Moonbeam said softly. "That makes me feel physically ill."

"Yes," Kane agreed. "And even now their suffering may not be at an end. They'll receive medical treatment and likely be funnelled into a women's shelter, but with that kind of mental trauma and no personal support systems or financial resources, most will likely end up on the streets again."

"They are welcome at our commune if they choose to come," Moonbeam offered. "We have experience in helping victims of violent crime, and the commune provides a safe haven for people who... choose to withdraw from the world at large. All we ask from our members is abstinence from alcohol and drugs and a willingness to contribute their share of labour to the vegetable garden and daily chores."

"That's very kind of you," Kane said quietly. "I'll put you in touch with Glen."

"Thank you..." Moonbeam began, but then went still, looking over my shoulder.

I spun, my heart lurching into my throat, but relaxed at the sight of Stemp approaching. A small glow of happiness warmed me. They'd get another chance after all.

"Good evening," he greeted us, and gave his parents a wary glance. "I apologize for my tardiness. I had to deal with an urgent matter at the office."

He looked tired, and remorse for my earlier judgement squeezed my heart. On call, 24/7. Who knew what deadly decisions he might have been making while we celebrated?

"Have you eaten?" I asked. "The caterers put the leftovers in the fridge if you're hungry."

"That would be most welcome."

"Come, dear," Moonbeam said, holding out her hand. "You look exhausted. Sit down and I'll fix you a plate."

"Thank you, Mother."

He and Karma and Moonbeam moved toward the garage, leaving Kane and me alone.

Kane glanced over at Daniel again, already tethered by the invisible bond between father and son, and I laughed with the sheer joy of knowing he'd finally gotten his heart's desire.

He turned back to me, smiling. "I feel as though I've been given the world. Something so immeasurably precious I'm almost afraid to accept it."

"Don't be afraid." I squeezed his hand. "You're going to be the best dad ever. Have you talked to your own dad yet?"

"Yes." His smile glowed. "He's absolutely over the moon. He's going to give us a week or two to get settled, but nothing will be able to keep him away from his grandson after that."

"So..." I hesitated. "How do you think 'settled' is going to look?"

"I... don't know." Kane sobered and cast another glance at Alicia and Daniel. Alicia gave him a tentative smile and he turned back to me, frowning. "I'm not going to go back to her, Aydan."

Startled, I blinked at him. "I didn't expect you to."

But he'd obviously thought about it.

"Don't make any snap decisions," I suggested. "I think you'd better count on spending quite a bit of time with them until you've gotten Daniel to the point where he doesn't have an anxiety attack as soon as you leave his sight. And you need to come to a truce with Alicia. Daniel needs two parents united in their concern for him, not divided by their personal issues."

"Yes," Kane agreed. "It's going to be a long process, and it's not going to be easy for any of us. But..." His face lit up again. "I can't think of anything more worth the effort."

"Get back there." I gave him a nudge. "Your family needs you, Dad."

He turned away smiling, his step light as he returned to swing Daniel up onto his shoulders. Daniel squealed with delight, grinning from ear to ear.

Drawing a long happy breath, I turned in time to see Moonbeam and Karma enfold Stemp in a three-way hug.

Heart full, I moved over to lean against the garage again as Hellhound stepped up beside the deejay's table, guitar in hand.

The crowd went still when he began to sing Bob Seger's Always In My Heart, his sexy rough-edged voice floating softly on the evening air. Listening to him croon the tender words of love and commitment he had never allowed himself to experience, I wrapped my arms over the pleasant ache in my chest.

One perfect evening.

For now, it was all I wanted.

Book 12 is available!

Visit my Books page at dianehenders.com/books for progress updates and announcements.

A Request

Thanks for reading!

If you enjoyed this book, I'd really appreciate it if you'd take a moment to review it online.

Here are some suggestions for the "star" ratings:

Five stars: Loved the book and can hardly wait for the next one.

Four stars: Liked the book and plan to read the next one.

Three stars: The book was okay. Might read the next one.

Two stars: Didn't like the book. Probably won't read the next one.

One star: Hated the book. Would never read another in the series.

You can help prospective readers by writing a few sentences about what you liked or disliked about the book.

Thanks for taking the time to do a review!

About Me

Before I started writing fiction, I had a checkered career: technical writer, computer geek, and interior designer. I'm good at two out of three of those. Fortunately, I had the sense to quit the one I sucked at (interior design).

When my mid-life crisis hit, I took up muay thai and started writing thrillers featuring a middle-aged female protagonist. ('Walter Mitty', you say? Nope, never heard of him.)

Writing and kicking the hell out of stuff seemed more productive than more typical mid-life-crisis activities like getting a divorce, buying a Harley Crossbones, and cruising across the country picking up men in sleazy bars; especially since it's winter most months of the year here in Canada.

It's much more comfortable to sit at my computer. And Harleys are expensive. Come to think of it, so are beer and gasoline.

Oh, and I still love my husband. There's that. So I stuck with the writing.

Diane Henders

And here's my "professional" bio, in case you need something more suitable for mixed company:

Diane Henders is the Kindle best-selling author of the NEVER SAY SPY series: Sexy thrillers packed with tension, laughs, profanity, and sometimes warm fuzzies.

The first book in the series, NEVER SAY SPY, has had over 450,000 downloads to date, and stayed on Kindle's 'Women Sleuths' Top 100 list for 60 consecutive months.

Diane enjoys target shooting, gardening, auto mechanics, painting (art, not walls), music, and martial arts; and loves food and drink almost as much as she loves her husband. They live in the wilds of British Columbia, Canada, where they get all the adrenaline rush they could ever want by growing fruit trees in bear country.

Want to know what else is roiling around in the cesspit of my mind? Drop by my blog and website at dianehenders.com, check out the extras, and don't forget to leave a comment in the guest book to say hi – I love hearing from you! Or you can connect with me on Facebook at:
https://www.facebook.com/authordianehenders.
See you there!